ZERO
at the
BONE

Jane
Seville

◈ Dreamspinner Press

Published by
Dreamspinner Press
4760 Preston Road
Suite 244-149
Frisco, TX 75034
http://www.dreamspinnerpress.com/

This is a work of fiction. Names, characters, places and incidents either are the product of the author's imagination or are used fictitiously, and any resemblance to actual persons, living or dead, business establishments, events or locales is entirely coincidental.

Zero at the Bone
Copyright © 2009 by Jane Seville

Cover art by Paul Richmond, www.paulrichmondstudio.com.

ISBN: 978-1-935192-80-0

Printed in the United States of America
First Edition
April, 2009

eBook edition available
eBook ISBN: 978-1-935192-81-7

Dedicated to every reader who has ever offered me praise, criticism, support or just acknowledgment. You know who you are. You have helped keep me writing for many years, and without that, I would not be the writer I am now, nor would I ever be the writer I still hope to become.

A narrow fellow in the grass
Occasionally rides—
You may have met Him,—did you not,
His notice sudden is.

The Grass divides as with a Comb,
A spotted Shaft is seen,
And then it closes at your Feet
And opens further on—

He likes a Boggy Acre,
A Floor too cool for Corn—
But when a Boy, and Barefoot,
I more than once at noon,

Have passed, I thought, a Whip lash
Unbraiding in the Sun
When stooping to secure it
It wrinkled, and was gone—

Several of Nature's People
I know, and they know me—
I feel for them a transport
Of Cordiality—

But never met this Fellow
Attended or alone
Without a tighter Breathing
And zero at the bone.
                    —Emily Dickinson

CHAPTER 1

THE smell of cheap motel rooms was comforting to him, like his oldest, rattiest T-shirt. Lysol, unwashed feet, and that sour tang of grime and desperation that tried to dress up and look nice with laundered sheets and those stiff bedspreads that felt like sandpaper on your ass, bargain basement art on the walls and the cheap paper-wrapped chits that weren't so much soap as a suggestion of what soap might be like.

Motel rooms like this had known many men without names, but he wondered if he was the first who'd let his go by choice. He signed a meaningless pseudonym to the register and paid cash. He could afford to stay in nicer places, but that would mean hauling out one of his impressive array of fake identifications, and he didn't use them unless absolutely necessary. Each one, when used, left a shallow footprint in the shifting sand dunes of his existence, which he preferred to keep pristine and featureless. Even if that hadn't been the case, he'd still prefer rooms like this. They fit around him snugly with the comforting security of anonymity. Every time he'd stayed in fancier digs he'd felt like he was rattling around in them like the last pea in the can. The eyes of the world could see him in places like that. Places like this, he could float through without leaving a trace, and the world's eyes looked away.

He shucked his jacket, smelling smoke and stale beer on himself from the bar he'd spent the evening in. He didn't know why he kept going. The bars, like the motel rooms, were always the same. He didn't go to the ones with fancy neon and clever drinks at the bar. He liked the ones with gravel parking lots and sagging roofs, the kind that sported hand-painted signs proclaiming that this was Somebody's-Name's-Bar. Folks went to those places for two reasons: to get drunk enough to forget their sorry-ass lives, or to pick up a piece of tail. Neither interested him. He wouldn't claim that his life couldn't stand some forgetting, but the booze had not yet been invented that could let him, and he sure as hell wasn't going to pick up a piece of tail.

Sometimes he thought he should, just to keep up the appearance of being part of the human race. It wouldn't have been hard. The skanks that hung out at these bars usually homed in on him the minute he walked through the door, sizing him up to see if he was good for a screw, a free meal, maybe shacking up in a double-wide and paying the bills. They'd flap around on the dance floor, presenting like monkeys at a zoo, and lean too close when they stood next to him at the bar, wafting an unpleasant mixture of Love's Baby Soft and flop-sweat.

The occasional notion that maybe he shouldn't sleep alone every single night of his life wasn't enough to actually make him take the initiative. It had been a long time since anyone got that close to him. In his line of work, he had to be careful. Close enough to fuck was close enough to shank him with a dagger hidden in the crease of some chick's jean shorts. Some part of his mind that remembered civilization knew that it wasn't normal to be this paranoid. Couldn't be helped. That ship had sailed.

So he went to the bars, had a beer or two, stayed quiet, watched the people, and left. If he stayed any longer, the eyes on him became too much. Always the eyes, looking at him sidelong, like they knew. What could they know about some stranger having a beer in a bar? They didn't know shit. But the eyes were always on him, and whether they knew anything or not, the idea that they might always drove him out.

He stretched out on top of the bedspread and lit a cigarette, staring at the ceiling. He could tell Josey that it was just a precaution, he could tell himself that it was paranoia, but here on the sandpaper bedspread where it was just him and the bargain-basement art, he couldn't deny that he was always alone in these godforsaken motel rooms because the tits and ass on offer just weren't that interesting to him. He didn't like to think about how far gone he was into the abyss that even the humanness of lust was now foreign to him.

At least he still felt hunger, and cold, and the craving for nicotine. How long until even those animal sensations left him? Would he eventually be left with nothing but a set of skills that suited him for only one profession, and a head full of things he didn't want to know? Maybe he'd disconnect enough that he would no longer sweat, or piss, or get stupid songs stuck in his head. He'd been told over and over again that he'd have to become a machine, but he hadn't really believed that he would. He knew better now.

He stubbed out his cigarette and shut off the bedside lamp. He wondered if he should try jerking off. It'd be nice if he were capable of even that level of self-love, but he hadn't managed to wring one out in a long time. Months? Years? He couldn't remember. The desert stripped most indicators of date and season from his memories. Everything was always hot and bright and seared crisp.

He set the alarm clock. He couldn't be late for Josey tomorrow, and it still was a long drive to Nevada.

JACK just wanted to wash the blood off his sleeves. It was ground into the creases of his knuckles and clotted into the hair on his wrists. He was elbow-deep in blood on a daily basis, but never without the shielding of gown, gloves, sterility… sanity. He couldn't stop staring at it, the edges of the stain bleeding into the white of his shirt, the darker blotches on his hands. He just wanted to be allowed to get up, leave the interview room, and wash it off. Or change his shirt. Or go home and cry.

The odds of this happening seemed slim. "Let's go over it again, Dr. Francisco."

He didn't bother to look up to see which of the suits was talking to him. They were all the same. They blended into one nameless entity of Suit With Questions that surrounded him in navy blue polyblend and poked and prodded and wouldn't let him go home. "I told you already."

"Tell us again."

"I was on my way to my car."

"In the parking garage."

"Yes."

"What floor?"

"The tenth."

"Why'd you park way up there?"

"I got to work late today; that was the first spot I found." He could hear his own voice, flat and uninflected. This was what it had come down to: a rote recitation of one of the worst days of his life. "I saw three people standing in the empty spot next to the car."

"What kind of car?"

"It was a black Escalade. I don't know what year. Late model. I didn't get the plate number. The woman was up against the side. I looked over to see if she needed help, then I saw the knife." He felt the shame rising in his chest again, wanting to choke off his words. "I should've helped her," he said.

"It's a good thing for you that you didn't, or you'd be dead too. Then what happened?"

"I ducked down behind a car. The tall one stabbed her. She didn't scream. There was this sucking noise, like a gasp. I heard her fall. The two men got in the Escalade and drove off." He gulped. "They didn't see me."

"And you saw the men clearly?" Jack nodded. "Then what'd you do?"

"I ran to her to see if I could help her. I tried to put pressure on the wound while I called nine-one-one." He swiped at his eyes. "She died before the paramedics got there."

Silence. Jack looked up. The suits were concerned. He glanced around. The suits were waiting for something. He didn't bother to ask what.

The door opened and another suit entered, carrying a folder. He didn't introduce himself or acknowledge the other suits; he just sat down next to Jack. "Dr. Francisco, the woman you saw killed was Maria Dominguez. She was scheduled to testify about her extensive knowledge of her ex-husband's drug-related activities."

"So… those men were…."

"Yeah." The new suit met his eyes. "I'm not going to bullshit you, Dr. Francisco. You're our winning lottery ticket here. We've never had a witness who could identify any of the Dominguez family in the commission of a crime."

"You mean you haven't had one that lived long enough to testify."

The suit sighed. "You'll live. I promise."

JOSEY was waiting at the drive-in where they'd arranged to meet. The place was straight out of the Twilight Zone. It looked like it had been abandoned for years; everything was bleached white from the desert sun. Listless brown weeds clumped around the bases of the empty posts that had once held the speakers, planted in regular rows like grave markers. He wouldn't have been surprised if some of them were. *Be a good place to bury some bodies,* he thought. *No one watching except this big blank eye of a movie screen.*

She was sitting on the hood of her car. "You're late, D," she said as he approached.

"Pick a meet site that ain't in the middle a fuckin' nowhere, then we'll talk about bein' late. What ya got fer me?"

"Nothing you'll take, probably."

"Must have somethin'. Ya called me here."

"I swear, I don't know why I keep you on the list. So fucking picky."

"Rules is rules."

She sighed and opened her briefcase. "Biggest ticket today is this one," she said, handing him the folder. He glanced over the file and knew within five lines that he wouldn't be taking it. "D, it's a hundred large," Josey beseeched him, as he handed the folder back to her. She always tried to palm off a few up front on him, although he couldn't imagine that after all this time she'd think that just this once he'd cave in and take it.

"I ain't doin' no woman just cuz her asshole husband's embarrassed that she fucked the pool boy. Next."

"This one?"

The second one only took two lines before he was handing it back. "Don't do cops."

"Okay, Mr. Fucking Moral Superiority, how's this one?"

He started reading, and kept going. This one was... possible. "Hmph."

"Oh, you're actually gonna consider this one? I might just piss my pants for joy."

"Never done no art dealer."

"Oughta be a walk in the park. A guy like this thinks he's untouchable."

He sighed. "How much?"

"Fifty."

He tucked the folder into his jacket. "Three days." He started to walk away.

"You know," Josey said. "All these other ones that you won't do? I just give them to one of the others. They get done anyway."

D stopped, but did not turn. "Yeah?"

"So if they're gonna get done, why does it matter you're not the one doing them?"

He shook his head. "You gotta ask why it matters, I ain't gonna bother answerin'."

JACK was sitting in his dim living room. Well, not *his* living room, technically. It belonged to Jack Macintosh, whoever that was. He had Jack Macintosh's driver's license in his pocket, and the mail in the hallway was addressed to this mythical man, wherever he'd come from. Who was he? What did he do for a living? Jack Macintosh was a professional at waiting. Waiting for it to be time to take an oath and tell a jury what he'd seen. At the moment, however, Jack Macintosh was scrolling through the cable guide, looking for something interesting on TV. Dr. Jack Francisco wasn't here just now. But Jack Macintosh had all the time in the world to reflect on the events that had led him here to this impersonal, pre-furnished home in Henderson, Nevada.

You had to have a cookie.

A cookie had landed Jack here, thousands of miles away from his old life. He'd been on his way out of the office when one of the nurses hailed him. "Have a cookie, Dr. Francisco!" she'd said. He'd hesitated. It was possible that this was just the latest assault in the ongoing campaign being waged by various nurses and fellow doctors to seduce him via baked goods.

He hadn't even been hungry. But mmm... cookies. So he'd had one. What was his rush, anyway? To get home to his dark apartment where the companion of his evening would probably be whatever was airing on TCM that night?

If he hadn't had that fateful cookie, he'd have missed Maria Dominguez's murder and he'd still be in that dark apartment, with his own furniture, and his own books, watching Robert Osborne introduce a film from the oeuvre of Bette Davis or Joseph Cotton. George Sanders, if Jack was very lucky.

Well, I still have Robert, Jack thought, changing the channel. If there was one thing you could count on in this world, it was that at any given moment, Robert Osborne would be talking about film from his fake living room at the TCM studios.

The Dominguez brothers knew that the state had a witness. Lucky Jack had seen Tommy Dominguez and Carlos Alvarez kill Maria. So now here he was in Las Vegas, his driver's license bearing a stranger's last name. "No one is from Las Vegas," his contact had said. "It's easy to hide there."

He was hiding until it was his turn to testify. And after that, he'd have to hide again. He was trying not to think too much about leaving his career behind. The idea of no longer being a surgeon, of not being able to do what he'd spent most of his adult life training to do, was heartbreaking. But what choice did he have? He had to help convict these men. He might have to give up everything he knew but he'd still be alive, which was more than could be said for Maria or the dozens of others these men had killed or would kill in the future if Jack didn't help stop them. This was what he kept telling himself. Sometimes it even worked. It wasn't much comfort when he lay awake in the middle of the night feeling sorry for himself, but it was all he had and he'd stick to it.

He put down the remote and settled back. *All About Eve* was just starting. Jack smiled. At least something was going his way tonight.

JOSEY had been right. The art dealer job was a walk in the park.

He waited in the man's bedroom, the last guest this man would ever entertain here. He sat on the bed, breathing evenly. It was a very nice bedroom. He wondered if the art dealer ever had sex in it, or if he just jerked off to his fancy art books. He wondered if what visitors there might have been were men or women.

The contract was simple. Obtain photographic proof of this man's misdeeds, then dispose of him. He'd already found the workroom and documented everything. It was a cold, bloodless little scam the man had going on here. He wasn't clear on the details, but from what he'd been able to gather, the guy took art with a shady paper trail, mostly pieces that had been looted by the Nazis, and laundered their histories so that collectors and art dealers could make a fortune selling it out from under the survivors' families.

That shit ain't right. It was what he needed to make it okay. It was enough… barely.

He heard the front door open and close. He waited. Patience was not a problem for him.

It took the little man an hour to come into the bedroom. He was barely in the door before D had the dart in his neck. He dragged him to the bed and laid him out. "You ain't gonna be able ta move," he said, "but you're sure gonna be able ta talk." He got out his iPod, plugged in the mike, and the man talked. They always talked. They never knew that D didn't care what they had to say. They never knew that it wouldn't help.

The man's eyes rolled in his head. D was put in mind of a deer he'd had to kill when his first shot hadn't gotten him clean. His father had stood at his shoulder, saying "Gotta finish what ya started." He'd used a knife, right to the animal's heart. "Finish it, son. 'Til the blood ain't pumpin' no more."

Sometimes he wondered about that, in light of his choice of profession. Sometimes he dreamed about it too.

The art dealer started trying to bargain with him, as they often did. He offered him double what he was being paid. He apologized for whatever he'd done to piss D off. D didn't bother to answer. It wouldn't do the man any favors to know that it wasn't D that he'd pissed off.

Two shots to the heart. D never went for the head; it was too messy.

He went to a Starbucks around the corner; he hated their coffee, but loved the Wi-Fi. He e-mailed Josey a blank message through an anonymous remailer, with the subject line "Get BiggER TITTTS ASAP!!!" That meant the job was done. The penis-enlarger subject line was for an abort, and the Hot Asian Sluts were for a delay. He downloaded the photos and the MP3 of the art dealer's confession, then saved everything to a stick drive. He slipped it into the envelope Josey had given him with the contract, then wiped the laptop's hard drive. He tossed the envelope into a mailbox on his way out, then the laptop into a passing garbage truck. The camera and the iPod were his; they went back into his pockets.

Walk in the park.

JOSEY wasn't at the next meet. He waited for an hour, but she didn't show up. D felt a fluttering of uncharacteristic worry in his gut. Supposedly such things had been trained out of him, but his rusty emotional core still sent up the occasional signal flare. They weren't exactly in a low-risk business, and any one of a number of unpleasant fates could have befallen his only compatriot.

He headed home to find an e-mail from her. The subject line was "Get VIAGRA Cheap!!!" That meant something was wrong.

He loaded up and got in his car, headed to the safe house. If there was trouble, Josey would meet him there.

There was, indeed, trouble, in the form of three large men who looked like they'd stepped out of the *Hired Muscle Weekly* catalog. D was hardly in the door before they were on him. He had a split second to wonder how they'd found the place before they'd pinned his arms and were dragging him inside. D whipped his head backward into a nose and heard a satisfying crunch. He pushed against the one still holding him and kicked upward across the jaw of the one in front of him. Clearly, they hadn't been expecting him to put up a fight.

Unfortunately, the element of surprise didn't last very long, and within a few seconds they had tossed him onto the living room couch. He stared up into two gun barrels, and was forced to rethink his thoughts of resistance. Josey was tied to a chair nearby, bruised and bloody. "You okay?" he asked.

She nodded. "I'm sorry, D," she said. Her voice sounded scratchy, like someone had been strangling her. "I don't know how they found me."

"Don't say nothin'," he reminded her. Probably unnecessary. Even beaten up and bound as she was, Josey was likely thinking three steps ahead.

The shortest of their new friends, probably the brains of the outfit, approached him. "We got a job for you," he said.

"I pick my own jobs, asshole," he snarled.

Brains tossed him a folder. "She says you wouldn't take this one if you had a choice. So we're not giving you a choice. You're taking it." D started to open the folder. "No need to open it," Brains said. "All you need to know is that you're doing it."

"Or what?" D said. It almost didn't matter. They were now in a position to threaten him in almost any way they chose. His own life, his identity, Josey's life, the target's slow, painful death against the quick one D would mete out.

As it turned out, they'd come prepared. Brains tossed D another folder, motioning for him to examine its contents. D opened it. "Fuck me," he said, clamping down on the dull horror that rose in his throat. The folder was full of pictures. Of him. Coming and going from the scene of every job he'd done in the past six months. All of them time stamped. He glanced over at Josey, the thought occurring that she might have sold him up the river, but the look on her face dispelled his doubts.

"You'll take the contract. We have evidence to tie you to half a dozen contract killings this year alone. You'll get six months in the electric chair." Brains smiled, and D thought again of that deer he'd killed. "You've got one week. After that, those photos and a number of other salient pieces of documentation will find their way to the FBI."

"And after it's done? I ain't gonna be your monkey forever," he muttered.

"My employer has no interest in you. You can go back to your regular… schedule. When it's done, it's done." He arched one eyebrow; D knew at once that this guy was one of those that was always imagining himself in a Tarantino movie. He knew the type. Same kind of guys that thought it was cool to hold their guns sideways, the way no one actually did in reality.

Brains and his pets left. D went to Josey and released her from her bonds. "I'm sorry," she repeated. "They made me bring them here and send you the trouble message."

"Don't matter," he said, his attention already turning to the contract they'd dumped in his lap. He opened the folder and started reading, knowing that he wouldn't like it, and he didn't.

Josey was watching his face. "I wasn't even going to show you that one."

"A fuckin' *witness?*" D snarled. "So now I'm killin' innocent bystanders on the say-so a some drug lords? Fuck." He tossed the folder aside and dragged a hand across his close-cropped hair. "How they been fuckin' tailin' me, anyhow?"

"I don't know. They must have been hacking my records."

"Thought that couldn't happen."

"Didn't think it could." He stood up and went to the window, feeling Josey's eyes on his back. "You have to do it."

"I know."

"No, I mean you have to."

"I said I fuckin' know."

"D… it's what you do."

"I know what I fuckin' do, and this ain't it."

"You get paid to kill people."

D ground his jaw. "When they deserve it."

Silence. "What's this guy's name again?"

He didn't have to consult the folder. One read-through and it was in his head. "Program got him in as Jack Macintosh. Real name's Jack Francisco." He shook his head. "Dr. Jack god-almighty-damn Francisco. Saw somethin' he wasn't s'posed ta see 'n' has the balls ta stand up 'n' say so. Now I gotta put a bullet in him for it."

CHAPTER 2

IT had been another long, hard day of doing nothing, and Jack was bushed.

His life, while conveniently unfettered by things like responsibilities and obligations, was starting to feel pretty damned pointless. He was alive for no other reason than to be life support for the brain cells that remembered Maria Dominguez's murder. After he'd spewed it out and had it recorded by some stenographer, entered into the public record and set in stone for all time in the tablets of the justice system, he might as well just blink out of existence. He tried to keep his mind fixed on the days after his testimony, but those days were starting to feel as cruelly insubstantial as the mirages that lay across the desert like oil slicks, changing colors and luring the eye. What did he even have to live for? It wasn't like he could go back to his job, which was all he really cared about.

He spent his days driving around, mostly. The tourist attractions and casinos of Las Vegas didn't interest him. He was drawn to the endless flat expanse of desert surrounding this chrome-and-steel oasis, to the grandiose gestures of nature that people skipped right over to get to the damned Cirque de Soleil show. He'd been to Hoover Dam, he'd been to Lake Meade, he'd explored the desert country in and around his Henderson suburban neighborhood. Sometimes he parked his car off some deserted road and hiked aimlessly, listening to the nothingness and feeling his skin bake. Today, he'd driven down the Strip for the first time, and was shocked at how strange it looked in daylight. What at night became dazzling and beautiful just looked misshapen and weirdly tacky under the unforgiving sunlight. It was like going to a nightclub at noon, when what was nocturnally glamorous revealed itself to be nothing more than a dirty black box where your shoes stuck to the floor.

He came into his house, sighing with relief at the cool blast of the air-conditioning (he kept his thermostat set at "meat locker") and tossing his keys on the hall table. His relief was short-lived.

There was a man sitting in his living room, looking at him.

Jack froze, his hand hanging in mid-air where it had started on its way to smooth his windblown hair. The spit dried up in his mouth.

The man looked relaxed, but Jack knew that he wasn't. He was wearing jeans, a white T-shirt, and a black sport coat. His hair was barely more than stubble all over his skull, and his eyes were hidden by sunglasses. Across his lap, he was holding a silver handgun with a silencer on it.

He stood up, his lanky frame unfolding with near-audible creases and crackles. Jack wondered how long he'd been waiting.

Jack's jaw felt stiff when he tried to speak; his face was numb in a way that made him think of shoveling the driveway in January. "Who are you?" he croaked. The man didn't answer. He crossed the living room in even, deliberate strides and grabbed Jack by the upper arm. He pulled him forward and sat him down in his Eames chair. The man stepped back and stood before him, all quiet menace and deadly intent. Jack stared up at him, nothing in his mind but blankness. The circuit breakers in his brain had tripped and stopped the flow of emotions. "How'd you find me?" he asked. It was less a stall question and more legitimate curiosity. Jack had half-assumed that the Dominguez brothers would find a way to get to him, but he'd been so impressed by the thoroughness of his relocation that he didn't know how on earth *anyone* could have found him here.

Still, it didn't exactly surprise him that someone had.

Jack took slow, even breaths. *I'm going to die any second.* The thought was surprisingly bereft of power. The idea of death didn't have much potency when confronted with the inescapable fact of it. It was a done deal. No use being afraid of it. It was almost a relief not to have to dread it anymore.

The man who'd come to kill him was just standing there, staring off into space at some point above Jack's head, his gun held loosely at his side. The man raised his free hand and rubbed at his forehead, then began to walk slowly back and forth in front of Jack's chair. Jack's eyes tracked him, his body glued to the chair as if he'd been strapped in. Something in the man's posture, his body language... a tiny, wriggling specter of hope worked its way into Jack's mind.

He doesn't want to do it.

Jack held his breath, watching his killer pace. *Don't be stupid. He's gonna do it whether he wants to or not.*

The man didn't look at him. He paced, those dark, blank lenses swiveling back and forth like the unfeeling eye of a security camera. Jack's brain made a random cross-connection and he found himself thinking of *2001: A Space Odyssey.* *"Open the pod bay doors, HAL."* That's what this man's shuttered stare reminded him of. The all-seeing cyclopean gaze of HAL. *"I'm afraid I can't do that, Dave."*

Don't just sit there like some dumb sheep waiting to get slaughtered. Do something, for Christ's sake. If you can't do something, at least say *something.*

Jack swallowed hard, hearing a click in his dry throat. "Don't do this," he said. *Nice one, asshole. Like this guy's never heard anyone beg for their life before.* Jack squared his shoulders a little. *I'm not going to beg. No matter what else happens, I'm not going to beg.* "You don't have to do this."

The man stopped pacing, then sat down on the couch facing him. He stared down at the gun in his hand. Jack watched him, trying to read something of his expression, which was damned difficult while his heart was pounding so hard it was making his vision shake. The circuit breakers were resetting. Terror was creeping into Jack's body, robbing him of whatever fortitude he'd been able to muster. *God, I don't wanna die. Not like this. Not like this.*

The man had his head down now, the gun clasped in both hands. Jack felt his tenuous self-control fading. He was shaking uncontrollably. *Please, just don't let me piss myself. I know I'll do it when the bullet goes through my head anyway, but not when I'm still in charge. Gimme that, at least.*

The man stood up and took two steps toward where Jack was sitting immobile, in his favorite chair. He raised the gun and pointed it at Jack's head. Jack sucked in a breath and closed his eyes, his mouth curling into a tortured ribbon of terror. His breath puffed in and out through clenched teeth like he'd just run a mile, and he waited. *What's it going to feel like? Will it hurt? Any minute now.... Will I feel it at all, or will I just be dead? I hope it doesn't hurt. Any minute now....*

Five seconds passed. Ten. Fifteen. Jack cautiously opened one eye. His killer was still standing over him, the gun pointed at Jack's head, but he hadn't fired. With effort, Jack looked past the gun barrel—it seemed to fill the whole world—and saw the man's clenched jaw and his lips, clamped tight in a thin white line.

He doesn't want to do it. The thought recurred, stronger this time. Jack stared at the mouth of the gun's barrel, that dark circle of death, and a sudden calm descended on him. All at once, he knew exactly what to do. *Talk. Play him. Get him to talk to you. Tell him your name. Make yourself a person.*

"You're not going to do it," he said, amazed at how calm he sounded. He'd stopped shaking.

His would-be killer's head turned slightly, cocked, interrogative. He still did not speak.

Jack shook his head. "You would have already done it." He lifted one hand, palm forward. *It's okay, I'm not a threat.* "What's your name?" he asked. *Great. Now you sound like a five-year-old on the recess playground trying to make friends with the coolest kid in the class and hoping he doesn't pound you for your trouble.*

His killer didn't respond, verbally or otherwise. He didn't appear to have heard him. "My name's Jack Francisco. I, uh… guess you know that, though. I'm a doctor. Did they tell you that? Maxillofacial surgeon." The man took a step backward. A little thrill of triumph ran down Jack's overtaxed nerves. *I'm getting to him.* "I'm from Baltimore." The man raised both hands to his face, his gun still clutched in his right. "Hey… it's okay," Jack said. "You don't have to do this. Do you even know why you're here? Or why I'm here? I saw somebody get killed, and now…."

"I know," the killer suddenly snarled, the first words he'd spoken. He'd snatched his hands away from his face and turned the blank dark-matter lamps of his sunglasses directly onto Jack. He could almost feel their high beams on him, like the rays of a black hole that sucked warmth from him instead of laying it on. "I fuckin' know what you saw," he repeated.

Jack swallowed hard. *Don't lose it now. You've got him talking.* "Look, I don't know what your bosses told you…."

"They ain't my bosses," the killer said, his lip still curled in a half-sneer, his voice a cornered-animal growl. "Fuckin' drug lords." He shook his head. "Ain't takin' no orders from the likes a them." The pacing started up again. "Don't own me. Motherfuckers. Ain't doin' no job on their say-so." Jack watched him. The man didn't really seem to be addressing him anymore.

Jack's brain was twirling too fast; the thoughts kept getting tossed off in all directions like kids that didn't keep their grip on a playground merry-go-round. He managed to snag one with his numb fingertips. *He doesn't want to do it, and he's chafing against being made to do it. Use it. Get under his skin.* Jack shifted in his chair a little. *But don't piss him off.*

Right. "So, you work for the Dominguez brothers?" he said. "They pay you well to do their dirty work?"

The killer paused in his pacing and, incredibly, chuckled. "You playin' me, Francisco?" he said.

Hearing his name spoken aloud by the man who'd been sent here to get it carved on a headstone gave Jack an unpleasant shiver. *Amateur,* he scolded himself. "I just want to know if you're going to kill me, or what."

The killer—Jack's mind was starting to think of him as HAL—swung around, his gun rising to target Jack's head again. "Could jus' do ya right now," he said. "Don't wanna waste yer time or nothin'."

Jack recoiled. "No rush." HAL nodded, then resumed his pacing. *Talk to him. The more you talk, the harder it'll be for him to execute you. The longer you stall, the less likely he'll be to pull that trigger.* "So you don't work for them, then."

"Fuck no."

"Then why are you here?"

"Ain't none a yer business."

"Are you going to kill me?" Jack asked.

HAL sighed. "I dunno."

"You could just leave. I... I won't tell anyone you were here. I won't call the police or the Marshals or anything. I swear."

He sniffed. "Think I care who you fuckin' call? Ain't the problem."

"Oh," Jack said, feeling abruptly out of his depth. This man wasn't afraid of the law. "The brothers? Guess they'd be mad if you don't kill me."

HAL shook his head, taking a seat on the couch again. "You ain't got no idea, doc," he grumbled.

THE guy wasn't a pussy, D had to give him that. Sat right there in that fancy chair and tried to play him. Needled him about being the Dominguez's bitch, slapping him with words to see if he flinched. He'd thought the guy would be a pussy. Big city doctor, some kind of specialist, from the file. Thought that he'd wet himself and start blubbering the minute he saw the gun. He hadn't, though. Just got that thousand-yard stare that he'd seen on lots of folks, that look that said they'd gone as far as they could, and now death was here and it was time to just present your belly and let it gut you. Fact of it blew a fuse in the mind, so the feelings didn't shut down the whole damned system.

But he'd come back pretty quick. Tried to get D to talk to him. Asked his name, told him his own. Tried to engage him in fucking *conversation.* D had heard plenty of begging and crying and swearing and bargaining, but he hadn't ever been on the receiving end of some guy's college psychology courses.

Now D wondered why he'd thought Francisco would be a pussy. Guy had the balls to testify against the brothers. He had to have at least a little lead in his pencil to do that, knowing what it'd earn him, namely a one-way ticket to Witness Protection and a lifetime of looking over his shoulder.

He'd been all set to do it. Spent two days talking himself through it so he wouldn't have to engage his brain when he got here, hoping that'd get him past. Just sit the guy down, pump a couple rounds into him, close your eyes if you have to, and leave. He'd done it dozens of times. Hundreds, maybe. This wouldn't be no different.

But it was different, and there was no use pretending otherwise. He was used to killing people who'd earned the kind of death he brought them. He'd even come to think of it as his contribution to society. Cleaning up the scum. People who'd killed, raped, hurt, stolen. Bad people. But Francisco, he wasn't bad people.

You don't do it, you know what's gonna happen. They ain't gonna even bother sendin' them photos to nobody. They'll just come after you guns blazin', and Francisco too. Probly got a couple on yer tail already, just ta make sure ya do the job 'cause they know you ain't so keen on it.

So why'd they pick you in the first place?

That was the question he couldn't get out of his mind. The brothers had gone to considerable effort to get *him* to carry out this hit, even going so far as to tail him for months. There were dozens of other professionals who would have taken Francisco out without batting an eyelash or losing one minute of sleep. They knew D wasn't one of those types. So why him?

Maybe they just wanted ta pop yer cherry and make ya kill an innocent man so's it's easier next time. Maybe they're gentlin' you inta executions like you'd break a horse ta the saddle.

That just brought him back around to the sleep-killing idea that Josey might somehow have engineered all this. She'd made no secret of the fact that D's disinclination to carry out certain hits was a burden to her. *Maybe she just wants ta make me do it. Maybe she's sick a my bullshit. Maybe she knows....*

He couldn't go near that, though. *Cain't be. If she knew, I'd already be dead.*

Now here was Francisco, thinking he understood a damned thing. "Guess they'd be mad if you don't kill me," he'd just said, like he'd discovered some earth-shattering revelation of the goddamned universe.

Mad, sure. The brothers will stomp their feet and say "Curses, foiled again" and then throw up their hands in surrender. "Guess we cain't stop Francisco from sendin' us to the hoosegow," they'd say, and sit back and wait to get hauled away.

Mad. Mad like a hornet's nest gets stepped on. Mad like a fuckin' hurricane, and that's about how strong they'd come after him. Not him... *them.* 'Cause if he decided not ta kill Francisco, he couldn't leave him here. They'd just send somebody else.

That's what they always do, a quiet voice, a familiar voice, whispered to him. *You won't kill no innocent folks, so they just send somebody else. Never bothered you before.*

That wasn't true. Not by a long shot. But this was different, anyhow. He ain't never had a gun in no one's face and then spared their life. In the sparing was the keeping, and if he wasn't gonna do Francisco himself, then no one else was gonna do him neither.

If you don't do him, yer gonna hafta run. And yer gonna hafta take him with you, 'cause he ain't gonna last two days once the brothers realize he's still breathin' and you took off.

Fuckin' Francisco. Couldn't he have been an irritating, snot-nosed fool who'd have gotten down on his knees and begged D to spare his sorry-ass life? Couldn't he have been a jerk-ass fucker who secretly strangled kittens or something? If he had been, maybe D could have pulled that trigger.

Just do it. Fuckin' do it. You can live with it. You cain't live with what'll happen if you don't, and that ain't no figure a speech. Only takes a second. Two shots. Shut them eyes a his lookin' at you like they see through ta yer bones. Fucker; why does he keep lookin' at me like that? Most folks look away. Look at the floor, at the ceiling, at their own hands, anywhere but at me. Biggest damned eyes I ever saw on any man, and bluer'n the sky down in Bryce Canyon. Big enough ta hold all the life in him so's I can see it, the life they want me ta take, the life I'll hafta stand here and watch leave him. Stupid motherfuckers killin' their own and makin' me clean up for 'em like they fuckin' branded me.

D sighed. It chapped his ass something fierce, but there was no choice.

"YOU ain't got no idea, doc," HAL mumbled. Then, to Jack's amazement, he reached up and removed his sunglasses. He shut his eyes before Jack could even see what color they were, his brow furrowing. With his free hand he pinched the bridge of his nose, like he was getting a headache. He sat like that for a few long moments. Jack felt like his senses were amplified, honed into hypersensitivity by the gun still grasped in HAL's right hand. He was aware of the hum of his air-conditioning, the stickiness of his damp skin where it rested against the leather chair, the rustle of HAL's clothes against the couch cushions, and the faint sound of cars passing and kids playing.

People are living out there. How can they? I'm in here with some kind of hired assassin and he has a gun with which he might shoot me at any moment and meanwhile, people are driving to the grocery store and screwing each other and cooking meals and watching fucking Oprah.

HAL dropped his hand and stood up. Jack managed not to recoil as he met the eyes of his would-be killer for the first time. Without the sunglasses, the machine quality was gone and he just looked like… a man. A man with strong, high cheekbones and brown eyes that might have been warm had they not been filled with such flat resignation.

He sighed, the sigh of a man about to shoulder a heavy load. "Get up, Francisco," he said.

Somehow, Jack peeled himself out of the chair and stood up. His legs felt like Jell-O. "Want to look me in the eye when you shoot me?" he said.

The killer gave him a little head shake that clearly said *God, the idiots I have to deal with.* "Pack a bag."

Jack blinked. "A… a bag?"

"Yer comin' with me."

"The hell I am!"

HAL raised the gun again. "You forgettin' who's in charge here?"

"Look, if you're not going to shoot me, just get the hell out of my house and we'll forget it ever happened."

The man shook his head again like he couldn't believe Jack's stupidity. "You think the brothers'll forget? I don't kill ya, they'll send someone else who will, probly someone who'll do it slow 'n' messy."

"The program will move me again. They won't find me."

"They found ya here. They'll find ya again."

"I'm not going anywhere with you."

"D'you have a fuckin' death wish?" HAL hissed at him. "Those fuckers are gonna come after me fer not killin' you, and they're gonna come after you fer not bein' dead yet, and no one can protect you from them! No one, ya hear? Not the Marshals, not the police, not the goddamned Neighborhood Watch! Yer only shot is ta stick with me!"

Jack blinked, not sure if he was hearing what he thought he was hearing. "What, you're saying that… now you want to *protect* me?"

"You wanna live? You gotta come with me. Is what I'm sayin'."

"You must be out of your mind if you think I'm going to trust you!" Jack shouted.

HAL seized Jack's shirt and yanked him forward until they were chest-to-chest, the gun barrel pressed underneath the shelf of Jack's chin. Jack stiffened but didn't drop the man's gaze. "You don't gotta trust me. You just gotta do what I fuckin' say. Now. Pack. A. Bag."

D PACED in Francisco's living room, smoking. The man was a goddamned caution. Giving him lip when he'd be better advised to just hop to. Thinking the damned Witness Protection Program would save his lily-white ass. D wondered what Francisco would say if he told him that the brothers had probably learned of his location by buying the information off someone in the Marshals' office.

Take Francisco's car. Probly got somebody watchin' the house. Since I come in the back, hopefully they don't know I'm here. We leave in his car, me ducked down, maybe they jus' think he's goin' out fer groceries or somethin'. Gotta try 'n' get a head start.

A head start to where? D had no idea where to go next. None of his usual safe places felt safe at all. The brothers probably knew about them if they'd been tailing him, or they could pound the information out of Josey. He thought back to hidey-holes he hadn't used in a long time, places no one else knew about, weighing their relative tactical merits.

He could hear Francisco thumping about upstairs. He heard something fall and break, and Francisco's angry "Goddammit!"

Yer an idiot, lettin' him pack alone. He could hide a gun or a knife or God knows what else in his bag, ambush you in yer sleep. Which was true. In a way, D half-hoped that Francisco *would* try something like that. At least it'd tell him what kind of man he was dealing with. One that'd offer his jugular to the alpha dog? Or one that'd bite at his neck to challenge him?

The man came half-tumbling down the stairs, looking frazzled and carrying a backpack over his shoulder. "Okay. I packed a goddamned bag. Satisfied?"

D crushed out his cigarette into the carpet. "I'll be satisfied we get five hours distant. Let's go. Take yer car."

JACK backed out of the driveway, D hunkered down in the backseat so that any observers couldn't see him. "All right, where are we going?" he asked.

"Head north outta town."

"Whatever." He drove quietly, being careful not to speed or run any red lights. The thought occurred that he could probably manage to flag a cop, or signal someone for help... but to what end? What help could be offered? And did he really need help? He wasn't being kidnapped, exactly.

I'm on the lam, he thought crazily. *On the lam with a hired killer who was supposed to execute me. What's next? A femme fatale? A car chase? Maybe we'll have a showdown in some abandoned warehouse like in some half-assed action movie they'd show on TNT on a Saturday afternoon.*

Jack shook his head in amazement. *Actually, if this were a movie, you'd be a beautiful woman and you'd be sleeping with HAL by the second act.*

"Check if anyone's following us," HAL said from the backseat.

"How do I know that?"

"Uh… look in the rearview mirror." Jack was getting a little tired of the subtextual *dumbass* that seemed appended to most of HAL's statements. And he was getting *really* tired of thinking of the man as HAL.

He kept a close eye on his mirrors for a few minutes. "No one's following us."

"You sure?"

"I'm sure."

HAL sat up, then peered over the dash. "Gotta stop 'n' get gas."

Jack pulled into the nearest gas station. He was just about to swipe his debit card in the pump when he felt a hand on his arm. "Cash. Pay cash. Cain't leave no trail." *Dumbass.*

"I don't have any cash."

HAL sighed wearily. "I got cash."

Jack watched his unlikely companion return after paying for the gas, bearing two bottles of water. "Lemme drive," he said.

Jack gladly gave up the driver's seat and buckled himself in. He uncapped his water bottle and HAL's, setting them in the cup holders. HAL glanced at him. "Thanks," he said, sounding surprised at this miniscule courtesy.

"Thanks for not shooting me."

HAL snorted as they pulled back onto the road. "I'd say no problem, but the truth is that it's a real big fuckin' problem."

They drove in silence for a few miles. "So *now* will you tell me your name?" Jack asked. "I can't just keep calling you HAL."

He frowned. "Why would ya call me Hal?"

"Long story. So? You know my name. Give it up."

"Less ya know about me, the better."

Jack shrugged. "Fine. Long as you don't mind being addressed as 'hey, you.'"

Beat. Sigh. "Call me D."

"D?"

"You asked my name, I told ya."

"Yeah, it's just that… well, most of the time in names, D is followed by some more letters. Like –onald, or –avid."

D stared at him for a few seconds, then seemed to relax. "D's good enough."

Jack nodded. "Nice to meet you, D."

CHAPTER 3

JACK said nothing as D drove in what seemed like aimless, meandering circles around the Vegas suburbs, taking his time and turning randomly right and left, doubling back on himself. His eyes were alert; Jack suspected he was still watching for someone following them.

Finally, D pulled into an alley behind a strip mall and parked the car. He reached into the backseat, pulled a laptop out of his messenger bag and booted up, balancing the thing on his knees. Jack tried to look nonchalant and unconcerned, as if he parked in alleys with hired killers every day of the week and this was nothing new.

He glanced over at D's laptop screen. Looked like Google Maps. "Uh... what are you doing?" he finally asked, when it became clear that D was not going to volunteer this information.

"Gotta get new plates fer this car," D muttered. The words were given up grudgingly, resentful at having to taste air to explain D's actions.

Jack frowned. "How? Don't think they sell those on Amazon."

That earned him a withering sidelong glance. "Hafta steal a set." *Dumbass.*

"Oh." He supposed he ought to feel uneasy at the thought of perpetuating petty theft, but after witnessing one murder and almost starring in another, he couldn't quite work up any indignation over a set of license plates. License plates.... A light bulb went off in Jack's head. "Wait! I know this! Airport long-term parking, right?"

D sighed. "Ya watch too many movies."

"That isn't right?"

The black HAL lenses of D's sunglasses swiveled toward him. "When ya leave airport parking, ya gotta pay the guy ta get out. Might remember somebody who came in and then came right back out again. Cain't afford ta get noticed." He turned back to the laptop.

"So... what are you looking for? The License Plates Store on eBay?"

A half-smile crept onto D's face. "Nope. Found somethin' better."

"YOU'RE kidding." Jack looked around, confused, as they pulled into the nursing home's parking lot. D drove around to the back, away from the visitor parking. He parked Jack's nondescript Witness Protection-issue Ford Taurus and got out. After a moment's hesitation (*petty theft*) Jack followed him. "A nursing home?"

D ignored him, his head turning back and forth as he surveyed the cars. Jack suddenly realized that these were the cars that belonged to the home's residents. Most of them were Old People Cars: sizable sedans, stolid and sedate, none of them too new. This parking lot felt neglected; many cars had dead leaves and other detritus piled around their tires and rain-dust streaking their windows. The back of the nursing home was secluded and not visible from the street; they were alone. Suddenly D stopped and his chin tilted down; he zeroed in on one car like a hunting dog pointing at a kill. "That one," he muttered, nodding toward a nearby Toyota.

"Why this one?" Jack whispered, feeling conspicuous but following D to the car.

"Dusty like it ain't moved in awhile."

Jack tugged on D's sleeve. "No, this one's better," he said, pointing to a Buick sedan a few cars down.

D hesitated. "Why?"

"The tags are six months expired. I don't think anyone's driving it at all."

The HAL lenses rested on Jack's face for a beat, and then D nodded. "All right," was all he said, but Jack detected (or hoped he detected) a note of admiration for Jack's deduction. *Maybe I could be a ninja assassin too,* Jack thought.

D took a Swiss Army knife out of his pocket, crouched by the Buick, and had the plates off in a few quick twists, then went around to the front and repeated the procedure.

They went back to Jack's car and D swapped out the plates, carefully peeling Jack's current registration tags off his plates and putting them on the stolen ones, then tossed Jack's plates in the trunk. "Shouldn't we put those on the Buick?" Jack asked.

D looked at him like he was crazy. "Why'n hell would we do that?"

"Well... no one would notice wrong plates on the Buick, but no plates might stick out."

"Look round," D said, impatiently. "Folks don't come back here much; by the time anyone sees we be long gone. Besides, we put yer plates on this car, if it gets reported they'll know we was here, and they'll know what plates we got!"

Jack nodded, feeling like he deserved that particular *dumbass.* "Right. Sure."

Back in the car, he said nothing as D drove out of town. As they put Vegas in their rearview mirror, the adrenaline began to leave Jack's body and he slumped against the passenger door, his head aching and his muscles twitching. In the past few hours he'd gone from the safe (albeit dull) life of a protected witness to being on the lam with a man who'd come to his house to kill him. A man who, it seemed, had decided not to kill him but couldn't be bothered to actually *talk* to him. It yanked all the moorings out from beneath his feet when he could see no more of his future than he could of the highway ahead. "Where are we going?" he finally asked.

"Quartzsite," D replied

That was about a four-hour drive to the middle of nowhere. "What's there?"

Sigh. "Gotta pick up some stuff." He sounded put out to have to answer even this simplest of questions, and pique rose in Jack's throat.

"You know, you could cut me some fucking slack," he snapped. D glanced at him briefly, then back at the road. "I am stuck in a car with some guy who was supposed to kill me and this is the *second* time in as many months that my whole life's been pureed and I'm just supposed to sit here quietly and not ask any questions? I'm real fucking sorry to *bother* you, but I'm the one with a bull's-eye on his forehead here." Jack crossed his arms over his chest and flopped back against the seat.

D's visible response to this little tirade was to purse his lips slightly. Jack watched out of the corner of his eye as the man's jaw clenched and unclenched. Suddenly, he yanked the wheel to the right and pulled off the deserted highway, then parked the car and turned in his seat to face Jack, taking off those damned HAL sunglasses. "Dominguez brothers want ya dead. I was hired ta kill ya. I cain't be entirely sure was them that hired me. So that's possibly two parties after ya. Plus the U.S. Marshals gonna be on the hunt for ya now that yer outta pocket. That's three parties we gotta steer clear of."

"Why can't we let the Marshals catch us? If you're so worried about my welfare, they're the ones—"

D cut him off. "Hate ta tell ya, but we gotta consider that whoever put out the hit on ya got yer location from inside the program."

Jack blinked. That was a disturbing thought. "How could they—"

D flapped a hand as if this were an insignificant detail. "Bought, stole, hacked, blackmailed. Don't matter. Point is, cain't trust 'em no more ta hide ya. Plus, since I ain't done ya, parties what hired me, be they the brothers or not, gonna be after *me*. Ya gettin' the picture?"

Jack swallowed hard. "A little too well."

"None a my hideouts gonna be safe. I got a stash hid outside Quartzsite. Goin' there fer money 'n' weapons. Then we gotta get new ID. Gotta go ta LA fer that, but need cash first." Throughout this speech, D's unblinking eyes didn't leave Jack's face but pinned him there against the passenger door like an amoeba under a microscope.

"Okay," Jack said, nodding.

D sighed. "But don't go thinkin' it's jus' you with a bull's-eye on yer forehead." He turned toward the road again and pulled back onto the highway.

They drove in silence for a good half hour. Jack watched the spare expanse of southwestern scenery scroll by outside the car, trying to empty his mind of thoughts... but one kept recurring. "What did you mean when you said it might not have been the Dominguez brothers who hired you?" Jack asked.

It took D long enough to answer that Jack started to wonder if he was going to. "I got no proof was them."

"Isn't them wanting me dead proof enough? I don't think anyone else is that mad at me."

D cleared his throat and shifted in his seat. "Mighta been more about me killin' ya than you bein' dead."

"I don't understand."

"Possible some parties wanted ta see if I'd do it."

"Why would they think you wouldn't?"

"Don't matter."

"Fine, whatever." Jack fell silent again. The sun was setting, and he was starting to get sleepy. He squinted into the spectacular sunset that was, sadly, lost on him in his distraction and let D's words percolate into his brain. He tucked himself into the corner of the seat and rested his eyes on D's profile as he faced relentlessly forward, both hands on the wheel, the picture of steely resolve even engaged in such a mundane task as driving.

With his shorn hair and stubble, D's head looked like it had been sandblasted and weather-stripped. Jack had spent most of his professional life cutting people's faces open, and his surgeon's eye showed him the bones beneath D's skin, although his seemed much closer to the surface than most people's. His jawline was like a flying buttress, his brow like one of the table mesas that lurked on the horizon. His skull was geologic in its architecture. One could only imagine the seismic events and plate tectonics that had gone on in his life to shape him into this... whatever he was.

Jack knew that he ought to be afraid of D, and in a way, he was, but he got no sense of evil or malice from the man. He just seemed so rigidly defended that Jack wondered if any emotional considerations were even possible, and yet he'd displayed emotion in Jack's own living room when faced with his homicidal task. Since then, however, he'd been about as accessible as the saguaro cacti dotting the landscape.

How accessible would you want to be if you were a hired killer? Jack suppressed a shiver. How many people had D killed? Dozens? *Hundreds?* How many had begged for mercy? How many had families, children, spouses to support? How many, like him, had done nothing but be in the wrong place at the wrong time? He looked away, having managed to give himself the creeps. *This guy could decide to kill you at any moment, Jack. Just because he gave you a pass today doesn't mean you're in the clear, and you better not forget that, not for one moment.*

Jack reconsidered the wisdom of trying to get away. He'd probably have the chance if he stayed on his toes. He'd already had chances. *Get to a phone and call your contact in the program.* It was tempting, but D had said that might not be safe. *He could just be making that up so you won't call the authorities.*

Jack rubbed his eyes. He was talking in circles, and giving himself a headache to boot. The plan D had described seemed like a good enough one to Jack, and he was just too tired to think of a reason why he shouldn't go along.

FRANCISCO had been watching him for most of the drive. D let him, not acknowledging Francisco's observation or asking why. If he were in Francisco's position, he would have been trying to figure some shit out too.

The deserted two-lane blacktop wasn't the fastest way to Quartzsite but it was the loneliest, and that was what he wanted. Easy to spot a tail, hard to get snuck up on. He was feeling off his game and unbalanced and wanted to give himself every advantage he could. He couldn't shake the feeling that they weren't in the clear, even though he'd seen no sign of surveillance at Francisco's house or since.

As for Francisco? The man had surprised him. The thing about the tags on the license plates they'd stolen had been a sharp note, and D had kicked himself a little for not picking up on it himself, but then his spy-novel ideas about long-term airport parking and putting the Taurus's plates on the Buick had taken him right back to a little kid playing cops 'n' robbers. Francisco might have had some book-learning and a little backbone, but in those eyes of his D could see the deep thread of gonna-be-okay running through him, made more remarkable by what he'd been through lately.

Francisco was still watching him, but now he was trying to hide it. He didn't know that D could feel anybody's eyes on him, the weight of their gaze sitting on him, heavy like a drop of rainwater. He hated being this close to the man and this easily watched. Wasn't anything personal; it just wasn't his way. And he'd have to keep him this close if he didn't want him bumped off right from under his own nose.

He saw Francisco shudder a little. *Probly rememberin' the gun ya had in his face a few hours ago,* D thought. *Oughta throw the guy a bone, leastways so's he knows you ain't gonna pop off and shoot him after all. Gotta make him trust ya a little, else he might try 'n' get away. Cain't have that. Cain't chance him goin' ta the cops or runnin' off on his own 'n' getting his damned fool head blown off.*

Goddamn, I hate this. D cleared his throat. "Hour ta Quartzsite," he said.

Francisco jumped a little at the sudden noise after an hour of silence. "Oh... uh, good. I guess."

"Find a motel, hole up fer the night."

"Okay." Francisco was sitting up a little straighter, and watching him openly again. "So... you don't work for the brothers normally?" he asked, taking the opening D had laid at his feet.

"Don't work for nobody."

"You're a free agent?"

D sniffed. "Guess so."

Francisco nodded, mulling this over. "Never thought men like you were real."

"Men like me?"

"You know. Hired assassins."

That surprised a brief snort of laughter out of him. "*Hired assassins?* How many Tom Clancy books you read, anyway?"

Francisco blinked, and then chuckled a little. "I guess that does sound kind of melodramatic, doesn't it?"

"Bit, yeah."

"You tell me, then."

D fished a pack of cigarettes out of his jacket pocket and lit one, cracking the window. "Just do what I do."

"But just so we're clear, what you do is murder for hire, right?"

Hearing it put like that made D's lips clamp down a little tighter on his cigarette. "S'pose so."

"So why would anybody have thought you wouldn't kill me?"

"Huh?"

"You said before that somebody might want to see if you'd kill me. Why wouldn't you?"

"'Cause ya don't deserve it," D said, quietly.

Francisco blinked at him. "What?"

"You ain't done nothin' ta bring it ta yer door, Francisco. You witnessed a crime 'n' were gonna help put them bastards away. Ain't no reason ta kill ya, not by my reckonin'."

Francisco had turned in his seat and was now staring at him with unabashed interest. "Are you telling me that you only kill people who *deserve* it?"

"Them's my rules."

"And who gets to decide that? You?"

"Who the fuck else?"

"What kind of people? Who deserves it, tell me that?" Francisco was getting agitated. D had thought this line of discussion would calm him down, but it sure wasn't working out that way.

"Well... some a them killers themselves. Done some child molesters. Done a few a them fer free, matter a fact. Lotta crime-boss types. Few pimps. Bad folks."

"Bad folks," Francisco repeated. "Like you."

D sighed. "I'm jus' cleanin' up the scum, Francisco." He shook his head. "Didn't mean ta piss ya off none," he said.

"I'm sorry," Francisco snapped. "I've just never met a professional killer before, and I'm having a little trouble with the degrees of morality here." He sat back in his seat, exhaling. "I guess I shouldn't judge. Your rules saved my life, didn't they?"

"Reckon so."

A few tense minutes passed until Francisco sighed and his shoulders sagged. "I'm...."

"Don't worry about it," D said, cutting him off. "Yer right. I *am* bad folks."

Francisco said nothing for a few beats. "I don't think you're bad," he murmured.

JACK woke with a start, a finger poking his shoulder. "Huh?" he said, sitting up straight. D was leaning over him, nothing more than a darker outline in the general darkness.

"We're here," D said. "C'mon, need an extra pair a hands."

Jack got out of the car. It was so dark he couldn't even see his hands in front of his face. "Christ, it's dark out here. How do you know we're in the right spot?"

The soft glow of a green LED screen briefly lit up D's face as he handed Jack a flashlight. "GPS." He turned on his own flashlight and Jack followed along. As his eyes adjusted he could make out hulking hills nearby, and the flat desert ground at his feet. D walked slowly, casting the beam of his flashlight around, until he saw a tall Joshua tree nearby with a distinctive pitchfork shape to its branches.

"How appropriate," Jack muttered.

D stopped at the base of the tree and shone his light on the ground, swiping at the desert soil with his foot until he exposed something metallic. He bent over and grabbed it, and Jack saw it was the handle to a trapdoor. D pulled up a cloth, exposing a combination lock. He spun it right and left, then yanked up on the trapdoor. It yawed open like a hungry mouth, revealing a short flight of stairs.

Jack followed D into the hole, a little apprehensive, but it was just an old bunker, possibly an abandoned bomb shelter. D pulled a cord, and a naked bulb illuminated the room. The bunker was dusty and stale; a number of aluminum cases were stacked on its shelves. D began pulling them down and opening them; Jack could see that most of them contained guns. He didn't know the first thing about firearms, but D seemed to know what he was looking for.

"Here, hold this," he said, handing Jack a duffel bag. Jack held it open while D tossed in weapons and boxes of ammunition. He added a smaller, leather case and then opened up an innocuous-looking coffee can and pulled out a very thick roll of bills secured with a rubber band. This, he stuffed into his pocket.

"Holy shit," Jack said. "Are we taking over a small country?"

D snorted. "Gotta be prepared." He looked up at Jack's face, frowning. "What?"

Jack shrugged. "It's just...." He sighed. "I'm starting to see words like 'accessory' and 'accomplice' floating around my head."

D barely reacted. "How about 'dead on arrival'? Ya like that better?"

Jack nodded, pressing his lips together. "Get more ammo. Ammo is good."

ONCE the deadbolt and chain were secured, D immediately felt better. The motel room's tackiness was familiar, and as he shut the drapes it was like shutting the world's eyes to them. No one could see them here.

Francisco was flopped on the bed near the bathroom, staring at the ceiling. D sat down on the other bed and removed his guns. He checked the loads and placed one on the nightstand, the other on the dresser. "I'm starving," Francisco said. "Can I order a pizza?"

"Pizza's good."

Francisco sat up, frowning. "Oh, you want some?"

"I'm hungry too." D watched Francisco's bemused expression. "What?"

Francisco shrugged, shaking it off. "I don't know. It's just weird that you, you know… eat."

D cocked an eyebrow. "Don't everybody?"

"You just seem like you'd be impervious to everything."

Damn, I wish. "Well, I ain't. And I like mushrooms."

"Me too." Francisco found a phone book and ordered their pizza. D listened, shaking his head, as Francisco turned on the charm and convinced the pizza joint to bring them a six-pack too. After he hung up, they waited in silence, Francisco on the bed, D sitting in the chair by the window. "Why'd you do it?" Francisco asked.

"Do what?"

"Agree to kill me. You said you didn't kill people who didn't deserve it, but you were going to kill me. Why'd you break your rules?"

D sighed and lit up a cigarette. *Motherfucker never stops talking.* "Had no choice."

"What, were they holding your cat hostage or something?"

"Don't got no cat."

"Why didn't you have a choice?"

"Men that hired me had pictures a me at other jobs I done."

"So they blackmailed you."

"Yup."

"What's to stop them from turning you in now?"

D turned and looked at Francisco, sitting there on the bed cross-legged like a kid telling ghost stories, so fucking naïve it made D's teeth hurt. He almost hated to be the one disabusing the man of all his well-meant notions. After the life D had led for the past ten years, it was nice to know that there were still people like Francisco in the world, who thought that life could be good and sweet. "Nothin'. They could turn me in at any time. They won't, though. I took the job 'n' I didn't do it, and now I'm tryin' ta stop anyone else from pickin' up my slack. They ain't gonna bother getting me thrown in jail. They're just gonna want me dead."

"You and me both."

"Yup."

"So… we're in this together?"

D sniffed. "Ya sound like ya hope we are."

"Frankly, if I've got people after me, I'd much rather be on the run with somebody like you than on my own. I can repair a cleft palate in my sleep but I'd be useless against armed killers."

"Ya sure would."

Francisco was quiet for a moment. D knew it wouldn't last, and it didn't. "So, how long were you in the military?"

D looked at him sharply. "How'd you know I was in the military?"

Francisco smiled. "I didn't. Now I do. Lucky guess. You just seem like the type. And you didn't start wearing your hair like that for high fashion."

D slouched down in his chair. It troubled him that Francisco could read something like that so easily. Usually, he prided himself on being unseeable. Black, like a new moon, no features visible. Either he was slipping, or Francisco was real fucking sharp. He sucked on his cigarette to avoid answering. "Yeah, went in when I was eighteen."

"How long were you in?"

"Seven years. 'Til ninety-five."

That seemed to surprise Francisco. "How old are you?" he asked.

"Thirty-six."

"Me too! Huh, you don't look thirty-six."

"That so?"

"No. I would have thought you were older."

D snorted. "Guess I oughta be insulted."

"Why'd you leave the… what, the Army? Navy?"

"Army. What the fuck is this, Twenty Questions?" D bit out, tired of the interrogation but also alarmed at the amount of personal information he was letting slip out. Josey didn't even know how old he was, and here he'd known Francisco about eight hours and he was spilling his goddamned life story. What was even *more* alarming was that he found himself wanting to say more. That shit had to be nipped in the bud. "We ain't friends, Francisco," he snarled, hoping he sounded forbidding. "You don't gotta know my business, I don't gotta know yours."

Francisco shrugged. "Fine, be that way. We're just going to be spending a lot of time together and we can't sit here in silence all the time."

"Why the fuck not?"

That seemed to take the wind out of his sails a bit. His shoulders sagged, and D felt a little tug behind his sternum at the hangdog expression on his face, like a puppy who just wanted his belly rubbed and didn't get how anybody could resist when he was laying there looking all cute. "Well… can't you at least call me Jack?"

D sighed. "Yeah. Guess I can do that." *And you know what, Jack? You can call me… call me….* But that wasn't happening. That name was no longer his; it belonged to a different man who didn't exist anymore.

Jack brightened. "Good. Progress."

Progress, D thought, lighting another cigarette from his first. *Wants ta make progress. Next he'll be wanting ta talk about our childhood traumas and our favorite colors and our deep innermost thoughts.* He waited for that idea to be repugnant, or horrifying, but it refused to be either. D stared out the window, shoving down the feeling that it might be real nice to sit here and tell Jack Francisco everything about himself, confess things he'd never told nobody, just to feel like somebody cared, and to keep those big blue eyes fixed on him for as long as he could.

CHAPTER 4

JACK blinked around in disorientation, his sleep-addled brain trying to make sense of the strange surroundings. *What the fuck.... Oh, yeah. Motel. Quartzsite. Almost murdered. Gotcha.* He turned on his side. D was sitting in the chair by the window, fully dressed in what looked like the same clothes, smoking a cigarette. He didn't appear to have moved at all since Jack had finally crawled into bed and fallen asleep the night before. Had D slept? Did he even *require* sleep? Maybe he'd been one of those MK-Ultra top-secret government genetically engineered super-soldiers who didn't need to sleep and had a photographic memory, but he'd rebelled against his superiors and their immoral experimentation and struck out on his own to right the wrongs done to him....

Jack rubbed his hand over his face. *He's right. I do read too many Tom Clancy novels.* "Did you sleep?" he asked.

D grunted. "Enough."

"Did you... use the bed?" The other bed didn't appear to have been slept in.

"Laid on top."

"Why? So you could leap into action if we were ambushed?"

D just looked at him, one eyebrow ever so slightly cocked. "We gotta get goin'," was all he said. "Ya want breakfast?"

"Let's just pull through a drive-up window or something. I feel like eating something really bad for me. Do they make bacon-covered donuts?"

In the end, the Golden Arches had been the lucky recipients of their patronage, and as they set out on the road to LA, Jack was mopping the grease off his mouth from the Egg McMuffin. "Damn, that was disgusting," he commented. "I'm not much for fast food, normally."

"Ate it all though, didn'tcha?" All D had gotten was an extra-large orange juice.

"I was hungry. You weren't?"

"Don't like ta eat in the mornin'," D muttered. "Stomach troubles."

"Oh, but that highly acidic orange juice will calm you right down. Fruit juice is pure sugar, you know." That got him The Eyebrow again, so Jack shut up. Briefly. "Where are we going, again?"

"Ta get ID."

"I know that, but where? No, let me guess. You know a guy."

"Right, fer once."

"You sure we can trust him? You said that...."

"We can trust him," D said flatly, his tone forbidding any argument.

"How long will it take to get new papers?"

"Dunno. We'll see. Easy ta disappear in LA. Oughta be okay. No one really looks at ya unless yer some kinda movie star, which we ain't."

They passed the drive in silence. Jack felt jumpy. He'd thought that he'd be more at ease the farther he got from Vegas, but the opposite seemed to be the case. The idea of going back where there were so many people was unnerving. The desert offered a lonely kind of security in its remoteness. It was hard to hide there. In the sprawling city, a city Jack had visited only once and disliked intensely, danger might lurk around every corner and behind every face.

JACK seemed a mite jittery. D wasn't surprised. LA did that to people, even him, although he wouldn't show it. He didn't like LA and only came here when absolutely necessary. In his business it was hard to avoid. Any illegal activity west of the Mississippi had to come through LA eventually. There were certain things you could only get here, like the papers he and Jack needed.

He didn't say so, but he was a little anxious about showing his face at the club where Dappa kept his shop. He was hardly the only one who used the man's services, and he might run into some of his competitors. Any one of them could already have heard about the price that was no doubt on his head. He hoped that for once, word had not gotten around too quickly, and they could be in and out without running into anyone he knew.

D drove around San Bernardino until he found a motel that looked generic enough for his purposes. Not nice enough to attract robbers, not grungy enough to be populated with lowlifes paying by the week. It was a fine line. "Are we getting a room first?" Jack asked.

"Gotta. I ain't drivin' inta the city with a duffel fulla guns, ammo 'n' money in the trunk." Jack nodded, and helped him carry everything into the room, where D locked it all into the aluminum cases he'd brought from the bunker and slid them under the bed. They both took a few minutes to freshen up a little, and Jack changed his clothes on D's suggestion. "Ya look like a refugee from a fuckin' softball game. Put on pants and a jacket."

Within half an hour they were back in the car and headed into the city. Jack stared out the window, looking like a kid from the suburbs seeing a ghetto for the first time. If he'd ever visited LA, which D guessed he probably had, he sure as hell hadn't come to this part of town.

Dappa's shop was beneath a nightclub. D had often wondered why it was that folks who were up to no good had such a damned fondness for setting up shop behind, underneath, above, or otherwise proximal to fucking nightclubs. Couldn't go anywhere without that goddamned bass line thumping around in your chest when all you were trying to do was buy black-market ordnance or launder some cash. This particular nightclub, a raunchy spot called Del Muerto that catered to the Hispanic crowd, was owned by Dappa's brother.

He and Jack made their way through the crowds outside, then through the door and past the bouncer with a quick high sign. Jack was sticking ridiculously close to him. D wondered if he ought to hold his hand like a scared kid at an amusement park. "Jus' don't say nothin'," he muttered as they entered. "Let me handle this."

Jack nodded vigorously. "Sure, sure. No problem."

They went down the dirty back staircase to the basement, through an Employees Only door, and into what looked like a supply closet. Cut into the back of the closet was another door. D knocked, and the door was opened by a large man in a beret that always made D think of those beanie-copters that kids in 1950s' cartoons wore. "Who's knockin'?" the man asked.

"The good and the bad, which I guess makes you the ugly, Carlos. Lemme in."

Carlos glanced past him at Jack, his dark, beady eyes sweeping him up and down. "Who's the twink?"

"My cousin. Step aside. Dappa's expectin' me."

Carlos shouted over his shoulder. "Boss? D's here." D winced when Carlos said his name out loud. *Don't fuckin broadcast it, asshole. Tryin' ta lay low here.*

"Let him in!" came a familiar, reedy voice.

"He got a preppy-lookin' friend with him."

"I said let him in!"

Carlos stepped aside, grudgingly. "Hafta take yer weapon," he said.

D reached under his coat and handed over his pistol. He felt Jack stiffen; likely he hadn't realized D was carrying. Ought to know by now that D always carried. "Happy?" Carlos just jerked his head, and they entered the workroom.

Dappa's shop just looked like a regular office, if a cyclone hit it. D had no idea how the man found anything. "He called me a twink," Jack muttered, as they lurked near the door, waiting for Dappa.

"Shut up."

"Is that good or bad? What's it mean?"

"Means a man who knows when ta fuckin' shut up, so clearly he was mistaken. Now shut up."

"Got your message," Dappa said, scurrying up. "I got things set up; just need to take pictures. You got the money?"

"Got it," D said, withdrawing most of the roll of bills he'd recovered in Quartzsite.

Jack leaned close as Dappa walked away. "It costs that much for papers?"

"Nah. Dappa's set me up with a new checking account so we don't gotta carry cash, usin' whatever name he's givin' me. He'll take my cash, put it in his front company, and then transfer that much cash inta the new account with papers listin' my alias as some kinda consultant or investor or somethin'."

"Huh. Seems so… boring."

"What'd you expect, sacks a gold coins like in pirate movies?"

Jack shrugged, looking out of his element and nervous. "How do you know we can trust this guy?" he asked, leaning even closer, his voice barely a whisper.

D sighed. He hadn't known he was taking on a full-time backseat driver when he'd taken Francisco on as a pet project. "He owes me in a real personal kinda way. Relax. Know what I'm doin'."

"Okay," Jack said, giving off an *if-you-say-so* kind of attitude.

Dappa took their photos with a little camera, the kind they had at the DMV. "Be half an hour or so, D. Why don't you guys go upstairs and have a drink? On the house."

D considered this. Exposing himself and Jack made him nervous, but Jack could sure use a drink to calm him down some, and a whisky sounded mighty good to him too. He didn't really want to sit here in this basement shop and wait with old Carlos giving him the hairy eyeball the whole time. He nodded curtly and left the shop, Jack sticking to his side like he'd been Velcroed there.

He scanned the crowd as they made their way to a shadowy corner of the bar. No one was paying them any attention. So far, so good. He ordered a whisky for himself, and to his surprise, Jack ordered the same. "Come here often?" Jack said, going for a joking tone and not quite getting there.

"Fuckin' hate LA," D said, turning his back to the bar and most of the patrons.

"Me too. Came here once for a medical conference and couldn't wait to get home." D watched Jack's face as a brief shadow of sadness crossed it.

"Ya miss Baltimore?" he asked.

Jack nodded. "Yeah. Guess I'll never be able to live there again."

"Probly not," D said, seeing no need to sugar-coat it for him.

They drank in silence for a few minutes. D was just starting to think that they'd get away with it when he spotted a dark-clad figure approaching from the other side of the bar.

Jack must have felt him tense up. "What is it?" he asked, looking around in a fine display of not-subtle.

"Calm down," D said. "Jus' drink yer drink."

"See somebody?" Jack said.

"Fella in my line a work."

"Shit," Jack hissed. "Competition?"

"Nah. A friend, sorta. Did a coupla two-man jobs together."

"Oh. That's okay then, right?"

"Don't bet on it. If the bounty on me's less than two million it'll be a fuckin' insult. Don't got no friends when yer hide's worth that much." He watched as Signor approached, being casual about it.

Sig walked right up, bold as you please. "D," he said.

D nodded. "Sig."

"This him?" He asked, with a jerk of the head toward Jack.

Shit. The word's out. "Nah. Jus' some guy buyin' me a drink. Mus' think I'm cute or somethin'."

"Sure, whatever. The shit's out on you, D. Hit went up this morning."

"How much?"

"Three point five."

D whistled. "I'll take that as a compliment."

"You better get out of here before someone sees you."

"You already seen me."

"I'm not taking that hit. Not on one of the brotherhood."

D snorted. Sig was one of those types that had pipe dreams of some kind of honor-among-thieves bond of fraternity among men who did their kind of work. D thought it was an assload of Hollywood crap, but Sig was a Hollywood crap kind of guy. If it helped, D would nod and smile through it. "Who else is gonna see?"

"Well, Rolan Bartoz just came in with his posse. Sitting at his table like king of the hill. He sees you, he'll have it to his guys in about five seconds and to everyone else in California in five minutes."

D knocked back the rest of his whisky. That was not good news. Bartoz's table was by the entrance. "Hafta go out the back way."

"You'll have to go past him to get your stuff from Dappa. Tell you what. I'll go downstairs and get your papers and meet you around back through the dancers' door. Cover you to your car. You park on top of the garage?"

"Yup."

"Okay. Better go now."

D nodded, clapped Sig on the shoulder, and beckoned Jack to follow him. He walked quickly past the stage, through the curtain, and past a few screeching half-dressed go-go dancers, popping out behind the club in a little-used alley. He let the door shut behind him and turned to Jack.

"Nice of your friend to help out," Jack said.

"He ain't helpin'. He's comin' back here ta kill us."

Jack froze, blinking. "But… he said…."

"I coulda got down to the shop without Bartoz seein' me. Sig didn't want me to go because Carlos has my gun and I'd a gotten it back if I'd gone for the case myself."

"So you're just letting him…."

"I let him think he was foolin' me. When he gets here I'll take care of it. You stay back. Stand next to that Dumpster. You get behind it any sign a trouble, ya hear?"

Jack nodded, his face white even in the darkness behind the club. "Christ, D… this is crazy! What if he kills you? What'll happen to me then? Let's get out of here before he gets back!"

"I need that case with Dappa's papers."

"What if he doesn't bring it? What if he brings an empty one, thinking he's just going to shoot us?"

"He won't. He wants the papers too. That way he can take all the cash in my brand-fuckin'-new bank account."

"Well… what if Dappa won't give him the papers?"

"He will. He knows we've worked together. Now will you hush up?" D hissed at him. "We gotta act casual when he comes up, like we don't suspect!"

"Then why did you even *tell* me?"

D blinked. That was a pretty fair question, actually. "Jus' stand over there and be ready ta duck."

Jack moved closer to the Dumpster, trying on various "casual" poses. Leaning against the wall, then arms crossed, then one hand on the Dumpster. It would have been funny if the situation were less tense.

Sig came walking around the corner bearing a briefcase. He glanced right and left as he approached. "Here you go," he said, holding out the case.

"Jus' put it on the ground," D said.

Sig hesitated for a moment, then bent and set the case on the ground. D was watching, so he saw Sig's hand steal into his jacket, and when the hand emerged holding a gun he was ready. He kicked out at the gun hand and the pistol went flying. Sig wasn't exactly surprised, either, so he just pistoned his shoulder into D's chest and slammed him up against the wall. D heard Jack yell something, couldn't tell what. He grabbed Sig's shoulders and jammed his knee upward into his stomach, then shoved him back.

Sig faced him, pale-faced and sweating. "Should have stayed clear, D," he said.

"Shouldn't a fucked with me."

EVEN though D had warned him (which he kind of wished he hadn't), Jack was still surprised when the other hit man (he hadn't caught his name clearly, it had sounded like Ziggy, which couldn't possibly be right) whipped out a pistol. D seemed to be ready and kicked it away, and then Ziggy slammed D into the wall. Jack heard someone yell, realized it had been himself, and ducked back behind the Dumpster as he'd been told to do.

"Should have stayed clear, D," Ziggy said.

"Shouldn't a fucked with me," D snarled, in a voice that made the hair on the back of Jack's neck stand on end.

Ziggy backed off, arms up in some kind of martial-arts pose. D just stood there, looking not the slightest bit ready, but when Ziggy came at him with the kung-fu action, D lashed out with one arm, then a leg, then a fist. Jack tried to watch but it was dark and they were moving so fast. Ziggy pulled a little knife out of his belt buckle and jabbed it at D, who just waited for him to swing it, then stepped forward, turning so his back was to Ziggy, grabbed the man's arm and cracked his wrist back, forcing him to drop it. D kicked it away as Ziggy staggered back, wrist hanging limply, cursing.

Jack was terrified, horror-struck, and afraid for D's life, but a part of him was fascinated. He wondered what kind of training D had. Ziggy seemed to be expending a lot of energy whipping himself around while D just stood there, relaxed, making a minimum of movements; the ones he did make were quick and decisive. It didn't look like karate, not that Jack was any kind of expert apart from having watched *The Matrix.*

Ziggy wasn't done, despite having what looked like a broken wrist (*scaphoid fracture possible ulnar fracture likely tearing of the ventral ligaments*). Jack guessed that 3.5 million could buy a gold-plated wrist splint. He came at D again but his balance was off. D swept the guy's leg out from under him and then grabbed him around the neck with his arm. D made a quick motion with his arm and his other hand, Jack heard a crunch, and Ziggy dropped like a stone.

Before Jack could even begin to process the fact that D had just broken the guy's neck, D was pulling him to his feet by his arm. "D... you... he...."

"He ain't a problem no more," D growled, picking up the briefcase and dragging Jack toward the mouth of the alley. "Smarten up. Look normal."

Jack somehow composed his face and clamped his arms firmly across his chest to still their shaking. He stuck close to D's side as they crossed the street, passing the crowd of people waiting to get into Del Muerto (he would have laughed at the appropriateness of the name if he wasn't so fucking petrified). They made it into the shadows of the parking garage and D quickly opened the briefcase, checking that his papers were there, and pulled out his gun. He tucked it into the back of his pants and they continued to the car. Jack stumbled a little. His arms and legs felt numb and his head was swimming. D's hand was suddenly holding his arm tightly. "C'mon, keep it together," he muttered in Jack's ear.

He tried, he really tried. He was gasping like he'd just inhaled something awful, trying to get the smell out of his nose. They climbed the stairs to the top where they'd left the car. "Oh shit," Jack choked, feeling it rise up his throat. He staggered into the corner and let go, everything coming up from his stomach. He shut his eyes and hung on to the wall until it was over then stayed hunched over, coughing and watching the stars dance in front of his eyelids.

He sensed D standing next to him, and then he felt a hand between his shoulder blades. "Y'all right, there?" D said, his voice surprisingly gentle.

"Fuck," Jack choked.

"Take a deep breath. Jus' relax." D's hand was rubbing the center of his back, almost like a father would to a sick child. *Is that how he sees me? Childlike?* In any case, the motion was comforting and Jack didn't want him to stop. The warmth of his hand through Jack's shirt and jacket was seeping into his spine, traveling up to his neck and flushing him with the contact.

Jack tried to relax, as D said, turning away from the puddle of vomit he'd left. D kept his hand firm on his shoulder. Jack swiped at his streaming eyes. His chest was hitching all by itself, like a rapid-fire case of the hiccups. "I'm... suh-suh-sorry...."

"S'okay. You jus' take it easy." D led him around to the passenger door and opened it for him like they were on a date. Jack folded himself in, his stomach still cramping, and D shut the door. He got in the driver's side and within a few moments they were blocks away.

"I'm sorry," Jack said again after a few minutes' recovery time. "I've just... never seen anything like that. Somebody getting killed right in front of me."

"But yer a doctor. Ain't ya never seen...."

"I've seen plenty of people die. Just... never like that." Jack sighed and made himself look at D. *He's a killer. That's what he does.* Jack wondered if deep down he hadn't hoped that it was just a figure of speech or something, that he didn't *really* kill people, that it was all just an abstraction. Well, the proof was in the crunching sound that guy's neck had made, the sound that was still in Jack's ears. "He was going to kill us, right?"

"Right."

"But... did you have to kill him? You broke his wrist. He couldn't have done much damage."

"No, but he could have told every lowlife in a hundred-mile-radius we were around. This way, hopefully no one else seen me."

Jack sat tucked into the corner of the seat, feeling weak-limbed and wrung out. "I guess. I just...."

"You don't gotta explain," D said, quietly. They pulled up to a red light and D turned to face him. "I'm, uh... sorry ya hadta see it."

Jack nodded. "Thanks."

D COULD smell the sharp ozone tang of fear and adrenaline coming off Jack, and he was surprised at how it was affecting him. When Jack looked at him, right after he puked... the expression in his eyes gave D a bad turn. Was like he was disappointed, almost, more even than scared, which he obviously was. Man wasn't hardened like D was. D had just reacted how he'd been taught, had done what he had to do to make sure they were safe. Signor had been in the way, he'd been a real immediate threat, and D had but one thought: neutralize. When he'd seen Jack's face in that alley, his stomach had flopped in a way it hadn't for years. Shame came over him, and he almost hadn't recognized it. *Broke a man's neck right in front of him, how's he s'posed ta trust ya now? Probly jus thinkin' yer a killin' machine again.*

Get him talkin'. Get his mind off it. Don't let him sit there and stew in silence. "So, uh... what kinda doc you say you were, again?"

"Maxillofacial surgeon," Jack said. His voice sounded dull and dusty. He sounded like those tacky motels looked.

"What the hell's that?"

Jack took a slow breath and released it before answering. "Maxillofacial surgeons treat injuries, diseases, and defects in the skull, jaw, neck, and face."

"Like a dentist?"

"I am a dentist."

"Thought you were a surgeon."

"I'm a dentist and a surgeon. I got my dental degree first, then went to med school. That's usually how it goes for doctors in my field."

"So... you could pull out these fuckin' wisdom teeth fer me, then?"

"Sure. Got a pair of pliers and a hammer?"

"What's the hammer for?"

"To knock you out before I start yanking."

D looked over at him. The ghost of a smile curled his lips as he cut a glance at D. *That's better.* "That's a fuckin' lotta school, Jack."

"Fourteen years."

D almost drove the car off the road. "Shitfire, fourteen fuckin' *years?*"

"Four in college, four in dental school, and six in medical school and residency."

"So... yer just barely done!"

"Just finished my final residency three years back. Now I'm an attending."

"Fuck me." D was legitimately impressed. He'd known Francisco was sharp, but he had to be pretty damned determined, too, ta get through all that. "So, what kinda diseases and defects? Ever see anyone with an empty skull?"

That got a chuckle. "Well, I might have thought so. I don't deal with the brain; I leave that shit to the neurosurgeons. You want to see insane, those guys are insane. I specialize in reconstructive surgery. I operate on people who were born with defects in the bones of their face, or were injured in accidents and need repair."

D pondered this. "So... you fix people's faces when they're broken."

Jack looked at him. "Yes." He turned to look out the window. They were on the freeway now, passing through a jungle of dark shapes of buildings laced through with ribbons of car headlights and streetlamps. "Just before the Dominguez thing, I operated on this little girl who'd been born with a really terrible congenital skull abnormality. She had no chin and virtually no forehead, her nose was practically inside out. It was the third operation I'd done on her. This one was to build her a functional nasal cavity. I had to take her face completely off," he said, a note of wonderment entering his voice.

D blinked. "Her face... off?"

"Yeah. I had to peel it all the way down to her chin from her forehead so I could work inside her sinus cavity. There was a moment when I just looked down at her, and I could see through her skull plate into her brain. And I thought, damn. This is a view that no one ever has on a living person. It was one of those moments when what I do really hit me, you know? I was giving that girl a face when she didn't really have one before."

"Damn," D said. "That's a helluva thing ta do, Jack. Whole lot more than most people will ever do."

Jack was quiet for some time. "D?"

"Yeah?"

"Does what you do ever really hit *you?*"

D stared straight ahead at the taillights in front of him. "Every damned day."

BY the time they got back to the motel, Jack's ass was dragging. "Fuck, am I tired," he said.

"Well, don't get comfy," D said, going ahead with the key. "We ain't stayin'."

"We're not?" Jack said, hearing the whiny note enter his voice but not being able to help it. "Can't we at least get some sleep?"

"Gotta hit the road. Too risky. Just took the room fer a place ta stash the guns 'n' such. You can take a shower if ya want."

"Gee, thanks," Jack groused, getting out his bag. "Where are we headed now?"

"Stockton."

"What's in Stockton?"

"Not a goddamned thing. That's why we're goin'."

"Then what?"

"Then...." D sat down on the bed with a weary sigh. "I don't fuckin' know. I need ta hole up somewheres 'n' gather my thoughts."

"I'm all for that," Jack said. "I got first shower." D just nodded as Jack went into the bathroom and shut the door.

He stood under the hot spray, as hot as he could make it, eyes shut, the water not quite loud enough to drown out that horrible crunching noise. He'd heard bones make a lot of sounds, some of which had been under his own hands, but never that grinding, wet crunch of vertebrae separating, spinal cord snapping. Jack bent over, feeling his gorge rise again, and put his head between his knees until the feeling passed.

When he emerged, dressed in clean jeans and toweling his hair, D was sitting shirtless on the bed peering down at some bruises on his chest. He moved his arm, hissing in pain a little. "Let me see," Jack said.

"It's nothin'," D said.

"Come on. Let me be the one with the expertise for once." D sighed and put his arm down, giving Jack a raised-eyebrow, come-on-then kind of look. Jack bent over him. There was an abrasion and the beginnings of a nasty bruise on the far right side of his chest, wrapping up into his armpit. "Can you move your arm?"

"Yeah. Little sore is all."

Jack palpated the bruise. It wasn't bleeding. He shrugged. "You're right; it's nothing."

"Gee, thanks, doc. You gonna charge me two hundred bucks now?"

"Least I know you've got it," Jack said, smiling. "Take two aspirin and call me in the morning." D started to smile back, but then it vanished like a puff of smoke. He turned away, mumbling something, and went into the bathroom.

Jack pulled on a shirt, frowning. The man was an enigma, that was for certain. He sat on the bed and flopped onto his back, letting his eyes fall closed as he heard the shower running in the bathroom.

He didn't know he'd drifted off until D was shaking him awake. "C'mon, doc. Gotta hit the road."

Jack hauled himself up and shouldered his bag. He took one of the aluminum cases, D took the other, and within minutes they were back in the car and headed for Stockton, and this time, that blankness ahead of them on the road was a comfort.

CHAPTER 5

D KNEW that if he were any kind of a normal person, he'd be struggling to keep his eyes open. It was after midnight, he hadn't had much sleep the night before, and he was driving at night on a really boring stretch of highway across the California no-man's-land. But he wasn't no normal person, and he'd had to acquire the ability to function on very little sleep long ago.

He glanced over at Jack, fast asleep in the passenger seat, curled up like a kid with his folded hands tucked under his cheek and his head resting against his balled-up jacket that he'd shoved into the corner. His forehead was furrowed with faint worry lines even in sleep, and every so often he'd mumble or shift, making little sleep noises and snuffling. D let his gaze linger for a moment and then turned back to the road, his jaw clenching.

He'd been arguing with himself for a good portion of the trip. *You oughta get him a new identity and dump him off somewheres. Ain't no good fer you ta keep draggin' him along. He's gonna get caught in the crossfire. You tryin' ta help might get him killed.*

But... ain't no one else can protect him like me. I know these assholes, I know how they work, 'cause I'm one of 'em. No cops, no Witness Protection know how ta anticipate what they're gonna do. He's safest with me.

But that ain't the real problem.

Shut the fuck up.

Yer gettin'... attached.

Toldja ta shut the fuck up.

Kinda like him, don'tcha? He ain't no preppy asswipe like ya thought he'd be, moaning about missin' his tee time 'n' afraid ta get dirt on his fuckin' J.Crew. Guy's got some smarts ta him, some nerve. Kinda guy ya could get ta be friends with.

Ain't gonna know him long enough ta be no friends.

Ya crossed that line when you was rubbin' his back while he fuckin' puked and ya know it. Gave you a bad feelin', didn't it? Ta kill that guy in front a his eyes? Don't want him ta think bad a you, do ya?

Need him ta trust me so he won't try 'n' run off.

Bullshit. You want him ta like you. You want him ta turn them big, pretty eyes on you and look atcha like yer his fuckin' hero. You wanna BE his fuckin' hero. Well, you ain't no hero, Anson Dane.

That ain't my name no more.

That's the name ya done cut off when ya cut yerself off... after. Thought you was done havin' feelins, didn'tcha? Thought you was safe? You ain't safe. Shut it all down 'cause no feelins at all was better'n all them bad feelins. Seeing their faces, hearing yer little girl's voice in yer head over 'n' over, callin' fer Daddy but you ain't comin'. No feelins was better'n THOSE feelins.

Don't know what yer talkin' about.

Sure ya do. Those feelins. Like fer girls. Except... maybe not.

Shut the fuck up. How many times I gotta tell ya?

You cain't tell me ta shut up, 'cause I am you, asshole.

D sighed and put that fight from his mind as he'd done a thousand times before, that voice of his long-ago self made wiser than his real self had ever been by watching his own folly and hearing his own torment inside his head.

Maybe you oughta jus' kill him. Maybe you get outta this alive if ya just do it. Do it quick, right now while he's asleep. He'll never know; he jus' won't wake up.

D gripped the steering wheel tighter.

You keep on, both a ya's gonna end up dead.

He looked over at Jack again, and his knowing that maybe killing him was the smart thing to do didn't affect the fact that he couldn't.

They passed a sign saying it was 100 miles to Stockton. He ran through what had to be done now. First, find a place to hole up for a few days. Get their shit together. Catch their breath. Make double damned sure they weren't being tracked. Eventually, Jack would have to contact the Marshals, because they had to be told that he still intended to testify. If he just disappeared without a word, the trial might get postponed. That'd be tricky, though. They'd have to do it in some way that the Marshals couldn't take him into custody, so D could continue to protect him.

He wasn't forgetting the threat to himself, either. The Dominguez brothers might want Jack's head on a pike, but the more he thought about it, the more he thought that they were not the ones responsible for his own involvement here. If they wanted a hit man, there were a lot less scrupulous ones than himself available, and for them to go to such lengths just to blackmail him into doing something that a dozen other men would do for the paycheck made no sense... unless it was somehow about him.

He had no doubt that the Marshals knew by now that Jack was out of pocket too. So that was possibly three parties on his ass, and it was starting to feel mighty crowded back there.

He pulled into a remote gas station just after four o'clock in the morning. He'd used this gas station before, feeling comfortable here because of its very remoteness and its lack of security cameras. The place was deserted, which was just fine with him. Jack twitched a little and blinked, straightening in his seat. "Are we there?"

"Not quite. Need gas."

"I gotta pee," Jack muttered, rubbing his stubbled face and unfolding himself out of the passenger seat. D had to smirk a little at Jack's bed-head as he shuffled toward the station. He hesitated and turned back. "You want a soda or anything?"

D almost responded with a knee-jerk "no," but then reconsidered. "Guess so."

"What kind?"

"Ginger ale. Vernor's if they got it."

"You drink ginger ale?"

D frowned at him. "What's wrong with that? Toldja got a bad stomach."

Jack shrugged. "Just thought you'd drink something more... intense."

"Which sodas are the intense ones?"

"I don't know. Mountain Dew?"

D made a face. "That shit is nasty. Rot yer balls off."

"There is no medical evidence that Mountain Dew has a bad effect on testicles," Jack said, smirking. "But I can't disagree that it's nasty." He resumed his course to the gas station while D leaned against the car, waiting for the fuel tank to fill. He was glancing around, staying alert for a possible tail. He was almost positive that they hadn't been followed from LA, but you could never be too careful.

He watched Jack through the windows of the dingy little gas station as he perused what had to be a limited pop selection. D shifted his weight, the comforting heft of the gun in his belt pressing into his lower back. He wondered if Jack had ever shot a gun. Probably not; didn't seem the type for sport-shooting, and he'd have no reason to do it otherwise.

D cleared his throat, eyes automatically picking out the lines of sight and the cover. The hair on the back of his neck was standing up. He was getting that feeling. The cornered-animal feeling. The rush of the gas from the nozzle, the dry chilly desert air, the buzz of the fluorescent lights overhead, it felt like every ambush he'd ever set up.

Then he saw it. The barest glimmer, a reflection off something shiny, around the corner of the gas station. He wandered nonchalantly a few yards away to light a cigarette and saw that it was the bumper of a car, parked behind the building where cars weren't supposed to park.

Jack came out of the gas station, walking straighter with his hair back in place, carrying a couple of bottles of soda. "No clerk," he said, frowning. "I waited and yelled, but there wasn't anybody there. I just left the cash."

D nodded. "Get in the car," he said quietly. "Driver's seat."

"What, my turn to drive?"

"We ain't alone here. Don't look around."

To his credit, Jack stayed calm and didn't look around. "The clerk…?"

"Already dead."

"How'd they find us?" Jack whispered, acting like he was counting out change to D. *Pretty good cover, Doc.*

"Dunno. Don't matter right now." In his head, D was wondering where on the car the tracker was.

"What do I do?" Jack said. He met D's eyes for a moment, his own wide and scared.

"Jus' get ready ta get us outta here. You'll know when." Jack went around to the driver's side and got in. D pulled the still-gushing nozzle out of the fuel tank and tossed it to the ground, well clear of their car, the hold-open catch letting gas puddle around the base of the pumps.

Two dark-clothed men suddenly materialized from the brush at the sides of the parking lot and rushed him, much more boldly than D had been expecting. A silenced shot spanged off the iron support at his right. "Jack, get down!" D yelled. He put a bullet through the first one's forehead and brought to bear on the second, but before he could fire he was wrenched around by what felt like a cannonball striking his chest, high under his left shoulder. He heard Jack shout his name. There was no pain, just a spreading numb pressure. He didn't look down, just brought his gun back around and somehow hit the second guy, who went down.

Now, the pain was coming. It was a lot worse than he'd always imagined it would be. D staggered against the car, his left arm useless. The second guy wasn't dead. In fact it looked like he'd only winged him… but he had his legs in the puddle of gasoline. D took a big drag on his cigarette to fire the ember and tossed it into the gas puddle, which went up with a low-frequency *fwump* that sent a wave of air pressure toward him.

Jack had thrown himself across the front seat and now had the door open. "Get in!" he said. D somehow managed to collapse into the seat and shut the door. Jack squealed out of the gas station lot just in time for them to see the entire place explode in the rearview mirror. D saw with relief that the station and the car that had been parked behind it both went up in flames. Jack wasn't wasting time watching; he was hauling ass away as fast as he could safely drive.

D lay in the passenger seat, the world graying out around him. Suddenly Jack's hand was clamped around his upper arm, bringing things back into focus. "How bad?" he asked.

"Whut?"

Jack tried to look over at him and see the wound, but he had to watch the road. "How bad is it? Are you bleeding out?"

D looked down at himself. The wound was in his upper left chest. His shirt was bloody but nothing was gushing. "Don't think so."

"Are you dizzy? Nauseated?"

Jack was speaking in a quick, clipped, answer-me-right-goddamned-now tone that D had heard from every medic he'd ever known. It was the Doctor Voice. "Little dizzy," he managed.

"Can you breathe?"

D took an experimental breath. "Yeah... mostly."

"Missed the lung, then." Jack shook his head. "I have to look at that. Where can I hide us, just for a little while?"

D gritted his teeth, holding his left arm tight against his chest. "Get off the freeway. Get ten miles, at least. Take a few turns. Find a motel. We gotta get the tracker off the car too."

"Tracker?"

"Mother*fucker*!" D yelled, as the car went over a bump and another wave of crushing pain cruised across his torso. *Shit, I thought I'd be a lot more stoic on gettin' shot,* he thought. *I'm disappointed in myself.*

"Shut your eyes and breathe quick and steady," Jack ordered him. "Quit moving around! Haven't you ever been shot before?"

"No!" D retorted.

"Oh," Jack said, sounding chastened. "I assumed you would have been. You know... considering."

"I ain't been 'cause I'm good at my job! Took havin' *you* around ta get me shot!"

"Lean forward," Jack said, in that Doctor Voice again. *Yeah, cuz it's jus' that easy,* D thought. *My body feels like it's made a concrete.* He somehow managed to cant himself forward and Jack's hand was on the back of his shoulder, feeling around. D gritted his teeth. "Bullet's still in you. No exit wound." Jack pulled him back again; D's head fell against the headrest.

"Gotta get the tracker before we stop. Pull over."

Jack did as he was told, killing the lights. "How do you know there's a tracker?"

"How else did they find us there?"

"But... they couldn't have followed us to the station; we'd have seen them come in! How'd they get there *ahead* of us?"

D shook his head, cursing his own habits. "My fuckin' fault. Too goddamned predictable. If someone's been followin' me fer months takin' pictures, they'd know I stop at that gas station. Like it 'cause it's outta the way. Tracker showed us on that road, pretty good chance be stopping at that station. Now. Look under the trunk lid, above the inside a the catch. If it ain't there, check the wheel wells, and underneath the trunk on the frame."

Jack nodded. "Are you okay?"

"No, I been fuckin' shot. Go do as I say."

He popped the trunk and went around to the back of the car. D shut his eyes, listening to the vague sounds of Jack's feet and hands, and then he heard him approach the passenger window and opened his eyes. Jack was holding out a small black device. "It was under the lid of the trunk."

D took it. "Shit. Fuckin' Feds." He handed it back. "Stomp on it, then throw it away."

Jack let the tracker drop, then D heard it crunch beneath his shoe. He picked it up and flung it as hard as he could off into the darkness. He got back behind the wheel and got them on the road again. "How do you know it was them... the, uh, Feds? When'd they bug my car?"

"They always put the goddamned tracker on the inside a the trunk lid. Think they'd learn ta change it up a little. And they probly put it on the car before they gave it ta you, so they could find ya if ya ever decided this Witness Protection shit was too much 'n' took off. When they realized you was gone yesterday, they activated it. Somebody else either hacked or bought the frequency 'n' found us, 'cause them guys back there sure weren't Feds." All this talking was making D very, very tired. When had talking become so strenuous? "Gotta stay awake," D mumbled.

Jack chuckled, incredibly. "That's for a concussion. You're not going to bleed to death. Go ahead and shut your eyes if you want." D turned to find Jack looking back at him. "I'll look after you. You did it for me."

I ain't trusted nobody else ta look after me fer over ten years, Francisco. The second I shut my eyes yer gonna drive me to a police station, or dump me outta the car, or take one a them guns and shoot me in the head. I can look after myself. He sighed, looked into Jack's eyes, and nodded. "Okay." He let his eyes close and it was a relief; not just a relief of minutes, but of years.

JACK scanned the road, a two-lane highway by now. They seemed to be the last people alive in the universe; he hadn't seen another car for five miles. D was passed out next to him. Jack could smell the familiar copper tang of blood, and it was almost comforting.

He'd seen D slammed back against the car and knew right away he'd been shot. His own reaction had been a surprise, even to himself. A shield of icy calm had descended over him and his mind had clicked over into trauma mode, triaging the situation, an instinct borne of months spent on ER rotation in a violence-ridden inner city. *Get an airway, get a pulse, stop the bleeding, dull the pain, prevent infection.* Except this had been *get him in the car, assess his wound, get away, get far, keep your head down, drive fast, don't get pulled over, find a cave.*

D was his patient now. It had been awhile since trauma rotation but some things didn't leave you. His wound didn't seem serious at first glance, but he'd have to excise the bullet and get some antibiotics into him as soon as possible. It might need to be stitched. He was unconscious, so Jack didn't see the harm in getting them a little farther away from the scene of the explosion. From the remote location of the place, he guessed it would take police a little while to get there, and once there, there was nothing to connect them or this car to the incident.

He drove for half an hour before finally pulling into a generic roadside motel. He drove around the place once, parking on the far side so the car wasn't visible from the street. He left D in the car, reluctantly, and walked around to the office, making sure he didn't have any blood on him before he went in. "Can I get a room?" he said to the tired-looking clerk. "I parked over by twelve."

"Suit yourself," the clerk said. "Fifty bucks."

Jack paid cash and showed the clerk his new Dappa-issue ID, which identified him as John Templeton. He signed the register, took the key and hurried back to the room. He opened the door and glanced around; grabbed a couple of towels and put them on the bed, then went outside and opened the passenger door. D was still out cold.

Jack retrieved his doctor's bag from the trunk and took out a vial of smelling salts. He cracked them under D's nose and put his hand on his forehead to keep him steady. The wound looked to still be seeping. "Whu... fuck!" D cut himself off as his sudden movement strained his shoulder.

"Shhh," Jack said. "Take it easy. We're at a motel."

D nodded sluggishly, and turned to get out of the car. Jack bent and got one arm behind D's back, helping him up and out. He kicked the door shut and staggered with D into the room, kicking that door shut too. D sat down on the edge of the bed. "Get the cases outta the car," he said.

"Don't lay back without a towel underneath," Jack said. "We don't want to have to explain bloodstains."

D blinked. "Towels'll get bloody instead." *Dumbass.* Except this time, Jack knew he wasn't such a dumbass.

"We can get rid of the towels. This place must have towels stolen daily. They might remember a missing bedspread, though."

D considered this for a moment, then nodded. "Yer not bad at this, ya know."

"I'll be right back," Jack said, hurrying out and hoping D hadn't seen him blush like a school kid at the praise. He gathered up their bags, the aluminum cases containing the guns, ammo and money plus their new papers, locked the car, and went back into the room. "Okay, now let's have a look at that," he said. D was holding his left arm tight to his side to minimize the movement in his shoulder.

Jack helped D get out of his jacket and shirt. D winced as the fabric stuck to his wound. Jack examined it; it didn't look like there was fabric inside the bullet hole. He spread towels on the bed and helped D lean back. He was sweating and pale. Jack went into the bathroom and wet a washcloth, then laid it over D's forehead. "Relax," he said, lapsing into calming-bedside-manner without thinking about it. He opened his bag and drew out a syringe and an ampoule.

"What's that?" D asked, looking a little suspicious.

"It's just Lidocaine," Jack said, showing him the bottle. "Trust me; you want me to numb the area. I'm going to have to go digging for that bullet." D nodded weakly, and Jack injected small dosages around the wound, conserving the drug in case he needed more later. Almost immediately, the tension in D's shoulder and arm eased off, allowing Jack to pull his arm away from his body and get a good look at the wound. He palpated it, front and back. He could feel the bullet about two-thirds of the way through D's shoulder. "You okay?" he said.

D nodded. "Lots better now."

Jack took out a pair of long-nose forceps and snapped on some rubber gloves. He wiped the forceps with a sterilizing wipe. Not as good as an autoclave but better than nothing. He tilted the lamp toward him for better light and pressed his fingers around the wound. "Now, this is still going to hurt some," he said. "I'll try to be quick." D nodded and shut his eyes; Jack saw his jaw clench. He took a breath, steadied the forceps, and plunged them quickly into the wound. They touched metal, he gripped and withdrew. "Huh," he said, holding up the bullet.

D opened one eye, then the other. "Is… that's it?"

"Well, *here's* your problem," Jack joked, showing D the bullet.

"Damn. Barely felt that. Sure are fast, doc."

"I'm a professional. Don't try this at home." He put the bullet in the ashtray on the nightstand and went back into the bathroom for another washcloth. He sat at D's side and washed the wound, then took another ampoule out of his bag.

"What's this one?"

"Ampicillin. Just an antibiotic. Don't want you getting infected." He injected the drug into D's arm. "That oughta do it, but we can always get you some pills if we need to. Come on, sit up." He helped D sit up and washed the blood from his chest and back. Neither of them spoke. Jack was glad that D couldn't see his face as he touched him, the muscles of D's back tight and defined under his hands, and he was pretty sure he wasn't imagining the little jumps and flutters of muscle where his fingertips grazed D's skin.

"No stitches?" D finally asked.

"Not a very big wound. Shouldn't need them. Unless you're worried about scars for your Playgirl shoot."

D snorted. "Smartass."

Jack began bandaging the wound with gauze, folding it into squares and wrapping strips around his shoulder, secured with adhesive tape. "It always amazes me that handguns, even at that range that you were shot, don't cause more damage."

"Handguns're low velocity, Jack. But it ain't the velocity, it's the energy transfer. If ya hit something hard, like a bone, or a tough muscle like the heart, you get fast 'n' hard energy transfer with lotsa damage. If ya don't, like this shoulder bit where I got shot, not much transfer."

"Huh. I guess I always thought handguns were really bad."

"They're bad 'cause they're easy ta hide, and ya don't know who's carryin', but in terms a lethal wounds it's rifles ya gotta watch out for. Rifle bullets got three, four times the velocity of a handgun bullet. Lucky fer us rifles aren't too convenient ta carry round on yer person."

"Well, I saw plenty of handgun wounds during my ER rotation, but no rifle wounds that I remember. The handguns did damage enough."

"Yeah. Some of 'em pack a wallop. Lemme see the bullet." Jack handed him the bloody, deformed projectile. "Looks like a thirty-eight. Nothin' fancy." D's expression shifted slightly as he stared at this murderous little piece of metal that had until recently been lodged inside his body. "Huh. Coulda killed me if he'd had better aim."

"Then let's be glad he didn't," Jack said, grimly.

D was watching him. "That bother you? Blowin' them guys up like I done?"

Jack sighed. "No. Not really." He met D's eyes. "It should have. Maybe I'm getting used to all this."

"It happens," D said. He sounded a little sad. He flexed his shoulder experimentally. "Huh. Thanks, Jack. Feels okay."

"Wait 'til the Lidocaine wears off and then tell me how good it feels." Jack looked around. "What now? Stay here? Move on?"

"Think we oughta move on, but I don't know where. Stockton don't feel safe no more. Too close. Don't wanna turn around and head south again."

"Well… you know, I might know a place we can go."

"Yeah?" D shook his head. "I ain't gonna be much use ta you for a little while," he said, glancing ruefully at his shoulder.

"I think we'll be safe there. It's my ex-wife's father's cabin on Tahoe. Only uses it during ski season."

D seemed to consider this. "Lotsa neighbors?"

"None. It's way the hell out in the woods."

"Could possibly get traced ta you, through yer ex."

"Well… there aren't any records tying him to the place. The place is still in his sister's name."

"That's good." D nodded. "Okay. Tahoe's only three hours."

Jack stood up and looked down at him. "As your physician, I'd like to recommend that you rest for a little while."

D stood as well, swaying a bit and still pale but clear-eyed. "I'm fine, doc. I'll rest when we're far away from here."

CHAPTER 6

JACK pulled up to the cabin, relieved that he'd actually remembered where it was. Surely it ought to be getting dark any minute now. Surely this day would be over soon, and he could retreat from everything into dreamless (he hoped) sleep. But no, it was only 3:00 in the afternoon. He was far too exhausted for it to only be 3:00 in the afternoon. Although, to be fair to himself, kind of a lot had happened.

D was either asleep or passed out in the passenger seat. Jack had given him the last of the ampicillin he'd had in his medical bag, and he hoped to hell it'd be enough. He reached out and touched the back of his hand to D's forehead, which felt a little warm, but without a thermometer it was hard to say if he was really feverish, or if he was just warm from the sun beating in the window of the car onto him. "Hey," Jack said, shaking him gently on his gunshot-free shoulder. "D?"

He opened his eyes, groggy but alert. "Wha?"

"We're at the cabin. How do you feel?"

D blinked and sat up straighter. "Uh... okay, I guess."

"Come on; let's get inside. You need to rest that shoulder."

"I'm fine," D said, flapping a hand at him. Jack kept an eye on him as he hauled himself out of the passenger seat, his left arm done up in a makeshift sling Jack had fashioned from a towel. He paused and looked up at the cabin. "Huh. Nice place."

"Yeah. Caroline's father is very well off. Just ask him. He'll tell you all about it." Jack shouldered his bag and went up the walk to the front door. The spare key was in a fake rock half underneath the porch. He heard D snort in derision at this half-assed attempt at security. He shot him a look. "Not everyone's on their guard against armed assassins and drug lords, you know. A fake rock's good enough for most people."

D followed him into the cabin. It was a nice place. Two bedrooms that shared a big bathroom, with another bathroom off the kitchen. Cozy living room and a deck that looked out over Lake Tahoe a few miles away. "Where are we, exactly?"

"About halfway between Carnelian Bay and Tahoe City."

"Still in California, then."

"Yeah. No one's around. Closest neighbor is two miles off to the east; you can't even see the lights through the trees."

"Good." D sat down heavily while Jack went back to the car for the aluminum cases.

"So... we're sure we weren't followed?" Jack said, shutting the door behind him and flipping the deadbolt.

"Pretty sure. Unless there's another tracker on the fuckin' car." D winced and let his head fall back against the couch.

Jack leaned over him and undid the top two buttons on his shirt, pulling it aside and lifting his bandage. He tried not to show it, but the sight of D's wound didn't reassure him. It was angry red around the edges and suppurating slightly. He was out of antibiotics. "When was your last tetanus shot?" he asked.

D looked at him like he was crazy. "Tetanus shot? Fuck if I know."

"You don't remember?"

"Shit, no. Got 'em regular in the Army, not since."

"So more than ten years, is what you're telling me?" Jack straightened up and ran one hand through his hair.

"Is that bad?"

"Bad? D, you got shot! You could get tetanus!"

"Thought that was from rusty nails."

"Anything metallic penetrating the body is a possible source of infection and that does include bullets. It's not too likely you'll get it, but if there was ever a time for better safe than sorry, this is it." He shook his head. "I'm going to have to get some tetanus vaccine somewhere."

"I'm fine. I ain't gonna get tetanus."

"You don't know that. And if you develop symptoms it'll be too late to administer the vaccine. Tetanus has a fifty percent mortality rate, D. You like those odds? Because I don't." D looked a little troubled by this. "I can't take the risk. And your wound... it isn't looking good. You're not looking good, either." D was pale and clammy.

"I feel kinda feverish. Didn't like ta say nothin'."

"You don't do that, you hear me?" Jack said, rounding on him. "You tell me how you're feeling! I can't take care of you if you're hiding things from me, and I can't have you dying of sepsis or tetanus or fucking necrotizing fasciitis because you didn't tell me you felt feverish in time for me to do anything about it!"

D just blinked at this tirade. "Fine. You the boss, doc. So let's hear yer big fuckin' plan. You gonna waltz right inta some ER and walk out with pockets fulla drugs? 'Cause I hear they crackin' down on that shit."

"I'll think of something." He sighed and fell back into the corner of the couch, watching D. "But not until tomorrow. I want to see how that wound does, and if you need more antibiotics. It takes at least two days to develop symptoms from tetanus so it'll be fine for me to go tomorrow."

"Go where?"

"I haven't figured that part out yet." He smirked a little. "C'mon, D. Trust me."

"Well... I guess I owe ya that much, don't I?"

The cabin was pretty well stocked with canned goods, so Jack put the microwave to good use. He hadn't really realized how hungry he was until he smelled the chili, crappy sodium-laced canned chili though it was. They sat at the little round table in the kitchen; Jack wolfed down his food while D picked at his. "You need to eat," Jack said.

"Ain't too hungry."

Jack paused. "You should be; we haven't eaten all day."

D glanced at him. "Feel kinda... mashed up." The admission of physical vulnerability seemed to embarrass him.

"How's your shoulder?"

"Hurts like a sumbitch."

"Hurts how? Is it a sharp pain, an achy pain, or a burning pain?"

"I gotta pick just one?"

Jack stood up and put his hand to D's forehead. He definitely felt warm. He went to his bag and pulled out a digital thermometer. "Under your tongue," he said, and D obliged him, though he didn't look happy about it. Jack withdrew the probe. "Well, you've got a one-and-a-half-degree fever. That's not so bad but it isn't good." He went to the stove again. "Go sit on the couch and wrap up in that afghan. I'm going to make you some tea."

D stood up slowly. "Ya sound like a fuckin' grandmother."

"Grandmothers were doctors before doctors were doctors. You need fluids."

When Jack came back to the living room, mug in hand, D was on the couch, wrapped up in the afghan as Jack had instructed. "Thanks," he said, taking the tea. Jack sat on the far end of the couch. D was looking around the room. "This place secure?"

"Secure?"

"The windows lock? Got a second entrance?"

"Everything has a lock. There's just the front door and the patio door." D grunted, sipping his tea. "You seem nervous."

D shrugged. "If I'm laid up, you ain't got no defense."

"You'll be fine."

"Best hope is that no one finds us here."

Jack nodded, curling up into his corner of the couch with another afghan. He studied D's face, flushed now with heat from the tea. "How'd you get into this business?" he asked.

"Jus' kinda happened."

"A person can't 'jus' kinda' become a hired killer."

"Well, I did."

Jack tried another tack. "Why did you join the Army?"

D shrugged again, as if these questions had no importance. "I was eighteen, didn't have no prospects, hadta do somethin'."

"You must have liked it to stay in as long as you did."

"It was okay. It liked me pretty well. Officers said I had the attitude for it, the right kinda personality, whatever the hell that means."

"You were in during Desert Storm, right?"

"Yep. Spent two years over there."

"Seriously?"

"Yep."

"What was it like?"

"I don't wanna talk no more."

"Come on, D. You know everything about me."

"Don't think that's so."

"Well, ask me. I'll tell you anything you want to know."

"Ain't nothin' I wanna know. Know enough. Ya saw a lady murdered and yer gonna say so in court, and ya don't deserve ta die. That's all I care about."

Jack said nothing, hurt more than he would have expected by D's lack of interest. He couldn't abide silence for long, though. "So... how does it work?"

"What?"

"The whole hired-killer thing. How does it work?"

D sighed wearily. "Got a handler. Contracts come ta her, she shows me the files, I take jobs I wanna take, client pays her, she takes a cut, pays me. Real simple. I work when I want, no more 'n' no less."

He didn't want to ask, but he knew he had to. Eventually, he had to, and he might as well do it now. "How many?"

D's face turned slightly toward him, his eyes still focused toward the fireplace. He didn't hesitate. "Sixty-seven." He said it without pulling the punch, like he wanted the blow to strike Jack hard.

Sweet Jesus. "How many of those were while you were in the Army?"

"None."

"None?" Jack asked, incredulous.

"Never even fired my weapon. Army trained me ta kill, but hadta leave it ta become a killer."

Jack was determined not to look away. "Who were they? These sixty-seven people?"

"You don't wanna know this, Jack." D was staring down into his mug again.

"I do. Tell me who they were."

"I don't want you ta know."

"Why?"

D suddenly turned the high beams of those blazing eyes full on him. "'Cause I don't wanna wreck that world ya live in, where folks are good and help each other out and you fix people's faces that's got hurt, and where ya step up and stand and fight when ya seen wrong bein' done, where ya take care a some man who was sent ta kill ya, and I don't want ya ta know how it ain't like that, not really, and 'cause I don't want ya touched by me and my kind and the world I know so's you can go back ta yer life jus' the way you are right now."

Jack stared, transfixed. That was the most D had spoken at one time, and it was the first time he'd heard that kind of emotion from him. D looked away, and then put his mug aside. "I'm goin' ta get some sleep." Jack just watched him go into one of the bedrooms, the afghan still clutched around him, and shut the door behind him.

He slumped down on the couch, one hand over his eyes. *Jesus fucking Christ, what have I gotten myself into?*

D STRUGGLED awake through layers of heavy fog, and that in itself was alarming. He usually snapped awake, directly to full alertness, a leftover skill from the Army that had saved his ass on more than one occasion. Jack was shaking him.

No, he ain't shakin' you, you jus' shakin', he realized. He was wrapped in an afghan and sweat was pouring off him, but he was shaking. His shoulder was on fire and he felt hollowed out, mind and body. He'd been sick a few times in his life, but nothing like this. This felt like burning alive, liquefying and pouring himself out of his pores.

He struggled to sit up, then got his feet on the floor, but stumbled and fell with his feet tangled in the afghan. He heard quick footsteps, then the bedroom door opened and there were arms lifting him back to the bed. "What the hell are you doing?"

It was a blow to D's carefully cultivated independence and detachment to realize how glad he was to hear Jack's voice. He had to restrain himself from clutching at him. He just felt so strong and calm and healthy and D had little experience with feeling needy. "Woke up... shaky," he managed.

"Christ, you're burning up," Jack said, pushing him back onto the bed and turning on the bedside lamp. He pulled D's shirt aside to look at the wound; D could tell by Jack's tight face that it didn't look good. He sat on the edge of the bed, much closer than D would ordinarily have tolerated, but he felt so low that he didn't care. "D, I have to get some more medicine for you."

"How?"

Jack sighed. "I'll drive into Carson City and sneak into a hospital."

D opened his eyes and focused on Jack's face. He sure as hell looked serious. "Jack, I was kiddin' when I said that."

"I'll buy some scrubs from a medical-supply store, a lab coat, take my stethoscope, and walk in like I belong. Isn't that how they say you get by? Walk around like you belong?"

"Yeah, guess so... but...."

"I can do it. I have to do it."

"No, it's too risky. You get caught... brothers might find ya...."

Jack leaned a little closer and fixed him with a determined stare. "D, I am not going to do nothing while you die of sepsis or some kind of staph infection. I know what I'm doing. I'll be quick, and I'll be back before you know it."

"You ain't goin' now, are ya?"

"No, I can't. I'd be more easily noticed at night, when there's less staff around. I'll go in the morning." He had two fingers on D's wrist, taking his pulse. "I wish I could go now, though. You're getting worse by the minute."

"I'm okay."

"Cut out that impervious-ruthless-killer act. When's the last time you were seriously ill?"

"Don't think I ain't never been."

"Well, it's a great equalizer. It makes everyone feel vulnerable, from the weepiest soccer mom to the toughest drill sergeant. You're not so tough that you're immune, you know."

D grunted and scooted away a little, like maybe that'd make him forget about the bolts of panic that ran through him at the thought of Jack going out. "Don't need no hand-holdin', doc."

Jack chuckled. "You say that now, sure." He got up and went into the living room, coming back with his bag and a glass of water. "Sit up," he said, and D was humiliated to find that he needed help doing this. "Here, take these," Jack said, holding out his hand.

"What are they?"

"Just aspirin, dumbass," Jack said, with a playful smirk that D didn't really understand. "Help with the fever and the chills. And drink this entire glass of water. I don't want you dehydrated on top of everything else." D took the aspirin and drained the glass as fast as he could. "All right, let's get you into bed. Come on, get undressed."

D looked up at him. "Ya mind?"

"Oh. Sorry. My brain gets into doctor mode where I forget that people have modesty. I'll get you some more water; you get undressed and get in bed."

Jack left the room and D struggled out of his clothes, a task made more difficult by the pain in his shoulder and the uselessness of his left arm. He managed to strip down to his boxers and climb into the bed, which felt soft and inviting. He settled back against the pillows with a sigh, feeling marginally better, but still like he'd gotten a real close acquaintance with the front end of a truck.

Jack came back in with a glass of water and a bowl of something. "Drink this, and I want you to try and eat something."

D's stomach cramped up at the thought. "Cain't eat nothin'."

"Then at least drink."

D took the glass and got a few sips down. Jack took the glass and examined his shoulder again. "I have to change this dressing. It's going to hurt."

"Okay," D said.

He was right. It hurt.

Jack looked a little ill himself as he disposed of the old bandage. He wiped D's face with a cool washcloth. "Sorry," he said.

"Nuh... don't...." *What was he going to say?* He was drifting away. He felt weightless and the room was coming apart, floating apart in pieces. He could hear Jack saying his name, but it wasn't his name, just one stupid letter, the least you could get away with and still call it a name. *Wanna hear you say my real name someday, Jack.* The thought floated through his mind, moorless and slick so he couldn't hang on to it. *Might be that yer the person I could tell why it ain't mine no more.*

JACK watched as D drifted into semi-consciousness. He took his temperature again. 101. Higher than before. And that was with aspirin in him. He had to get some stronger antibiotics, and fast, before the infection spread and made him even sicker. He hated that he now had to wait until morning.

He took D's laptop out into the kitchen and set it up at the small table, hoping he could pick up a network. He was pleased to discover that at some point, Warren had wired this place up, so he was good to go. He found the location of Carson-Tahoe Hospital and copied down the directions from MapQuest, and did the same for a uniform store where he could buy scrubs. Their Web site said that they could even embroider his name on a lab coat while he waited, which would lend a touch of believability to his disguise. Was it really a disguise? He was a doctor, after all.

D was right about one thing. He couldn't walk into the ER and grab a couple of handfuls of drugs and tetanus toxoid. Emergency rooms had pretty good security these days. But if this hospital was anything like the ones he'd worked at, there would be little to no security at the employee health center. One nurse on duty, who would have plenty of antibiotics and probably tetanus vaccine in her office. All he had to do was wait for her to go to lunch or something. He even found the floor plan of the hospital online and located the employee health center. He sat and studied the floor plan until he had it pretty well committed to memory. It'd be hard to look like he belonged there if he was wandering around with a lost look on his face.

You could just run, you know. D's in no condition to give chase, and he won't have a car. Drive to Reno and call the Marshals. Have them put you back in protective custody. This man's dangerous. He's said there are people after him apart from the ones after you. The last thing you need is a traveling companion who makes you an even bigger target. Get away from him. Far away.

Jack got up and went back into D's room. He was sleeping, not entirely peacefully. Jack crossed to the bed and sat down on the edge, looking down at his unlikely ally with a head full of troubled thoughts. In sleep, the bedrock guardedness that D wore like a second skin was gone, and he looked vulnerable, human and frail. Jack put the back of his hand to D's forehead again. Still hot. Who was he kidding? He couldn't leave D. Not now. He'd saved Jack's life at least three times. He might be a vicious killer, but Jack couldn't bring himself to judge him. There had to be something that had driven him to it, because Jack had looked but he hadn't seen the kind of coldness or cruelty that he had to believe would be there for a man who'd truly chosen to make his living by killing others.

It was his turn to do the rescuing, and he'd do it, by God.

D shifted in his sleep, a quiet groan escaping him. "D?" Jack said, wishing he knew the man's real name. "You all right?"

He seemed to be dreaming. Something frightening, or upsetting, by the looks of things. "Unnhhh... no," he moaned. "Juh... Juh...." For one alarmed moment, Jack wondered if D was about to say his name. "Jill...," he finished. "Juh... Jill...."

Jill? Who's Jill? Does he have a wife? Or a child? The notion of D having a family didn't quite fit in his mind. *Maybe he left some family behind somewhere. Maybe he's got an ex-wife who left him and took the kids.* Jack had no evidence of this, of course, but it seemed logical that a man in the hired-killer business might pay a steep price if people close to him learned what he did for a living.

"It's okay," Jack said, trying to be soothing. He hesitated, then reached out and took D's hand. It was large and strong, callused between the fingers and thumb. "Shhhh," he said, making meaningless noises of comfort. "You're going to be fine, D."

"Jill...."

"We'll find her again. Just try and relax."

D nodded. "Yeah... gotta find her...."

"We'll find her. I promise."

"Lemme go...." D drew his hand away and rolled on his side, away from Jack. He stayed where he was, watching as D fell into a deeper sleep, and then moved to the easy chair in one corner. He sat there, watching his patient, until he fell asleep himself.

CHAPTER 7

JUST past ten o'clock in the morning, a surgeon who didn't exist walked into Carson-Tahoe Hospital. He wore blue surgical scrubs and a white lab coat; his name, Dr. John Templeton, was stitched in blue over the pocket. A stethoscope hung around his neck and he was flipping pages on a clipboard as he walked, just another surgeon reviewing a chart before a procedure, or a consultation, or grand rounds.

No one paid him the slightest bit of attention, except for the nurse at the desk who saw him walk by, wondered who the handsome new doctor was, and promptly forgot about him the moment he was out of sight.

Jack had thought that the act would be hard to keep up, that his nerves would make him awkward and obvious, but this environment was reassuring. It ought to have been; he'd done this a million times when it wasn't an act. He'd spent the past five years walking hospital corridors in scrubs, looking at clipboards and not paying attention to where he was going, a stethoscope around his neck. This wasn't awkward; it was familiar. Hospitals were all the same, and he knew the lives of these nurses and PAs and interns and attendings as well as if he were a resident here.

He watched as a patient on a gurney was wheeled by in a big hurry. He wondered what was wrong with the patient. He wondered if he could help. *Maybe I could just pop down to the ER and lend a hand. Intubate a head trauma... maybe assess some surgical candidates... even just stitch up a couple of scratches, anything....*

He resumed his course toward the employee health center. *Get a grip, Jack. D needs you to not fuck this up. Focus.* He thought of his feverish patient alone in the cabin, and steeled himself to continue. When he'd left, D had been sleeping fitfully, his temperature spiking higher and his wound suppurating. He had to do this quick, and the hospital was not the only stop he had to make before he returned.

He walked straight into the employee health office. Just like the one at Johns Hopkins, it was an ordinary-looking office with a reception desk and a couple of exam tables, plus a cot. The nurse, a middle-aged woman with fire-engine red hair, smiled broadly at him as he entered. "Hello!" she said.

"Hi," Jack said. "I'm Dr. Templeton."

"Are you new, Doctor? I don't think I've seen you before."

"No, I'm from Reno. I'm just here consulting on a case. Listen, I had some bad sushi last night. Do you have any compazine?"

"Sure!" the nurse said. She looked glad to be having an actual visitor. "Are you having any cramping? Have you thrown up? Diarrhea?"

"No to all," Jack said, thinking rapidly about which responses would be the least memorable and produce the fewest follow-up questions. "Just feeling a little nauseated."

She got up and went to the cabinet by the exam beds. Underneath the counter was a small refrigerator. It wasn't locked. That was where Jack would find what he needed for D. The nurse pulled a small bottle out of the cabinet and returned to the desk. "You just want two?"

"That'll do for now, thanks." Jack took the pills, smiled, and left the office.

He walked down the corridor a short distance and then sat down on a couch, pretending to study the "chart" on his clipboard. *Now what? Sit here and wait? I feel like I'm wasting time. I don't dare leave; what if she goes for lunch and I miss it?* He leaned back and watched the doctors and nurses walking to and fro, full of purpose, patients to see, people to fix. The directory on the wall told him that the operating rooms were on the third floor. *Maybe I could just pop up there and scrub in on a cleft-palate repair.* The thought was ridiculous, but seductive. He hadn't had a scalpel in his hands since the day he'd witnessed Maria Dominguez's murder, and he missed it more than he would have imagined possible. Wielding the knife, parting the skin, repairing the damage, fixing what had gone wrong... it was all a heady experience, and he could easily see how surgeons developed God complexes. He hoped he didn't have one of his own brewing. The delusions of omnipotence displayed by his supervisors and mentors had been irritating enough that he and his fellow residents had sworn never to think so well of themselves, but he'd started to suspect that it just came with the territory.

I ought to look on the bright side, he thought. *Maybe my profound helplessness at the hands of drug lords and being a fugitive will keep me from getting a swelled head.* Mortal danger seemed like a high price to pay to avoid a God complex, all things being equal.

He pulled out a cell phone. It wasn't his. It was one of a half-dozen cloned, untraceable cell phones that D had retrieved from the bunker in Quartzsite. He'd brought it along in case D needed to reach him, although he wasn't entirely sure that D had understood him when he'd explained. His eyes had been open, but his attention had been fading in and out. At least it was useful as a prop. Jack held an imaginary conversation with a colleague, keeping one eye on the employee health office, which he could just barely see from his vantage point on the couch.

He took some notes, spinning an ever more elaborate tale in his head of a four-year-old patient with severe Treacher Collins syndrome. He told the phantom pediatric plastic surgeon he was not talking to about the bone grafts he'd need, the imaging they'd have to have done before surgery, the stages of facial reconstruction, and the post-op care that the girl—little Susie, he'd decided she was called—would require.

He got so caught up in his fictional patient that he almost *did* miss it when the red-haired nurse left the employee health office. He caught a glimpse of her retreating back, and the small placard she'd hung on the door handle. He casually wrapped up his conversation with thin air and got up, trying to project nonchalance, and walked back down the corridor. The placard said "Back in One Hour." Perfect.

Jack took a quick glance up and down the hall, and then slipped inside, leaving the placard where it was. He went right to the fridge and opened it up. Tetanus vaccine was the first item on the shopping list; he had a bad moment when he thought she didn't have any, but then he found it in the corner. Two vials of Ancef ought to be enough to knock out D's infection. He added a third just to be safe, taking the vials from the back of the row so it wouldn't be noticeable. He opened up her cabinet drawers and pulled out a few syringes. The entire heist took less than a minute.

Jack left the office and rejoined the traffic flow in the corridor. No one seemed to have taken the slightest note of his presence. He walked quickly but calmly out of the hospital, got in his car and left, profound relief washing over him as the building disappeared from his rearview mirror.

LYING in bed in the grip of a raging fever, D discovered, was kind of like hanging for hours in that not-awake-not-asleep hinterland where dreams started and stopped every few seconds and reality seemed hazy, like a bad acid trip.

Not that D had ever dropped acid. God knew what he might do or say. Too risky.

Sweat was pouring off him, but he felt like he was freezing. His shoulder throbbed with a sharp ache that spread in waves through his whole torso and his stomach was rolling in unpleasant flip-flops of nausea. He had a vague recollection of Jack making him drink water and take an aspirin before he'd... he'd....

He fought his way back to consciousness. "Jack?" No answer. "Jack!"

He's gone. Took the money and the guns and the ID and left ya here ta die. Better'n you deserve. You'll probably just dehydrate and fall asleep, which is a nicer death than you ever expected ya'd get. Fuckin' left ya.... His eyes fell on the cell phone sitting on the nightstand and he sagged, remembering Jack hovering over him, saying he was going for the medicine D needed, that he'd be back soon. *Use the cell phone if you need to call me. I programmed in the number of the one I'm taking.*

D picked up the cell phone, his muscles feeling about as forceful as wet noodles. He opened the Contacts menu and saw the single, solitary entry, the name glowing there in blue letters: Jack. His finger hovered over the Send button. *Call him. Just put yer mind at ease. Find out when he's comin' back. No, don't call him. What are you, some kinda little girl cain't be left alone for a coupla hours? He's gonna think yer a first-class pansy. Jus' put the fuckin' phone down and go back ta sleep, and you'll wake up when he's back.*

He put the phone down. Just its existence was good enough for the time being.

JACK fought to keep himself from speeding, running lights, taking unnecessary risks as he went through the other tasks he'd set himself. First, the drugstore. Bandages, hydrogen peroxide, Tylenol, sterile gauze, a proper sling, some Epsom salts, topical anaesthetic, and anything else that seemed like it might be remotely useful. Next, the grocery store. Some fresh food. Bread, juice, lunchmeat. Ginger ale—they had Vernor's—and teabags. Meat for grilling, vegetables, pasta. D would need to get his strength back up, and fighting an infection was very tough on a body. He'd be weak for a few days at least. Some beer, just because he suspected he'd need to knock back a few himself.

Finally, he was back on the road to the cabin just after one o'clock. He'd been gone for about four hours.

It took him three trips to unload the car, between the groceries and the bags from the drugstore. The precious vials of medicine were carefully unloaded from the glove box and placed in the cabin's refrigerator. He locked the front door again and went into D's room to check on his patient.

He was lying sprawled, half-uncovered, a sheen of sweat over the skin that Jack could see and dampness darkening his T-shirt. He had the cell phone Jack had left clutched in his hand and resting on his chest. Jack bent over him and felt his forehead. If anything, his fever was higher than when he'd left, and one look at his wound told him that the risk he'd taken to obtain the antibiotics had been necessary. He pried the phone from D's hand, which made him jerk and stir. "Whu… huh…." He flopped like a fish for a moment, disoriented. Jack sat down on the edge of the bed and held him down, one hand on his damp forehead.

"Hey, it's all right. Shhh, lie still. It's just me. I'm back."

D's eyes focused on him, bleary and fever-clouded. "Oh," he exhaled. "Ya came back."

"Of course I did!" Jack shook his head. "I guess it tells me something about the kind of people you're used to dealing with that you thought I might just abandon you here to die like an animal."

"How'd it go?" D's voice was thin and weak. It didn't sound like him at all.

"It went fine, actually. No problem."

"Anybody seen ya?"

"Well yes, people saw me, but I don't think anybody took any notice of just another doctor in scrubs and a lab coat. I'll be right back." He went into the kitchen and washed his hands, then got the syringes, the vials and the bags from the drugstore. "Okay, let's do this. You've been malingering in bed long enough, don't you think?"

"Ha, funny," D rasped.

"Roll on your side."

"Why?"

"Because, genius, both of these shots have to go in your ass, I'm sorry to say."

D grumbled, but rolled on his side. Jack lowered his boxers just enough to expose the injection site near his hip. He swabbed the site with alcohol, drew the tetanus vaccine into a syringe, and made the injection. D winced. "Ow," he said.

"Sorry. That one hurts, I know. It's a big dose, goes deep. The Ancef won't be as bad."

"Ansawhat?"

"Ancef. It's a broad-spectrum cephalosporin. An antibiotic. It ought to kill whatever bugs are eating you." He drew the dose and injected him. "There, all done." D rolled onto his back again.

"How long… 'til…."

"Hopefully your fever will break by tonight. That's when I'll know you're really on the mend, but I'm going to keep dosing you with this stuff until I'm damned sure you're clear of it. I got plenty. Here," he said, giving D more aspirin and a bottle of water. "Drink all that down, now. And I'm going to make you some broth, which you will eat without arguing with me, and I got you Vernor's."

D looked up at him. "Ya… got me Vernor's?"

"You said you liked it. And ginger ale is good for stomach upset, which the Ancef might possibly give you."

"Thanks," D said, sounding amazed. Jack wondered if anyone had ever done anything considerate for D ever before in his life, because by the look on his face, no one had. That couldn't be possible. Maybe he'd just become so accustomed to expecting nothing that even this tiny kindness of remembering his favorite soda seemed like a grand gesture.

"You're welcome," he said. "And if you save my life a fourth time, maybe I'll even spring for a Slurpee. Come on, I need to clean that wound and change your dressing again."

GODDAMN, if I ever say anything rude, dismissive or remotely condescending about the nursing profession ever again, please let me be immediately struck by lightning. Caring for a sick person, nonstop, as opposed to breezing in and breezing out while bestowing the gift of his wisdom upon them, was exhausting. And in a relative sense, D wasn't that sick. He had an infection but it hadn't gone into sepsis and he'd heal. And he was Jack's only patient. He didn't know how nurses did it. He kept him dosed with aspirin, administered additional injections of Ancef, kept him hydrated, cleaned his wound, made him drink broth and water and Vernor's and sponged his goddamned brow. D drew the line at helping him into the bathroom, though. He insisted on staggering in and back by himself, despite Jack's reassurances that he'd seen penises before and he was a doctor and therefore capable of medical detachment, and furthermore he'd be damned if he was going to go back into town and steal an orthopedic surgeon when D fell on his ass and broke his leg.

In between, he sat on the couch and watched TV, drifting in and out of a fitful doze, and blessed his own good health. He'd been sick like D was a few times in his life and not only was it unpleasant, it made you feel weak and vulnerable, two conditions that he knew had to be antithetical to D's very existence.

Just after midnight he shuffled into D's room. The only sound was deep, even breathing. He flipped the lamp on and felt his forehead. It was cool. The fever had broken. He sighed, relieved, and sat down in the easy chair in the corner. *Just sit here for a minute....*

And then he was waking up, a hand on his shoulder. "Hey. Jack."

He blinked, the sunlight—*sunlight?*—hitting his eyes hard like a slap. D was leaning over him, some color in his cheeks, a quilt wrapped around his shoulders. "Oh shit... what time is it?" Jack stammered.

"Bit past eight. You been here all night?"

"Guess I fell asleep." He focused on D again, remembering their situation. "How are you? On your feet, I see."

"I feel better."

"Sit your ass down. I'll be the judge of that." D sat on the edge of the bed and behaved himself while Jack listened to his chest, checked his temperature, and inspected his wound. It was still reddish but wasn't suppurating anymore; it was beginning to crust over and heal. "Well, thanks to the extraordinary gifts of your physician, I believe you're on the mend."

"I feel kinda... weak. Like I couldn't walk more'n a few feet."

"That's to be expected. We ought to get you up and about if we can, though. Let me give you another shot—"

"Another one? My ass ain't no pincushion."

"For prophylaxis."

"Prophyl-whatsis? Ain't that a condom? What the hell you plannin', doc?"

Jack chuckled. "Prophylaxis is any preventative measure, like flossing to prevent gum disease. Condoms are sometimes called 'prophylactics' because they're a preventive measure against insemination. More antibiotics are to prevent resurgence of your infection."

"Oh. Guess so." He sat still for the injection, then got to his feet. "I'm dyin' fer a shower. And *no*, I don't need no help with that!" he snapped.

Jack smiled, watching him shuffle into the bathroom. *He must be feeling better; he's all grumpy again.*

D HAD to pause every few minutes and lean against the shower stall to gather his strength, but the hot water felt damned good. He had two days' worth of sweat and sickness on his skin like an oil slick, and all he wanted to do was rub himself raw with the puffy scrubby thing he found hanging from the faucet handle.

Weakness was something he'd been taught to hate, and had been forced to deny by his lifestyle. It was something he could never afford, either to experience or to show. Funny that something as stupid as some bacteria on a bullet could do what a number of big strong men hadn't been able to do, namely to lay him low. What was worse was that he hadn't been alone; there had been a witness to his weakness, and what made it even worse than that was that his witness was somebody D had wanted to be strong for, stronger than the men who wanted him dead, stronger than the law, stronger than his own fear of exposure.

But was he strong? No. It was Jack who'd been strong. Jack who'd gone out into the hostile world and committed a crime, Jack who'd chased away the monsters that had been waiting to prey on him in the dark.

When was the last time D had trusted someone with his life? He couldn't remember. Probably he had done so in the Army, but that time was so distant and hazy, shoved as it was behind a veil of anger and betrayal and loss and horror. No, before Jack there was only one person D trusted, and even then, it had to be someone whose face D had never even seen.

He dried off and put on some fresh clothes from his duffel, which Jack had thoughtfully brought into his room. He could smell food cooking, and his stomach growled. All at once he was hungry enough to eat a horse. A dead horse. With maggots.

Jack had set the table, and was at the stove cooking something. Grilled cheese, it looked like. D blinked, looking out over the little setup, which was disturbingly domestic. "Feel better?" Jack asked.

D grunted. "Cleaner."

"Here," Jack said, leaving the stove and picking up some kind of cloth contraption with straps and Velcro. "This is for your arm. You're going to want to keep your shoulder still so it can heal."

"Don't need no fuckin' sling."

"You need a sling and you'll wear a sling." Grumbling, D let Jack help him on with the damned thing, although he had to admit that having it on took some of the pressure off the wound. It didn't feel like it was pulling at itself anymore. "Now sit down."

D obeyed. "You gonna gimme a time-out next, doc?"

"Nope. Tomato soup and grilled cheese." He put a plate in front of him, and D's appetite outweighed his self-consciousness. He had half the sandwich gone by the time Jack sat down in the other chair. "Damn, you must have been hungry."

"Ain't had nothin' fer two days."

"You're really looking much better."

D nodded, a mouthful of soup making it hard to answer. "Got me a good doc," he said, allowing himself a brief flick of the eyes to Jack's face, just long enough to see the pleased smile that spread there.

JACK spent the afternoon compulsively cleaning the cabin while D napped. He hadn't even *used* the other bedroom yet, having been taking his sporadic sleep either on the couch or in the easy chair in D's room. He went outside and moved the car around to the far side of the house, thinking it might be prudent for the cabin to appear uninhabited at a glance. He took a quick inventory of supplies with an eye to another trip to Carson City in a day or so, to do laundry and get more groceries. He didn't know how long they'd be here, but it'd be at least a week before D could comfortably use his arm, and the longer he rested it, the better off he'd be. He didn't know if D would agree to stay put that long, but on the other hand, the longer they stayed here without detection, the more that meant that they were well-concealed. Didn't it?

D joined him on the back porch just before five. "Goddamn," he muttered, looking out at the view of Lake Tahoe. "This is... somethin'. Yer father-in-law must be some kinda rich."

"Oh, yeah," Jack said. D sat down in the other deck chair.

"You 'n' Caroline split in ninety-eight, right?"

Jack looked at him. "How'd you know that?"

"Seen yer file. Know lots about ya."

"Oh. Yeah, nineteen ninety-eight, after six years of marriage."

"Married young, then."

"Twenty-two, the both of us. I was just starting dental school. She was studying business, and the dental students and the business students shared a parking lot. We must have had classes at the same time because I always seemed to see her coming and going when I was."

D snorted. "Yeah. Classes. Sure."

Jack frowned. "What?"

"She was stakin' you out, doc."

"Huh?"

D sighed. "She was takin' note a when you was comin' 'n' goin' and made a point ta be there so's she could chat ya up, dumbass."

Jack blinked. Another well-deserved *dumbass* for him. "Never thought of that."

"Course ya didn't, 'cause yer mind don't work like that. Mine does. Caroline mighta made a good hit man. Women do real well at it, 'cause no one never suspects 'em."

"You know any women hit men? Uh... hit women?"

"Couple. My handler's a woman. Was a woman, I oughta say."

"She's dead?"

"No, but I cain't exactly say she's my handler no more, now that I'm off the fuckin' reservation, can I?"

Jack sat back, embarrassed. "Guess not."

"So, why'd ya break up?"

"Why are you asking me all these questions?" Jack bit out. "You don't care."

"Who says I don't care?"

"*You* do! You said that all you needed to know about me was witness, truth, don't deserve to die, blah blah blah and that was all you cared to know!"

Now it was D's turn to look a little embarrassed. "Oh. Guess I did say that, didn't I?" He said nothing for a minute. "Maybe I wanna know now."

"Don't do me any favors. I don't need any pity conversation. We can sit here in total fucking silence for all I care." Jack crossed his arms over his chest. *You're pouting; cut it out.* He *was* pouting, and he thought he was justified. D, however, wasn't responding. He just sat there like a statue. Pouting wasn't much fun when its target audience wasn't cooperating. "Look," Jack finally said. "I took care of you because you needed it, and I'm a doctor and that's what I do. Don't feel you have to suddenly be a different person because of it."

"Different person how?"

"You know. Friendly and interested."

D grunted. "Gee, thanks."

"You know what I mean. You're a certain way, and I get why you've had to become that way, and I'm not going to try and get you to change just to make me more comfortable."

"Ain't 'cause a you," D said, his fingers twitching in a way that let Jack know that he was craving a cigarette. "Jus'… curious. About regular folks. Ain't been one fer so long. How do normal folks like you 'n' Caroline break up?"

Something in the way he asked the question jagged in Jack's mind like a fishhook. "You were married, weren't you?" he said.

D shot a sharp glance at him, and then looked away again. "Long time ago, yeah."

Jack watched his profile for a moment, that geologic skull underneath growing-in stubble of hair, and then plunged ahead. "D… who's Jill?"

He saw D's jaw clench. He shifted in his chair and crossed his legs at the knee. "How you know about Jill?" he asked, quietly.

"When you were sick, you said that name. You were delirious."

D raised a hand to his head and pressed in on his forehead, like he was trying to hold something inside. "Jill's my daughter," he said.

"Where is she now?"

"I ain't doin' this, Jack."

"But—"

"I ain't," D said sharply, meeting Jack's eyes. "Some things don't get out. Not yet."

Jack nodded. "Okay." He let the moment pass, and the silence return and make itself comfortable. The man really was a caution, as his mother used to say. Tiptoe, tiptoe around the edges, look out for the guards posted, and maybe find a hole dug under the fence where you could get your head in for a peek before you got hauled out by the ankles to walk the perimeter again, waiting for another chance.

He got up for a beer, bringing one out to D as well. "Am I s'posed ta have this with all these drugs?" D asked, accepting the bottle.

Jack shrugged. "You're not on any narcotics. Should be fine. You might get buzzed a little faster than you normally would." He took his seat again. "You want to know why Caroline left me?"

"Asked, didn't I?"

"Because she finally met the guy she'd married me to escape."

D frowned, and Jack could see this answer refusing to compute. "Huh?"

Jack smiled. "Her dad, whose hospitality we are currently enjoying without his knowledge, had it in his head that she was going to marry the son of some business associate of his. Like it was Shakespeare and they were going to unite the families and rule the empire together as a single dynasty, or whatever. Spent half of Caroline's life talking this guy up to her. Pete McFarland is so athletic, won't he make a nice husband someday for some lucky gal, Pete McFarland will inherit a fortune, Pete's handsome, Pete's fantastic, you get the idea. By the time Caroline was eighteen she hated Pete McFarland even though she'd never actually met him. Warren kept after her, wanting to arrange for them to meet, trying to set things up, and she got so fed up that when we met she just grabbed onto me and before I knew it we were married, and Pete McFarland was no longer a threat. Warren was not pleased."

"Guess not," D said, with a sage nod.

"Well, I was in med school and she was working at a brokerage when guess what? She met Pete McFarland. And guess what else? He was handsome, funny, charming and a great businessman. Hell, I'd have married the guy if I was a woman. It damned near killed her to admit her daddy'd been right. Anyway, by that time it was already clear that our marriage was a bust. We were barely more than roommates. We had a real friendly divorce, no kids, split everything, and she married Pete McFarland with my blessing. Warren was so happy that he even forgot how he'd hated me, and to hear him tell it now I'm some kind of hero for letting his daughter have a life with her soul mate, or however he's phrasing it these days."

D shook his head in amazement. "So this is how normal folks pass the time?"

"Not entirely. Sometimes we go bowling too."

As their laughter mingled and rolled down the hill toward the lake, Jack could almost believe that they were just a couple of buddies come up here for a weekend of fishing to escape their daily grind and responsibilities. Crack open a beer, shoot the shit, smoke cigars in the open air, and laugh about things that had once been painful while keeping silent about things that still were.

CHAPTER 8

BEHIND the cabin, there was a sloping yard with some rudimentary landscaping and a couple of isolated sitting areas, all of them with views that could have made the devil praise the Lord. D was sitting in one of them now, staring out at the impossibly blue surface of the lake, the craggy snow-capped peaks surrounding it like the torn edge of a piece of paper.

It was two days now since Jack's expedition into Carson City, and D was starting to feel like something approximating himself. His energy was returning and the pain in his wound was down to a dull throb. Jack inspected it often, checking for signs of recurring infection, but the skin around the bullet hole had returned to a healthier hue and the wound was knitting itself up. At Jack's insistence, D kept his arm in the sling to avoid tearing the wound open again. Being hamstrung like that was galling, but he thought he at least owed Jack the courtesy of taking his advice. It'd be pretty asshole-ish of him to reinjure himself after what Jack had risked to treat him.

Jack was still asleep, or at least D hoped he was. Now that his patient was on the mend, Jack had finally taken possession of the cabin's second bedroom and had been sleeping. A lot. When D had left the cabin just before ten, there was still no sign of life from him. The guy needed some rest, and D was glad he was getting it.

He was also glad for some time alone, because at any moment his pocket was going to vibrate, and he didn't want to have to concoct some kind of explanation.

He willed his mind to go blank, which wasn't such an easy task given the graffiti all over it. The scenery laid out before him was working pretty well as an eraser. He couldn't discern any signs of civilization. From this vantage point, no other houses or structures were visible; he and Jack might have been the last people on Earth.

The unexpected sense of freedom that came from this notion was interrupted by the pocket vibration he'd been waiting for. He pulled out one of the cloned cell phones from the bunker and thumbed open the text message.

r u ok

D took a breath and let it out slowly. He held the phone with his thumbs over the keypad for the brief conversation he'd been waiting for all morning.

y
Wher
cant say.

safe?

y

jf?

ok

u?

shot but ok

u r vnishd no wrd

good

nxt mve

dunno

need hlp?

not now mybe l8r

ok u no how 2 cntkt me

thx 4 msg

no prob b careful

will do

wtch back

alwys

He slipped the phone back in his pocket, marginally reassured. He heard the back door of the cabin open. "D?"

"Out here," he called back.

"You want some breakfast?"

He stood up and headed back to the cabin. "Comin'."

Jack was putting out bowls of oatmeal when D came in the patio door. In the past days, D had learned that Jack was more than competent at cooking but damned irritating about it. Wouldn't make bacon and eggs, but insisted on oatmeal and lectured him about cholesterol and saturated fat. "What were you doing out there?" Jack asked.

D shot him an irritated glance. "Why you gotta know?"

Jack shrugged. "Just curious."

"Takin' the air. Oatmeal again?"

"It's good for you. Complex carbohydrates."

"Don't we have any eggs?"

"How are you feeling?" Jack asked, ignoring D's question.

D shrugged, sitting down and starting in on the oatmeal without further protest. Much as he was craving a nice big cheesy artery-clogging omelet, he guessed that as long as Jack was doing all the cooking he could shut up about what was put in front of him. "Pretty good."

"How's your shoulder?"

"Hurts. Not as bad as yesterday."

Jack sat down to his own breakfast. They ate in silence, putting their bowls aside when they were finished and moving on to coffee. D had noticed that Jack's sermonizing about proper nutrition stopped short of denouncing caffeine.

He yearned for a smoke, but Jack had thrown all of them away. Somehow, in the course of treating his gunshot wound, Jack had appointed himself as D's personal health and well-being traffic cop. If asked, D would have said that he hated the intrusion, Jack's presumption and being deprived of grease, nicotine and starchy foods, but just between himself and the lamppost he could admit that it felt kind of nice to have someone worrying about him, and looking after him. He'd been looking after himself for so long that he'd forgotten what it was like to know that someone else actually gave a shit if he lived or died or came down with emphysema. He didn't kid himself, though; Jack was looking out for himself in the process. D was the only thing standing between him and hordes of angry drug lords, after all.

Jack seemed a little distracted this morning. D could sympathize. He was trying to see his way clear to their next step, but the way ahead was still murky and ill-defined.

When Jack spoke, his voice sounded sharp, a blade cutting into their silence. "Tell me about these sixty-seven people," he said.

D sighed. He wasn't going to let this go. "You don't wanna hear all that."

"Don't tell me what I do and do not want to hear."

"Jack, there's things about me you'll be easier in yer mind if ya don't know."

"There are good things about you," he said, meeting D's eyes. "But I need to know the bad things too."

D drained his coffee cup, looking out the patio doors at the lake. He had little experience talking his way around his job. Most of the time it wasn't an issue. "I don't think—" he began.

"I deserve to know," Jack interrupted. "This isn't you saving my ass anymore, D. We're in this together, aren't we?"

He sighed. "Reckon so."

"You trust me?"

That was a harder question to answer. For more than ten years, probably longer, D had only trusted one person, and that trust had been paid for in blood. He didn't know if he trusted Jack. He did know that he shouldn't. His trust was dear, and it wasn't earned by a short acquaintance or even medical treatment. Not when Jack had so much to gain by keeping D on his good side. And certainly not when Jack might have it in his power to get D arrested or killed.

But none of that changed the fact that in his heart he wanted to trust Jack, and hoped that he could, and that was unsettling to him. He knew that it was a short ride from wanting to trust someone to trusting them too soon, and from there an even shorter ride to a knife in the back. And if there was one thing that he already knew, it was that any knife in his back that had Jack's name on the handle would hurt worse than just the wounding of it, and he didn't care to think too long or hard on why that might be.

Jack was waiting for an answer. "No more'n you trust me," D said, which was as vague as he could stand.

Jack wasn't fooled. "Well, whether you trust me or not, you owe me."

"I don't owe you shit," D snapped, rankling at the idea, its truth notwithstanding. "Don't go thinkin' 'cause you patched me up that I'm obliged. I'd still be well advised ta kill you and serve up yer head ta the brothers, ya know."

He could see that this not-so-veiled threat didn't faze Jack all that much. "What are you afraid of?" he asked. "That I can't handle it? That I'll run screaming into the woods? I know you think I'm some kind of city-boy softie—"

"I don't think that," D said.

"Whatever," Jack said, flapping a hand. "Point is that I've done time at hospitals in neighborhoods that even you'd be scared to walk around in. I've seen things that'd make you puke up your whole intestinal tract, so don't treat me like I'm made of bone china and can't handle hearing about what you do."

D sighed. "Usedta do, ya mean."

"So let's have it. All of it."

He met Jack's eyes, blue and chipped, and he couldn't think of another reason not to tell him what he wanted to know. "All right. You asked for it." He started in on another cup of coffee. "What you wanna know?"

"Who was the last one?"

"Art dealer. Thief, really. Took art that the Nazis looted and made it so it couldn't be proved, so he could sell it for a bundle a cash when it belonged ta the families a the survivors."

Jack blinked. "And you thought he deserved death for that?"

"He was a bad man. And it wasn't me wanted him dead, anyhow."

Jack had his hands folded on the table. He looked like he was processing this information, to uncertain results. "So... what about the rest?"

"What, you want a complete list? Hafta check my day planner."

"Are you trying to piss me off?"

"No, I am tryin' ta tell ya that there ain't no point ta me quotin' ya chapter 'n' verse about all the people I killed in my time!"

"I just want to know who they were!" Jack exclaimed, his face reddening.

Understanding bloomed in D's mind and spread. *He don't wanna know who they were. Wants ta know how much like him they were. Wants ta see how close he came ta bein' one more.* He sighed. "A lot of 'em were killers theirselves. If you only knew how many a them guys get off on technicalities, it's enough ta turn yer stomach. Some were rapists, or child molesters... court cases real hard ta prove fer those types." Jack was nodding along.

"But... who pays to have them killed? You get, what, contracts? Who puts them up, and how? You can't exactly look up 'killers for hire' in the yellow pages."

D chuckled. "Not really, no. Actually...." He hesitated. "I shouldn't be tellin' ya this. Lotsa times, my services are paid for by families a victims. Sometimes the cops 'n' lawyers pitch in too. It ain't talked about. And most a the time, the family gets an anonymous letter, or a card, tellin' 'em who ta call."

Jack's eyes were getting wide. "Who's sending these cards?"

"Most a the time somebody like Josey, my handler. They keep careful track a the big cases. Court TV, newspapers... they got people watchin' all over the country that tips 'em off too, so they know when some low-life killer's got off, or some rapist got acquitted. On occasion, when the case is real bad... well, sometimes, a cop or a lawyer clues the family in."

"Seriously?"

"Anonymously, a course. They cain't be condonin' what I do. But sometimes they jus' cain't take it. Bad folks gettin' off 'cause the system's set up ta prevent mistakes. I get why. Better the guilty go free than the innocent go ta jail. If the guilty go free... well, there's folks like me ta deal with it." He refilled Jack's coffee cup. "Big part a my business. Most a the rest is criminals bumpin' off their own. Warrin' amongst themselves. Some are folks doin' bad that ain't never been caught, or ain't never gonna be caught. Folks the law cain't touch."

"So someone calls your handler—"

"Right. Calls Josey, tells her who they want done, she does an assessment, quotes 'em a price. Price goes up for a high-profile target, goes up for high-risk, like if the guy's got bodyguards or anythin', goes up for a rush job, stuff like that. Part a that price is her fee, rest goes ta me if I take the job."

"Who are these people that you won't kill?"

D shook his head. "Jack, people want other people dead for all kinds a reasons, not all a which wash with me. A lot a those hits that come up are witnesses, like you. Ton a those. I've seen hits on cheatin' wives, and hits on kids ta punish their parents fer whatever, and hits out on whistle-blowers and business competitors and just people pissed someone off."

"And you see those files, and... what? Just say 'Thanks but no thanks'?"

"Pretty much."

"What happens to those hits then?"

"Well... Josey keeps 'em... until...." He was treading on very dangerous ground here, and by his darkening expression, Jack thought so too.

"Until she can give them to someone else who will take them, right?"

"Reckon so." D stared down at his coffee cup.

"So you've seen these files on these innocent people, kids and women and whistle-blowers and witnesses, and you just pass on by, knowing that someone else will do what you won't, and what do you do? Do you do anything?"

"What'm I sposed ta do?"

"Warn them?"

D shook his head. "I cain't warn 'em. Give myself away sure as shit."

Jack stood up and took a few steps backward. "Then why the hell didn't you just kill them yourself? Why the big act, like you're too good for it? You knew they'd be killed, you did nothing... you might as well have gotten paid for it!" he shouted.

"Jack, calm down."

"Don't tell me to calm down!"

"Ya knew who I was when ya asked."

"I knew what you told me, but you didn't tell me all of it, did you? You told me you only killed people who deserved it."

"Right."

"You left out the part about standing by and doing nothing while people who didn't deserve it were killed by others!"

D gripped his coffee cup hard. *He cain't know. Not yet. He cain't fuckin' know. Keep yer stupid trap shut, no matter how much ya wanna tell him.* "Weren't my job ta save them," he said.

Jack's face twisted into an expression of such disgust that D had to look away. "You're no better than the ones who did kill them," he spat. "I should have let you die of that gunshot wound." He turned around and stalked into his bedroom, slamming the door behind him. D could hear him pacing, then he heard something smash where it was thrown.

He sat where he was, the coffee cup pressed between his palms, and stared at the tabletop until it stopped swimming.

THIS is a fucking fine situation you've gotten yourself into, Jack. Stuck in a cabin with a killer in the middle of nowhere while the bad guys prowl around trying to find you and kill you.

He'd been lying on his bed for over an hour, working himself up into a lather… or trying to. Cursing D, picturing the innocent people who'd died because he did nothing, imagining him putting bullets through people's heads (Did he shoot them through the head? Or somewhere else?), imagining him waving off some file about a charity-donating, volunteer-working, church-going mother of five who someone wanted dead and not giving her fate another thought, going about his business, eating bad food and smoking like a chimney and maybe picking up hookers just for kicks.

I want to hate him. Why can't I hate him?

He saved me. He should have killed me. He didn't, he couldn't. He saved me again, and again. He put himself in danger.

Why for me, and not for any of those others? Why am I so goddamned special?

There was a quiet knock on the door. "Jack?"

Jack sighed. "What?"

He heard an awkward throat-clearing. "You, uh… gonna stay in there all day?"

"Maybe!"

There was a pause. "Well… I was jus' thinkin'… reckon we oughta talk."

Jack sat up, glaring at the door. "Oh, now you want to talk, huh?"

"C'mon, Jack. Lemme in."

He flopped back onto the bed. "It isn't locked."

The door edged open a crack and D peered in. Seeing Jack just lying there, he came in further and lurked near the door, seeming loath to intrude on Jack's personal space. "Let's go out ta the porch, somethin'."

"Why? I spent enough time in your bedroom when we first got here."

"But it's… such a nice day 'n' all."

Jack laughed. "Oh, of course! Beautiful day! Like you care. We'll walk among the trees and hear the pretty birds and sing tra la la."

D rolled his eyes. "Will ya cut that out? I don't much like you like this."

"Oh! You don't like me! That is rich!"

"Look, it must be real nice and comfy on top a that high horse," D said, suddenly snarling, "but you ain't lived in my world and it's jus' fine fer you ta judge when you don't gotta make them kinda choices."

"Oh yeah?" Jack said, jumping off the bed to face him. "How about deciding whether you're going to treat the woman with the head trauma or the drunk driver who mowed her down? Or whether to let a man die of gunshot wounds because you know he shot a cop on his way down? How about treating a woman who's been beaten nearly to death and having to watch her walk out the door back to the husband who nearly killed her while she tells you that he didn't mean it, not really! Don't you fucking talk to me about hard choices, and harsh reality. Just because I didn't tote a rifle around Kuwait and never put a bullet between someone's eyes doesn't mean I live in some world of sunshine and rainbows, D. I live in a world where I spend months putting a four-year-old's face back together after her own father smashed it in with a bowling ball. You think you've got it so hard, and maybe you do, but the shit is tough all over. Fucking suck it up, man."

He held D's furious gaze, willing himself not to blink first. After a few moments, D sagged and the fight seemed to go out of him. He sat down on Jack's bed, holding himself carefully like he was in pain, or expected to be at any moment. He spoke quietly, his tone measured. "I couldn't help them folks," he said. "I wanted to. Saw their faces and knew what they were in for, and I can still see every one a those faces. I learned ta shut it off, shut everythin' off, and the best I could do for 'em was ta pass 'em by." He sighed. "The jobs come ta me first 'cause I'm the best, Jack. I get it done, I don't get caught, and I don't flinch. So all I could do was hope that whoever took them other jobs would get sloppy. I know it don't sound like much, but more woulda been the death a me in short order. Maybe that woulda been better fer everyone. I sure as shit don't know what I was protectin' myself for, or livin' for."

The dead, uninflected recitation of this fatalism chilled Jack straight through. He sat down at D's side, his anger sidelined for the moment. "How'd you get yourself into this?" he asked. "What happened to you?"

He shook his head at once. Jack could see the reflexiveness, as if he'd hit his knee with a hammer to see it jerk. "Don't matter."

It does matter. It matters to me. You matter to me, and that is scarier than anything you can tell me about yourself. "If it didn't matter, you could tell me," Jack said.

D looked up at him, then away again quickly. "Don't wanna say."

Jack tried another tack. "What did you want to be when you were a kid?"

"A cowboy," D said, almost immediately.

"Really?" Jack didn't think he could be more surprised if D had said that he'd wanted to be a ballerina.

"Yeah," D said, smiling a little ruefully at himself. "Stupid, huh?"

"No, not at all."

"Worked on ranches when I was a kid."

"So… why didn't you—"

"Enlisted when I was eighteen. Hadta."

"Why?"

D took a deep breath and let it out. "Had me a brand new wife in the family way, Jack. Not too many options."

Jack watched his profile, the stillness there, the control of every muscle and tic down to the roots of his hair, each strand standing up at regimented attention, brutally cut off when they got long enough to bend their own way. "What's your wife's name?"

"Sharon. Course she ain't… wasn't—"

"You told me your daughter's name was Jill."

D nodded. His mouth was tightening like a drawstring, closing off the hood, shutting away the face.

"D, where are they now? Do you get to see Jill?"

He straightened by degrees, like putting on a suit, then turned to face Jack, his face that granite shadow again. "They're dead, Jack. Is that what ya wanted ta know? Sharon 'n' Jill are both dead, and it's on my head." He stood up and went to the door. "You let me know when yer done judgin' me, 'cause we got some shit ta work out and we cain't stay holed up here forever. I'll be out back." He shut the door behind him, leaving Jack sitting there on the bed, staring at the depression D's body had left in the mattress where he'd been sitting.

CHAPTER 9

JACK emerged from his bedroom after a good hour of lying on his bed berating himself and D in turn.

Why'd you have to keep pushing him? The guy's wound tighter than a suspension bridge. So why is it up to you to unwind him, jerkwad?

He didn't have to tell me.

Probably did it just to shut you up. You should have guessed that something awful had happened to him.

What am I, the Amazing Kreskin? He doesn't give anything away.

He didn't want to talk about it, and you kept at him until he lost it.

He didn't lose it. He never had it; he never lets it go.

Finally, he'd just put it aside and gotten up. It was done with, after all.

D wasn't in the house. Jack found him outside, sitting in his favorite chair on the patio. *He's a killer. He doesn't deserve your pity, or your sympathy, or your gratitude, or your... whatever else.* Jack could tell himself that, and he could even agree, but that didn't change the fact that whether D deserved them or not, somehow he had all of those things.

He didn't give any sign that he'd heard Jack come out the patio door. He came up behind D's chair and stood there for a moment, waiting to be acknowledged. *You're going to be waiting a long fucking time,* he thought. He lifted a hand; it hovered there in the air for a moment, undecided, before finally falling on D's uninjured shoulder. He felt D twitch just a little at the contact, but he didn't move. His skin was warm through his T-shirt. "When did it happen?" he finally asked.

D shifted in his chair, looking away from where Jack stood behind him. Jack stepped to the side, letting his hand slide from D's shoulder, and sat down in the chair he usually sat in, on D's right side.

D shook his head. "Ain't sayin' no more about that jus' now."

Jack shoved down his curiosity with difficulty. "Okay."

Finally, D turned and looked at him. "You ain't gonna yell at me for bein' a crazed killer lettin' innocent folks die no more?"

Jack drew one knee up. "It bothers me, and I won't say that it doesn't just to make you happy."

"You lyin' wouldn't make me happy."

"The world's full of people trying to atone for things they regret."

"That what you think I'm doin'? Makin' amends?"

"Maybe. And maybe you're trying to atone for more than just the contracts you didn't take."

D snorted. "Maybe I oughta lie down on a couch fer this psychoanalysis, ya think?"

"You can play it off all you want, but there's something eating away at you, D. I've known you less than a week and I can see it plain as the nose on your face."

He took a deep breath and let it out, nodding. "Well, if somethin's eatin' away at me it mus' be getting awful hungry, 'cause there cain't be much left a me ta eat." His fingers were twitching. "Jesus, I wish I had a cigarette."

"Over my dead body."

"That can be arranged," D said, but he cut Jack a sidelong glance that had a bit of a twinkle to it so Jack knew he wasn't serious.

They sat in silence for a few minutes. Jack stared out at the lake, letting the nothingness crowd out the noise inside his brain, just for a short time. A very short time. "So, you said we had things to talk about," he finally said.

D made a noncommittal grunting noise. "Gotta decide what ta do."

"About what?"

"Cain't stay here forever. Someone'll find us."

"But… we've been here a few days now and no one's found us. Doesn't that mean we're pretty safe here?"

D just looked at him, the *dumbass* written all over his face. "Jack, that's like sayin' that if you ain't got cancer by the time yer forty that yer safe. Gets riskier the more time passes, not safer. More time goes by the more's the chance somebody'll dig inta yer past and find yer connection ta this place. Besides, yer father-in-law'll get wise soon enough."

"I told you he never comes here except for—"

"He sure as hell might notice a big increase in the electric bill on this place and wonder why, though."

"Oh," Jack said, feeling like an idiot for not having thought of that.

"At some point we're gonna hafta tell the Marshals that you ain't dead too. Let 'em know that ya still intend ta testify. You jus' vanish, and the trial's like ta be postponed if the prosecutor can swing it, or worse it'll go ahead without you on the stand and that's real bad."

"We've got a few months 'til the trial."

"Yeah, and I'll bet that prosecutor's spittin' nails about you bein' off the reservation too."

"I only have one contact. I guess I could call him. But what do I say? He'll want me to come in, and put me back in custody."

"You jus' say you don't feel safe, that someone found ya and was gonna kill ya but ya got away, and yer hidin' out on yer own but you'll be in Baltimore fer the trial. He ain't gonna like it but he ain't gonna have much choice. You don't mention me."

"He's never going to believe I got away from some hired killer."

"Probly not, but he ain't gonna have no grounds ta challenge ya and he'll have no way ta track ya, so he'll hafta live with it."

Jack imagined what it would have taken for him to have actually gotten away from D if he'd decided to carry out his order after all. The thought was a bit daunting. "D?"

"Hmm?"

"When you were fighting that guy in the alley?"

"Yeah?"

"What kind of fighting was that?"

D frowned. "The bare-ass desperate kind. Whaddya mean?"

"No, I mean… you were trained in hand-to-hand combat, right?"

"Yeah."

"What kind? Like, judo or something?"

D laughed. "Nothin' that fancy. Military uses this fightin' called Krav Maga. It's real… useful. It's all about savin' yer energy and usin' it where it counts."

Jack turned in his chair, the idea surging into his head with urgency. "Teach me."

D just blinked at him. "Teach ya?"

"Teach me to fight. Don't you think I ought to be able to defend myself a little?"

"Jack, I cain't fuckin' teach ya ta fight in a coupla days and I sure as hell cain't teach ya with a bum shoulder. Takes a long time ta get comfortable with that, and I can tell jus' by lookin' at ya that you ain't never had a hand laid on ya in violence."

He had a point, Jack had to admit. "Well, then… can you teach me how to shoot a gun? That can't be as hard."

"Oh, hell yes it can." D hesitated, his lips pursing and unpursing. "Ain't a bad idea, though."

Jack had never even touched a gun. The idea of holding one and shooting it was suddenly appealing in a way it had never been. He supposed there was nothing like near-death experiences to make a person appreciate the utility of weapons. "So can we do that?" he asked, sounding absurdly like a kid asking permission to go to the zoo or something.

D turned to him, a half-smile on his face. "Yeah, we can do that."

THEY set up a target along the longest clear path they could find in the backyard, and D produced some earplugs from somewhere in one of his magic aluminum cases. Jack lugged one out onto the porch and D began unloading guns. "You know anything about guns?"

"They shoot bullets."

"Well, that's a start. First thing about guns is safety. Y'always assume they're loaded, don't never point 'em at nobody you don't mean ta shoot at, and always remember that yer holdin' in yer hand a piece a human ingenuity designed ta cause harm, and ya better goddamn respect that, got it?" Jack nodded. "Okay, then. This is a revolver," he said, handing Jack a gun. "Revolvers are kinda old-fashioned but the mechanism's simpler and they're less likely ta jam up or misfire." He drew out a sleeker-looking black pistol. "This is a semi-automatic pistol."

"What's the difference between a semi-automatic and an automatic?" Jack asked. "I've just heard people say 'automatic'."

"Same thing. People say automatic when they mean semi. It jus' means that the bullets come up from the cartridge by themselves so you can fire shots one after another without cockin' it. Fully automatic means you jus' hold the trigger and bullets keep comin' 'til ya let up, like a machine gun."

"Are there fully automatic pistols?"

D arched an eyebrow. "Yeah, but that's some heavy shit. You don't wanna mess around with that. Anyway, I ain't got any here."

"What do those look like?"

"Uh…." D squinted. "Didja see *The Matrix*?"

"Sure."

"That part where they was shootin' up that lobby fulla SWAT dudes? They was packin' machine pistols fer the most part there. Ya hold 'em in one hand. Nasty bit a weaponry. Don't use 'em, myself. Don't got much call fer fully automatic guns in my line a work. Handguns 'n' rifles, mostly."

"Rifles?" Jack said, perking up.

"Hold on there now, Tex. I ain't got no rifles with me, and they ain't fer beginners. It's one thing ta shoot a handgun but somethin' else ta fire a rifle." He took the revolver and handed Jack the black pistol. It felt natural in his hand, like it had been made to fit it, which Jack supposed it had. It felt weightier than its mass, and deadly. "That's a Beretta ninety-two. That's standard military issue in the U.S. Spent a lotta time with one a them on my hip. This one's a Glock seventeen, real common with police departments and such. Nine millimeter."

"What's that mean?"

"That's the caliber a bullets it fires."

"What about ones that are… what, three fifty-seven? Or thirty-eight?"

"Damn, you do watch a lot of movies. When they say thirty-eight that's also the caliber, but that's inches. Them are used with American-made guns. Glocks are Austrian so it's metric."

"What's that really big scary one?"

D smirked and reached into his case again, withdrawing a pistol that dwarfed the other two. "That'd be this one, I guess," he said. "It's a Desert Eagle. I don't think yer gonna be firin' that thing. Tell ya the truth, it ain't so useful as a handgun. Too big. Might come in handy if ya hadta shoot an elk or somethin'. Here, try this one," he said, handing him a slimmer one. "That's a Walther PPK. Look familiar?"

Jack looked at the gun in his hand, frowning. "Kinda."

"That's James Bond's gun," D said. "I like that one."

Jack blinked and put the gun down. "I guess… you've used all these, huh?" he said.

D sat down. "Yep."

"To kill people."

"That's what they're for." He sighed. "That's what I'm for."

Jack looked up at him, slumped to the side with his arm in its sling, his eyes on the array of death dispensation spread before them on the table. "That's not all you're for."

"It is, or so you say. Killin' or lettin' people be killed." D picked up a cartridge and began loading it with bullets in quick, precise movements. "Now yer wantin' me ta teach ya how, and ain't that jus' fuckin' ironic." He loaded the Glock. "Only thing I was ever good at," he said, quietly. Jack watched his face, transfixed. "And I was damn good. Too good, 'cause it got me inta this fucked-up business." He handed the gun to Jack. "Come on, doc. Let's get this over with."

He led Jack to the far side of the yard, facing the target. "How do I…," Jack began, but D was already moving around him, showing him with quick nudges and pulls how to position himself.

"There ya go. Plant yer feet. Support yer firin' hand in the other one… yeah, like that. Brace yer shoulders; it will kick some." D moved around to stand directly behind Jack. Close behind, so Jack could feel D's breath on his ear. "Okay. That's about fifty feet, no problem. You sight along the barrel, then let yer breath out and hold." Jack did as D said, trying to find some center of stillness inside him while his entire body felt jumpy and fluttery, not only with the strangeness of the activity but with D's sheer physical proximity, the effect of which was unexpected, although not entirely unfamiliar. "Then ya fire. Don't pull the trigger; squeeze it."

Jack took another breath and let it out, held it, sighted and squeezed. The gun jumped, a loud *crack* issuing from it. He looked up at the target to see that he'd hit it about a foot from the bull's-eye in the center. "Hey, I hit it!" he said.

"Huh. Not bad fer a first time. Again."

JACK had fired a full cartridge from all the semi-automatic pistols, and he was starting to feel somewhat comfortable with the sensation. It was a heady thing, to hold this tidy little feat of engineering in his hand and dispense bullets from it, bullets that could maim or kill if they found their mark.

After the first couple of rounds, D had backed off a little and observed him from a few steps away. Jack finished firing a full magazine from the Beretta and lowered his arms. "Hey, what's that thing where you hold the gun sideways?" he said, grinning.

D snorted. "That's called being a punk-ass punk," he said. "Might look good in rap videos. You see anybody holdin' a gun like that ya know they're cake, 'cause they're more interested in what the gun looks like in their hand than what it can do, and they're probly dumber'n a fuckin' bag a hammers too." He was loading the Walther again. "See if ya can group 'em better this time. Yer accuracy ain't bad, but the precision is fer shit."

"What's the difference?"

"Don'tcha know? Ain't you a scientist?"

"Physics 101 was a long time ago."

"Accuracy is how close ya come to the mark ya wanna hit. Precision's how consistently ya hit the same spot. See, if I take all them holes ya made and average 'em out, yer hitting on average close ta the bull's-eye, but they're scattered all over. Left, right, high and low. Not too precise."

"Which one's more important?"

"Depends."

"On what?"

D smiled and handed him the gun. "On how badly ya gotta hit what yer aimin' at and how many chances yer gonna get ta do it."

Jack looked down at the gun, then up at D. "Thanks."

"Fer what?"

"For teaching me this. For trusting me with it. I mean... you're teaching me how to kill you, in a way."

"Uh, you coulda done that real easy a few days ago, Jack. Woulda died a infection if ya hadn't—"

"I know, but... you know what I mean."

"Yeah." D sobered, then waved at the target. "Go ahead."

Jack sighted, planted his feet, and breathed carefully, trying to group his shots close together. He was peripherally aware that D wasn't really watching him, but was walking slowly back and forth to his right. He emptied the magazine, one shot at a time, then lowered the gun and grinned. "Hell yeah, that's what I'm talking about! D, look at that, they're all within...."

Jack turned quickly, his arm swinging in enthusiastic gesticulation, not realizing that D was right behind him. His hand struck D square on his bullet wound. "Shit," D hissed, stumbling back a step. Jack dropped the gun.

"Oh Christ, D, I'm sorry, I didn't see you there."

D was gritting his teeth, his other hand pressed to his shoulder. "Shoot me again while yer at it!" he snarled.

"I said I was sorry! Let me see," Jack said, pulling D toward him.

"No, it's fine—"

"I said let me see," Jack said, prying D's hand away from the healing bullet wound. D resisted, breathing in quick shallow pulls, but finally relented. Jack pulled D's shirt aside and checked the wound. "Oh, it's okay. Doesn't look like it's opened up again. It isn't bleeding."

"Hurts like a motherfucker," D said, his face gray.

"Come on inside. I've got a few Demerol left."

"Them things make me feel like my head's stuffed fulla cotton." He didn't resist as Jack drew him into the cabin, though.

"You'll live," Jack said. He sat D down on the couch and fetched his bag, along with a glass of water. He shook out two Demerol and handed them to D, then pulled out his near-empty bottle of Lidocaine.

"Gonna shoot me up?"

"Just a bit of a local 'til the Demerol kicks in." He injected D's shoulder near the bullet wound. D relaxed almost immediately.

"That's better," he said, leaning his head back and letting his eyes close.

Jack put the bag aside and hitched one knee up on the couch so he was facing D. He watched his face for a few moments, their earlier conversation recurring. "I'm sorry," he said.

D shrugged. "Ya didn't mean ta hit me."

"No… I'm sorry," he repeated, letting the words carry some more weight than they normally did. "I'm sorry about your family."

D turned his head and met Jack's eyes. "Thanks." He held Jack's gaze just long enough for it to start becoming a little squirmy, then looked away again. Jack sat back on the couch at his side.

"So," he said, attempting a light-hearted tone. "How'd I do for a beginning marksman?"

D chuckled. "I've seen worse."

"I want to shoot that big one. Such a cliché, isn't it? I never thought I'd be one of those guys who'd want to shoot a big gun. So much transparent symbolism. But I don't care; I want to shoot that big one."

"You don't need ta shoot that Eagle. That gun's bigger'n you."

"You shoot it, and you're no bigger than me."

"I'm a professional."

Jack thought for a moment. "It's different when you're shooting at a person, isn't it?"

"I hope you never hafta find out."

"You don't like to see me shooting, do you?" D gave a half-shrug. "Why not?"

"I dunno, Jack. You jus'… ain't that guy."

"Which guy?"

"A guy like me. Yer...." He broke off with a frustrated sigh. "You ain't spoiled. Yer whole. I didn't want ya touched by all this."

Jack watched him, half-silhouetted by the setting sun. "I'm not some innocent schoolboy, you know. I've—"

"Yer a babe in the woods, Jack," D cut him off. "Take it from a guy who's seen some evil men, and what they do, and who's done some evil things."

"So, what? You decided you weren't going to just save my life, but my soul or something? I don't need you to guard my virtue, D."

"Thought if I could keep ya like ya are, then...." D trailed off, staring down at his slung hand, his other hand resting next to his leg. He shook his head, chewing on his lip. "I cain't never go back ta that. But if I kept it from ya, maybe I could...." He looked away, and Jack saw him blinking. "I dunno what I'm talkin' about. Fuckin' Demerol's talkin' fer me."

"Maybe it should keep talking for you, if you're going to say things that are this important."

"It ain't important."

"It is, D. Maybe more than anything else."

D lifted his head and looked down into his lap, his lips twisting. "There is some fuckin' dark shit around me, Jack. Sometimes it's like I cain't see nothin' else."

Jack shifted a little closer on the couch and spoke softly. "You thought if you could keep the dark away from me, that maybe some of it would leave you too."

D turned to look at him, and Jack saw something naked and exposed in his expression, set free by the narcotics. That stoniness was gone, and Jack could see the child D had once been, and the father, and the husband. The young soldier, the hopeful family man, and it damned near broke his heart to see that man buried so deeply within the man D was now, a man he clearly detested but could not escape. His eyes were wide and shining. "I cain't remember what things look like without it," he said, his voice hoarse and shaky.

Jack didn't know what to say to that. He couldn't place himself in D's position, or even begin to imagine the kinds of things he'd seen, and done, and wished he could prevent. He looked down and saw his own hand resting at his side, just a hairbreadth from D's. He took a breath and held it, then slowly stretched out his pinky finger until it just grazed the side of D's hand; a tiny stroke of tentative contact. D didn't withdraw; instead, his hand flinched a little closer. Emboldened, Jack covered D's hand with his own; D turned his palm up and their fingers slid together, interlacing and fitting against each other like they'd been waiting for nothing else but the chance to do so.

D exhaled and let his head fall back again, his eyes closing. Jack just sat there at his side, his shoulder pressed to D's, their clasped hands hidden between them like lock tumblers, two sides separated by a harsh wooden barrier but joined by an unseen mechanism, waiting only for the right key to align them.

CHAPTER 10

JACK moved his knight to QB4. D frowned, staring at the board, then shook his head. "Wish I knew how ta play this fuckin' game," he said, moving his rook.

"Yeah, me too," Jack said.

"I mean... I know the rules, but I wish I knew how ta play, for real, with strategy and shit. Feel like I oughta be better at it."

"Why? Does the hit man business involve a lot of strategic tactics?" Jack said, a sarcastic edge to his voice that D had never heard there before.

"You'd be surprised." He moved his king's knight. "Uh... check." Jack didn't move. He met D's eyes, looked down at the board and then back up again. D frowned, re-examining the pieces. "Oh, wait... checkmate!"

Jack heaved a weary sigh. "Best two out of three?"

"I'm hungry. Let's rustle up some dinner."

He seemed only too eager to abandon the chessboard. "Thought I'd grill some burgers tonight," Jack said, going to the fridge.

"Burgers're good," D said, staying in his chair for the moment. He hoped he was putting up a good front, because he felt like he was crumbling and losing cohesion by the minute.

The afternoon had passed in a haze of Demerol. He could remember sitting on the couch with Jack, and holding his hand, and all he'd wanted was just to let his head fall to Jack's shoulder or lay right down on his lap. Give it up, give it all over, and let Jack take care of him. Jus' the fuckin' Demerol. Sure, that was a nice fairy story.

Jack kept glancing at him, little sidelong looks that he probably thought were subtle, tiny appraisals that all said one thing: *What the fuck, dude?* D wished he knew what the fuck, dude. After a good half hour just sitting silently on the couch, Jack had pulled him to his feet and made him go to bed for a nap, not releasing D's fingers until he had him tucked in. Crazily, D almost asked him to stay. *Jus' sit on the side a the bed, okay? Maybe pull up a chair? Don't gotta say nothin' or do nothing. Jus' please... don't let go a me.* But Jack had let go, and D had let him, because what else? Nothing else.

He shut his eyes and imagined his vault. The vault was his friend, and he had built it plate by plate, one weld at a time, until it was impenetrable and watertight. Inside it was everything that was no longer his, the things that had been taken from him and the things he had put from himself to survive. Most of what had once made him human was in that vault, but these days the door seemed to be cracking open, and he could feel wisps escaping, shadows of their stronger selves that remained safely locked inside. *Oughta put*

Jack in the vault, he thought. *Before he gets too big ta fit in there and I hafta build a fortress ta hold him.*

He got up and flexed his shoulder experimentally. There was a twinge and a pull deep inside the wound, but the pain was abating. Soon he'd be able to put this sling aside, and that would be a relief, if for no other reason that he wouldn't feel so hogtied if there was trouble, an eventuality that felt more inevitable by the day.

He went to the small kitchen where Jack was forming the burgers. "Want a beer?" D said, opening the fridge.

Jack glanced at him. "Uh… no thanks. You shouldn't have one either on top of that Demerol."

"That was four fuckin' hours ago."

He shrugged. "Fine, have one."

D cleared his throat. "Guess I'll have lemonade," he said, hauling out the pitcher and pouring a glass. He expected Jack to smile or comment, but he just kept his eyes on the burgers.

"Better start the grill," he said, and headed out the patio door. D watched him go.

He's freaked out. The bullets and the near-assassination and the fiery gas stations were okay, but the hand-holding freaked him out.

Ya sure it's him yer talkin' about?

D shut his eyes again. *You ain't done nothin'. You didn't hold his hand; he held yours. He started it. You were all hopped up on Demerol, didn't know what you was doin'.*

Oh yeah? Well, was you on Demerol in the desert? But that was in the vault, and there it would stay. It ain't like that. *I ain't like that. Jack's my responsibility. He ain't... I don't....* Every sentence he tried to start wound up with its tail in the vault, the clang of that door slamming shut, cutting off his every thought.

D shook himself and went outside. Jack was bent over the grill, opening the propane tank. He glanced up at D's approach, and then straightened. He squared his shoulders and faced him. "How's the shoulder?" he asked.

"It's okay. Don't hurt no more."

Jack nodded. "Good, good. Listen, D, I'm really sorry about that. I should have been more careful. I didn't realize you were right there—"

D held up a hand. *Is that what's eatin' him?* "You don't gotta apologize, Jack. Was an accident."

"Well, I'm supposed to first do no harm, and here I am getting all excited about shooting a goddamned gun, like I'm some violence-obsessed teenager, and hitting my patient where he's hurt.... I could have opened up the wound again."

"Hey," D said, stepping closer. "Don't take on so."

"You must think I'm the world's biggest dork," Jack said, half under his breath.

"Nah," D said, going for a casual tone when his mind was spinning. *Christ, he's talkin' like... like he thinks I'm one a them cool kids from high school and he's afraid I'm gonna make fun a him. That what he thinks? Oughta tell him he got it backwards.* "No harm, no foul."

Jack met his eyes and held them for a moment, and seemed reassured by whatever he was seeing there. "Okay," he said. "I'll get the burgers."

D stood by the grill and drank his lemonade, then set the empty glass on the patio table. He took a deep breath—it didn't twinge his shoulder for once—and looked out at the view of the lake, a view of which he had yet to tire. Jack came back out bearing the plate of burgers. He put them on the grill and shut its lid, then came to stand at D's side, a little closer than he might have the day before. "Nice day," D commented, hoping he sounded neutral.

"Yeah," Jack said. D felt their fingers brush slightly. *Move away. Just take one step. Don't hafta be obvious about it, even though he'll know.* And yet the seconds ticked by and he kept not moving. He just stood there motionless as Jack reached out, moving nothing except his hand, and cupped his fingers around D's. D cut a quick glance out of the corner of his eye and saw Jack staring resolutely forward, as if unaware of what his left hand was up to and claiming no responsibility for its actions. Jack's hand was warm and dry, and his fingers were strong; his grip was one that could lead and guide. Maybe lead D to places he'd sworn never to return, places he'd even disavowed knowledge of. He didn't respond at first, wondering if Jack would just let go if he did nothing, but when he did not, D was left with no other choice. He squeezed Jack's fingers briefly, then released them and stepped away. He picked up his lemonade glass and made as if to drink from it, then realized it was empty and put it back down again. Jack was going back to the grill to turn the burgers, and the whole exchange went unremarked upon.

A topic. I need a fuckin' topic. "So, this contact ya got in the Marshals," he said. "What's his name?"

"Churchill," Jack replied.

"That his first name or his last?"

Jack looked up, blinking. "I have no idea. We only talk about official stuff."

"You trust the guy?"

He shrugged. "I guess. Don't have much choice, do I?" He put down the tongs and sat on the arm of the nearby deck sofa. "Do you really think someone bought my location off somebody inside the office?"

"Not really. Witness Protection is pretty damned airtight. But I do think it might be possible for somebody slick enough ta hack the information out. That's why if ya call this Churchill guy, ya cain't tell him where we are. Even if he's trustworthy, it could still get out. I ain't trustin' nobody."

Jack nodded. "Will they be able to track me with the phone call?"

"Not if ya use one a my cells. They're untraceable."

"Then what?"

"Then we gotta find someplace ta hole up 'til your trial. Someplace without no connection ta you at all."

"The trial's two months away! Are you really going to—" Jack cut himself off. "That's a long time, D. I can't ask you to—"

"To what? Finish what I started? Jack, I am gonna see you on that witness stand unharmed or die tryin'."

"I don't want you getting hurt again," Jack said, his eyes so large and blue as they bored into D's own that everything else seemed washed-out and pale.

D shrugged it off. "No one's gotten the better a me yet, don't you worry."

"Where will we go?"

"I got a coupla ideas." He wiggled his slung arm. "How long 'til I'm free a this contraption?"

Jack stepped closer, that doctor face sliding over his features, and pushed D's shirt aside so he could lift the bandage and examine the wound. He palpated it gently. "Another day or two. But that doesn't mean you're ready for full mobility with it yet."

"I got it. But we gotta wait ta head out 'til I got most a the use a this arm."

"Two days sound all right?"

D nodded. "Okay." He looked up; abruptly aware of Jack's proximity. He could smell him as he reaffixed the bandage and straightened D's shirt, his hands smoothing the fabric over the knob of D's shoulder joint. His eyes remained lowered as one hand trailed down D's arm, gently enough that it might have been an accident.

D stood up and stepped away. "Don't wanna let them burgers burn," he said.

They ate in silence, and it seemed that there was a third person at the table with them now, an uninvited guest who'd come breezing in on a magic carpet of Demerol and now refused to leave.

D kept thinking of their shooting lesson that morning. Jack had been right; D didn't like to see him firing a gun, although he could appreciate the practicality of him learning to do so. It was just yet another way that D's life was infecting Jack and pulling him further and further from the life he'd started to lose the day he'd witnessed that murder. *Looked good doin' it though, didn't he? Looked natural. Did real well fer a first-timer, better even than ya let him think he did. Got them steady surgeon's hands and a sharp fuckin' eye. Little trainin' he could be a helluva marksman.*

"You want to tell me about your nightmares?" Jack said, out of the blue. D looked up, startled by the abrupt question. There was a challenge in Jack's eyes.

"What?"

"Might help to talk about them."

"What nightmares?"

Jack swallowed a bite of burger and shook his head, as if wearied by D's obtuseness. "The ones you have every damned night, D. Or anytime you sleep."

"How d'you.... What the fuck?" D snapped, a cold ball of fear settling into his belly. *How's he know? What am I fuckin' comin' to?*

Jack's expression was edging toward sympathetic now. "Jesus. You really don't know, do you? You aren't just fucking with me."

"If you tell me what the hell yer talkin' about maybe I can help you with that question."

"D, every night since you got over your infection, you've woken me several times. Yelling, thrashing, banging against the wall. I almost said something before, because I was afraid you would injure your shoulder in your sleep, but... I don't know, I didn't like to."

D stared at his plate. He never dreamt. The vault kept everything that might show up in his dreams locked up tight so that not even his unconscious mind could get to it. He couldn't remember having any nightmares here, but he didn't doubt Jack's word. *Fuckin' vault's leakin'. God knows what's bubblin' up.* "I don't remember no nightmares," he said. "What was I sayin'?"

"Well," Jack began, looking a little uncomfortable now, "you say your daughter's name a lot." He glanced up at D's face, then quickly away.

Jill, D thought, queasiness rising up with that forbidden name. "Oh," he managed.

"Lot of it isn't intelligible," Jack went on. "I hear you say 'no' sometimes, like... you're begging."

D picked up his burger. "Maybe you oughta invest in earplugs or somethin'," he grumbled.

"Don't just brush this off. You're saying that you don't remember having nightmares? That isn't normal, you know."

D laughed. "Normal fer me. Much as anythin' about me can be called normal."

"Maybe your unconscious mind is trying to tell you something, or trying to get you to face something."

"So yer a shrink as well as a maxiwhatsis surgeon, that it? Ya fix the outsides a their heads 'n' then the insides? Two fer the price a one?"

Jack recoiled a little. "I'm just trying to help you."

"I don't need yer help. Not on this subject."

"According to you, there's nothing to this subject!"

"I don't wanna talk about it."

"No, of course not," Jack said bitterly, stabbing at his potato salad viciously. "You just go and do what you always do, D. Back off and shut down. I guess that's just your way of dealing with everything, isn't it?"

"Works fer me."

"Sure. Works so well you have screaming nightmares and can't handle the slightest emotional investment in anything."

D narrowed his eyes at him. "Investment? Like what?"

"Like… this!" Jack said, making vague motions in the air between them. "You know!"

"No, I fuckin' don't."

"You do; you just won't admit it."

"Maybe you oughta think twice before gettin' up in my face, Jack."

"Yep. That's the next step. Go hide behind that big scary hit man thing. Well, I'm not scared of you!" Jack shouted. His face was red and a vein was throbbing in his neck. D was glad. Anger, he could deal with. The angrier Jack got, the cooler and more in control D felt. It was an autonomic response, and comforting in its reliability. He calmly laid his hands in his lap and watched Jack with a flat gaze.

"You should be," he said. *Don't do this. Don't make him afraid a you. Ya don't want him ta be afraid a you, do ya?*

No, a course I don't. But it'd be better fer both of us if he was.

"I should be a lot of things," Jack said. "I should be living in Baltimore and operating on little girls with cleft palates and spending my Saturdays watching an entire season of *24*. But am I? No, I am here in a cabin in the woods… with you." He stood up and tossed his dishes into the sink with a clatter. "I'll be in my room. Minding my own business. I guess that's what you want, isn't it?" He stomped off without another word, and D heard his door slam.

He sat there quietly for another few minutes, then got up and slowly went outside. Jack had, apparently, cleaned up their target practice detritus while he'd been sleeping; the target had been taken down, the guns were gone. Looked like nothing more than a quiet backyard, a vacation house, a retreat. Except for D there was no retreat, not from anything. The mistakes of his past refused to be quieted. He'd infected Jack with violence, and now he'd infected him with the proclivities that had trapped him in this outlaw existence.

Maybe ya want him trapped too. So you'll have company.

That couldn't happen. He'd be safe, and he'd be left alone, and that was just how it was going to be.

D retrieved the cell phone he'd been using and checked his text-message inbox. Nothing. He wasn't surprised—X rarely contacted him first—but he was disappointed nonetheless. He could send a message, but he had nothing new to say or ask, nor any requests to make, and he and X had maintained only-when-necessary communications for eight years, a streak he didn't particularly feel like breaking today. Besides, he had another call to make, one he'd been putting off. He sighed and parked himself under a tree on the far side of the cabin, where Jack could not possibly hear him, and dialed a number he'd long ago committed to memory.

He heard a series of clicks and relays, different ringtones denoting different lines and extensions, until finally a female voice said "Switch, nine two six."

He shut his eyes. "Relay, alpha two one zero."

Tap tap tap of fingers on a keyboard at the other end. "Clearance?"

"Seven six, bravo four five mark eight."

Tap tap tap. "Hold, please" Click, click. Dial tone. Click, ring.

It rang three times before it was picked up. D had no idea where this final relay was answered, always by the same man, who would only tell D to call him Stan. "Switch, six two nine."

"It's me."

"Do you have Francisco?" the man asked. No preamble.

The question threw D for something of a loop. He'd expected to have to explain the situation. "That's affirm," he said.

"Are you secure?"

"Much as can be expected."

He heard a sigh. "I heard through another informant that you'd accepted the hit on him. I didn't want to believe it."

"Didn't have no choice. Payin' fer that now, make no mistake."

"How?"

"Bullet in my shoulder, fer one. If I didn't have a doctor here with me, I'd be dead fer sure. And I'm through in the business, which I guess is bad news fer you guys."

"You've done enough. I'm glad you're getting out."

"Don't go gettin' all warm 'n' fuzzy on me, now."

A low chuckle. "What's the plan?"

"I'm gonna have him call his Witsec contact tomorrow. Guy name a Churchill. You know him?"

"Yeah."

"You get word ta this Churchill ta expect Jack's call, but he's gotta act surprised. I don't want Jack ta know about me pullin' no strings."

"Got it."

"Jack's gonna call, tell him that he don't feel safe after the attempt in Vegas, and he's gonna lay low on his own 'til the trial. You make sure this Churchill agrees. Jack's under my protection; he will be on that witness stand, ya got it?"

"Yeah. He isn't going to like it."

"He don't have no choice." D hesitated. "He a good man, this Churchill?"

"He is. You should talk to him. Might have some mutual interest goin' on."

"Might do, but later. After Jack meets him, we're movin' on. Not sure where yet, but once we're there, might ring him and set his mind at ease. Ya hearin' any whispers from the brothers? Do they know Jack's not under Witsec's wing anymore?"

"I don't know; it's hard to say. They have other witnesses to worry about besides Jack. You don't think it was them that blackmailed you?"

"Not really, no. If they'd known that Jack was in Vegas, they'd have just taken him out."

"Well, they're worried about something. They brought Petros in."

D sagged. "Fuck me."

"Don't you let anyone get wind of where Jack is."

"You don't gotta tell me. I seen that man work up close 'n' personal."

There was a hesitation on the other end of the line. "You sound strange."

"Strange how?"

"I don't know. You sound… like you care. Is it Francisco? What's he like?"

D let his head fall back against the tree trunk. "He ain't what I expected. He's tough and smart, and he ain't no fool."

"You like him, huh?"

"Yeah," D murmured. "I like him well enough. Enough ta be glad I didn't kill him."

Another pause. "How close did you come?" Stan asked, his voice very even and quiet.

D closed his eyes. "I don't wanna think about that." *Real fuckin' close. Too fuckin' close. Ta think I almos' put a bullet between them eyes, and took that life that now I'd die ta save, and I never woulda known what he was in the world, and who he was or could be, and I woulda never even known what I was missin', nor known how right it could feel just ta lay my fingers alongside his.*

"That close, huh?"

"They had the shit on me. All of it."

"Any thoughts on who put you up to this hit, if it wasn't the brothers?"

He sighed. "That is what's really burnin' my toast. I got no fuckin' clue. But that'll hafta wait ta puzzle out, 'cause I got other things ta think on now. I just gotta get Jack through this call to Churchill and then get us hell and gone."

"I'm glad you called in."

"I didn't want this Churchill to go all SWAT on us and yank Jack away in the back a some government-issue Taurus where I cain't protect him."

"Huh."

"What?"

"You do care, don't you?"

D sighed. "More'n I should." He hung up and sagged back against the tree. *You wanna know if I care? Jus' ask me how hard it was ta let Jack be mad at me, and sit there doin' nothin' while he yelled at me and turned his back, knowin' it was best, wantin' ta close that vault door, but also wantin' ta throw it wide open and let everything out, 'cause he's the first one ever made me think I could look inside there without goin' crazy, and the first one I wanted ta know all of it. First person made me ever think I might wanta reclaim some a what I locked away… or think that I might even need, or deserve, ta have it back.*

CHAPTER 11

JACK lay in bed, arms crossed over his chest, staring at the ceiling. He heard the door open and close as D went outside.

Fine. Don't want to talk about your really awful-sounding nightmares, that's no skin off my nose. I don't give a shit how you sleep.

Which was a lie, of course. He cared, and he wanted to know. He wanted to know what was in D's mind, what drove him, what scared him. He wanted to know it all.

And why's that, Jack? Why are you so interested? Do you want to know what's wrong so you can fix it? Be the hero, heal the wounded man?

Maybe. Was that so terrible? Was it so offensive that he might want to help?

You just want him to let you in to his closed-off self, because he doesn't let anybody in. If you get in, that means you must be special. You're important. Important to a man who makes a point not to form attachments. And if there's an attachment despite his nature, it must mean you're even more awesome than you thought you were.

Jack turned on his side, curling his hands under his cheek. Was that all this was? Some play for validation on his part?

I just want to know if I mean something to him... the way he means something to me.

Jack rolled onto his stomach and clutched a pillow over his head. Sure, no problem. Testify against some drug lords. All in a day's work. Get a new name and get yourself relocated thousands of miles away. No sweat. Assassins coming after you? Check. Conscience-ridden hit men spiriting you away? Check. Hiding out in a remote cabin? Oh, got that one covered. Develop unseemly crush on ruthless hired killer?

Jack sighed. *I am one incurable illness away from a Lifetime Movie of the Week.*

D STOOD outside Jack's bedroom door for a good five minutes, trying to figure out what to do. *Knock? Yell? Barge right in? You fuckin' asshole, you can plan an infiltration of a goddamned Federal Reserve branch but ya cain't figure out how ta wake up yer... yer....*

What was Jack, anyway? His mark? His companion? His protectee? His friend? D's vocabulary wasn't up to that task.

He knocked. "Jack?" No answer. "Jack!" He heard a vague mumbling from inside. "C'mon, get up! It's almos' nine, and ya gotta call that guy."

Jack made an incoherent, irritated-sounding noise. "Does it have to be right this very minute?" he said through the door.

"Uh... guess not. Jus' thought... ya know... ya might wanna get up." *'Cause ya been in there since eight o'clock last night and yer freakin' my shit out.*

He heard a thump, then footsteps, then Jack yanked the bedroom door open. "You just want me to get up because I'm freaking you out," he said.

D blinked. *Shit, did I say that out loud?* "What makes ya think that?"

"You're stammering and you sound freaked out."

"Oh." D shuffled. "Well, now yer up, let's have some breakfast."

"So you just got me up to cook for you, is that it?"

"No! I'll cook! What the fuck is yer problem, anyway?" He stomped off to the fridge and pulled out the milk.

Jack went to the table and sat down. "I don't know." He sighed. "I'm sorry. Guess I just went to sleep mad and woke up still mad."

D brought over the bowls and cereal. *Hope this'll do fer cookin'.* "Mad about me 'n' my nightmares, ya mean."

"Well... yeah." There seemed to be something else lurking behind Jack's shuttered gaze, something he wasn't letting past himself. D didn't pry.

"I jus' cain't share everythin' with ya," D said. "Ya jus' keep pryin' and nosin' and I know ya mean well, but...." He sighed. "I kep' things locked up my whole life and it ain't so easy. Them hinges are rusted damned near shut."

"I know," Jack said, his voice sounding gentler. "I shouldn't push. You don't owe me any kind of confessions or revelations. I'm just... concerned."

D poured the milk. "I ain't exactly used ta havin' nobody be concerned fer me."

"Well, get used to it." D met his eyes and saw the smile there. He felt himself smile back. They ate cereal in silence for a few moments.

Jack got up to refill his coffee and returned to the table, looking a little disgruntled. "I don't want to call Churchill."

"Gotta."

Jack shook his head. "He is not going to believe that I somehow got away from a trained killer."

"Won't have much choice."

"He'll just think I'm making the whole thing up."

"So what? He cain't prove ya are."

Jack was still shaking his head, like he was bound and determined to argue with every damned thing D said. "What if he tries to come and get me?"

"How's he gonna do that? With his magic X-ray vision? He cain't track this phone. You could be anywhere in the lower forty-eight and I doubt he's got some magic reindeer ta pull his sleigh. Will ya relax?"

"Well, I'm sorry if the idea of talking to a man of some authority, who, I might add, has done nothing but try to protect me, and telling him a bunch of fairy stories and hoping he believes me is a little strange to me."

"You'll be fine." D handed him the phone. "No time like the present."

Jack took it, his eyes widening a little. "Now? Seriously?"

"Get it over with."

He stared at the handset like it was a sleeping snake that might wake up and bite him at any time. He stood up. "I'll go outside."

"What, ya don't want me ta hear?" The idea of not listening in was vaguely upsetting, although D knew he had no right to eavesdrop.

"Just... want some privacy," Jack muttered, and then headed outside to the patio. D sat and watched him go, then returned to his cereal with a sigh.

JACK dialed the number from memory, his mind racing with all the things he'd have to say and not say, mention and not mention, reveal and hide. "Witsec, Churchill."

"Uh… yeah, it's Jack Francisco."

"Jack? *Jack?* Are you kidding me?" Churchill sounded like he was on his feet and running somewhere already.

"No, it's me."

"Where the hell are you? I have been looking for you for a week!"

"I know… I'm sorry. I'm okay."

"What the hell happened? Why'd you leave?"

"Why'd you have a tracking device on my car?" Jack snapped. *Jesus, where'd that come from?* he thought.

There was silence for a moment. "It's just a precaution, Jack. I figured you must have found it when we lost the signal. Why did you leave Vegas? You were safe there!"

"Safe, right. So safe that some hit man showed up at my house to kill me."

Silence again. "That isn't funny."

"No, I didn't think so, either."

"Are you serious? Someone came for you?"

"Came home and found him sitting there in my living room with a gun."

"Fuck. How'd he find you?"

"That's what I'd like to know, seeing as you and your agency were the only ones who knew where I was."

"No one here gave you up, Jack. I hope you know that."

"I'd like to believe it."

"You could have been spotted on the street, just a random happenstance."

Whatever. "It doesn't matter how he found me, just that he did."

"How'd you get away?"

"Threw a vase at his head and ran."

"Jack… we didn't find any broken vase in your house. There was no sign of any struggle there."

Shit. Jack thought fast. "The vase didn't break. One of those heavy pottery pieces. He probably took it with him when he left so his blood wouldn't be found in the house." *Does that make sense? Sounds good to me. Too late now.*

Churchill sighed. "Well, that makes some kind of sense. And… you just ran? How'd you find the tracker?"

"I thought someone was following me. I didn't know who it was, so I lost them and pulled over and searched the car."

"Where are you now?"

Jack sighed. "I'm not comfortable sharing that information."

"Let me bring you back in. We'll relocate you."

"I tried it your way once and it didn't work out. I'll take care of myself. I don't feel safe with anyone knowing my whereabouts."

"I can't allow you to stay out there on your own, Jack."

"What are you going to do about it?" Silence. "Yeah, that's what I thought. Look… I am absolutely going to testify. Okay?"

"I don't mind telling you, the prosecutor's on the phone to me six times a day. He's about ready to have an aneurysm."

"Tell him I will be there. I will check in with you twice a week, you can keep me updated on when I'm supposed to appear, and I will get myself there. Until then... I'm just going to lay low and hide out."

"I don't like this, Jack."

"You think I like it? This is not what I signed up for, but I'm going to have to live with it until the trial."

"I think you've got someone helping you."

"I'm on my own, and it's going to stay that way."

"You're talking like a professional. You're a surgeon, not some kind of operative. Who's helping you?"

"No one, and that's just how I like it. Now, are we okay? We understand each other?"

"What's happened to you? You were such a babe in the woods when I put you in Vegas."

"Well, you grow up fast when hired killers come after you." *And when you live with one for a week.*

"I didn't want this for you, Jack."

"I know. I'll be in touch." He hung up before Churchill could get another word out.

Jack stood and looked out across the backyard for a moment, going back over the conversation he'd just had. He didn't like lying to Churchill, but he didn't have much choice. He turned and went back into the house. D was still at the kitchen table, staring at a bowl of soggy cereal.

"Well, it's done," he said.

D looked up, his gaze guarded. "What'd he say?"

"About what you expected. Didn't like it, didn't have a choice, thought I was getting help. He seemed to buy it, though."

"Good." D turned back to his cereal, twirling his spoon in the sodden mess.

Jack nodded, tapping the phone against his leg. "That's all you have to say? 'Good?' I just lied to a government official, D. That's got to be some kind of violation of something. Witsec has promised to help me and I just told them a bald-faced lie to help protect the man who came to kill me."

D stood up slowly and turned to face him. "Wasn't on my behalf ya done that, doc. Was on yer own. You ain't protectin' me none."

Jack shook his head and tossed the phone to the sofa. "I can't believe any of this is real. Fuck me. What the hell am I thinking? I ought to tell Churchill exactly where I am and ask him how fast he can get here!"

"If that's what ya want I won't stop ya."

"You'd just let me tell him everything? You'd stand there and do nothing while I gave him the whole damned story?"

"Nope. I'd be gone. You can tell him whatever ya want, but I sure as hell cain't stick around ta meet him. So I guess all ya gotta decide is whether ya think yer better off with me or Witsec. I'm jus' tryin' ta protect you, Jack. I think I can do it better'n they can. You don't agree, then go ta them with my blessins and best wishes for yer safety."

"You'd let me turn myself over to them? Just like that?"

"Jus' like that." D narrowed his eyes and peered at him. "Sounds like that troubles ya some. Ya think I'd wanna fight ta keep ya, is that it? That I'd feel some remorse or regret on seein' the back a you? You ain't wrong. This is a hard business, Jack, with no room fer friends or fond feelins. Ya gotta do what's practical, and what's immediate, and what'll keep ya from getting killed or arrested or both. Havin' a friend's the quickest way to a knife in the back."

Jack looked at D's face, his hardened and weathered face, and wondered just how much he was speaking from personal experience. "That's the saddest thing I've ever heard," he said.

D shrugged. "It's a hard fuckin' fact a life. It is what it is."

He got up again and went to the window, keeping his eyes averted. "Well... whether there's room for it or not... I'm your friend, D."

He heard D sigh. "I wish I could say I was yours, Jack." He heard footsteps, and then the back door opening and closing again.

D SAT on what he'd started to consider "his" bench for hours. The sun climbed overhead, then started its slow descent across the sky. He stared at ants trundling by on the patio, wondering what he was waiting for. Was he hoping Jack would come outside and make him talk about it? Ask him to come back in? Was he waiting to see how long it would take?

The cell phone, the one Jack had used to call Churchill, was in his pocket. He'd swiped it off the couch while Jack's back was turned, and it felt heavy with expectations. The call he was putting off making would get no easier with time. Finally, he got up and walked a short distance into the trees, and redialed the last outgoing number.

It only rang once before it was picked up. "Witsec, Churchill."

"This is D."

He heard the other man settle in, clear his throat, take a breath. "Been expecting your call."

"We understand each other?"

"Give me one good reason I shouldn't come find you and put you down like a dog."

"I'll give ya two. Ya cain't, and ya shouldn't."

"You accepted a contract on Jack Francisco's life."

"A contract I didn't carry out."

"I'm supposed to trust you because you had some last-minute attack of conscience?"

D counted to five before answering, his voice tight and controlled. "The Bureau talk ta you?"

"Yeah."

"Then ya know just how long my attack a conscience's been goin' on."

"I don't give a shit what you've done for the Bureau. My concern is Francisco."

"That's my concern too."

"But it's not your only concern."

D sighed. "No. I got somethin' of a situation myself. Someone blackmailed me inta takin' that hit on him, and now they're in a state. Dodged a couple of 'em on the road ta Stockton. Figure they found us by piggybackin' on yer very own tracker, so don't ya go getting on yer high horse when yer little lodestone almost got the both of us killed."

"That gas station that went up?"

"Yeah. What'd you find there?"

"Nothing. Car rented under a false name, two bodies without ID, you know the drill."

"Well enough ta sing along."

"So these persons unknown are on your trail."

"That's in addition to the brothers, who are still gonna be looking fer Jack even if they don't know nothin' 'bout what's happening with me. You hear who they got in fer help on this?"

"Petros, I heard."

"Yeah. Look, I know ya mean well, but I am tellin' ya that you cain't protect Jack like I can."

"I can't leave one of my witnesses in the hands of a mercenary."

"You call me whatcha want, but I know these people and you don't."

Churchill sighed. "Look, D... whatever your name really is... Jack Francisco is a good man. He's a rarity in my business: a truly innocent bystander. Most of our witnesses are insiders turned state's evidence, so I end up protecting the lives of people who have a long list of crimes of their own to atone for. Francisco is different."

"You don't gotta tell me about Jack." *I probly know him a helluva lot better'n you do, you Witsec son of a bitch.* "I know what kinda man he is, and what he saw and what he's gonna do about it. So you better believe me when I tell ya that anyone comin' fer him is gonna hafta go through me, and if they get him ya better know that it means I'm lyin' dead in front a him, you hear me? Sittin' in yer nice safe office wherever ya are and tryin' ta call the shots? I am here in the shit with him with a three-point-five-million-dollar price on my head fer my trouble and listenin' ta you bitch 'n' moan about how yer sposed ta trust me. I don't give a fuck. You jus' gotta give me the room I need ta do what I gotta do ta keep him 'n' me breathin' long enough fer him ta get ta that witness stand. After that, you can take over and make him inta someone new 'n' my job be over. You got that?"

There was a long silence. "Yeah, I got it. I just have one favor to ask."

"What?"

"Jack's going to check in with me twice a week. You do the same."

D sighed. "Yeah, I can do that."

"And you keep him safe, you hear me?"

"Ya got my word on that." D hung up, and returned to his bench. He sat down and watched the lake as the sun angled across its surface in ever-deepening shadow.

JACK had spent the day on D's laptop, watching pointless videos on YouTube and reading three weeks' worth of back posts on one of his favorite music forums. He certainly wasn't waiting for D to come back inside, or wondering what the hell he was doing out there, or asking himself what had happened to the ease they'd established between themselves. Somehow it seemed that now all they were doing was walking circles around each other and getting snappish.

You know why, genius. You feel it, and he feels it too.

He sighed and clicked over to CNN, but he'd reached critical mass for self-delusion and denial and he abruptly shoved the laptop away with a frustrated sigh. He let his head fall into his hands and stared at the tabletop, giving in to all the thoughts that had been crowding against his mental barriers for days.

It was difficult to admit that he was attracted to D. That hadn't been part of the plan, if there'd ever been a plan apart from not getting killed. It had taken Jack a long time, most of his adult life, in fact, to admit to himself that he felt far stronger attractions to men than to women. He had buried this fact during his marriage, although at times he wondered just how successfully he had hidden it from Caroline, who was sharp as a tack, but that wasn't important now. He was not a stranger to the bodies of other men, but his experiences had never ventured into the emotional realms. He had slept with men, but he had never... did he even dare think it now? Was it even true? He didn't know if he had any actual experience of that four-letter word he wasn't letting too close to himself, no means of comparison to the bubbling cauldron he'd been steeping in for days.

It was all moot, anyway. D was about as accessible as Mount Everest. Jack's mind stubbornly went back to that moment on the couch when they'd held hands, that tiny glimmer of possibility, but that had been nothing but Demerol-induced passivity. When Jack had tried to re-create the moment the next day, D had politely but firmly ended it.

It didn't matter. He had to put it out of his mind, and fast. He'd be spending a lot of time with D in the coming weeks, maybe months, and he had to nip it in the bud before it made him miserable.

He got up from the table and went to the cabinet over the fridge, where he knew there was a mostly full bottle of Wild Turkey. He trudged to the sofa and sat down heavily, uncapped the bottle and took a swig, wincing over the bite of the whisky.

He'd drunk another four swallows before D finally came back inside, the setting sun silhouetting him in the doorway. "Gettin' drunk, Francisco?" he grumbled.

"What's it to you?" Jack said, feeling his tongue slow and stupid already. *Jesus, you're a lightweight, Francisco. Couple of pulls and you're already half in the bag.*

D came over and took the bottle, but instead of putting it away he upended it and drank two long swallows. He sat down at the other end of the sofa and passed the bottle back. "Jus' don't wanna listen ta you bitch about bein' hungover in the mornin'."

"Why, we got something to do?"

"Gotta be leavin' soon. Once ya give my arm the seal of approval." He flexed it in Jack's direction. He'd stopped wearing the sling the day before.

"No rush," Jack said, taking another drink and handing the bottle to D, who did likewise.

"Nope, no rush."

They sat silently passing the bottle back and forth for a good half hour, staring into the flames of the gas fireplace. Jack began to feel weighty and relaxed. Words were rising unchecked to his tongue and it was only with effort that he barred their way.

Some escaped, though. "How long since you got laid, D?" he asked.

D made an indistinct grunting noise. "Why?"

Jack shrugged. "Dunno. Middle of a bit of a dry spell myself. Betcha it isn't hard for you, though. Mysterious black-clad specter of death; bet the babes can't get enough."

D shook his head. "You drunk already?"

"That isn't an answer."

"I don't do that, all right?"

"Do what? Fuck?"

D's jaw was grinding. Jack watched his profile. "I don't... I'm not...." D sighed and reached for the bottle, taking another swig. "I jus' cain't," he said, quietly.

Jack's brow furrowed. "Whaddya mean, you can't?"

"Don't feel nothin'. Ain't no kinda human bein'."

"Well... but...." Jack hesitated. "You don't feel nothing?"

"Jus' shut up about it."

"What, you can't get it up?"

D turned to face him, his eyes glittering in the dimness. "You watch yer mouth, Francisco. Ain't too late ta kill ya, ya know."

"Oooh, I'm so fucking scared. You're not kidding, are you?" Jack hitched one knee up and turned to face D. "You're telling me that you've dug yourself into a cave so deep you don't even have a libido anymore?" D's silence was confirmation enough. Jack shook his head. "That is hard core, D."

There was a long silence, and more passing of the quickly dwindling bottle. Finally, D spoke again, his voice low and sibilant, almost as if he were talking to himself. "I do things," he said. "Too many ta count or measure. Gotta cut it off ta bear it. Cut it all off." His chin set in a hard line of determination. "You tryin' ta sew it back on and it's too goddamned late." He stood up abruptly and went into his room, shutting the door behind him.

Jack faced forward again and drained the rest of the bottle. He slumped into the corner of the couch and gazed numbly into the fire until his eyes closed themselves.

WHEN the crash woke him, Jack was dreaming about shooting a gun. He was in the backyard with D's Glock in his hands, firing away, trying to aim, but the bullets kept coming back toward him and he had to duck time and again.

He sat straight up, disoriented and still a little bit drunk. It was deep night, he couldn't read the clock above the stove, and his head felt muzzy and thick. What the fuck was that? It had sounded like something heavy falling.

He heard something else. Another thump, not as loud, and an incoherent half-muffled cry. *Shit, it's D. He's having another nightmare.*

Previously, Jack had let him alone during his nightmares. Best to let him sleep through them. But now, sitting right outside D's door, still half-asleep… he stumbled to his feet and over to the bedroom. He pounded on it with one fist. "D? Wake up!" Another thump and a strangled yell, no words.

Jack opened the door. D's head was thrashing from side to side on his pillow, his hands clutching at the bedsheets. He'd knocked his lamp off the side table, which had probably made the crash that had woken Jack.

Jack didn't think. He staggered to the bedside and grabbed D's shoulders. "D! Wake the hell up! Just a nightmare!"

D spluttered a few nonsense syllables and then snapped to lightning-quick action, grabbing out blindly and shoving Jack away. He fell backward onto the foot of the bed. D was sitting up now, but Jack didn't think he was really awake yet. He sat back up and seized D's upper arms. "Calm down! It's me, Jack!"

D lashed out, struggling against Jack's grip, and all was confusion and tangled arms and Jack took a glancing blow to the side of the face that made him see stars. Jack grabbed D's arms and held them fast between their bodies. D's forehead was against Jack's, his chest heaving. "J… Jack…," he stammered.

"Yeah, it's me… it's okay," Jack whispered. "You're… you just…."

He trailed off, his own breath quickening. D's fingers were gripping Jack's forearms and everything was crackling, snapping like a static charge off a doorknob, heavy like the air before a lightning storm. He was practically gasping for breath; they both were.

Jack drew back a little and looked into D's face, flushed and sweaty, his eyes lowered. Jack felt himself hardening. *Oh Jesus, get out. Just get out. He can't see you like this. He probably won't remember… just don't let him see….*

D's eyes flicked up to meet his, wide and surprised like Jack had never seen them, the pulse visible in D's throat, quick and fluttering. Jack could smell the sharp tang of D's sweat and feel his muscles taut and thrumming beneath his hands; he held D's gaze, eyes side-lit by the glow from the living room, and saw there something raw and scrubbed blank by time and neglect, creaking to life and crawling out of the darkness.

Jack would never know how he'd let himself do it, but without lowering his eyes he took his hand from D's shoulder and slid it down between his legs. D hissed and flinched, his eyes slamming shut. Jack felt D hard beneath his hand. He leaned his forehead against D's again. "You feel it," he whispered, barely breathed, not really a question.

D just shook his head, turning against Jack's, but it wasn't a denial. Jack felt arousal spiking through him, clouding his mind with the wanting, wanting this man, all of him, black and tarry, rotted with disuse, glorious and fractured and spilling out of the cracks.

His hands went on their own to his belt buckle and fumbled it open. D's hands were on his neck now, gripping and squeezing it, kneading the damp skin. Jack heard him suck in a breath and hiss it out, and then suddenly he seized Jack's shoulders and turned him toward the bed, onto his stomach, pulled to his knees. *Oh Jesus, this is happening.* He felt the humid air of the bedroom hit his bare skin as D yanked his jeans down off his hips. The bed creaked as D moved up behind him; he could hear D's breath scraping in and out in harsh bellow pulls, a faint mumbling beneath it, the heat of his hands on Jack's hips. He put his head down and tried to relax; then a press and a deep throb and D was inside him.

Jack groaned and grabbed at the sheets, wincing against the pain; D let out a strangled cry and Jack felt his hips tight against his ass, his weight pressing him forward, his hands hanging on to Jack's shirt, then scrabbling beneath for skin. He pushed back, the discomfort fading, D thrusting forward again and again, rough and eager with denial. Jack's brain emptied of all thought and he let himself go, giving himself over to D's urgency, low-pitched whines coming from D's throat and then Jack lost it, crying out as he came without even a hand to himself, D's hands on his back beneath his shirt greedy, then seizing and holding as D thrust deep and came into him without a sound, rigid and overtaken before he flopped forward with a quiet groan, bearing Jack down onto the bed with him, slipping out of him and rolling to his back. Jack turned on his side, whirling and dizzy. He kicked his jeans off and lay there in just his T-shirt, pulse slowing and sleep racing to overtake him, cautiously extending one hand to rest on D's chest before it caught them both.

CHAPTER 12

D WOKE up slowly, the curtains blocking most of the morning sun. The room felt humid and closed in, and he was unusually warm.

That's cuz there's somebody else in the bed with ya, dumbass.

He turned his head and saw Jack's sleeping face, half-buried in the pillow, his hands curled under his cheek. He stayed very still so as not to wake him, because as long as Jack stayed asleep D would not have to school his expression, wouldn't have to erase any trace of alarm or regret or confusion or even tenderness that might have shown in his own features. He could just lie here and look at him for a moment, and try not to think ahead, or wonder what the hell had happened, or how he'd allowed it, or what it meant, or if it was too late to take it back.

One of his hands drifted toward Jack's face, all by itself. D stared at it hanging there in the air, then drew it back. Jack stirred slightly and D turned away, slowly sliding his legs out from beneath the covers. He rose from the bed and tiptoed into the bathroom, which was shared by both bedrooms. He made the water as hot as he could and abraded himself with the stupid little fluffy scrubbie thing, squinching his eyes shut and letting the steam surround him like a shield of invisibility.

You fucked a man last night. How about that? You gonna think about that? When ya gonna start dealin' with it? Or with the fact that it may a been the first time ya did it, but weren't the first time ya wanted to?

He rubbed soap through his hair, being careful of his still-tender shoulder wound. He rinsed his head and stood there blinking, unsure of what came next. He'd washed everything, but he didn't want to leave the sheltered dimness of the shower quite yet.

Finally, he made himself turn off the water. Jack would probably want a shower, and not a cold one, so it wouldn't be too nice of him to use up all the hot water just because he was scared to face life outside the bathroom. He stepped out and toweled off, eyeing the bathroom door. Was Jack still asleep? Was he sitting in bed, waiting for D to come out so they could have some kind of heart-to-heart conversation about What It All Meant? Worse, was he waiting there for D to come back so they could... do it again? Would it be weird to walk out naked? He wasn't sure he wanted Jack to see him naked.

That ship's kinda sailed, ain't it? You've screwed him but ya don't want him seein' ya in the buff?

Well, ya cain't stay in the fuckin' bathroom all day.

He eased the door open and peeked out. The bedroom was empty, the covers on the other side of his bed thrown back, and he could hear Jack out in the main room. Heaving a sigh of relief, he hurried out and yanked on clean clothes.

He paused at the bedroom door, shut his eyes, took a deep breath, and walked right out like it was any other morning, and he and Jack would be having breakfast as if they hadn't had sex the night before. Jack was at the counter making coffee. He'd put his jeans back on.

"Morning," he said, casting a quick glance over his shoulder.

"Mmm," D grunted.

"You done in the bathroom?"

D blinked. *No, I jus' took a little breather in the middle a my mornin' beauty ritual ta come out here 'n' chat with ya. A course I'm done.* He restrained himself to a simple nod. "All yers," he muttered.

Without another word, Jack went into his own bedroom. A few moments later, D heard the shower running. He leaned on the counter and stared at the coffee dripping slowly into the coffeepot, concentrating on a caffeine fix to keep himself from thinking of Jack in the shower. Naked in the shower.

He'd more or less put the image out of his mind by the time Jack emerged, fully clothed and shaven, a task D hadn't had the mental wherewithal to remember. "That's uh, the last of the coffee," Jack said. "Are we leaving soon? For good, I mean."

"Dunno."

"If we're not, we need to get some groceries."

D made himself turn and look Jack in the face for the first time. He looked the same. *What'd you expect? A big pink triangle on his forehead? A giant letter Q on his chest? A course he's the same. Jus' like yer the same. Same old Jack.* Except it wasn't. Jack looked the same, but he wasn't the same, and neither was D. He felt it in himself, and he saw it in the stiff set of Jack's shoulders and the fidgety way he had his hands shoved in his pockets. Mostly he saw it in Jack's eyes. They were veiled, cautious. He looked... defended. He didn't know what was going to happen now and he was bracing himself against whatever did. D knew the feeling. "Ya want some breakfast?" D asked, turning back to the stove.

Jack sighed. "Sit down. I'll do it. You could burn water."

D glanced at him, detecting a slight trace of normality in the jibe. Jack's lips were curled into a hard, tight little smirk, but he didn't look D's way. "Yer the boss," he said, and adjourned to the table.

Jack made eggs and toast, lifting the cholesterol embargo for the time being. They ate in silence. D concentrated on his food, not lifting his eyes from the plate in case they should see anything that would require him to respond.

The silence wasn't fooling anyone, though. It was miles from the easier, more companionable silences they'd enjoyed just a few days ago. D could practically feel the tension thrumming in the air, like he was vibrating with it and through him the chair, the floor, the table, and all the way over to Jack.

He pushed his plate away and folded his arms on the table. "We'll head out tonight," he said. Just making a definite statement about something—anything—felt like progress.

"Where are we going?" Jack asked. He sounded like he was a little afraid of the answer.

"Redding."

"What's in Redding?"

"A place we can hide out, maybe until the trial." *Wait. Did that sound like some kinda come-on? Get all comfy and cozy and intimate in some house somewhere? Does he think I'm.... What if he thinks I mean.... Fuck it, I don't even know what I mean. Good Christ, I am fuckin' bad at this. Whatever "this" even is.*

"A house?"

D nodded. "My brother's house."

There was a pause. D risked a glance upward to find Jack staring at him in amazement. "You have a *brother?*"

"Had. He's dead."

"You… had a brother?"

D shrugged. "Yeah. What's the big deal?"

Jack shook his head and shrugged. "I don't know. Just… it's weird to think of you having relatives. Like a normal person would have. Siblings and parents."

"A course I got parents. Ya think I sprung up outta the desert sand full-grown?"

Jack blinked. "Kinda, yeah."

D sighed. "Well, my parents died when I was a kid. My brother 'n' sister took care a me. Didn't see neither a them again after I left the army. My brother died in a car crash five years ago and left me his house. I put it in a fake name, one a my aliases, so it couldn't be traced ta me."

"Where's your sister?"

"Dunno."

"What do you mean, you don't know?"

D glared at him. "Which part's givin' ya the trouble? I. Don't. Know."

"You could find out!"

"Don't care ta. She don't wanna see me nohow. Anyway, she's part a… who I used ta be. That man's dead. Jus' me left now, and I ain't got no family."

D waited for Jack's reaction, but it wasn't what he expected. Seemed like only a few days ago that his "the man I used ta be is dead" speech would have gotten some awe, or quivery-chin empathy, or some damn humility at being in the presence of such hard-bitten emotional deadness. Now, Jack just shook his head with a cynical half-smile on his face. "Sorry I asked," he said, his tone clipped and sharp. "You know, your fear-me-for-I-do-not-exist routine is getting pretty fucking old." He stood up abruptly and stalked over to the sink, tossing his dishes in. He just stayed there, his back to D and his head bowed.

"Old, huh?" D said, more as a placeholder than an actual question.

"Yeah, old. And it's insulting that you're even laying that line of bullshit on me anymore, after… everything."

"You'd like ta think it's a line a bullshit, wouldn't ya?" D snapped, his temper flaring. "Be nice fer you ta believe it's all some kinda act and that I got a nice little life tucked away somewhere ta go back to when I'm done playing Hit Man. Well, it ain't no act, doc. I ain't never bullshitted you, not about that." He stood up and went to the patio door. "We gotta go into Carson City fer some supplies before we head out. Leave in ten minutes."

"Whatever," Jack muttered as D escaped into the backyard, his bench calling to him and promising quiet, if not peace.

JACK stood in the aisle, both hands on the shopping cart, staring sightlessly at the rows of coffee cans. *Need coffee. Do we need a big can? Will there be coffee at the new place? Better get the big can. Which one does D like again? He didn't like the last one. I'll get this one; it's expensive so he'll have a hard time bitching about it. D and I had sex last night.*

All morning it had been like that. A string of ordinary thoughts capped off by another jolt of reality to yank him out of the careful scrim of normalcy they were both maintaining.

The ride into town had passed in excruciating silence that they had both passed off as casual. The conversation in the store had been confined to which granola bars to buy and if they should get a case of Red Bull for the road.

He didn't even know why they were here. To his knowledge, there *were* grocery stores in Redding. If they were leaving that evening, they didn't need to come here and get supplies now. *He's trying to fill the time with busywork.* Then why didn't they just leave immediately?

Maybe he's putting it off. Maybe he doesn't want to leave the cabin. God knows I don't. The cabin was their little safe place, tucked away in some enchanted forest like they'd gone through the back of a wardrobe to get there. A bubble of peace where they could spend hours doing nothing, talking about unimportant things, easing each other along into something still unnamed. Leaving the cabin felt like being shoved back into a hostile world where it meant a lot of things to sleep with another man, not all of them good or comforting, where it would become real in a way that it wasn't yet, and where they might once again be found by the dizzying array of people who wanted one or both of them dead.

Jack just wanted to leave the shopping cart, get back in the car and get back to the cabin as fast as they could. Lock the door, turn off the lights, take D's hand and lead him into the bedroom, get under the covers and hide there, wrapped up together. It was a cowardly impulse. A head-in-the-sand impulse. If he just stayed very still, nothing bad would happen. If he just pretended that D had feelings for him, that he'd ever in a million years express them or act on them, that the two of them could hide away in the cabin, fall madly in love and spend the rest of their days taking care of each other, then maybe reality would leave them alone for just a few more days. But D was right; they would probably be found eventually.

For a short time this morning, Jack had wondered if maybe D didn't even remember what had happened between them the night before. He'd had some whisky, after all. He hadn't seemed blackout-drunk, but sometimes it was hard to tell. He'd quickly put the notion aside, though, once he'd seen him. Of course he remembered. He'd woken up with Jack in the bed next to him, after all. And it was all over the way he was avoiding Jack's eyes.

He's sorry. He wants to forget. He can't believe it happened. He doesn't want it to ever happen again. He can barely speak to me.

"Jack?"

He jumped and turned. D was standing there holding a bag of oranges. "Huh?"

"Didja get the coffee?"

"Uh... yeah," he said, grabbing the nearest can and tossing it into the cart. He walked off down the aisle, D falling into step beside him.

"Maybe we oughta get some—"

"We don't need to get anything," Jack said. "Why are we buying groceries *now?* Wouldn't it make more sense to wait until we get to Redding?"

D flushed slightly. "Well... I guess... it's jus'...."

"What?"

He shrugged. "Don't like ta be seen 'round town."

Jack peered at him, trying in vain to read something in those flinty eyes. "Do people know you there? People from your past?"

"Nah, not really. But some of 'em know me as the guy owns my brother's house. Might be a connection."

"That's pretty damned paranoid, even for you."

"Well, I ain't dead yet, so I'll keep bein' jus' as paranoid as I always have been, if it's all the same ta you."

"What if it isn't the same? What it *nothing's* the same?" Jack said, the words tumbling out.

D looked at him blankly. They weren't talking about groceries anymore. "Let's jus' get this shit and get outta here. I got a bad feelin'."

"What kind of feeling?"

"Like I been still too long. Like I'm bein' watched."

"It's your imagination."

"My imagination's saved my ass more times'n I can count."

"But...."

D rounded on him. "Jack, give it a rest, huh? Jus'... gimme a fuckin' break, okay?" He walked off down the aisle, leaving Jack with the cart amongst the Cremora and Earl Grey.

THEY arrived back at the cabin just after one o'clock, and it was a relief to be there. D hated being out among... people. He saw their faces and their mundane little lives and marveled that he'd ever remotely been one of them. They drove their cars and watched TV and fucked their spouses and fed their kids and read *People* magazine and had no idea that they'd brushed elbows at the supermarket with a man who'd murdered more than sixty people in cold blood. It made him wonder who they really were. It made him wonder who *he'd* brushed elbows with without knowing it.

Jack had driven on the way back, silent and tight-jawed, his eyes fixed on the road ahead. D found his eye wandering to Jack's strong thigh, the cords in his forearm as he gripped the wheel, and had to continually drag them away. *Ya want him. Ya wanted him last night when ya took him, but also the night before that and the night before that too. Ya mighta wanted him since he looked past yer gun barrel at yer face and saw you, really saw you.*

Ya want him, but ya cain't have him. You ain't doin' that to nobody ever again, 'specially not ta him. He don't deserve it. Jus' get him through ta this trial and then cut him loose, and never see him or think about him again.

They left most of the bags in the car, seeing as they'd be loading up their things and leaving in a few short hours. They went inside, shuffling into the main room, picking things up and putting them down again. D headed for the patio purely on instinct. "Goin' ta get some air," he muttered. He'd almost made it out when Jack's voice stopped him.

"You're really not going to deal with it, are you?"

D stayed where he was, one hand on the door handle, head down. "Deal with what?" he said.

Jack made a disgusted, dismissive sound. "You are too fucking much for me, D. It's been... what, five hours?"

"Since what?"

"Since we woke up in bed together, you cold-blooded bastard."

D made himself turn and face him, keeping his face tight and composed. "And?"

"And… I…." Jack's hands were waving in the air like the words were dancing away from his grasp, his mouth opening and closing again. Finally he shrugged and let his hands fall. "I guess that's all I need to know, isn't it?" He looked away and headed for the front door.

"Where ya goin'?"

"Out for a walk."

"Don't go too—" The door slammed. "Far," D finished, sighing. *Nice goin', slick. But better cut it off now than later, when it'll hurt more.*

He went out to the patio, wishing more than ever for a cigarette. Damn Jack and his health-nut crap, all he wanted was a drag. He shoved his hands in his pockets and turned his face upward, trying to do that thing he'd heard other people talk about where they basked in the sunlight and got some kind of feeling of well-being and oneness with nature. All he felt was vaguely warm.

He wandered down toward the grass, kicking at the flagstones on the patio, telling himself that he didn't care if Jack had been hurt, or if he was pissed. In fact, it would be better if he *was* pissed. They didn't have to get along for D to protect Jack.

He'd just about convinced himself that it'd be the best thing for everybody if he and Jack ceased all but business-related contact when he reached the big tree down by his bench and his eyes fell on the grass at its base. All thoughts of his relationship with Jack were sliced neatly off by the sight of four cigarette butts crushed into the dirt and the small patch of trampled grass surrounding them, neither of which had been there this morning before they'd left for Carson City.

D darted behind the tree and stood on the trampled patch. *Fuck. Perfect view a the house from here.* Panic poured into his veins, in a way that it hadn't done in years and years. He ran in a half-crouch around to the side of the house, then sprinted to the front drive. "Jack?" he called, looking around and trying to sound casual in case someone was listening. "Hey, Jack?"

Nothing.

D ran past the front door to the other side, scanning the trees for Jack's blue jacket. *Oh god oh god oh god oh god* ran the litany in his head as ran down the drive, where Jack was likely to have walked, looking for any sign of him.

He turned in a circle when he got to the intersection where the drive met the road. "Jack!" he shouted, past caring who heard him now. Nothing but birds.

He ran back up to the house, his heart pounding. Then it skipped a beat and he screeched to a halt before the porch steps.

Jack's jacket was hanging on the front door, held there by a large dagger stabbed through it into the wood. "Oh no oh no no no no no," D muttered under his breath, barely aware he was doing so. He bounded up to the porch, yanking the knife out and clutching the jacket to his chest. Underneath the jacket was a scrap of paper; it fluttered to the ground as D freed it.

He fell to his knees on the Welcome mat and picked it up. Just four words, scrawled in messy block letters: "Stay by the phone."

He crumpled the note in one spastic motion, flinging it aside like he could undo what it said if he just put it from him with enough force. He was hugging Jack's jacket and breathing much harder than he would have liked; he made himself relax a little. "Jack," he whispered, looking down at the newly ventilated jacket.

He wasn't sure how long he stayed kneeling there on the porch, but it was only necessity that dragged him back into the house. He felt gutshot, and the sensation was a surprise. What was also a surprise was the realization that he couldn't handle this alone. He'd encountered very little in the past ten years that he couldn't handle alone.

He found his cell phone and made himself sit down and take a few deep breaths before sending the message.

sos

He waited. He sat there at the kitchen table and held the phone in both hands, staring at it, willing it to vibrate. After a few minutes, it did.

?
need help
call?
plz

He waited again, and in a few seconds the phone rang. "I need your help," he said into it.

"What's wrong?" X's voice, as usual, was filtered through a masking device. It didn't even read as male or female.

"They took him."

"Took who?"

"Jack!" D exclaimed, thumping one hand on the table. "They took Jack!" *Christ, listen ta you. Get ahold a yerself.*

"Who took him?"

"I dunno. I'm waitin' fer the call."

"Well, it can't be the brothers."

D blinked, not following. His usually sharp thought processes felt dipped in molasses. "Why not?"

"They'd just kill him. If they're going to call you, they must want something. Probably a trade."

"So it's whoever set me up with this job, then."

"Most likely. They'll want you to trade yourself for him."

"Okay. They can have me."

"D, you can't just give yourself up."

"It'll be a relief."

"Who'll protect Jack if you're dead?" D sighed. "Yeah, I thought so. Look, just wait for the call. Get back to me, tell me where the trade's going down. Just do like you're going through with it."

"Then what?"

"I'll take care of it."

D shook his head. "I don't like this."

"What's to like?"

"But…." He hesitated. "They staked the place out. Whyn't they jus' take me? Why take him?"

There was a pause. "I don't know, D. Do you?"

"Maybe… ta see if I'd do it."

"They must think you won't."

"They're wrong, then. I been ready ta die ta save his life from the first."

CHAPTER 13

DON'T panic. Don't panic.

Good advice, but easier said than done. Jack kept repeating it to himself, but it kept not working. Panic was rising in him like the tide and he knew he'd only be able to keep it down for so long.

His eyes were covered and his ears were plugged; the world was dark and silent. All he knew was that he was indoors, and he was tied to a chair. He didn't know if he was alone, he didn't know if anyone was talking, he didn't know if it was day or night. Judging by the painful knot on the back of his head he'd been knocked out, and he'd woken up here. Wherever "here" was.

The darkness and silence were more unnerving than he could have possibly imagined. Someone could be about to torture him with needles and he'd never know about it until he felt the pain. He could be about to die, and he'd have no warning.

You sit tight now, and don'tcha worry. I'm comin' ta get you.

D's voice, clear as a bell. If only it were true. If only he could convince himself that D was coming to rescue him. He didn't even care that he was the damsel in distress in this scenario. Damsel he was not, but in distress he most certainly was, and if it took D swooping in and rescuing him to get him out of said distress, he'd gladly suffer the blow to his masculine pride.

But for all he knew, D didn't even know that he was gone. He had no idea how long it had been since he'd been so efficiently removed from the cabin. And even if D did know, he might not know where Jack was, or how to find him.

Or he might just be saying "good riddance" and going on his merry way.

Jack didn't really think that was true... but he was still afraid it was.

Focus. Think.

His first thought was that the brothers had found him, but that didn't make much sense. If they'd found him, they would have killed him. Why keep him here, and make sure he didn't know where he was or who had him? The brothers would want him to know.

The only other explanation was that these people had some beef with D. Jack was still a little confused about the labyrinthine connections that led from D to the shadowy figures pursuing them, but he knew that D suspected that it wasn't the Dominguez brothers who'd blackmailed him into taking the contract on Jack's life, but someone else entirely. Maybe this someone else had decided to swipe Jack and use him to put the screws to D.

But that assumed that whoever-it-was knew that D would care what happened to Jack. Why would anyone think that? Unless they'd been watching them….

That was a disturbing thought. Jack put it out of his mind.

Either they know that D and I have made some kind of… connection… or they think that D would try and save me no matter what. But why would they think that a man like D, who kills for a living, would care if I lived or died? They'd have to know him. They'd have to—

Jack was suddenly struck across the face, hard. The blow drove the wind from his lungs with surprise; his head rocked to the side. He could hear, very faintly, the rumble of someone talking, but he couldn't make out any words.

Oh Jesus God please just get me out of here I don't care who's got me or what they want or who they're after or what they know I just don't wanna die yet, please.

A WATCHED pot never boils. A watched phone never fuckin' rings.

D had been sitting on the couch with his phone in his lap for more than an hour. Since hanging up with X, he had been doing as he'd been bidden: waiting by the phone.

He didn't know what to do. Didn't know how he felt. Didn't know what to think. He was putting off trying to figure anything out until he knew Jack was safe, and who had him, and what they wanted. They had to want something, or they would have just killed him.

At least, that's what he kept telling himself.

His eyes drifted shut, and right away it started. Images of Jack, of him and Jack, of what he was really trying not to think about. Every time he closed his eyes he saw it. D sighed and let his head fall backwards to rest against the couch cushions and gave in, letting the memory of Jack's skin and his body and how it had felt with him to wash over him like the surf, hard and pounding on the rocky shore and obscuring its rough breakers and jagged edges.

Jesus, Jack. Don't fuckin' do this ta me. Don't dig up all that shit I locked away.

D got up and paced. It was pointless, but at least it made him feel like he wasn't losing it completely. Had been a time, though it seemed like a mirage now, that nothing affected him. He was goddamned bedrock, and everything rolled right off without leaving any trace. But Jack Francisco was like a million years of rain, carving channels and caverns all through him, sinkholes down into the dark depths that he never thought would see the light of day again. Right now he felt about as rock-solid as Swiss cheese.

They can't know that when they call. You gotta be cold as a fuckin' glacier. Cain't give it away that ya give a rat's ass what happens ta him cuz that'll jus give 'em more leverage.

The phone rang. D jumped, then immediately cursed what was left of his nerves. He picked up the phone, took a few breaths, and answered it. "D here."

"Ten miles west of here on Highway 267 there's an old gravel access road that splits off just past Harlan Creek Road. It'll lead you over the Truckee Gorge Dam. Be on the east end of the dam in one hour."

D cleared his throat. "And, uh… what's s'posed ta happen there?"

"Do you want Francisco back alive or not?"

"You think I give a shit?"

"You do, or you'd already be a hundred miles away." D sighed. They had him there.

"What d'ya want?"

"Just you."

"Me for Francisco?"

"That's right."

D bit his lip. "What ya want me for?"

"Does it matter?"

"How do I know he ain't already dead?"

"He isn't."

"Lemme talk ta him."

"I don't think that's necessary."

"I ain't comin' unless I know Jack's alive."

"He's fine. And even if he isn't, you'll come anyway just in case he is."

Fuck. And I thought I had ice water in my veins. "I guess you think ya got me all figgered out, don'tcha?"

"I don't know any more than what you're telling me, D. I had heard you were smart and cautious. My informant must have been thinking of someone else."

D ground his jaw tight and somehow managed not to unleash a comeback. "One hour. I'll be there." He hung up and sank down onto the couch, already dialing X.

He (she?) must have been waiting for his call, because he picked up on the first ring. "What'd they say?"

D repeated the instructions he'd been given. "Not much ta go on."

"No. Jack could be dead, and they could be planning to just shoot you when you show up."

"Seems like an awful lotta trouble ta go to just ta shoot me."

"Agreed. They're probably going ahead with a trade, which means they'd need Jack alive and walking so you could switch places. They know you wouldn't give yourself up until you saw him."

"So? What do we do?"

"All you do is get there on time. Leave it to me."

D blinked. "I cain't jus' leave it ta you."

"Isn't that why you called me?"

"I ain't that guy."

"Which guy?"

"The guy who goes along with the plan. I'm the guy with the plan."

"Fine. Let's hear your plan." D's mouth opened but no sound came out. "Yeah, I thought so. Besides, you shouldn't be calling the shots here. Your judgment isn't trustworthy right now."

D's temper flared. "Why the hell's that, then? Was good enough for you in the past!"

"You're emotionally involved. You can't make rational decisions in this state."

"My decision-makin' saved yer life, as you've told me a million times, or didja forget?" D snapped. There was a pause, just long enough for him to wonder if he'd crossed the line.

"I haven't forgotten," X said, and D thought he heard a little sadness coming through the synthesized voice-masking. "Which is why I want this to go right for you."

"I'm sorry," D mumbled.

"Don't apologize. Just do as I say."

"Okay," D said, half to himself. "Okay."

"Go ahead with the trade however they want you to do it. I'll take care of the rest. Be ready to move fast."

"Always am." He frowned, a thought occurring. "How's it that yer close enough ta get ta the site in an hour?"

"I'm in Tahoe, D. Have been for a week."

D was blindsided. "You watchin' me?"

"Not directly. I just… want to make sure that you do what you're trying to do. I've been waiting a long time for you to want out of the business, and this is your way out." An electronically distorted sigh. "One thing you should probably know, though."

"What's that?"

"I wouldn't have let you kill Francisco." The line went dead. D stared at it, his mind and expression blank, trying and failing not to pay attention to the man behind the curtain.

ONCE they were in the car and moving, Jack's blindfold and earplugs were removed. He hissed at the sudden assault on his retinas. Everything seemed very loud. He squinted out the windows at the passing trees but didn't recognize anything. "Where are you taking me?" he asked, hoping he sounded confident and defiant instead of terrified, which he was.

"Letting you go now," one of the two men in the front seat said.

"Just like that. Sure."

"Well, we're getting something in return."

Jack swallowed hard. "D?"

The henchman (as Jack could only assume these men were) chuckled. "Heard he was such a hard-ass, but he rolled over like a puppy and gave himself up."

"Wh… what are you going to do to him?"

"That isn't any of your concern," the driver said, speaking for the first time and glancing at Jack in the rearview mirror. Jack shrank back against the seat, his mind racing. There had to be something he could do. He couldn't just let D trade himself.

Why not? Might be a fitting end for him. A chance to redeem himself.

Jack's jaw clenched as he thought about D taken, beaten, hurt, killed. *I don't care if he's never redeemed; I just want him safe with me.*

D PULLED up to the dam right on time. There was a nondescript black car parked on the other side. "Motherfucker," he muttered.

He couldn't see Jack in the other car. He turned off the motor and sat there gripping the wheel for a moment, hating everything about this but most of all the fact that he didn't know exactly how X was planning to handle this. He could guess that it probably involved a sniper rifle and a couple of dead henchmen, but there was just too much wiggle room in that scenario for his liking.

He got out of the car and stood by the hood. The doors of the other car opened and two men in suits got out. "Lemme see Jack!" D yelled.

"Step away from the car," the driver said.

D took a few steps forward. "I ain't comin' no further 'til I see Jack," D said.

The driver nodded at the other henchman, who opened the rear door of the car and drew Jack out. D felt relief rush through him as he saw Jack, alive and apparently unharmed. Their eyes locked like they'd found magnetic north. The henchman undid Jack's cuffs and shoved him forward. Jack started walking, not taking his eyes off D's. The driver pulled out a gun and aimed it at Jack. "Don't try anything, D," he said. "I can still kill him."

D nodded and started forward. Jack's eyes were full of questions. *How are we getting out of this? You've got a plan, right? I'm ready to go along. Just let me know. You've got it all under control, right?* D tried not to let his own uncertainty show as they drew nearer.

"Get in the car," D hissed at Jack when he got close enough to hear. "Anythin' happens ta me you jus' drive. All our stuff's in the trunk. Got it?"

"What's going on?" Jack stage-whispered. "What do I do?"

"Jus' get in the fuckin' car and get outta here."

"You're not really going to...." They were passing each other now. D saw Jack's arm twitch as if to reach out to him, but he didn't. The urge to just grab Jack and hit the deck was strong, but he resisted.

"Don't worry about me, jus' do as I say." D kept walking, not allowing himself to look back. He took slow, deliberate steps, watching the driver's gun aimed past him, keeping a bead on Jack's retreating back.

"That's right," the driver said. "Don't be a hero."

"I ain't no hero," D growled. Behind him, he heard the car door open and then shut again. The driver swiveled his gun toward D.

"Okay. Now get in the car."

D actually felt the breeze past his ear before he heard the faraway, faint spit sound. A circular hole appeared in the driver's forehead, drilled with laser precision. He went stiff and D saw the life leave his eyes; it was a familiar sight. He glanced at the other man, who didn't even yet realize what had happened, just in time to see an identical hole appear in his forehead.

Both men fell in heaps. D ran forward and grabbed the driver's gun. He tucked it into his waistband, reached inside the car, and popped the trunk. All at once Jack was there, ducking and covering his head. "What's happening? Who's shooting?"

D seized the driver under the shoulders. "Grab his feet. Let's get these guys into the trunk."

Jack picked up the driver's legs and tucked them under his arm. They hauled him off the ground, Jack looking a little green. "Oh, God... he's still twitching."

"You okay?"

"Shut up and let's just get him in the trunk," Jack said through gritted teeth, red-faced. They carried him around the back and put him in the trunk.

"Other one now," D said, glancing at Jack to see if he could take it.

Jack nodded. "Let's get it over with."

D had just shut the trunk when his phone rang. "Yeah?"

"I'll dispose of the car. You guys get lost."

"You sure?"

"You've got less than an hour before somebody realizes they aren't coming back with you. How far away can you be by then?"

"Right." D took a breath. "Thanks."

"Watch your back."

"Are you still going to be watching it?"

Pause. "I'll let you wonder about that." The line went dead.

D stared at the phone for a moment, and then slipped it into his pocket. "Come on," he said to Jack.

"We're just leaving their car? With bodies in it?"

"It's bein' taken care of. We gotta get outta here."

They ran back to the car. "Where are we going? Redding?" Jack asked as he buckled his seat belt.

"Yeah." D shook his head. Was it really only five o'clock in the afternoon? This day was never going to end. He backed off the dam, did a Y-turn and headed back to the highway. He glanced over at Jack, who was sitting stiffly in the passenger seat with his arms crossed over his chest. "You okay?"

"I'm fine."

"They didn't… hurt ya or nothin'?"

Jack shrugged. "Hit me in the face a couple of times."

D frowned. "Lemme see."

"I'm fine."

"Get a black eye or anythin'? Did they—"

"I said I'm fine," Jack snapped, tossing a glare at him. D let it go and kept his eyes on the road. *Trade yerself fer a guy and get yer head bit off fer yer trouble, I guess.*

A few moments passed in tense silence. "You wanna tell me what's up yer ass?" D said, immediately regretting the unintentionally loaded metaphor.

Jack didn't seem to notice. "Who the hell was doing the shooting, D? Someone else you haven't told me about?"

"Now look here, who says I gotta tell you about every damned thing in the world?" D said.

"When somebody's shooting a rifle in my direction and narrowly missing your head I'd like to be kept in the loop."

D sighed. "Jus' a friend a mine. Well… not a friend, really. Somebody I trust." *Somebody who may or may not have been watchin' me without my knowledge fer weeks now.* "Is that what yer ticked off about?"

"Who says I'm ticked off?"

"Yer actin' awful pissy if you ain't."

Jack stared out the passenger window, his chin on his hand. "If your friend hadn't been able to help you, would you still have traded yourself?" D didn't answer. No answer was required. Jack sighed. "Yeah, I thought so. I just…. I almost got you killed."

"Wasn't you."

"The hell it wasn't. You would have given yourself up to save me. Why?"

D's jaw tightened. "Right thing ta do."

"I don't know what the right thing is anymore."

"Yeah. Story a my fuckin' life, Jack."

THEY arrived in Redding just before ten. D pulled up to a comfortable-looking ranch house in a quiet neighborhood. They'd barely spoken for the entire trip, but it had been excruciating anyway. Seemed like the air was shimmering inside the car, like heat rising off a highway, zinging around in the space between them like they were giving off radiation. The kind that burned you.

D could tell that Jack was tense. His whole body was giving it off, that keep-it-together vibe. What was it that he wanted to say? Or do? Did he want to touch D, or make some kind of heartfelt confession that neither of them were ready for? D prayed that they could pass the time inside this forced proximity without incident, and was profoundly glad to climb out of the car and away from that shimmering that laid on his skin like a night sweat.

He found the key to his brother's house, a new trepidation rising in his chest as he approached the front door. He'd never brought anyone here before, and it felt dangerous. It was too close to what he'd left behind. There were things inside that connected him to who he used to be, things that Jack would undoubtedly ferret out with his nose for the sensitive spots, things that D wasn't ready to confront or explain.

He opened the house and they carried their things inside, leaving them in the middle of the living room for the time being. Jack put their groceries in the fridge, opening a bottle of water for himself. D checked the doors and windows, making sure everything was locked up tight.

When he returned to the living room, Jack was standing at the window looking out, silhouetted by the glow of the streetlight outside. D just stood there and watched him, paralyzed by indecision, struck mute by too many years of self-censor.

Yer fuckin' foolin' yerself. Or tryin' to, and not doin' such a good job. You want him. You need him. And it's got ya so petrified you cain't even reach out ta him after ya both just narrowly escaped gettin' killed.

D shut his eyes, every cell in his body pushing and pulling at him... pulling him toward Jack, pushing him away, a tug-of-war where nobody won.

He shuffled forward, slow and hesitant steps that drew him up behind Jack. He didn't turn from the window although he surely knew D was there. D's hand rose from his side, a marionette arm on strings, his breath going shaky and panicked like a spooked horse. Jack didn't move.

Fuck it. D let his hand fall to Jack's shoulder. He felt him flinch a little at the contact, but he didn't turn. The feeling of Jack beneath his hand, warm through his shirt and solid and strong and alive, sent another blast against that vault door, shuddering it on its hinges. He put his free hand on Jack's other shoulder, his head sagging down. He could feel Jack thrumming, like putting his hand on the hood of a car with the engine running.

D gave up. He couldn't fight this, at least not now. The horror of seeing Jack's jacket pinned to the front door of the cabin, the fear of what had happened to him, the ease with which he'd decided that he'd trade himself for Jack, and now the relief of having him back safe—it was all too much, even for him. He tilted forward until his forehead was resting against the back of Jack's neck. A great exhale rushed from him and he found himself hanging on to Jack's shoulders for dear life.

Jack didn't move. D didn't really need him to; he just needed to stand there, feeling the warmth of Jack's body and the pulse in his throat, the life that he'd spared and to which his own had quickly become secondary.

All at once, D felt the tension leave Jack's shoulders. Jack turned quickly and pressed hard against D, a sharp exhale rushing from his throat. D sucked in a breath and shut his eyes, clutching Jack to his chest and holding him fast, Jack's arms around his shoulders.

"I can't believe you came for me," Jack whispered against D's neck.

"Hadta," he said.

"Why?"

"Shhh," D said. "Jus'…." He hesitated. "Jus' lemme hold ya fer a minute, okay?" he whispered. Maybe if he was quiet enough, it wouldn't really be him saying it. "Don't ask me no questions. Jus' lemme feel yer safe."

Jack sighed and his arms tightened around D. "D?"

"Hmm?"

"I might want to hold you longer than a minute."

"Hmm. I s'pose."

CHAPTER 14

STANDING there in front of the window with D's arms wrapped around him, Jack had to wonder if it hadn't been worth being kidnapped and roughed up after all.

He would have stood there forever, but predictably, D pulled away. "Hmm," he grumbled. "S'have a drink." He stepped back and patted Jack's shoulder. *Like we're goddamned drinking buddies having an after-work beer.*

He followed D into the kitchen and sat down at the round table in the breakfast nook. He looked around; he'd been too distracted to notice much about the house when they'd first arrived. "Nice place."

"Keeps the rain off," D said. He poured two glasses of scotch and sat down at Jack's side. Jack guessed that they'd have to have some kind of conversation now. Anything to keep from acknowledging that it was late, the traditional time for sleeping, because that would lead to talk about sleeping arrangements, which would mean that they'd have to at least let it enter their heads that there was some kind of question about who might sleep where and in whose company.

Jack picked up his glass. *So much for beer.* He took a swallow. "So, are we going to talk about what happened on the dam? Or just pretend it's business as usual in our exciting lives?"

D snorted. "Mine, maybe. Not yours." He peered at him. "You sure yer okay? That's a helluva shiner."

It was pretty damn sore, but Jack sure wasn't going to let D see how much. "I'll live."

D got up and went to the freezer. He got a towel out of a drawer and put some ice cubes from their cooler on it, then wrapped it up into a cold pack. "Here," he said, returning to the table. "Put this on it."

"Who's the doctor here?" Jack said, taking the pack.

"I had enough black eyes in my time, I don't need ta have no MD ta know how ta treat 'em." He reached out and pushed Jack's hand and the towel tighter against his bruised eye socket. "You hold that close up, now. Help with the swellin'."

Jack held the ice to his face, propping his elbow on the tabletop. "I didn't even hear them coming," he said, quietly. "They must have knocked me right out. I have a lump on the back of my head. I'm fine," he said, off D's furrowing brow. "I know the signs of a concussion, so quit clucking. All I know is one minute I was walking on the drive, the next minute I was waking up in the trunk of a car."

"Did ya see or hear anythin'?"

"They had me blindfolded and my ears plugged. I didn't see or hear a thing." He looked at D, who was staring morosely into his untouched scotch. "Did you know those guys?"

He shook his head. "Not those guys in particular, no. Sure's shit they were just hired muscle."

Jack swallowed. "Hired by whom?"

D looked at him, the first time he'd done so since they sat down, and chuckled a little. "Listen a you. 'Hired by whom.' Talkin' 'bout hired guns 'n' yer all usin' correct grammar."

"Are you going to answer my question?"

"Would if I had an answer."

"You must have some idea."

D knocked back the entire shot of scotch, grimacing. "Guess so."

Jack waited. "Well?"

He was just sitting there, staring at the empty glass, turning it around and around in his fingers. Jack reached out a tentative hand and laid it on his forearm. D jerked and glanced up, then sighed. "I guess you got a right ta know. It's yer ass as much as it is mine now. They came after you ta get ta me."

"Who, D?"

He put the glass aside and turned to face him, visibly steeling himself. "Jack, I got some stuff ta tell ya. 'bout myself."

Jack took a breath. "About… your family?"

D blinked in confusion. "What? No, no. This ain't about that."

"What, then?" D still hesitated. Jack ducked his head, trying to meet his eyes. "D… you know you can trust me, right?"

D fidgeted a little. "S'a hard thing. I only trusted one person fer a long time. Not so easy with somebody new."

"But… do you?"

He raised his head and their eyes met. "Yeah. I do."

"Then tell me. Tell me the truth."

D nodded, and squared his shoulders. "You 'member when I told you about them contracts I would never take? Never forget what ya said. Might as well have shot 'em myself if I knew they was in for it and did nothin'."

Jack nodded. "I remember. I guess I said some pretty harsh things."

"You ain't said nothin' that weren't true. But I'm tellin' ya now that…." He sighed. "Well, I *was* doin' somethin'."

Jack frowned. "What do you mean?"

D shut his eyes for a moment and opened them again, and Jack could all but see him flinging himself off the edge of the cliff and into the chasm. "Thing is… I been workin' with the Bureau. Goin' on three years now."

Jack's mouth dropped open. "The FBI?"

"The same. Real hard fer them ta get a handle on folks in my line a work. Like ghosts, we are. No connections, no identities. Hard ta track. Damn near impossible to anticipate. When I saw one a them contracts, the ones I wouldn't never take… well, sometimes I'd give the Bureau a little heads-up."

"Only sometimes?"

D sighed again. "If I did it every time, it wouldn't take long fer somebody ta get wise." He snorted. "I guess somebody did."

"You think somebody knows about what you're doing and is trying to... what, exactly?"

"Take care of it. But not just that. They want ta take some revenge too. I got my suspicions that somebody out there wants ta make me suffer for it, so they made me take yer contract. Reckon if I'd a done the job, they'd a made sure I went ta the chair for the murder of a witness. Kinda like poetic justice, ya see? Make me do myself in by way a killin' you?" Jack nodded. "But 'cause I didn't, now they jus' want me dead. Probly with malice aforethought, as they say."

Jack was still taking this all in. *I knew he wasn't bad. Not really. I just knew it.* "D, I'll be honest. I'm glad to hear you've been trying to do something about all this."

He shrugged. "I didn't dream a bein' a cold-blooded killer when I was a boy, Jack. There's reasons I am how I am, and why I'm doin' what I'm doin'. Time came them reasons weren't enough no more."

"Helping save people... that must have made it easier to take, huh?"

"Made it harder."

"How's that?"

"Jack.... Christ, I ain't never talked about this. You jus' keep draggin' shit outta me, Francisco."

"It's a gift." Jack smirked a little, but it was wasted on D, who was keeping his face studiously averted.

"Somethin' happens ta you when... well, when ya do what I do, and... ya lose things. Cain't let nothin' out. Lock it all away. Had it down pretty good. Still do, as ya may a noticed."

"What, you? Closed off? Nope, hadn't noticed."

D went on as if Jack had not spoken. "It's easy when ya jus' put yer head down and ignore it all. But then I hadta start really lookin'. How d'ya decide which a four innocent people yer gonna try'n save? Couldn't save 'em all, or else I'd be no good to none of 'em. Made it worse. Hadta lock up even tighter. Hard enough when yer not lookin' at the ones ya cain't save. Gets even harder when ya start takin' peeks."

"You still killed people, though."

D nodded. "Ones I thought had it comin'."

"And that's your call to make?" *Shut up, Jack. This is not the time for this discussion.* Too late.

His head swiveled back toward Jack. "Who else? The fuckin' justice system? You gotta be kiddin' me. The same justice system where a small-time dope dealer gets ten years while a child killer gets three? Them're some fucked-up priorities. I ain't got that problem."

"No, vigilantes sure don't have to deal with due process and all that crap."

"The more guilty a man is, the more due process don't help. Folks I kill? Not the kind what gets convicted by a jury a their peers. They ain't got no peers on juries. Ya know who's their peer? I am. I'll do the convictin'."

"And the executing."

"Pays the bills."

Jack felt a chill go up his spine. "Stop it."

"Stop what?"

"You know what."

"No, I fuckin' don't."

"Stop playing Bad-Ass Assassin. You're just trying to scare me or creep me out or something so we won't have to talk about it."

D regarded him with a flat, lizard-like gaze. "About what?"

"You know."

"I am gettin' real fuckin' tired a these guessin' games."

"About what's going on between *us*, D." *There. Chew on that.*

D just sat there grinding his teeth for a few beats, then rose and went to the sink where he carefully set his empty glass. "Nothin' ta talk about."

Jack nodded. "I guess not." There was more Jack wanted to ask—who had saved their asses on the dam, for starters—but the conversation seemed to be over. For now. He stood up, tossing the ice pack into the sink. "I'm going to bed."

"Go on, then. Pick a room."

Jack retrieved his bag from the living room and went down the hall, not sparing D so much as a glance as he went by, determined to take the biggest room for himself.

JACK lay in bed on his side, arms tucked under his head, watching the line of light visible beneath his bedroom door. He had put his things in his chosen room, going so far as to unload his few articles of clothing into the dresser, and then showered, brushed his teeth, and climbed into bed, all without seeing or hearing D at all. Judging by the smell, though, he could deduce that D was sitting somewhere in the house and smoking.

Smoking in the house. Where'd he get more cigarettes? That's going to stop pretty damn quick.

Jesus, Jack. What are you, the guy's wife?

Soon after he'd retired and shut his door, he'd heard D moving around. Footsteps in the bedroom next door, into the bathroom. Drawers opening. Shower running. More footsteps. The line of light from the hallway broken by moving shadows of legs and feet as D crossed back and forth in front of his bedroom door.

The steps went into the bedroom next door and stopped. Suddenly, there was a loud thud and a curse; Jack felt the house shake slightly. D had just hit the wall, or else he'd thrown something at it. His pulse jacked up a bit; what was going on?

The steps went further into the other bedroom. He heard the bed creak. Then again. The steps came back.

Jack turned onto his back and stared at the ceiling, the covers pulled up to his chest. He wasn't wearing anything to bed tonight; whether this was laundry-related necessity or just optimism wasn't something he wanted to think too hard about. He saw D pass before his door into the bathroom again. The light dimmed as the hall light was turned off, leaving just the bathroom light on.

The leg-shadows came to his door and paused. Jack held his breath. He heard a soft thump; he was pretty sure it was D's forehead hitting the door.

He waited.

After what felt like an eternity during which those shadow-legs didn't move, the knob turned and his door swung open. D huddled there against the jamb, looking at the floor, dressed in pajama pants. Jack rose up on his elbows. D was gnawing on his thumbnail, looking everywhere but at Jack. Finally he risked a quick glance.

Jack stretched his arm across the neat, unrumpled bedclothes, extending his hand toward the door. "Come on," he whispered.

D shuffled forward, his shoulders rounded, eyes still on the floor, arms crossed over his stomach. When he reached the bed he turned his back and sat down on the edge with a weary sigh, as if the journey across the carpet had just been too exhausting. He braced his hands on the edge of the mattress and hung his head like a man contemplating his last words.

Jack waited. He could feel the heat from D's body slipping over the sheets to caress him. The muscles in D's back were twitching and he just kept shaking his head slowly back and forth, back and forth. Jack stretched out a hand and gently touched D's shoulder. He felt the flesh flinch away at the touch, but D didn't move. He flattened his palm against D's skin and slowly ran it down the outside of his arm. "What?" he murmured.

"You…," D rasped.

Jack sighed. "What?"

There was a long pause. "You deserve better," he finally said, almost too quiet for Jack to hear.

Jack's heart broke a little. "So do you," he murmured. D turned his head slightly to look at him, his face shadowed in the faint light from the bathroom. Jack took hold of the blankets and folded them back, exposing his nakedness and the flat expanse of empty sheet, a silent invitation. D just sat there immobile for a few beats, then stood up. For one awful moment Jack was sure he was going to leave, but then his hands went to his waist and he quickly shucked his pajama bottoms. He slid under the covers and drew them back up. He lay there on his back, staring at the ceiling, the sheets tucked primly under his arms.

After a few moments of tense silence, D snorted. "What'm I fuckin' doin' here?" he muttered.

Jack was tired of dancing around it, and knew that if he didn't do something they might lie here all night. "D, do you want to have sex with me?" he asked, trying to sound forthright and confident, which he was not.

D shut his eyes with a sigh, then nodded. "Jus'… don't got the excuse this time," he said.

"What excuse?"

"Bein' drunk."

Jack chuckled. "Oh, yeah."

"That is… I'd mean it this time."

That gave Jack a moment's pause. "Didn't you mean it last time?"

D turned his head and their eyes met. "Yeah," he croaked. "But Jack, I… I don't… dunno if I can—"

"Shh," Jack said, putting a hand on his chest. "Let me, okay?" D nodded, sighing in relief. *You wondered if he felt anything for you? Well, look at this, Jack. He's letting you see him like this. What more do you need to know?*

Jack slid close and pulled D into his arms. He was tense like a man being defibrillated, but came into them as best he could. Jack pressed his face into D's neck, the heat of his skin bringing sweat to his brow, and ran his hands up and down his back, the nervous thrumming in D's muscles quieting a little bit at a time. Jack molded himself against the body he'd longed to touch like this, twining their legs together, feeling D's hands tentative on his own back, touching him with cautious fingertips as if he was afraid Jack's flesh might burn him.

He nuzzled at D's face, seeking his lips, but D kept pulling away. Finally, he lifted a hand and seized his jaw, holding his head still, and looked right into his eyes. D cut his own away, tensing up again. *Okay. One thing at a time.*

Jack backed off and slid his mouth instead down the cords of D's neck, feeling him shudder, and also feeling with his leg that D was still flaccid. He himself was painfully aroused and trying not to take it personally. He just persisted, touching D where he'd like to be touched, caressing the tension from his muscles, urging him on with his hands, trying to tell him with his body *it's okay, it's okay to want me, it's okay to feel it, it's safe to show it.* D's hands on him were growing bolder, greedier, and then a strangled groan escaped him and his body abruptly went from tense and trembling to loose and demanding, and Jack was enveloped by a crush of stroking hands and writhing legs, D's mouth on his neck, his chest, everywhere. D rolled him onto his back and Jack knew that neither of them could wait. He reached out for the jar of Vaseline he'd found in the bathroom earlier and put on his bedside table, just in case, and somehow opened it one-handed. D propped himself up on one hand and Jack reached between them, slicking him with a couple of fast, desperate strokes, D hissing at Jack's hand on him. "Come on, come on," Jack mumbled; he sucked in a breath and pushed out just as D slid himself in. He was big—bigger than Jack remembered—but he didn't have much time to ponder the matter because D was going crazy.

Mumbling unintelligible syllables like he was speaking in tongues, D dropped his head into the hollow of Jack's shoulder. The man was frantic; all Jack could do was hang on, and even that was barely possible. He nearly bucked himself off a few times; Jack grabbed his ass in both hands, trying to keep him close. The angle wasn't so great for him; he already knew this wasn't going to get him off, but at the moment that didn't seem so important, because something else was happening here. D was pouring himself into Jack's arms, his body, and the deluge was fierce; Jack clung to him like a barnacle, holding him fast in his arms. *I've got you. I've got you. I've got you.* The thought ran over and over in his mind as D heaved great swoops of breath past Jack's ear, swoops that had sobs caught at their dregs, as if he'd found something old and unexpressed at the very tidal bottom of his lungs now dragged into the open air by the exertion.

I'm not letting go of you.

D's body stuttered and stiffened; he cried out his release and collapsed, damp with sweat and limp as a dishrag, Jack's arms and legs wound around him. "Jack… Jack," D breathed, the name sighing out on each exhalation as if it had gotten inside and was escaping like steam from a pressure cooker. He buried his face in Jack's neck. Jack cupped the back of his head and sighed. D drew back and looked at him. "Uh…," he said, sounding like he was rebooting his voice. "Ya didn't… y'ain't…."

"Don't worry about it."

D watched Jack's face for a long moment, then suddenly slid down the bed, shoving the covers aside, and took Jack in his mouth. Jack gasped in surprise. *Jesus, I'd have been happy with a hand job. I never thought he'd… oh goddamn….*

Jack rose up on his elbows so he could watch, because this was something he did not want to miss. The sight of D, this tough-guy hit man who knew a dozen ways to kill you with a straw, doing this to him was almost more arousing than the feeling of it. D, who was too butch to let being shot slow him down, who was too macho to talk about… well, anything… who Jack guessed he could now call his lover even if he didn't yet know his real name, was surely too much of a he-man to perform this most homo of sexual acts even if he wasn't above screwing another man. And yet, all evidence to the contrary.

"Oh God... D," Jack moaned, his head falling back on his limp neck. "I'm... I'm gonna...." D pulled off and grasped him, stroking him firmly until Jack came with a cry. "Jesus Christ," Jack sighed, falling back against the pillows. D crawled back up to the head of the bed and drew Jack close; he rested his head on D's chest and pulled the covers up around them.

He felt the slight rumble of D's silent laughter beneath his cheek. "Better now, doc?"

"Mmm. Huh?"

"Guess that answers that." Jack felt D's arm tighten around his shoulders and he snuggled closer, almost as amazed that D was allowing post-coital cuddling as he'd been at the oral sex.

When D spoke again, his voice was subdued. "Ya know how long it's been since... well, I was with anybody?"

"How long?"

D sighed. "More'n ten years."

Jack gaped. "But... that'd be...."

"Since my wife, yeah."

Jack didn't ask how it was possible for a man to give head like that without having done it before. It didn't seem the right time. "You must have had the opportunity."

"I told ya before. Didn't wanna. Couldn't, even. Hell, I ain't even wrang it out in years. It's like...." He sighed, looked up at the ceiling. "Like I stopped bein' human. Sometimes was a surprise I still needed ta piss and eat. Half waitin' ta wake up one day and find I didn't have a pulse no more, like some kinda zombie."

Jack reached out a finger and touched his cheek. "Well... you feel alive to me."

D bit his lip. "That's... well...."

Jack frowned. "What?"

"Inside, it's like maybe...." His voice dropped to a near-unintelligible rumble that Jack had to strain to hear and watch his lips to understand. "Startin' ta feel a little human again. Like wakin' up from a long sleep fulla bad dreams."

Jack nodded. "Since you started working with the FBI."

D met his eyes, frowning. "No, Jack. Since I met you." Jack was struck dumb, the words hitting him in the gut like a hard punch with some mustard on it. He held D's gaze until it became uncomfortable, which didn't take long. D shifted, his jaw working; Jack could tell he thought he'd said too much. He just lowered his head to D's chest again and put his arm across him. *I'm not letting go of you.*

He felt D relax a little at a time; the day they'd both had made sleep a swift and easy captor. Within minutes it had them both.

Just as Jack was right on the edge of dropping off, he felt D shift slightly, and then—although later he could not swear it wasn't his imagination—a brief kiss, pressed into his hair, and just as quickly withdrawn.

CHAPTER 15

JACK knew he was alone in bed before he was fully awake. He had expected to be. This morning, though, his solitude didn't alarm him.

He yawned and rolled onto his back. The other side of the bed was rumpled and slept-in, the covers not tossed aside but carefully folded back; D must have risen gently so as not to disturb him. Jack took a few deep breaths, easing himself bit by bit into waking, scratched his chest and glanced at the clock. It was after nine already. D had probably been up for hours.

Jack had woken just after two a.m. needing to go to the bathroom; when he'd returned, he hadn't gone right back to sleep but had sat up in bed, momentarily transfixed by the sight of D lying in bed next to him on his stomach, deeply asleep, his arms wrapped around a pillow. The angles and planes of his face were softened in quiet peace, his breathing slow and even.

It didn't matter that he wasn't waking up with D this morning. He'd slept next to him, and at his side D had slept peacefully, hardly moving all night, and Jack didn't need to be told that a night's rest like that was a rare occurrence in D's life.

He rose, wincing slightly at the ache born of last night's sex, and put on sweatpants and a T-shirt. The smell of coffee was drawing him out of the bedroom.

D was sitting at the kitchen table reading the paper, a cup of coffee at his side. He looked up as Jack entered, one eyebrow cocked. "Well, look who decided ta get outta bed t'day," he muttered.

"I never claimed to be a morning person, you know. Anyway, it's only nine."

"I been up since six-thirty."

Jack poured coffee. "Hey, where'd you get the paper? You can't be getting it delivered here."

"Went out and bought it," D said, slowly. *Dumbass.*

Jack nodded, feeling stupid. "Yeah."

"Brought back donuts."

"You... brought me donuts?" Jack blinked.

"Well, I did intend ta eat a couple myself. Ain't jus' fer you."

Jack sat down at his side and rummaged in the donut box, coming up with a glazed chocolate. "Anything happening in the world?"

D shrugged, folding up the paper and putting it aside. "Same shit, different day."

He glanced around. "So... this is your brother's house?"

"Was, yeah."

"How do you know they won't find us here? I mean, if they found us at the cabin—"

"Was a trail to us from that cabin. Yer ex-wife, her father, his sister. Ain't no trail leadin' ta me from this place. I don't own it. Deed belongs ta one dummy company which is a front fer another which is owned by a shell corporation, and on and on. And even if somebody managed ta get back to a name it wouldn't be mine, seein's I don't even have one."

"So we're safe here?"

"Much as we can be, yeah. Providin' we ain't been followed." He held up a hand at Jack's alarmed expression. "We ain't been."

"Are you sure?"

"Ain't nothin' ever sure."

"That doesn't exactly fill me with confidence."

"You got a better idea?"

"A string of anonymous motels?"

"Too risky. More travel means more exposure."

"Cave in the woods?"

"The hell you say."

Jack sighed. "Okay, I give. I'll defer to your expertise. Oh, and speaking of, let me have a look at your shoulder."

"It's fine," D said.

"I'll be the judge of that." He got up and leaned over D, pulling the neck of his T-shirt aside to check the wound. It was almost completely closed; they were down to a small bandage. Jack peeled it away and palpated the skin. It appeared pink and healthy; the wound itself was scabbed and receding. He nodded. "Good." He let his hand linger on D's shoulder, his thumb sweeping across the skin over his clavicle. D was facing forward, his eyes lowered to the tabletop. All by itself, his hand slid up and over Jack's hip, slipping beneath the hem of his shirt to rest against the small of his back. Jack watched D's profile but his expression didn't change. The intimacy of the touch sent warmth radiating from the point of contact, but Jack didn't try anything. He knew that wasn't how it was supposed to go. He straightened up and went back to his chair, D's hand falling away as stealthily as it had come.

"Looks good," Jack said, deliberately sweeping his eyes up and down D's chest, but the double meaning was wasted since D wasn't even looking at him.

"Glad ta hear it," he said, draining his coffee cup.

"So... now what do we do? Sit here until the trial?"

"Pretty much, yeah."

"Well. Looks like I'll have plenty of time to clear out my Netflix queue." He leaned back, resting his foot on the rail of D's chair. "This probably happens to you all the time, right? Just holed up someplace for weeks and weeks?"

"It happens."

"Don't you get bored?"

D shrugged. "Kinda. Like ta read, if I got some books. Or even... go fishin'."

"Fishing, huh?" Jack wasn't surprised. Fishing, with its stillness and patience, seemed suited perfectly to D's temperament. He sighed. "D."

"I know. We got more shit ta talk about."

"Who helped us on the dam? One of your FBI friends?"

"No. Least... don't think so."

"Then who?"

D thought for a moment, then met his eyes. "I dunno."

"You... don't know?"

"Well, I know. I jus' don't know who they are."

"You lost me. Way back there."

"You 'member I told ya once was only one person I trusted?"

"Vaguely."

"Well...." D cleared his throat and seemed to be weighing his next comment. "First of all, that ain't true no more," he said, flushing slightly, flicking his eyes to Jack's face. Jack smiled. "But that someone I meant, thing is... I don't know who they are."

"You trust them but you don't know who they are?"

"Only know 'em as X. Don't even know if it's a man or a woman."

Jack was struck dumb for a moment. "X? Seriously? What, do you meet them in darkened parking garages? Do you have a Bat-Signal or something?"

"Why ya getting all riled up?"

"I'm sorry. It's just... Jesus Christ. When does it end? Just when I think I'm getting down to who you really are there's another layer of cloak-and-dagger bullshit."

"Hey! That bullshit kep' me alive more'n once, so I'll thank ya not ta comment!"

Jack put up his hands. "Okay, okay."

"Keepin' who you are a secret's like breathin' ta them what lives where I live," D said. "And I suspect X has got their own reasons fer not bein' real forthcomin'." He folded his arms on the table. "'Bout eight years ago, when I was still kinda green, I started gettin' the feelin' that someone was lookin' out fer me. Stuff kep' happenin' that ended up helpin' me, more'n you'd expect. Folks I knew had it in fer me would end up in jail... or dead. Thought it was jus' my imagination at first."

"But it wasn't?"

D shook his head. "One day I was out doin' normal stuff, ya know, Laundromat, grocery store, and I come back ta my car ta find it's unlocked. That put my guard up right off, but when I looked in, I saw somethin' on the passenger seat. I get in the car and turns out it's an ignition trigger."

"A what?"

"S'a little jobbie ya put on someone's car that detonates an explosive when ya turn the key. Real popular with the family men."

"Yeah, right."

"Anyhow, there'd been one on my car, but somebody found out, took it off, and left it fer me there so I'd know ta watch out. Similar shit happened couple more times over the next year. Started ta feel like I had me a guardian angel. Turned out I did."

"Who?"

"Got a call one day. Voice was masked. Person said they was the one who'd been helpin' me. Knew they were bein' straight; they knew stuff 'bout me. Was still kinda pissed, though. I mean... didn't like the idea a somebody spyin' on me, watchin' me, even if it saved my ass now 'n' again. I asked who the hell they were, but they wouldn't say. Jus' said that they owed me."

"Why?"

"Cuz I saved their life."

"You did?"

"Yeah, that's what I said. Still don't know how or when I did that. I guess I believe 'em, jus' 'cause it's hard t'imagine somebody doin' what they done fer me jus' fer their health. If I saved anybody's life, I didn't know it. But I knew fer damn sure they'd saved mine, so when they asked fer my help this time, I gave it. Been that way ever since.

Kinda watch out fer each other. Well, it's mostly them doin' the watchin'.... I cain't exactly keep an eye on somebody when I don't know who they are."

"So when I went missing...."

D nodded. "Yeah, I called X. Said he'd take care of it, that I should jus' show up ta the exchange and go through the motions, and be ready ta move fast."

"Do you think they know where you are right now?"

"If it were anybody else I'd say no way, but I've learned that X has a damn spooky ability ta know where I am and what I'm doin'. I stopped wonderin' 'bout it years ago."

"Could he have you bugged somehow?"

"Don't see how. I switched vehicles so many times, no way nobody could keep up with it. Don't keep the same clothes fer long. I ain't got no kinda device implanted in me; I been X-rayed and gone through plenty a metal detectors."

"Maybe he's psychic," Jack joked.

D wasn't laughing. "I'm almost ta the point that I'd entertain the notion, weird-ass as it might be."

"Well... I'm glad you called him," Jack said.

D sighed. "Didn't have no choice. I had ta get...." He stopped, cleared his throat, and went on. "Had ta getcha back," he finished, almost under his breath.

Jack stared at the top of D's lowered head, counting the beats as they passed in silence. Abruptly, D stood up and left the kitchen. Jack heard the patio door open and shut again. He sat at the table for a moment, then got up and refilled his coffee cup.

WHEN Jack went outside just before lunchtime, dressed, D was... gardening? No, that wasn't quite right. "What're you doing?" Jack said.

"Oh, these trees leave all kinda shit all over the lawn. Fallen branches and them little twirly things. Jus'... tidyin' up."

Jack watched him painstakingly gathering seed pods and leaves, depositing them in a garbage bag. "You want me to get out the vacuum cleaner so you can do the job right?" he asked.

D shot him a dirty look over his shoulder. "Jus' messy, is all."

"I know." Jack rolled up his sleeves. "I'll help you."

They put on gloves and found a chainsaw in the garage. A tree had fallen on the edge of the property, and once the yard was tidied, they moved on to this larger task without discussing it. D ran the saw while Jack hacked smaller branches off the trunk with a long-handled trimmer. They walked back and forth to the ditch by the road, dumping off the pieces and the bundles of branches until the yard was clear, leaving only the raw white flesh of the broken-off tree gleaming wetly in the hard sunshine. D grumbled when Jack wouldn't let him lift anything heavier than an armload of branches, but did as he was told.

Jack stretched, taking off his gloves. D came up next to him and nodded. "Good," he said. He turned and started to head for the house, but hesitated as he drew close to Jack's shoulder. D's features tugged inward, like he'd just remembered something. Jack didn't move. D blinked a few times, and then slowly leaned closer, lowering his face toward the crook of Jack's shoulder. Brow furrowed, he inhaled. Jack saw his eyes flutter closed and his features smooth out as if he were falling asleep right where he stood, falling into a daydream or a memory.

"Oh," he sighed, long and weary, the sigh of sinking into a favorite chair after long hours of standing. "Ya smell like sun," he murmured. D's voice was raw, like a man under hypnosis. "Ya know that smell? That toasty-skin smell, like ya get after goin' ta the beach?" He nodded a little. "I love that smell." He straightened, eyes lowered to the ground. "Reminds me a workin' on the ranch, when I was a kid. Ridin' with my brother, up in the hills, sun beatin' down turnin' our necks brown, our hands."

Jack didn't dare speak, or breathe, or make the tiniest move to disturb the so-rare reverie. This glimpse into D's secret mind was like having a skittish deer approach him on a wooded trail; one false move and it would dart away into the brush, leaving him with only a flash of white tail before vanishing.

D looked up then, the spell broken. He harrumphed and seemed a little embarrassed. "Anyhow. Gonna get a beer." He strode off toward the house, darting off into the brush, too late for Jack to take even one step closer with his hand out to gentle him closer still.

JACK used D's laptop to check the news and the blogs he read, and spy on a few forum conversations in which he could no longer participate. He shut it down, sadness creeping up his spine. Soon there'd be nothing, nothing left of the old. It'd all have to be new. He could carry nothing forward except his memories and his own self, if he could manage to even hold on to that.

His mind barely skirted up to the edge of the thought that D might be a part of that life before skittering away again. Too soon, way too soon for that. And pointless to even consider it, because it was just too... too everything.

He got up and went out to the patio. D was sitting on a bench by the grill, which they'd used to cook hamburgers for supper, staring off toward the valley behind the house. Jack frowned. What was he doing? Staring into space? He did that a lot, and Jack always wondered what was going through his mind.

He came up behind D, who surely knew that he was there but gave no sign. Drawn like wind to a vacuum, he put his hands on D's shoulders. Encouraged by the lack of withdrawal on D's part, he began to rub the tense muscles slowly, digging his thumbs into D's shoulder blades. He could have told himself that he was just being nice, or that he was angling for a return treatment later, but why bother lying? He just wanted to be near him, and touch him again as he'd barely been able to do all day long. Maybe if D couldn't see his face, it wouldn't seem so scarily intimate. Fear of intimacy seemed like it ought to be ridiculous after the night they'd spent, but that had been different, somehow. Being intimate in a bedroom, in the dark, during and after sex, was one thing. Casual intimacy in daylight, clothed, during ordinary activities was something else. It implied something else, something that had a name, a name no one had spoken or even dared allow to pass through his mind.

D resisted for a short time, maintaining his upright posture and his overall clench, but soon enough he gave in. He let his head fall forward and his shoulders slumped, making Jack's task much easier. "There you go," he murmured. "Geez, it won't kill you to relax."

"Hmm. Minute I relax somethin' awful always seems ta happen."

Jack knelt down behind him so they were the same height. He left off the backrub and slid his arms around D's waist, resting his chin on D's shoulder. He felt the chest beneath his hands expand in a sigh. "I could almost forget about everyone wanting me dead today," Jack murmured.

"Don't never ferget. That's when they find ya."

"Getting late," Jack said after a moment. "Come inside."

"I'm okay."

Jack sighed. "I didn't ask because I thought you weren't."

"Why, then?"

"Maybe I just want your company."

D said nothing, but his head tilted just a bit, just enough to rest against Jack's. "I ain't such great company. Don't know no amusin' anecdotes."

Jack squeezed him a bit. "I don't need you to amuse me."

"What you wanna talk 'bout, then?"

"Whatever we feel like talking about."

D was silent. Abruptly, he got up and walked several paces away, his shoulders drawing down like a turtle's shell. Jack rose to his feet but stayed where he was. D shook his head once, hard. "Don't fuckin' do this ta me, Jack."

"What am I doing to you?"

"You know, damn you."

Jack crossed his arms over his chest. "Suppose I want you to say it."

D shoved his hands in his pockets and kicked at the grass. "Ain't that I don't... ya know. 'Cause yer you, and a course I... shit."

"D, what?"

"I cain't need nobody. Not again," he said in a rush. "I cain't take it." He turned around and met Jack's eyes. "It ain't in me no more."

"That's not true."

"Has ta be. Better be goddamned true 'cause I spent ten years makin' it true."

Jack took a few steps toward him. "I know it's not because I've seen you. Not this," he said, motioning to D's clothes and appearance, "but the real you."

"Ain't no real me. I know...." He looked away again. "Ya think I'm strong but I ain't. Maybe I'm strong in the world, outside, but...." He chewed his lip. "I am fuckin' damaged goods, Jack. Ya got no idea how little's left in here. I can protect ya and make sure ya get that new life yer due. But I cain't give ya no more'n that. I cain't be no more'n that ta you."

Jack closed the distance between them, reached out and took D's hand. "If you can't, how come you already are?" he said. D didn't answer, just stared into his eyes and hung on to Jack's fingers. Jack nodded. "Okay." He turned and walked away, tugging on D's hand and leading him back to the house.

"Where we goin'?" D asked.

"Inside. I'm taking you to bed."

"Jack, I—"

"Shush. I don't care if you're damaged, or if you're not strong inside. Guess what? Nobody is. Whatever you have left is enough."

CHAPTER 16

CRICKETS still chirping outside, the moonlight slanted in across their bed, leaving the rest of the room darker past its reach. Faint red glow from the corner where D's cell phone was recharging with its tiny demon's eye.

Jack was a silvery form above him, his rhythmic breathing bringing D along into the trance as he rocked back and forth, head thrown back so the shadows fell long down his neck and spilled onto his chest, riding D slow and languid like they had all the time in the world, which D guessed they did. He stared up at him, eyes roving over his body; he looked like some kind of prehistoric man-god in a sweat lodge, smoke rising all around him to the hole in the ceiling, drums beating in the distance, caught in the hypnosis of a sex rite and ready to spill his own blood to sanctify them.

Jack's head lolled on his neck as his hips thrust across D's groin. His eyes were closed and his mouth open, strong fast breaths like a distance runner, flush rising to his throat and sweat trickling down his chest.

D lay there, unsure what to do with himself since Jack was doing all the work. They'd never done it like this, with Jack on top, and it felt strange. His hands itched to control, to flip Jack over and take him hard, or haul him to his knees and do him that way. That was how it had been for the past three days, each night and parts of each day spent here in Jack's bed, taking everything out on each other's body, while the bed in what was supposed to have been D's room sat pristine and untouched.

Jack bore down harder and D groaned, his thoughts flying to pieces, shattered by what Jack did to him, a hard hammer-blow on a slab of ice. It had been so damn long since he'd felt like this—in fact, he couldn't remember ever feeling this. His hands, worrying at the sheets, let go their safe handholds and slid up Jack's hips and around to grip his ass, feeling the muscles clench and flex under them. Jack looked down at him, his deep-set eyes hooded in shadow; he covered D's hands with his own and lifted them away, interlacing their fingers, then leaned forward and braced himself against D's elbows. The shadows fell from his eyes and the moonlight lit them from behind. D was pinned in place by those blue searchlights.

His jaw clenched as Jack pulled him higher and farther, white knuckles and gasps — all D could feel of Jack was their fingers clenched together and himself buried inside. Dangled over a precipice and held by a few thin threads while he writhed toward the long, long drop. *He'll never let go of me. Not ever.*

He came with a surprised cry, startled by its suddenness, the warmth of Jack's release spilled on his stomach, straining up with planted feet to bury himself deeper, spend within Jack's body and let it fly. Jack fell forward against his chest. "Jesus Christ," he murmured into D's neck.

D didn't say anything. He just lay there and listened to Jack's breathing and felt the weight of him against his body until he finally rolled away onto his back. Minutes passed. "Mm," he said.

Jack chuckled. "Is that all I get, then? A grunt?"

"What, you want I should sing ya a song?"

"If you're taking requests, I'd like to hear 'Bei Mir Bist du Schoen.'"

D snorted. "Yer awful pleased with yerself."

Jack rolled over and tucked close to D's side, their legs intertwined, Jack's head in the hollow of D's neck where it seemed to fit so naturally. D let his arm drape across Jack's shoulders, his fingers lightly grazing the skin. "Yeah, I'm pleased. That was... damn."

"Mm," D said. "Always is," he muttered. He felt Jack smile, then he ran a hand up D's chest.

"Still can't believe you let me do this," Jack said.

"Do what?"

"You know. This. The, uh... cuddly part. I always thought you'd be one to get off, roll over and go right to sleep."

"Huh. Didn't realize you'd given it so much thought ahead a time."

"Come on. The idea of... this... crossed my mind more than once before it happened." He lifted his head. "Didn't it cross yours?"

Did more'n cross, bud. Moved right in and opened a goddamned curbside hotdog stand. "Mmm... well...."

Jack shrugged. "I won't make you say it. Still... you said I was the first man you ever... you know."

D nodded. "Yeah. Kinda."

"Kinda? You mean you wanted to before."

"Why's it matter?" D said, exasperated.

"I know who I am, D. I'm still just trying to suss you out. You didn't put up much of a fight. You couldn't have thought you were straight."

"Ain't no point. Ain't much a the me that was in who I am nowadays."

Jack chuckled. "When I figure out what that means I'm sure I'll feel enlightened." He propped his head on his hand so he could meet D's eyes. "You never thought that you might be gay?"

"Who says I'm gay, then?"

Jack arched one eyebrow. "Let's ask my ass and see what it thinks."

"Don't even hardly know what that means, gay."

"Well, it means that when two boys care about each other very much, then—"

"Shut the fuck up," D snapped. The teasing light went out of Jack's eyes, which suited D fine. That light was meant to hide Jack's insides, where he was just as confused as D was, and he didn't see the point in hiding that. "I ain't a little kid. You don't gotta patronize me."

"I didn't mean to," Jack said, quietly.

"Such a fuckin' smartass, sassin' off ta me. I could kill ya with my little finger, ya know."

Jack gaped at him, then burst out laughing. "I'm sorry," he said, choking it back and waving one hand before his face. "Just... where'd you hear that line, a Bruce Lee movie?"

D let a begrudged half-smile curl his lips. "Somethin' my handler usedta say. Kinda like an in-joke."

"You keep getting off the subject."

"Don't much like it."

"Have you had feelings for men before? Before me, I mean. That is, uh... if you have feelings. I don't mean to assume that...." Jack stammered, his face flushing. D could feel the heat of his face against his shoulder. "Didn't mean those kind of feelings, just the sex feelings, you know what I mean."

"Jack," D said. "You shush now," he said, softening his tone. He sighed, knowing he wasn't escaping this conversation. "Yeah, I had them feelins before."

"And?"

"And I don't wanna talk about it."

"Why not?"

"Jesus, you jus' gotta know everythin', don'tcha?"

"Yes."

"I said I don't wanna talk about it."

Jack was peering at him with those eyes that sometimes seemed to have the ability to see past D's defenses. "There was a man, wasn't there?"

"I jus' told ya there was."

"Did something happen? Was this in the Gulf?"

D sighed and shut his eyes. "I'm gonna say this once, I'm gonna make it quick, and I ain't gonna answer no questions, got it?" Jack nodded. "Was a guy. Knew he was givin' me the eye, tried ta pretend I wasn't givin' it back. Went out together on a recon. Hadta wait two hours fer pickup, ended up... uh, ya know. Jerkin' each other. Didn't talk about it. Next day he came at me with a knife, which I took from him with some prejudice. He got court-martialed and sent home. End a story."

Jack stared, wide-eyed. "He came at you with a knife?"

"That's what I said."

"Why?"

"I said no questions."

Jack laid back down, his arm still across D's chest. "Jesus, no wonder."

D tightened his arm around Jack's shoulders a little, seeing not the ceiling above him but that day, the bright sun, the hard metal smell of diesel fuel and desert sand, and Porter with the knife. The shock of it, first cold up the spine and then heat to the skin and blood to the muscles. The tent flap opening, first Porter's face, a flush of pleasure to see him, the nervousness of what-we-did and will-we-do-it-again, the heat in his belly, the shame of the act so much greater than the shame of mere fantasy, half wanting to kick Porter's ass and half wanting to throw him down, all of it cut short by that glint of metal. Then quick, so quick, and had to act, Porter's clumsy lunge and his mad, twirling eyes and the all-at-once knowing that Porter was crazy. Maybe had been all the while, maybe had been made so by this place. He wouldn't have been the first. Maybe had been made so by... what they'd done. And there D was (except it hadn't been D but a man named Anson, this day being the first of many in his long, slow death), the evidence, the proof, the only one who knew. So, the knife. The hands that they'd used to touch each other used then to fight, to ward off the knife, take it quick and efficient, two blows, gut and neck, standing then over his friend, out cold. Explaining to the CO, leaving out the most important bit, no sir he just come at me, no idea why, maybe the heat's just baked his brain like a damned pot roast and he's all peas-and-carrots upstairs. Not too many questions asked. Shit happened. Tough old world, tough old war.

Going back then to business as usual. Eyes front, soldier.

He sighed and shut his eyes, seeing that scene again, except now it was not Porter coming at him with a knife; it was Jack. And he stood there and did nothing, just watched as the knife was plunged into his cold, dead heart.

JACK jerked awake. It was still dark. He choked back whatever sound had been on its way up his throat—a cry, a cough, a scream, even. He held his breath and listened; D's breathing was slow and even. He relaxed, exhaling and blinking away the remnants of the nightmare. It wasn't the first. As always, it didn't stay still to be examined but fled back into his subconscious, leaving impressions in his mind like footprints. Blood, and pain, and dark laughter and death, and all of it starring himself.

You're okay. You're safe now. If only he could really believe that. He put on a brave face because he didn't have much of a choice, but in his heart of hearts he didn't really think he was safe anywhere. The men who pursued him had grown in his mind from flesh-and-blood humans into all-seeing, all-knowing monsters who would bat D aside like a troublesome insect and then Jack would be eviscerated. Slowly.

"You okay?"

Jack jumped, the low voice from behind him jerking the tenuous calm out from under him. "Jesus," he breathed.

"Sorry. Heard ya wake up."

"I'm okay."

"Yer heart's beatin' fast."

"What, do you have mutant hearing now?"

"I can see the pulse in yer throat, dumbass."

"It's nothing. Bad dream."

"Mmm." D fell silent, but Jack knew he wasn't going back to sleep. Jack felt D's hand touch his shoulder, lightly. "C'mere," D said, the word barely a puff of air. Jack turned over and was drawn into D's arms. He sighed and relaxed a little. "Better?"

"Yeah." He stayed where he was for a few moments, the steady thump of D's heart in his ear, D's hand on the back of his head. "I'm scared," he finally whispered.

"I know."

"I keep telling myself everything's okay, and I should be brave—"

"Bein' brave don't mean not bein' scared. And we don't know if everythin's okay."

"Gee, that's a comfort."

"I ain't got much comfort ta give."

Jack burrowed closer to him, sliding his arm around D's waist beneath the sheets. "Feels like enough to me."

"You got good reason ta be scared," D murmured.

Jack sighed. "You aren't scared, though. It's embarrassing."

"Who says I'm not?" Jack could feel D looking down at him.

"Well... you never act like it."

"I wouldn'ta got far in my business if I wore it on my face." His arm settled around Jack's shoulders. "I ain't scared fer myself. Haven't been in a long time. Now, I'm jus'...." He hesitated.

Jack lifted his head and looked at him. "What?"

D met his eyes, then looked away quickly. "I'm scared I won't be ready if they come fer you. I won't be fast enough, or smart enough." He shrugged and harrumphed. "Scared I won't be able ta protect you."

Jack didn't know what to say to that. He let his head rest on D's chest again. They didn't speak for a long time.

"What were you like as a kid?" Jack finally asked.

"Huh?"

"What did you like to do?"

"Hell, I dunno. Was like any other kid, I guess."

"No, I want to know."

"Know what?"

"Anything. Whatever."

D sighed, exasperated. "What's this about, huh?"

"D, I sleep with you every night and I hardly know anything about you."

"What I did as a kid ain't gonna tell ya the important stuff."

"The unimportant stuff's what I want to know, though. What was your favorite kind of candy?"

"Hmm. Hafta think about that."

"I used to love Pixie sticks."

D chuckled. "Paper tubes a delicious straight sugar, huh?"

"That's the stuff, man."

"My grandma always had chocolate-covered cherries," D said, his tone curled at the edges, like he'd surprised himself with the memory. Jack slid up a little so he could watch D's face. "Usedta love them things. The way they'd kinda bust open when ya bit 'em, and that syrupy stuff inside, then the cherry. I'd bite off one side a the shell real careful-like, so none a the syrup spilled, then suck all the gooey out, then fish out the cherry with my tongue, then I'd just have the chocolate shell left and I'd nibble on it 'til it was gone. She'd only let me have one or two so I hadta make 'em last." He glanced at Jack, who was just staring at him, his mouth open. "What?"

"That is the sexiest thing I've ever heard."

D flushed and fidgeted. "Aw, hell."

"Seriously. Ask me how much I want to go get some chocolate-covered cherries right now just so I can watch you eat them."

"Shut the fuck up," D said, but Jack could tell he was a little pleased. D always got uncomfortable when Jack told him he was sexy, or commented on his appearance.

"Hey, you're the one who had to say it all sexified like that."

"My arm's goin' ta sleep," D said, changing the subject.

Jack rolled away onto his back and held out his arm. D just looked at him. "Well? Come here."

"I don't, uh... umm—"

"What, you're too macho to be cradled in my manly embrace?"

"Ya gotta say it like that, huh? Goddamn, you 'n' yer smartass comments."

"The fact that I get snarky when I'm uncertain should no longer surprise you. Get over here. We're having intimate bed conversation and I won't do it with a foot of mattress between us."

"Shit, yer gettin' bossy." D slid over and turned into Jack's side, letting Jack embrace him. His protestations notwithstanding, the tension seemed to gradually leach from his body the longer he laid there, his arm draped across Jack's midsection.

"See? This isn't so bad."

D shook his head a little. "Nah. Feels... kinda nice." He sighed.

"Tell me about the house where you grew up."

"You writin' a biography?"

"Well, it'd be one worth reading."

"Doubt that." D shifted a little; Jack rested his cheek against the top of his head, not speaking, trying to be a sponge, a quiet receiver for whatever had to be said. "Had a treehouse out back."

"Yeah?" Jack said, smiling.

"My dad built it when I was a kid. Big old tree in the back, with the ladder-rungs nailed ta the trunk, the whole works. Spent a lotta time up there."

"You were probably one of those loner kids, weren't you?"

"And I bet you were the most popular kid on the block."

"Where was your secret place?"

"How d'ya know I had one?" D asked, lifting his head to look at Jack, one eyebrow arched.

"You did."

D shrugged and laid back down. "Was an abandoned farm 'bout a mile down the road from us. Usedta go up ta the hayloft. Smelled like summer all the time." He hesitated. His hand had begun moving slowly back and forth across Jack's chest all by itself; when he spoke again, his voice was hushed. "Usedta go there 'n' pretend I was the last survivor. Last man on Earth. Hadta build my own shelter, forage fer food, kill wild game with jus' my wits 'n' whatever I found lyin' about."

D went on, his voice going from hushed to choked. "One day I been out there fer hours 'n' hours. Pretendin' ta hunt. I caught a rabbit 'n' killed it." Jack stayed very still and quiet, resisting the urge to fidget or speak. "I didn't know," D said. "Didn't know what it meant. Thought it'd be like a game, but... couldn't take it back. Sat there with that bunny, blood comin' outta its mouth, held it on my lap... weren't no game. Was for keeps." He sighed. "I buried it. Cryin' like a goddamn girl. Went home, thought everybody'd see it on my face, what I done. But no one saw nothin'. Was like any other day. Went back the next day ta see if maybe I dreamed it, but no; bunny still dead."

Jack felt tears rising to his eyes. He pressed his lips to the top of D's head and drew him closer. He waited.

"Jack, I... I dunno how—"

"It's okay. Take your time."

"I gotta tell ya...." He trailed off again.

"I know."

"Don't... don't let go a me." This last was so quiet as to almost be inaudible.

"I won't. Not ever."

D took a deep breath and let it out. "Got married 'cause she was pregnant. Dunno why I got her that way. Jus' was what ya did. Went inta the Army. Maybe it lasted long as it did 'cause I was gone so much. Love my little girl. So sweet, she was. Firs' time she call me 'Daddy' jus' thought I'd melt away. So smart, and jus' lovin', wanted ta love on everbody, me mos' of all. Real Daddy's girl, she was. I tried ta be good ta her mamma, but... well, guess you know why she ain't never done it fer me. 'Fore too long we had nothin' ta say ta each other. I weren't no kinda husband to her, so she left me.

"She hadta support her 'n' Jill, a course. I sent her money but weren't enough. We'd been livin' in North Carolina—she moved away with Jill while I was still at Fort Bragg. She'd got a real good job workin' fer the Social Security Administration. Had her a cousin there got her an interview. So she hadta go where the office was. Fifth floor a the Murrah Federal Buildin' in Oklahoma City."

Jack sucked in a breath, his arms tightening around D reflexively. "Oh, my God."

"She was workin'. Jill down in the day care."

"Oh, Jesus, D."

D's voice was flat and uninflected. "The bombin' killed 'em both. I saw it on the news 'n' I knew right then my little girl was dead. Knew that was her mamma's buildin'. They kept tellin' me ta have some hope, might not a got her, might be okay, but I knew. And it couldn't be took back, 'cause I put her in that buildin'. If I'd been there for her 'n' her mamma, they wouldn'ta hadta move there. That happened, was like all the lights went out inside. Just waited 'round for the next thing. Buried my little girl 'n' her mamma, went back ta work only ta find out that it was some crazy Army guy done this. One a my own, fer fuck's sake. Made it even worse, somehow. Was a lotta talk goin' 'round that he had friends still in the service. Militant motherfuckers lookin' ta take us all down from the inside. 'Bout a year after the bombin' one a the higher-ups come ta me 'n' said he'd heard I was a man could get things done. Said they'd found out some major'd helped that asshole get his materials 'n' plan the bombin'. Wanted it taken care of, off the books if ya know what I mean, asked if I'd do it. Didn't even hesitate, said okay. I went and took care of it. Next day resigned my commission, and went out lookin' for the next one."

He fell silent. Jack's mind was reeling. It was almost too much to take. He had so often wondered how D had gotten into his line of work. To find that he'd been driven by grief and misplaced vengeance was both strange and oddly fitting. D was not a man controlled by his emotions. At least he wasn't now.

"I ain't never told that ta nobody," D said, sounding hollow.

"I'm so sorry, D. You've had so much tragedy in your life."

"Guess."

"But... what happened to your wife and daughter, it wasn't your fault."

D snorted. "The hell it wasn't. If we'd stayed married—"

"But she left you, right?"

"Drove her off."

"You couldn't have known."

"Don't matter." He abruptly pulled away and sat up. "Jesus, listen ta me go on. Yer probly tired."

"I'm fine. I—"

"I'm gonna go take a walk or somethin'."

"It's three a.m.!"

"I'm restless. Be okay."

"But—"

"Jack, I said I'm okay." He tried to slide away but Jack grabbed his arm and held him back.

"No, you're not. It's all right not to be." D looked back at him, blinking. "I said I wasn't letting go of you, and I'm not going to." D dropped his eyes and stared at the bedsheets. Jack sat up and put his hand on D's face, making him meet Jack's eyes. "You're not the last man on Earth. Not now."

D stared at him, his eyes misting over. Two tears spilled over his lids and slid down his cheek. Jack wiped them away with his thumbs and leaned forward until their foreheads were pressed together. He could hear D's ragged breathing; he felt another solitary tear drip onto his leg. How long had it been since this man had allowed himself an emotional release? How far could he really expect him to come back in one night?

Suddenly D drew back and grasped Jack's face in his hands, an intent expression in his wet eyes. "Why?" he demanded. "Why's it like this with us?"

Jack struggled for a good answer but came up blank. "I… I don't know."

D nodded. "Good. Me, neither." He sighed. "Ain't never been nobody like this fer me, never."

Jack smiled, a little shaky, and lifted his hands to D's face. "Me, neither." He leaned closer, his eyes flicking to D's, waiting for him to draw back as he had always done.

He didn't.

The first touch was tentative, careful. The ghost of D's lips beneath his own, not moving, still as a statue. He brushed his mouth over D's again, waiting for a response, feeling D's breath. He drew back and met his eyes, questioning. D's eyes dropped to his mouth, his hands drew Jack's face forward and this time, he didn't hesitate.

KISSING Jack wasn't what he'd expected. Not letting himself do it for this long now seemed kind of stupid… or a lot stupid. What had he been afraid of? Too intimate, too romantic, too… just too. Sex was okay, even sucking dick was okay. That was to get off. Kissing, though… that you did only because you had something to say that words didn't quite do it for. That meant feelings and messiness.

Messiness came in more forms than just kissing, though. He'd just unloaded a whole pile of messiness, hardly able to believe he was doing it even as he heard the words coming out of his mouth. All of it. Sharon, Jill, his first job, all of it tumbled out. That vault door was standing wide open now, all its secrets disgorged and seeing air for the first time in forever. And he'd opened it willingly. He'd turned the lock and taken out his most closely guarded truths and placed them in Jack's hands, because he trusted him. It was a strange feeling. He was the one who was supposed to be doing all the protecting, but the truth was that Jack made *him* feel safe.

At the moment, Jack was making him feel something else entirely. His lips were soft and full, his body was warm and firm in D's arms and it was right, so goddamned right. He ran his tongue across Jack's lips and they opened to him without hesitation. He plunged his hands into Jack's hair and dove into him, restraint leaving without a backward glance, Jack's hands grasping at his back and shoulders, pushing his tongue into D's mouth. D drew back to kiss his lips some more, Jack's stubble rough against his cheeks and chin, soft little noises coming from Jack or from himself or from both of them, he couldn't tell; he just knew they were sitting on this bed, half in each other's laps, making out like horny teenagers in the backseat of Daddy's car.

Jack pulled away, holding D's head in his hands. "What?" D said, wanting nothing more than to be kissing those lips again.

Jack grinned, his eyes glimmering in the fading moonlight. "Just... I don't know. You."

"C'mere." D pulled him close, his hands sliding down his back to cup his ass, and kissed him again. "This kissin' stuff's workin' real good fer me."

Jack chuckled against his mouth, one hand sliding between D's legs. "Hmm, I can tell," he said. "Better make up fer lost time."

"No argument here," D said, cupping one hand around the back of Jack's head, tilting into him, mouths working each other over.

"D," Jack breathed, as D kissed his way down Jack's arched neck. "What do you want?"

"Want you," D said, coming back to Jack's mouth. "Want ya so damn bad."

Jack groaned and pushed D onto his back, falling on top of him, still kissing him. D wrapped his arms and legs around him, arching his groin into Jack's. "Jesus God," Jack gasped.

"C'mere," D said, pulling Jack's mouth back to his, their groans lost into each other's mouths as they rocked together on the bed, Jack bracing himself on his elbows, D's hands gripping Jack's ass and pulling him closer and tighter, their mouths sealed together. They came in quick succession, rushing impatient toward it, no time for anything but this, this which went on as they came down, laced tight together, their kisses slow now and languid, stopping only as they fell down into sleep, lying where they'd fallen.

CHAPTER 17

JACK blinked and stretched, yawning himself awake. The sun was pretty high on the wall; it had to be after nine at least. He wasn't surprised to be alone in bed. He rolled over and checked the clock. Yep, quarter after nine.

He got up and put on his track pants and a T-shirt, then shuffled out into the kitchen, still yawning. D was lighting a burner on the stove, a mug of coffee in his hand. "Morning," Jack said.

"Mmm," D grunted. "Want some eggs? Just 'bout ta start."

"Sure, thanks." Jack bent and got out the toaster, then the bread.

"How?"

"Scrambled." Jack leaned over D to get a mug for himself out of the cupboard, catching D eyeballing him as he drew back. He smiled, getting a little lip-twitch in return.

"You, uh… okay?" he said, watching D's profile.

D glanced at him, frowning. "Yeah, why?"

"Well, you unloaded some things last night. Things you'd been carrying for a long time. I just wondered if now, you know, in the light of day…."

D turned toward him. "What's done is done. Ain't no use dwellin' on it; couldn't take it back anyhow."

That answer wasn't quite what Jack had been hoping for. "But, I…," he stammered. "Well, I guess it doesn't matter," he said, turning around to fill his mug.

He heard D sigh behind him, a world-weary sigh that practically spoke full sentences, sentences like *Jesus Christ, what've I gotten myself into?* "Jack, I ain't regrettin' that I told you them things," D said, his voice low.

Jack turned. "No?"

"No," D said, shaking his head. He took a few steps toward Jack. "Never expected it," he said, staring at the floor, his hands in the pockets of his jeans. "I thought all that shit was locked away for good, and glad for it ta be so. I never wanted ta show it ta nobody." He flicked a quick, shy glance up at Jack's face. "Not 'til now."

Jack swallowed hard. "I'm glad."

One side of D's mouth curled into a half-smile, a glint of mischief coming into his eyes. "C'mere," he murmured, reaching out and grasping Jack's upper arm. Jack came toward him willingly, still holding his mug, but didn't make a move. D's glance flicked to Jack's mouth and back up to his eyes. Jack just arched one eyebrow. *Well? What are you waiting for?* D leaned forward, hesitant, waiting to be met halfway, waiting for it to be Jack's kiss and not his, waiting for Jack to take over, which he had no intention of doing. Jack stayed where he was, watching D's face, the twitchy eyes, the flush rising to his ears. D stopped and glanced up at Jack again. He tried once more, angling his jaw forward, his tongue sneaking out to wet his lower lip, but Jack held his ground and D stalled out halfway home.

D drew back with a sigh, shaking his head. "Fuck you, ya smug bastard." He chuckled, then pulled Jack tight to him, his free hand going around the back of his neck; a grin broke over Jack's face but barely saw daylight before D's mouth was on his, hungry and demanding, his hand in Jack's hair. Jack fumbled behind him in what he hoped was the general vicinity of the countertop and let go of his coffee mug; he heard it tip over but thankfully not all the way to the floor. That hardly mattered now that both hands were free to grab big handfuls of D's T-shirt, arms wrapped around his waist, a shiver running through him at this first intimate contact outside the bedroom. Whatever this was, it was now drug out into full view, not shuttered behind closed doors where it could be written off as a fluke or a need.

D's hand was up underneath Jack's T-shirt, warm and dry. The initial rush past, their lips were meeting now in a quiet, undemanding lazy-Sunday sort of acquaintance: stroke and rub, pull and taste, smile and breathe without parting and shift into each other like drifting dunes molding beneath the wind. The touch of D's tongue stealing into his mouth, tentative to make Jack want to weep for him, rejection so harsh a master, but warm and wet and his, his to claim and draw out.

Jack sighed, wondering if he might swoon like some kind of Victorian damsel. *I could get used to this.* D drew back, his eyes averted, his flush creeping down to his cheeks now. *Like a kid stealing kisses on the porch at curfew,* Jack thought. He smiled, forgetting for a moment to school his expression and rein in his emotions; all of a sudden it zinged up his spine and exploded in his skull like a time-lapse photo of a blooming flower. Jack exhaled sharply. *Jesus. Is this what it feels like?*

He stepped out of D's arms and turned to rescue his coffee mug. "Shit, I spilled the hell out of this, didn't I?" he said, keeping his back turned while he went for the paper towels.

"Guess… start breakfast then, huh?" D said, sounding a little confused.

"Sure, sounds great."

No one spoke for a few moments; the only sounds in the kitchen were of D cooking. Jack stood at the patio door and looked out into the backyard, drinking his coffee. "Better go ta the store today," D said. "Gettin' low on… stuff." He half-swallowed this last word, letting Jack know that D had noticed that they were running low not only on coffee and bread but also on lube.

Jack took a deep breath and rejoined D by the stove. "Can we swing by a bookstore or something? I'm dying for some new reading material."

D shot him a look. "Ain't no 'we' here, bud. I'll be goin' by myself."

"Oh, you've got to be kidding me," Jack said.

"I ain't kiddin'. Too risky fer you ta be out 'n' about."

"What, you think armed assassins will be staking out Albertson's on the off chance that I'll wander through?"

"It's possible."

"No, it isn't. You're being paranoid."

"Paranoid's saved my ass more'n once. Now it'll save yers."

"D, I have got to get out of this house."

"Got the yard there out back."

"I'll just pretend I didn't hear that. I am not a house pet!"

"Great. Now yer getting pissy," D grumbled, stirring the eggs more forcefully.

"Maybe I am. We've been here a week, nothing bad's happened, you yourself say we're safe here, why shouldn't I go out?"

"Because I don't wanna push our luck, all right?" D exclaimed, banging the pan down on a cool burner. "Willya just stay here, please? Gimme a fuckin' break, Jack."

Jack's temper flared. *Oh no, he did NOT.* "Give *you* a break? Sure, why not? I've only been uprooted from my life twice now, had to abandon my career, my home, my friends and family so I could be a hunted fugitive, but I guess you need a break, huh?" He threw his mug into the sink and walked away, the frustration surprising him with its ferocity. He banged through the patio doors and stomped off into the backyard, stopping when he reached his favorite tree. He sat down with his back to its trunk.

Jesus. Get a grip. But he'd been getting and holding that grip for weeks now, and his fingers were getting slippery. He'd pushed so much of the reality of his situation far from his mind so he could concentrate on other things, like surviving, but now in this place that was starting to feel safe, it was creeping back. Likely he'd never see his parents again, or Caroline, or his friends. The coffee shop on the corner by his apartment, the cranky nurse who worked the OR intake desk.

He found himself thinking of Julia, a little girl he'd been treating for nearly two years. She'd been born with some severe jaw deformities and had required a series of surgeries to correct them so she could speak and eat normally. She was only four years old but her face was like sparkling sunshine. She knew that every trip to the hospital meant pain and discomfort, but still she hugged him when she arrived, calling him "Dr. Jacky" in her distorted speech and giggling when he tickled her. He remembered her face when she'd demonstrated to him all the new words she could say with her new jaw and how she'd been brave and hadn't cried when she realized it was time to go to surgery again, though her lip had trembled and her big brown eyes had filled with tears.

Who was caring for Julia now that he'd gone? Was that doctor holding her hand? Was he visiting her in recovery and waiting to see her eyes open? Did he care about minimizing her scarring, was he being careful with her gums so her permanent teeth could come in later? Did she remember Dr. Jacky and wonder why he wasn't taking care of her anymore? Did she feel abandoned?

Julia was just one of many patients he'd had to leave behind, whose care he had been forced to entrust to colleagues. Most of them hadn't even gotten the courtesy of a conversation with him first; things had happened just that fast.

Jack felt a tear spill over and fall down his cheek. He dashed it away with an impatient swipe of his hand. *You're alive. Be grateful.*

Jack leaned his head back against the tree trunk. He'd expected his whole life to change, but he hadn't expected to meet somebody he'd have feelings for, feelings that frankly scared the shit out of him… mostly because he was having a hard time imagining any other outcome than one in which he got his untested heart truly and thoroughly broken.

D WATCHED Jack storm out of the house, a little relieved. Jack had been Mr. Okay-With-It nearly since he'd met him, cracking wise and coaxing D out of himself to a degree he would never have believed possible, and that was bound to get old sooner or later. It was good to see him feeling it, whatever it was. It wasn't an easy thing he was doing, and it wasn't going to get any easier.

Yer not makin' it easier by fuckin' him eight ways from Sunday, neither. As if you 'n' him gonna have some kinda loving supportive relationship. Not too fuckin' likely, but ya know he's thinkin' it. Jus' gonna get him hurt in the end, and ya think he needs this shit on top a everythin' else?

He stood there leaning against the counter, stuck as a long-tailed cat in a room full of rocking chairs. Two weeks ago, he would have let Jack be and gone about his business, but it wasn't two weeks ago. Part of him was pulled out there, wanting to go to Jack and get him to talk, or maybe just….

He sighed, shutting his eyes. *Admit it, asshole. Part a you wants ta jus' go out there 'n' comfort him. Put yer arms 'round him 'n' hold him 'til he feels better, dry his tears, maybe kiss him 'til he forgets why he's upset.*

Jesus. What was he turning into? A fucking girl? One of those sensitive New Age guys who'd run their mouths for hours about their feelings without saying a single thing that made any sense?

One of those… gay guys?

Jus' let him alone, fer cryin' out loud. Would you want him bargin' in on ya when yer havin' a moment? He'll be fine, come back inside all his normal self again.

He sat at the table, his back resolutely toward the patio doors, and ate his eggs and toast. He didn't taste much of it. He made a list of things to get at the grocery store, adding items he knew Jack would like without realizing he was doing it.

He put the dishes in the dishwasher. He scrubbed the pan he'd used for the eggs. He put away the toaster and rinsed the coffeepot, and when he could stall no longer he took a deep breath and went out into the backyard.

Jack was pacing, arms crossed, eyes on the ground. D was pretty good at reading body language and everything about Jack's was saying "Fuck you, fuck me, and fuck off."

He stopped a few feet away and just waited, at a loss for what to say, or if he should say anything at all. Jack didn't acknowledge him. "Hope it ain't me's pissin' you off," D finally said, going for a little levity.

Jack glanced at him, and then shook his head. "No. Just… I guess some things are hitting me all at once, here. I'm sorry."

"Don't you fuckin' apologize, y'hear? You been through hell these past weeks, yer entitled ta some frustration. I been amazed at how calm ya been, frankly. Most folks woulda lost their fuckin' minds by now."

"Yeah, well. That's my way, isn't it? Put on a happy face, pretend it's all fine so no one else has to be bothered." He raked his hand through his hair. "Swallow it and smile. That's me in a nutshell."

"You don't gotta put on a front for me."

"No, it isn't for you. I don't know who it's for, actually. Who am I trying to please, anyway?" He kicked at the grass, his face creased with anger and frustration.

D saw what Jack was about to do before he did it, saw it in the tension of Jack's shoulders and the twist of his hips. He started forward, one hand out. "Jack, don't—" was as far as he got before Jack hauled off and punched the tree, hard.

"MotherFUCKER!" he yelled, staggering back, his bruised hand held out before him. D grabbed him from behind, holding his arms to his sides.

"Jesus, Jack! Cut that shit out!"

"Ow ow ow ow," Jack muttered, half-laughing through it. "Goddamn, I am such a fucking idiot."

"Lemme see, come on," D said. Jack held out his hand. The knuckles were scraped and bloody. "Can ya move yer fingers?" Jack wiggled his fingers, wincing a little. "Okay. Let's go wash it off." He started to walk Jack back to the house.

"That really hurt, D," Jack said.

"Yeah, I know."

"Somehow I didn't expect that. I don't get it."

"I do," D said, leading him into the bathroom and sitting him down on the toilet seat. "I've hit a lot of things. Punching bags, sparring gloves, people's faces. Hard things too, like boards and yeah, a few walls. You can know in yer head that they're hard, but when yer all riled up and ya jus' wanna punch somethin', it's like somewhere inside yer head ya secretly believe that they'll give."

Jack was nodding. "Yeah, that's it, exactly. I thought it would give."

D knelt on the bathroom rug and wiped Jack's hand with a wet towel, then some hydrogen peroxide. "Be sore fer a bit," he said.

"My own damn fault."

"Hope it made ya feel better, at least."

Jack sighed. "I don't know. I don't know what's wrong with me. I was okay, I really was. I had my shit together... well, mostly together, until...." He trailed off. D looked up and met his eyes. "Feelings come in packs, D. Let one loose and they all want to run together."

D held his gaze for a moment until it became too intense and he had to look away. He wound some gauze around Jack's hand and secured it with a butterfly clip he found in the first-aid kit. "There. All better."

"My mom used to kiss it and make it better," Jack said.

A smartass comment sprang to D's lips but he bit it back. He looked down at Jack's poor hand and felt that tug of responsibility again, and the quiet warmth of Jack's fingers in his own. He lifted the hand, bent his head and kissed the bandaged knuckles, letting his lips rest there for a moment. He felt Jack shudder, looked up and saw his eyes filling with tears, gaze haunted and far away, then he tilted forward and slid off the toilet to the floor into D's arms, folding against him like a little boy. D held him, sentinel silent.

AFTER D left for the grocery store, Jack went downstairs. The basement was finished off as a kind of rec room, with a pool table and some old couches, a stereo and a larger TV than the one upstairs. One corner held some exercise equipment; Jack had a mind to run on the treadmill for awhile and work off some nervous energy.

There were a couple of doors set into this far wall. One led to the laundry and utility space, but the other one he'd never opened. Jack stared at it, wondering why he'd never investigated this; his inherent nosiness had taken him into most of the rest of the house by now.

No time like the present. He opened the door and stepped through. On the other side was an office of sorts, with a desk and a recliner and some bookshelves. Scattered about were photos and mementos that drew Jack like a magnet, fascinated as he was by any glimpse into D's family past.

Photos of people he didn't know. Souvenirs from destinations he couldn't identify. Memories of lives he'd never heard about. He stood staring around at the detritus of this man's life and felt a surge of resentment yet again that D still held so much back from him. They shared meals and activities and could be comfortable in a bathroom together but he still didn't know where the man had come from, not really, or what his life had once been like. He shared his bed, but didn't know his name.

He picked up a photo of three blond children and held it up to the light from the window-well, his chest tightening as he recognized D in the center. He looked about ten, but it was him, no mistake. Those same brown eyes, that same nose, that same tight-lipped not-quite-smile. Jack smiled, one finger stealing out to touch the little face, blond curls blowing in a long-ago wind. "Jesus, D," he breathed. This little boy looked like he enjoyed playing Parcheesi and making his action figures mount a sneak attack on the family-room ottoman. The tragedy of all he could have been and what he had become instead was near enough to knock Jack flat.

Where had this been taken? It looked like a park, maybe a family outing, or even a vacation. D had implied that his childhood had been poor, so a vacation wasn't too likely. Jack turned the picture over and popped off the felt backing. There was a woman's spidery handwriting on the back of the photo.

June 1980, Yellowstone. Darrell, Anson, and Merle.

Jack held his breath. He blinked and looked again, but it was still there.

Anson. It clicked into place in his mind as if there'd been a fitted slot just waiting for it to pass through and fall in.

He flipped the picture back over and stared at the boy's face. "Anson," he whispered, touching the image again. He looked over his shoulder; was the name an incantation that would summon the man himself if spoken?

For long moments he stood there staring at the picture, not moving, the name echoing up and down the corridors of his mind, a mind that was so full of D—of Anson—these past weeks that his presence had squeezed out other things that had been contained.

Why hasn't he told me?

But Jack knew why. This boy was dead, as far as D was concerned. He'd killed him when he'd taken up a weapon against another human being in cold blood. That name no longer belonged to him, and D no longer thought he had any claim to the things this boy had: a family, an identity, a place in the world where he was understood and welcomed.

The temptation to be hurt by this last omission was strong, but Jack resisted. D had told him so much, and Jack knew without needing it spelled out that D hadn't told anyone else what he'd told him. His Army experiences, his first kill, his family's deaths, his guilt, his blame, his rage, his conflict. These were things that D had shut away for long years and was only now allowing out into the sunlight, but it wasn't over. He wasn't done. And until he was, that name would never be his.

Jack put the picture back in the frame, replaced the felt backing, and carefully put the frame back where he'd found it, a line bare of dust on the shelf guiding it into its place. He backed away and nodded once.

He heard the back door open. "Jack?"

"I'm coming," he said, climbing the stairs. D was putting bags of groceries on the counter. Jack went to the car and hefted the other two bags, balancing them in one arm while he grabbed a case of beer with the other. He kicked the door shut behind him and put the bags down with the other ones. "See any hit men in the produce section? Hiding amidst the arugula?"

"Real fuckin' funny, asshole," D grumped. "It's the ones ya don't see ya gotta worry 'bout."

Jack busied himself putting things away. Bread, chips, D's goddamned beef jerky, cheese, ketchup. "Did you get the—"

"Yeah. Hadta get generic; they didn't have that brand ya wanted."

Jack shrugged. "Pickles are pickles. I just get cravings for them from time to time. It's probably the salt."

D snorted. "I could say somethin' but I won't."

"No, go ahead, make the predictable pregnancy joke. I'll pretend it's funny and we can all go back to our lives."

He turned around; D was opening a beer, leaning casually against the counter, his groceries unloaded. Jack folded up one empty bag, and then peered into the other one, throwing an exaggerated pouty face in D's direction. "Huh. That's it?"

D mumbled something under his breath.

"What? Didn't quite catch that."

"I said, I ain't buyin' no chocolate-covered cherries."

"Oh, come on. You know you want to."

D shook his head like Jack was just too much to be believed. "I do not either want to, and them candies make me think a my grandmother, so it's real fuckin' weird that you turned 'em inta some kinda sex fantasy, okay? 'Cause then I get all mixed up in my head where I'm in my grandma's livin' room makin' Play-Doh french fries while you suck my dick and that's just ten kinds a wrong. Even I ain't *that* fucked up."

Jack laughed. "Not yet, you aren't." He looked at D's face, smiling, laughing with him, as open as he'd ever seen him, leaning there against the edge of the counter. Jack sobered.

Anson. His name is Anson.

D frowned. "What?"

"What what?"

"Ya jus'… got a funny look on yer face there for a second."

Jack thought a minute. "Can I ask you something?"

"Go on."

"You're… well, you're more okay than I thought you'd be. With this. Us, I mean."

"Okay in what way?" D said, crossing his arms over his chest.

"If I'd had to guess I would have thought you might be a guy who'd wail and rend his garments over having had sex with a man, protesting about how not gay he was, denying everything and making himself miserable."

D thought for a moment. "Well, it don't make too much difference when it's jus' you 'n' me here, does it?"

"It won't be just you and me here forever, though."

He looked at the floor and shuffled his feet a bit. "Don't wanna think 'bout that jus' now."

Jack took a step closer. "We'll have to think about that eventually."

"Eventually don't mean today." D met his eyes.

Jack held his gaze for several beats. *I know your name, D. I don't have to wait until you decide to tell me. I can say it right now and watch your face as you realize that I have something of yours that you didn't let me see. Then maybe I could stop waiting for you. Maybe if I called you by your name, you would be mine, as surely as I am yours.* He opened his mouth.

D spoke again, cutting him off. "Cain't think no further ahead jus' now, 'cause today I got you here and I cain't think 'bout that time comin' when I won't." He was shaking his head. "Nobody knows me but you, Jack," he said in a hoarse whisper. "Weren't nobody in here ta be known before you, and after yer gone be nobody in here again."

Jack shut his mouth, struck dumb by this unexpected confession. He couldn't think what to say, so he said nothing, just reached out and embraced him, D's arms coming around him at once.

He pressed his face into D's neck. "You were never nobody," he murmured. "Not to me, D."

His name is Anson. And he'll tell me when he's ready.

CHAPTER 18

THE sun was warm on the back of Jack's neck as he scooted forward on his knees, yanking at the weeds with boredom-fueled enthusiasm. He'd taken on the yardwork as a project to distract himself and hadn't done so half-heartedly, spending hours at a time weeding and mowing and edging and pruning, sending D on mission after mission to the nursery and Home Depot. He fervently hoped that D would get tired of running his errands and let him actually leave the house, but so far he'd made the frequent trips without comment, showing no signs of changing his mind.

As of today, they'd been in this house for one month. Jack was starting to feel alarmingly... *settled.* The life in which he and D had found themselves unlikely co-participants no longer felt balanced on the knife-edge of catastrophe; it just felt like routine. D got up early every day and did some kind of calisthenics that looked kind of like tai chi but weren't, then made coffee and sometimes breakfast. Jack would stumble out of bed around nine and usually found D at the table with the paper, though he often made himself scarce soon after Jack rose. D was not much for casual company. He was always close by, but he got antsy when they were in each other's pockets for too long.

They got groceries. They argued over whose turn it was to do the dishes. They watched mindless TV together. Sometimes they holed up in different parts of the house, other times they hovered close.

At night they would retire to what had long ago become their bedroom and go at each other for as long as they could before collapsing. Jack had discovered a reservoir of sexual need in himself that he hadn't suspected, and as for D... sometimes it seemed like he was discovering sex for the first time. Jack would often catch him with a look of amazement on his face, as if he were thinking "Holy shit, I didn't know I could do *that.*" Jack looked forward to this time, because it was only here, in their bed and in his arms, that D relaxed his guard and let Jack see him, even if it were only a small part of him.

The only place he did take Jack was to a nearby firing range. They went every few days and Jack was becoming quite handy with the guns in D's personal arsenal, although he was still not allowed to shoot the Desert Eagle. Now D was teaching him about gun handling: how to get the weapon out of a hip holster fast, how to hold it, react with it, and really be comfortable with it as an extension of his hand. Jack was finding this much harder than just learning how to point and shoot.

He tried not to ask about the scenarios that D was seeing in his head that led him to put Jack through these paces. He had a feeling he'd rather not know all the awful ways D imagined him being attacked, shot at, or otherwise interfered with.

He stretched, hoping he wasn't burning. He was wearing a strappy T-shirt, his early-summer tan all but faded away since leaving Vegas. He heard a few vertebrae crackle in his spine and decided a break was in order. He got to his feet and turned.

D was lurking in the patio door, watching him, a beer dangling forgotten from his fingers. Jack just stood there and let him watch. D set the beer bottle on the railing and crossed the yard. He gazed off into the distance for a moment, then wordlessly held out his hand, keeping his eyes averted.

Jack shucked off his gardening gloves and took D's hand, puzzled. D turned away and led him back to the house, still silent. Jack followed along, feeling a bit foolish at being led by the hand like a child at the zoo, but something in D's manner compelled his silence.

D led him straight to the bedroom, shut the door (against whom, Jack had to wonder) and only then did he turn and look at him. He stepped closer, a look of forced concentration on his face, and grasped the hem of Jack's shirt, pulling it off over his head in one swift movement. His hands ran up Jack's sweat-damp chest and then back down again to his shorts, which he had off in a few seconds. Jack stepped out of them and let D guide him to the bed, shuffling backward so he wouldn't lose eye contact.

He let himself be laid down. D's hands on him were possessive, each stroke and pull telegraphing *mine, mine, mine.* He stretched out on the bed, hands behind his head to better display himself, and watched as D stripped off his own clothes. When he was naked he met Jack's eyes again, his expression guarded.

Jack slid over to make room; D climbed onto the bed and propped up on one elbow at his side so he could look down at Jack's body. He began to touch him when looking was no longer enough, maddeningly slow on his chest, his legs, his arms, D's eyes blazing trails up and down him for his hands to follow. Jack stayed still; somehow he knew that was what was required of him just now. He lay quietly and just watched D's face. He gave so little away that Jack had had to become expert at reading small cues. The slight clench near his temple, the pull at the corners of his mouth, the sag of his eyelids: this was all he had to go on, but what he saw told him that D needed something from him right now. He just wished he'd tell him what that was.

With no warning, D left off his exploration of Jack's body and rolled into him, his mouth claiming Jack's hard and fast. Jack sucked in a sharp breath through his nose, his arms coming around D's shoulders. He wound their legs together, angling his torso toward D so they could wrap around each other. This close was just not close enough. Jack clutched what he could of D's short hair, D's weight pressing him back into the pillows. He felt D's hand between them; he tilted his hips and groaned into D's mouth as he was penetrated, D surging up over his body, pressing forward with his hips socked tight between Jack's legs, gripping D's biceps hard as he propped himself up.

D dropped his head into the crook of Jack's shoulder, still eerily silent except for the rasp of his breath, rolling and thrusting like the tide against him, Jack letting himself go pliant to take him in as far as he could, his hands on D's back. He itched to say something, *do* something. Push D over on his back and ride him until he begged for mercy, perhaps. But he didn't. He just hung on and held him, cradling him in his body, one hand going to the back of D's head.

Suddenly, D stopped and lay still on top of him. For a long moment, they just lay there breathing. D drew back and met his eyes. "Jack," he murmured, the name barely more than a puff of air.

Jack nodded. "Harder," he whispered.

D reared back on his knees, pulling Jack's hips with him to keep them connected. He hooked Jack's legs over his forearms, shut his eyes and thrust forward once, hard and deep. Jack hissed, grabbing at D's wrists. "Like that?" D breathed.

Jack was almost too shocked that D was vocalizing something having to do with their sex life to respond, but managed to nod.

D thrust forward again, his head lolling back, and then again, and again until he was pistoning fast into Jack, holding his legs up and apart, every muscle in his chest and arms standing out like carved marble. Jack was transfixed just by the sight of him.

Before too long Jack's head was lolling on the pillow, helpless grunts all the sounds he could muster; D took a few deliberate, shallow strokes right over Jack's most sensitive spot and he arced as if electrocuted, coming with a strangled cry and feeling D follow him seconds later in typical silence. He lay there spent, gasping and watching his own chest vibrate with his heartbeat. D pulled out and turned partly away to sit on the edge of the bed, his legs over the side, his shoulders sagging. Jack felt like a limp dishrag, aching and hollow in all the right ways, shaking with adrenaline rush.

He came back into himself little by little until he'd regained enough awareness to be concerned that D was sitting there like he'd just lost a puppy. He reached out and touched his thigh. "Hey. What's up?"

D sighed. "Sorry, doc."

"Sorry? Why?"

D glanced at him quickly. "Went at ya kinda hard there."

"You don't have to apologize for giving me what I asked for."

He sighed again, shaking his head. "It's jus'...."

Jack sat up and folded his legs under him. "What?"

"Saw you out there in the garden. Looked so damn... fine," he said, quietly. "Was like I hadta have ya, right then. Bubbled up like... I dunno, puke or somethin'."

Jack chuckled. "You sure have a way with words, D."

D turned halfway around and looked at him. "Never wanted nobody like I want you," he said, swallowing hard. "And now it's... I'm...." He trailed off, his eyes drifting toward the floor.

Jack reached out and put a hand on his arm. "You're what?"

"I'm queer, ain't I?"

Jack smiled. "D, I have known a lot of men in my time, queer and straight, and I think I can state with some confidence that you are as gay as a spring parade."

D laughed, looking surprised at himself. "Shit."

Jack scooted up close behind him, linking his arms around D's shoulders from behind and resting his chin on his shoulder. "Hey. It isn't as bad as all that."

"A course not. I'm jus' a fuckin' gay hit man. Sounds like a setup fer a bad joke."

"You're not a hit man anymore," Jack said.

D's hand came up to rest on Jack's forearm. "No, I ain't." He sighed, leaning his temple against Jack's, then turned his head to the side, burrowing for Jack's lips with a soft grunt. Jack craned his neck to meet D's mouth, soft kisses and slow breaths, a gentleness in D's touch that still felt like a surprise after all this time.

D twisted around and drew Jack to him again, pushing him down onto his back and stretching out next to him; he rolled over and pulled Jack on top of him. Jack settled against him, their mouths opening to each other, warm richness against his tongue and the smell of D and himself, that toasty-skin smell D had found so alluring, D's hands on his back and then on his ass, his legs parting so Jack slid snug between them. He felt D's hips tilting....

Jack drew back, blinking. D was looking back at him, face tight, eyes shuttered. He turned his head to the side and closed his eyes. Jack sagged into his arms, exhaling, his mouth against D's ear. "You want that?" he whispered. He felt D's short, shallow nod, his zigzag breaths like a scared rabbit against Jack's chest, the pulse in his throat speeding. "You want me inside you?" Jack breathed, less words and more lips around air, wanting to make sure. That quick nod again. *Don't make me say it; just do it. Let me pretend I'm not asking for it.*

Jack dragged D's mouth back to his to occupy himself while he pulled his brain back into coherence, hard rough kisses like fighting, D's muscles tense like rope. Jack kissed his mouth, his face, his neck. It had been a long time since he'd topped for a man who'd never bottomed. The thought of doing this with D was both unbearably exciting and nerve-wracking. "You gotta relax," he murmured. "Turn over."

D did as Jack asked and Jack rose above him, straddling his legs, and laid hands on him in long, smooth strokes like raking a Zen garden, lines and curves carved into the sand and into D's flesh. He bent and kissed the nape of D's neck then pressed the heels of his hands hard into the large muscles of his shoulders, his back, his arms, feeling the tension leave his body a little at a time. The ridges of scars passed beneath his palms. A knife wound here, some road rash there, markers in the haunted moor of D's body, what it had done and what had been done to it.

Jack leaned over so more of his chest was pressed to D's back, his hands working over D's outstretched arms, the flesh now loose and pliant. "Turn on your side," he murmured. D hitched his hip beneath and turned; Jack settled behind him, one hand stroking southward around D's ass, his fingers delving between the cheeks. He retrieved the lube and squirted some into his hand before returning to press close again, mouth on D's neck and chest to back, guiding D's breathing with his own.

He wrapped both arms around D from behind and just held him for a moment, forcing down some performance anxiety. *God, I can't believe he wants this. I have to make it good for him, I have to.*

He didn't need to be told that face-to-face would not be the best way for the first time. He gently eased D onto his stomach and crawled around behind him, grasping his hips in his hands. D let Jack pull him to his knees, but he kept his shoulders and face down close to the bed, crossing his arms and resting his forehead on them like he was hiding. Jack hesitated.

"You don't have to do this," he murmured.

D pressed back against him, his head turning slightly.

Jack nodded. "Okay." He applied more lube to himself and pressed up close. D exhaled when he felt it, the top of his head pressed to the bed, and Jack slid slowly inside. "Jesus," he breathed, watching D's body take him in. D was silent but still relaxed. When he was fully sheathed he just stayed still, eyes shut, hands stroking D's flanks and concentrating on not losing it right then and there.

He withdrew and surged again, D pushing back against him, his shoulders rising off the bed and his arms bracing his torso up, his head hanging down. Jack stared at the sheen of sweat shining on D's back as he thrust, gently at first, smooth and steady. "Shit," D groaned. Jack grasped his shoulder in one hand and snapped his hips harder, D's responses urging him on faster than he would have gone on his own.

Abruptly, D pushed himself upright, his back against Jack's chest, his hips settling back into Jack's lap as he fitted his knees between D's spread thighs. Jack wrapped his arms around D's chest from behind, their hips bucking and lunging in concert like they were riding tandem. D's hands reached back and seized Jack's hips, pulling him in tighter, his head lolling back into the hollow of Jack's shoulder. Jack slid one hand down D's taut abdomen and grasped him, heavy and hard in Jack's hand. D clenched around him in a way that made Jack's eyes go a bit crossed. "Jack...," D gasped. "Fuck... gonna come...." Jack stroked him until he came over Jack's hand, sagging forward. Jack held him fast around the waist, resting his cheek against D's spine, all control lost until he toppled over the edge, spilling into D's body with a strangled cry.

They stayed like that, sitting folded together on their knees, breathing hard and coming back to the world. Jack pressed his forehead and then his lips to D's back.

D was shaking.

Jack pulled out, slowly, and crawled around in front of him. He encircled him in his arms and drew them both down onto the bed, pulling the blanket up around their hips. D just lay there against Jack's chest, his arms tucked around his own stomach.

Jack said nothing. He just held him, one hand stroking the back of his head, where his brutally short haircut was giving way to soft curls. Jack was too overwhelmed to muster the ability to speak. In the haze of post-coital euphoria he wanted to tell D that he loved him, that he'd never loved anyone else, that he'd die for him or kill for him or whatever else people said when they didn't think about it first, that he didn't care what happened to him or the trial or his life as long as they could be together.

So he shut his eyes and let himself fall asleep before any words could escape, words that shouldn't be said, not now and maybe not ever.

THE nightmare came again, fucking sneaky bastard of a vision behind his eyeballs, blood and death, his little girl screaming, buried under the rubble, calling for her daddy to come save her. D tossed aside debris like it weighed nothing but more kept falling, her voice getting farther away, and then there was a hand on his arm, a hand he knew, and he turned to see Jack beckoning him away.

No, I gotta find Jill.

Jack's smile like peace on the water. *It's okay, Jill's safe. Come with me.*

No... but my baby... she's out there hurt 'n' scared....

She's waiting for you back here.

Jack took his hand and led him from the ruins but there was no way out. They wandered and wandered, D hearing Jill's cries still, clapping his hands to his ears, but it didn't stop the sound. Nothing stopped it.

Cain't ya hear it? I gotta help her! She's cryin' fer me!

Hear what? Jack's face blank. *I don't hear anything.*

Ya gotta hear her! It's so loud... it's getting louder....

I can make it stop.

Jack's lips on his and all is quiet, all is peace, but now there are faces rising from the grass, grass like a meadow with trees and the faces are all around him....

D jerked awake, hearing his own moans as they died out, hands on him shaking him. "Wha... the fuck...."

Jack was leaning over him. "It's okay," he said, sounding eerily as he had in the dream. "You were having another nightmare."

D sagged back against the cushions. *Motherfucker.* "Shit," he muttered, swiping at his damp brow. Jack was stroking his belly like you'd gentle a horse. "M'okay," he grunted.

"Jill again?" Jack said. D looked over at him. Jack shrugged. "You were saying her name, like you always do."

D nodded. "Same as always." He sighed. "I wish it'd stop. Sorry if it's botherin' you. Cain't be fun ta keep getting woke up by my damn nightmares."

Jack said nothing, just kept making slow circles with his hand. D looked up at him and saw tears in his eyes. "Jack... what?"

He shook his head. "It's nothing."

"C'mon, what?"

Jack met his eyes. "It's just... it was different this time."

"It was?"

"Usually you thrash around, and call for Jill, and sometimes you cry a little."

"And?"

Jack slid closer and laid his hand on D's face. "This time, after you said Jill's name...." He hesitated, his jaw working. "You called for me."

D said nothing. The look on Jack's face was too much for him. He just let Jack snuggle close to him and keep his illusions, illusions he wished he could share.

"D?" Jack said, after a long pause.

"Hmm?"

"Will you do something for me?"

"What?"

"Teach me to fight."

JACK was bouncing on the balls of his feet in the backyard, jabbing at the air like a boxer. D shook his head as he set out the pads he'd gotten at the sporting-goods store that morning. "Okay, Sugar Ray. We ain't takin' corners here." He began buckling himself into the body pads.

"You told me once what kind of fighting you use. Mango something?"

D laughed. "Krav *Maga.*"

"What's that mean?"

"It's Hebrew for 'close contact.' It's an Israeli fighting style. Them Israelis don't fuck around. I guess a couple thousand years a livin' in a war zone'll do that to ya."

"So how do I start? You going to teach me some fancy moves?"

"There aren't any."

Jack stopped bouncing and frowned. "What do you mean, there aren't any?"

"No forms, no choreographed moves. This ain't a sport, like karate or judo. It's survival. And it's somethin' different for everybody who learns it."

Jack was looking a little dubious. "Oh," he said.

"This ain't sportsmanlike, Jack. Three basic principles. One, don't care about how much ya hurt the other guy. Two, cause as much damage as possible and run, and three, don't drag it out: do what you gotta do and get gone. Ya grab whatever's handy, ya take the initiative away from whoever's on ya, and ya turn the fight on yer attacker as quick as ya can."

"But… what do I *do?*"

"Whaddya think? Punch, kick, poke, pull. Whatever you can think of. Go for the eyes, the crotch, wherever's the most sensitive."

"That's fighting dirty, isn't it?"

D straightened up. "You get that notion outta yer head right now, ya hear? That's a buncha honor-soaked bullshit from them Eastern fightin' forms. I ain't sayin' they're bad, or worthless, but they're clean-and-tidy sportsman's fightin'. The quickest way ta get dead in real life is ta worry 'bout fightin' 'fair,'" he said, making air quotes with his fingers. "The only dirty thing you can do in a fight is let yerself get killed or hurt. All this assumes the other guy's wantin' you dead. You wanta not be dead? You better do whatever you gotta do ta make *him* dead, or at least hurt bad enough that he cain't get ya. You wanna learn pretty moves and high kicks and worry 'bout yer honor? Go join a dojo. You wanna learn how not ta get dead? That, I can teach ya."

Jack sighed. "This isn't what I expected."

"That's 'cause ya watched too many movies growin' up. Honor's great, fair's all well 'n' good, and if ya let that get in yer way when yer fightin' fer yer life, you'll be a real honorable corpse."

"Yeah, I guess I get that, but… how do I… I mean, what do I do?"

D sighed. "Jack, ya got the same ideas in yer head every other person gets when they first learn ta fight. You don't need no fancy ballet moves or special precision ways ta lift yer fuckin' leg or no particular way ta position yer damn elbow. Jus' react. Defend, then attack. Jus' fuckin' have at it."

"And… that's it?"

He nodded. "That's it."

"But that sounds so… simple."

"Well, if I'm gonna teach ya, it's my job ta make it not simple until ya feel like ya know what yer doin'." D buckled the last pads in place over his shins. "Now that I look like the fuckin' Michelin tire man, you ready ta kick my ass?"

Jack smirked. "I can think of one or two things I'd rather do to it, but yeah."

D felt himself flush. "All right, smartass. We'll see how that mouth a yers is doing in an hour or so."

JACK was drenched in sweat, but he thought he was getting it.

The first time had been… humiliating. D had even warned him. "I'm gonna come at ya," he'd said. And he'd made what even Jack could see was a clumsy, lumbering near-slow-motion lunge… and Jack had still skittered out of the way and backed off like a scared kitten. D had just hauled him off the ground and told him to try it again. Jack didn't know whether to be happy that he wasn't mocking him or disturbed that D wasn't surprised by his wimpiness.

Now, Jack braced himself and tried to tell his brain to react, not avoid. D swung an arm toward him and Jack grabbed it blindly, staggering a little with the force behind it. He saw that this left D's side open, so he flailed a leg out and kicked him in the kidneys. D doubled over and Jack yanked on his arm as hard as he could, bringing him down and around, then he punched his chest and pushed him down on the ground. "Ow!" he said, shaking out his hand.

D got up. "That… wasn't too bad," he said.

"That hurt!"

"You'll get the hang of it."

"You were going easy on me."

"What, you want I oughta turn it up to eleven on your first day?"

Jack sighed, chagrined. "No, I guess not."

D was unbuckling his body pads. "That's enough fightin' fer now."

Jack nodded. "I'm exhausted."

"Yer gonna be real fuckin' sore too."

"Great."

D paused and looked at him, cocking his head. "Hmm."

"What? Oh god, what are you going to make me do now?"

"Nah, jus thinkin'… maybe can help ya with the sore part."

"Oh yeah?" That sounded promising.

"Give ya a rubdown or somethin'."

Jack grinned. "Oh yeah?" he repeated, giving the words a flirty curl this time.

D shook a finger at him. "Don't get cute. Purely therapeutic, a course."

Jack sobered, nodding. "Of course. Therapeutic. You got it."

Out of the body pads now, D stepped closer, shaking his head and smirking. "Damn doctors," he muttered, then put his hand behind Jack's neck and pulled him in for a brief, hard kiss before continuing into the house.

D PULLED the car into a vacant parking lot and took out his cell phone. Had to make this brief; Jack wouldn't buy that it took him half an hour to run out for ice cream. Plus he'd be expected back for *CSI*.

He dialed the number and waited. "Churchill."

"Reportin' in as ordered," he said, snarling over the last two words.

He heard Churchill sigh. "You know, it's been a month. You could ease up on the attitude a little."

"Jack already call ya? He said he was gonna do it tonight."

"Yeah, just got off the phone with him. He said everything's calm."

"Yep. Ain't seen shit."

"You almost sound disappointed."

"Fuck, no."

"Well, if you're missing the excitement, I have some news for you."

D sat up straighter. "Trial date?"

"Yeah. Two weeks from Monday."

Shit. "That's kinda… fast, ain't it?"

"The prosecutors are hauling ass on this one. Jack's not the only witness, and the faster they can get to trial the less chance one of the others will turn up dead. You'll need to be in Baltimore on the twenty-third."

"We'll have to leave in a week, then. Take better part of a week ta drive it."

"We could arrange secure transport by air."

"No. Any secured transport takin' off or comin' inta town might be spotted, and I cain't be seen ta be helpin' him. Fact, we'll hafta arrange fer you guys ta pick him up outside a town, like in Frederick or Annapolis, and let me come inta town on my own so he ain't seen ta be in nobody's company."

"Good idea."

"You shoulda thought a that," D said, sharply. He was trusting Jack's safety to this man, to some degree, and the fact that he wasn't anticipating these kinds of concerns wasn't reassuring.

"And you're too damn paranoid."

"It's got us this far, ain't it?"

Churchill was quiet for a moment. "Yeah, it has. Listen, I want you to know that I do appreciate what you're doing for Jack. We all do. Frankly, we're not prepared to deal with the kinds of threats that have come up in this case."

"I know. That's why I exist. 'Cause y'all ain't prepared."

"I've spoken to your contact at the Bureau. He says your assistance has saved dozens of lives."

D sighed, letting his head fall back against the headrest. "Drop in the fuckin' bucket."

"He's hoping you'll come work for them full time... after."

"After what?"

"After Jack's testimony and he's settled in his new identity. I mean, you can't continue as a freelancer."

"That's for fuckin' sure."

"Stan's been talking to his superiors about creating a position for you."

"Well, that's real considerate a him ta do without consultin' me."

"You saying you wouldn't want it?"

"I'm gonna have a shitload a stuff a my own ta deal with, ya know. Whoever it was put me up ta do Jack's murder still wants me dead. Besides, I uh... got some plans fer the brothers once the trial's over."

"They'll be in jail."

"Yeah, well I'll believe that when I see it. Even if they are, it ain't jus' them ya gotta worry about."

"What are you thinking?"

D sighed. "I got no intention a lettin' Jack give up his name and his career. I aim ta make sure he can keep his name, his life, and still be safe."

"D, there's no way... I can't hear what I think you're saying."

"You don't know what I'm sayin'. You don't know nothin'. Now listen. The second Jack's seen in Baltimore the hits are gonna start flyin' around fast 'n' furious. You keep an eye out for Petros. You got vitals on him?"

"Yeah, he's in the Bureau database."

"You look real hard fer him. Arrest him fer anythin' ya can think of. Jaywalkin' if ya hafta. Get him off them fuckin' streets because he will be their final solution if nobody else gets ta Jack."

"What'll you be doing?"

"You let me worry about the other hits. I still got connections, and a few other identities I can whip out."

Churchill hesitated. "This is really personal for you now, isn't it?"

D fiddled with his keychain. "Yeah."

Another silence that felt like questions that weren't being voiced. "Well... I told Jack about the trial date. He still doesn't know you're talking to me?"

"No."

"What reason is there to keep that from him?"

"Because we're gonna hafta separate here pretty soon, and he'll be with you. We're gonna hafta make a clean break. He'll be under yer protection then, and he cain't think I'm still pullin' the strings."

"You *aren't.*"

D chuckled. "You don't even think there *are* strings, do ya?" He hung up and sat for a moment, thinking.

He jumped several inches when the phone rang in his hand. He looked at it, expecting to see that it was Jack, but the number was unknown. A shrill squeal of fear went up his spine. "Hello?"

"Calling phone sex lines again?"

D blew air through his teeth, his relief at hearing that digitally masked voice hitting hard. "Jesus fucking Christ, you scared the shit outta me."

"I was waiting until you were off the phone."

D sat straight up, looking all around. *X could see him.* He could not see anyone, or much of anything at all. It was pitch black out. "Where the fuck are you?"

"Nearby."

"Now yer creepin' me out."

"Sorry. You know how it is."

"You been here the whole time?"

"No. I've popped in a couple of times a week to check up on you. Jack's getting pretty good at the handfighting, isn't he?"

D shut his eyes, shuddering at the thought of being observed at their private hideaway, even if it was by a friend. "You gotta spy on us like that?"

"Better me than Petros."

"He ain't found us, has he?"

"No. He thinks you're still in Nevada somewhere. The brothers found out Jack had fled Vegas and he tracked you guys to the cabin. His boys tore it apart."

D sighed. "Shit. That belonged ta Jack's father-in-law."

"Don't worry; I covered it. Faked an electrical fire and burned it to the ground. Mr. Hapscomb will collect a tidy insurance settlement and be none the wiser."

D felt surprisingly melancholy at the thought of their idyllic cabin on the lake, where he'd first touched Jack, a smoking ruin of cinders. "Well... thanks, I guess."

"I do what I can."

"We'll be leavin' for Baltimore next week."

"I know."

"Shit, were you listenin' in?"

"Churchill's a good guy. You can trust him."

"You know him?" D asked, perking up at this clue to X's identity. If he knew Churchill, perhaps he, too, worked in some government chop shop.

"In a way."

"Look, I gotta get home. Don't wanna leave Jack fer too long."

"D... watch yourself."

"Always do."

"This is a new situation for you."

"Avoidin' crazed killers ain't no new situation."

"It is when you're in love with the man they're hunting."

D sat stock still for several beats, his heart thudding against his chest. "Who says I'm—"

"You aren't fooling me, you know."

D shut his eyes. "Son of a bitch," he drawled.

"I have a feeling we might meet face-to-face soon, D."

"Yeah, same here."

"And it will probably not be under the best of circumstances."

"No. But listen… you owe me some kinda debt, and I ain't never been sure what that is, but it's just there, right?"

"Yes."

"Then…." He sighed. "If somethin' happens ta me, will ya…." He trailed off.

"I'll protect Jack if you can't, D."

D sagged against the car door. "Yeah. Thanks."

"Have a safe trip."

"Feels like goin' ta my damn execution."

"Into the lion's den."

"Nah, not that. 'Cause… well…."

Silence. "I know. But you'll see him again."

CHAPTER 19

D HESITATED outside the door that led into the house from the garage. *Remember, ya don't know 'bout the trial date. Let him tell ya and don't forget t'act surprised.* He nodded to himself and went in.

"Hey," he heard Jack say. "What took you so long?"

"I, uh...."

"Well, hurry up. *CSI*'s starting."

D shucked off his jacket and went into the living room. Jack was sprawled out full-length on the couch, arms crossed over his chest and the remote clenched in one hand like a sword before a duel, his face turned toward the TV. D lifted up Jack's feet and sat at the other end, resettling them on his lap once he did so. "You call Churchill?" he asked, hoping his tone sounded neutral.

Jack said nothing, just kept his eyes on the TV, his face stony.

"Jack? Ya hear me?"

He sighed, then muted the TV and looked over at him. "Yeah, I called him."

"And?"

Jack rubbed at his eyes with one hand. "And he says the trial starts in two weeks."

D let a few beats pass in silence. "Oh."

"Yeah."

"Well... then we gotta leave in a week."

"Yeah." Jack turned his head back toward the TV but didn't turn the sound back on. "I ought to be glad," he said, quietly.

"Glad?"

"To be getting it over with. To have this trial start so it can finish and I can get my new identity and try to move on."

"Yer sayin' yer not glad?" Jack just shook his head. "Why not?"

At this, Jack looked at D with a cocked eyebrow. "What, are you fishing for compliments? You know damn well why not."

D just grunted, staring at the silent TV screen with his hand cupping Jack's calf where it lay across his thighs. "Best thing fer you is ta get yer testimony over then getcha gone, and good."

Jack just lay there, blinking. "You could pretend to at least be a *little* sorry," he said, his voice rough.

D stared at his profile, silvered by the pale glow of the TV. He toed off his shoes and brought his legs up, then stretched out on the sofa, tucking his body between Jack and the cushions. Jack said nothing, but scooted forward a little to make room. D wrapped his arm around Jack's waist and slipped his hand under his shirt so it rested on Jack's warm belly. He slotted his other arm above Jack's head, his fingers lacing through Jack's hair. He sighed and let his eyes fall closed, knowing that he couldn't tell Jack what he wanted to hear.

He pressed his mouth into the crook of Jack's neck. "Ya think I won't be sorry?" he murmured, his hand stroking Jack's stomach and dipping lower, his fingers sliding beneath the waistband of Jack's jeans. "Huh?" He had Jack's jeans open now. Jack kept quiet, but his breathing quickened as D stroked him, his hips making shallow thrusts into D's hand. D wrapped his other arm around Jack's shoulders, holding his chest close against his own.

Jack reached back and shoved his hand between them to cup D through his jeans, then grabbed at his own and pulled them down. D left off stroking Jack and quickly yanked his zipper down. They didn't have any lube so he just slipped between Jack's legs. He wet his palm and took Jack in hand again. "Think I ain't sorry?" he hissed into Jack's ear. "Show you sorry." He barely knew what he was saying; Jack was writhing against him and squeezing him with his thighs. "Fuckin' sorry...." Jack reached back and grabbed a handful of D's ass, his head arched back into D's shoulder, the remote falling forgotten to the carpet with a muffled thump.

A few minutes of thrusting and stroking later and they were both coming with swallowed cries. Jack lay still for a moment, then sat up. "Shit," he muttered, looking down at himself. He stood up, holding his jeans around his waist. He sighed and glanced down at the couch where D was still lying there. "Yeah, I'll bet you're sorry," he said. "Sorry to lose a warm place to stick your dick." He stalked off to the bathroom.

D just lay there as the shower started up, staring at the featureless popcorn ceiling, feeling the trial date rushing toward him like a freight train.

one week later...

PACKING didn't take long. Clothes, toiletries, some snacks for the road, a cooler full of bottled water and ginger ale for D.

All Jack wanted was one sign. One indication that this departure was as painful for D as it was for him. All week he'd waited for it. Now, he had little choice but to conclude that this departure simply *wasn't* as painful for D as it was for him.

He couldn't have misread everything. He couldn't be *that* wrong-headed. D *did* have feelings for him. What kind of feeling was less clear, but there was something. There had to be.

He's shutting himself off so he won't be distracted by it, he told himself. *And you shouldn't be surprised. He dealt with all those years of killing by detaching from his emotions. No wonder he's doing it again now.* But then he thought he might be flattering himself that D's feelings for him were such that the prospect of separation was on a level with committing murder, and enough to make him retreat behind the emotional barriers he'd spent years building around himself.

They'd have the road, this cross-country trip they had to make by car for security, and then... that'd be it, probably. D would hand Jack over to Churchill in Frederick, Jack would testify and go into Witsec, and he'd likely never see D again. The thought of it was almost enough to make him say *Screw the trial; let's just disappear.*

On top of everything else, D was acting shifty. Ducking off for private cell-phone conversations, probably thinking that Jack didn't notice. Keeping his phone on him at all times and furtively checking for text messages. Stepping up the amount of gun and hand-to-hand practice they were doing together, not to mention the amount he did by himself.

He's getting ready for something. Jack sat on the front porch, waiting for D to come out with the last of the metal briefcases they'd retrieved from that bunker in Arizona so long ago. *Yeah, he's getting ready to run from whoever set him up for all this. Probably be on the run for the rest of his life. You may be facing testifying and losing your identity, but once he leaves you, D has a whole new set of problems to deal with.*

Jack hated to think of D like that. Hunted, hiding, looking over his shoulder, always wondering, never relaxing. D was the hunter, not the prey. He couldn't help but feel responsible. *Wasn't your fault somebody set him up. You were just the means to their end. The end of D.*

As much as he hated to think of D on the run, the thought of him being caught was too awful to even hold in his mind for very long. He saw in his mind's eye D dead on the ground, shot or tortured or beaten to death, and he felt sick to his stomach. What made it worse was knowing how profoundly helpless he was to do anything about it.

Since that night on the couch when they'd gotten the trial date, their physical relationship had been strained. Jack could still feel D's breath on his neck as he growled "think I won't be sorry" while he humped Jack roughly, demonstrating just what he'd be sorry to lose. Jack and D had had sex many times now, but that had been the first time Jack had felt used.

Since then, the bedroom thing had just not been working. D's close-mouthed stoicism was back in force and it wasn't conducive to good sex, and Jack's dejection over their looming departure made everything seem hopeless and doomed. Two of the nights since they'd just slept side by side, not touching. This morning, the last in this house that had started to feel so much like theirs, had begun with D leaping out of bed without a word and Jack lying there trying not to feel abandoned.

D came out of the house with a cigarette clamped between his lips, his mirrored sunglasses on his face, the last aluminum briefcase in his hand. Jack saw with vague dismay that D had also shaved his head back to the quarter-inch of stubble he'd had when they first met. "Let's go," he said, going to the car and putting the case in the trunk. Jack got up, looking around. *That's it? Just, "Let's go?" Not one comment about leaving our house, not one backward glance, nothing?* D looked at him from where he stood by the driver's side. "Lock up, will ya?"

Guess that's it. Jack tugged the door shut and checked it; it was locked. He slung his jacket over his shoulder and went to the car. They got in their respective doors and put on their seat belts. D started up the car and backed out of the driveway, and then they were gone.

Jack watched out the window as the house receded from view until he couldn't see it anymore. He crossed his arms over his chest and faced forward. *No use looking back. At least, that's what he'd say. If he were saying anything at all.*

HE'D thought that driving for four days straight with D at his most D-like would be excruciating, but it was surprisingly easy. They sat side by side staring out the windshield, not talking. Jack spent a lot of the trip listening to audio books on his iPod and watching the scenery scroll by out the passenger-side window. He kept waiting for D to ask him to take a driving shift, but he never did.

Each night they stopped at a remote motel and paid cash. Salt Lake City, then North Platte, Nebraska, then Chicago. Too tired to do much more than swallow some fast food and shower, they slept in the same bed, more out of habit than anything else, it seemed. Jack waited for D to make a move, but he didn't. He debated making one himself, but couldn't quite work himself around to it.

The second night, at the motel in Nebraska, Jack woke up in the middle of the night to find that in his sleep, D had rolled close to him and wrapped him up in his arms tight enough that Jack could barely move. He lay quietly, sweating from D's body heat, until D grunted in his sleep and turned over, releasing him and rolling away.

And finally, Frederick. Last stop.

They rolled into their last nondescript motel. D went to the office to get their key, as he always did, while Jack got their bags from the backseat.

They moved the aluminum briefcase into the room with them, locked and chained the door, and sat down, each on their own separate beds.

Jack took out his cell phone and called Churchill. "I'm here in Frederick."

"Good. Tell me where you're staying and I'll come get you in the morning."

Jack glanced at D, who wasn't supposed to exist as far as Churchill knew. "Why don't I just meet you someplace?"

"All right. Um… meet me in Baker Park, at the corner of Church and North Bentz. You got that?"

"Yeah. Nine?"

"That'll be fine. Trial starts Monday, so we'll have the weekend for the prosecutors to prep you, which they're damn mad they've had to wait until now to do."

"Oh, they're damn mad, are they? I'm the one with hired killers on his ass here."

"I know. It's taken extraordinary restraint on my part not to point that out to them." Churchill sighed. "You be careful."

"I will." Jack hung up. D had moved to the junky little motel room table, his sunglasses clamped on his face and a cigarette between his lips, staring out at the parking lot. Jack stood up and paced off a few steps in each direction, about as far as he could go in the confines of the small room. "So I'm going to meet Churchill tomorrow morning," he said, as if D hadn't been listening in to his half of the conversation.

"Mm."

"They'll take me into Baltimore."

"Mm."

"And that'll be that."

D just nodded.

Jack felt tears pricking the corners of his eyes and blinked hard. "That's it, then? That's all you have to say to me?"

He saw D's shoulders rise and fall in a quiet sigh. "Whaddya want me ta say?"

"Oh, I don't know. I guess nothing. I guess that's all I can expect from you. I guess that's all you have to give me. Nothing."

D stared and stared out that window. "Told ya that's all I had."

"But it wasn't. You had more, and don't you sit there and tell me you didn't. Don't you *tell me* that it all meant nothing to you!" Jack found himself shouting without realizing he'd started.

D stood up and whipped off the sunglasses. "What the fuck ya want from me, Jack?" His eyes were angry and challenging, but Jack wasn't impressed.

"Nothing. I don't want a goddamn thing from you, D. I just want to get out of here so I can start trying to forget you." He stomped across the room to the door.

"Don't go out there," D said. "Might be dangerous."

Jack rounded on him. "What the fuck do you care, anyway?" He stepped outside and slammed the door behind him, got in the car and drove away with no thought in his mind as to where he might be going.

JACK didn't return to the motel until nearly midnight. He'd found a Denny's a few blocks away and had sat in a corner booth drinking coffee and eating pancakes, because pancakes sounded good and he wanted them, dammit. The waitress didn't ask him any questions as he continued to sit there hour after hour, sucking down coffee and staring into space.

It's better this way. Make a clean break. Don't muddle things up with last-minute declarations or some kind of half-assed attempt to wring a promise out of him that's clearly not forthcoming. Let it die, let it be what it was, take your memories and run, and try not to think about it. Accept what he's been able to give you, don't ask for or expect anything more, and just be very glad that you never told him how you really feel.

And how do you really feel?

Like I'll never recover. Like I'll never draw another breath without half of it being a wish for him.

He pulled up in front of their room and shut off the engine. The window was dark, but he knew that D wasn't asleep. Still, he tried to be quiet as he unlocked the door and entered, just in case.

He shut the door behind him and leaned back against it. D was sitting on the bed nearest the door, fully clothed, only his sunglasses off, his elbows resting on his knees as he smoked what smelled like his hundredth cigarette. He didn't look up as Jack entered. For a long moment they both stayed where they were, not speaking.

"You tryin' ta punish me fer somethin'?" D finally growled, his voice rough with cigarette smoke.

Jack shook his head. "I can't punish you for who you are."

"You been gone a long fuckin' time."

"Had some things to think about."

"Like what?" He lit another cigarette.

Jack sighed. "Like how I've been expecting a lot from you, more than you could give. It's just that the way you were in Redding... I don't know. Maybe it got my hopes up too much."

D shook his head a little. "What is it yer hopin' for, Jack?"

"Oh, nothing much. Stupid things like you and me in a house with a dog and a vegetable garden, and Sunday mornings in bed with coffee and the paper."

D was silent for a long time. "Jus' 'cause somethin' ain't possible don't make it stupid," he finally said, quietly. "And I shouldn't a... well, I shoulda been more careful. Don't know how I let it go as far's it did."

"Are you sorry?"

He looked up and met Jack's eyes for the first time, glittering in the dimness. "I ain't said that."

Jack nodded, breaking D's gaze to look down at his shoes. "I'm going to get up early and head out. I'll call a cab so you can have the car."

"All right."

"Look... let's just leave it there, okay? I don't know if I can take saying goodbye to you, D." D said nothing, cigarette dangling limply, his hands clasped loose between his knees. "So I'll try not to wake you, and if I do, just... pretend to be asleep until I'm gone." D wordlessly stubbed out his cigarette in the ashtray at his side. "Just let me go, all right?" Still no response. Jack nodded, taking D's silence as all the acknowledgment he could expect. He took off his jacket and started toward the bathroom.

He was drawn up short when D reached out and grabbed his hand in a fast, convulsive jerk like he'd tried to stop himself but his hand was quicker. Jack stopped where he was, then looked back over his shoulder. D was still sitting there in the same position. Only his hand had moved and was now clutching Jack's hard enough to pinch.

Jack stepped back a little and turned to face him. He watched, speechless, as D drew Jack's hand close and rubbed his forehead across it. He grasped it with both hands and pressed it to his face in an unlovely, helpless clutch, whipsaw breaths exhaling moisture onto Jack's fingers. "D...," he whispered.

D pulled on his arm and reeled him closer, then dropped his hand and pressed his face into Jack's belly, his arms going around Jack's hips. "I cain't," Jack heard him murmur. Jack wondered what it was that D couldn't do. There were too many choices.

Jesus. I can't take this. Jack wished, just for the moment, that he were the kind of man who could remain impassive and resolute at such a time, but he wasn't. He sagged into D's arms, wrapping one of his own around D's shoulders and cupping the back of his head with his other hand. D was just sitting there, his face still pressed into Jack's stomach, breathing in long, emphatic pulls like he was getting ready to free-dive, saturating his insides with Jack before the deep plunge.

Jack slid to his knees within the circle of D's arms so they were face-to-face. He cupped D's face in his hands and made him meet his eyes. "What?" he asked. "What is it?"

D just shook his head. "I'm sorry," he whispered. "I'm sorry."

"Why?"

He stared into Jack's eyes, his own blank and confused. "I didn't wanna let it get me," he said, sounding hoarse. "I didn't wanna feel it. I'm sorry."

Jack nodded. "I know."

"I dunno what ta do."

"Me neither."

"I cain't let ya leave like that, like ya said you was gonna."

"I didn't want to. You were making me."

"I know. I'm sorry."

"Don't you be sorry." The tears had escaped and were running down Jack's face by now.

"We coulda had that whole trip together—"

"Shh. It's too late for that now. We still have tonight."

D nodded, then seized Jack's face in shaking hands and kissed him, a hard, frantic kiss that pushed quickly through Jack's lips and made him push back, gripping D's shoulders to keep from toppling over backward. D broke off and stood up, pulling Jack to his feet and going for his clothes. Jack shoved D's jacket off, then yanked at his shirt until it yielded. They push-walked each other around the bed, kicking off shoes and disentangling from mischievous pant legs that wanted to trip them up until they crawled together into the bed, naked and sighing their relief into each other's mouths, murmuring nonsense syllables to fill the stark memories of the past two weeks.

In the hours that followed, it seemed to Jack that the dingy walls of the motel room flew apart and left them wrapped up in the center of some vast plain of emptiness, clinging together to keep it at bay, hardly daring to speak or let their lips part company or else it would dive in and take them too soon. He shut his eyes and arched his neck as D rocked into him, their limbs tangled together and laced like clasped fingers, moaning with pleasure and hearing D whisper in his ear, flipping them over so he was on top and could ride D hard, looking down into his face.

They'd barely caught their breath before D was reaching for him again, sliding down the bed to take Jack in his mouth, then crouching over Jack's face at the head of the bed. They collapsed into a tangled heap, Jack holding D tightly to his chest and feeling the thump of his heart through both their skins. They dozed in fits and starts, waking each other with touches which turned time and again into sex until by the time morning came they were both rubbed raw, exhausted and limp.

Eight o'clock. Jack sat up and swung his legs out of bed. He heard D roll toward him, seeking his warmth again. "Hmm," he grunted. "Timezit?"

Jack sighed. "Eight."

Long pause. "Oh."

"I have to shower and get going."

"Uh-huh."

Jack got up quickly and went into the bathroom, hoping he'd make it. He managed to hold it in until he had the water going strong, then he stepped under the spray and cried, hoping the shower would cover the sound. When he'd calmed down enough, he washed quickly, smiling ruefully at the many red marks D had left on his body. He stepped out of the shower and shaved, then brushed his teeth.

When he emerged, D was sitting at the end of the bed, the sheets pooled around his naked hips, smoking. He glanced up at Jack. "You look a fair sight perkier'n I feel."

"Looks can be deceiving. I'm fucking exhausted."

D nodded. "But it… was worth it, weren't it?"

Jack smiled wearily, then leaned over and kissed his forehead. "You bet it was."

D cleared his throat and looked away, uncomfortable as always with expressions of tender feeling. "You, uh… pick which one you wanna take."

Jack frowned. "Which one what?"

"Gun, dumbass."

"You're *giving* me one of your guns?"

"You put in the time on 'em. You oughta have some protection on yer person."

"Won't they take it from me?"

"Ask yer friend Churchill if he can get ya a permit ta carry concealed. Seein's as you got death threats hangin' over ya that shouldn't be no problem."

Jack nodded. "Okay." He hauled the gun case off the floor and opened it on the motel table, looking across at all D's guns, many of which were now familiar as old friends to him. "I think I'll take the Glock."

"Thought you'd pick that one," D said. "Yer good with that weapon."

"It's my favorite. Still wish you'd let me shoot that Desert Eagle, though."

D chuckled. "Hell, I hardly ever use that one myself. Too much gun. Now, I want ya ta stay sharp with yer hand-ta-hand too. Lotsa martial-arts studios are offering Krav Maga workouts these days. See if you can find one."

"Okay, I will."

"I ain't gonna be 'round ta pick up yer slack, ya know. And them instructors out there in the real world ain't gonna coddle ya like I done." D was smirking, so Jack knew he was just taking the piss.

Jack loaded the Glock and slipped it into his bag along with several boxes of ammunition. He turned slowly and looked at D sitting there, looking uncharacteristically defenseless, naked with a haze of smoke hovering around his head. Jack sat down at his side. "I have to go soon," he whispered.

D nodded.

"D, I… I don't know what to say to you."

"Don't hafta say nothin'."

Jack stared at his lowered profile. "Thanks for my life."

D lifted his head and met Jack's eyes, and for the first time, Jack could see Anson looking back at him, the façade that he called D worn thin and threadbare. "Thanks for mine."

Jack reached out and twined their fingers together. His heart was breaking; there just wasn't a way to put a nice face on it, and there was no way to say it to him.

"So yer gonna go testify," D said, staring at the carpet. "Then yer gonna go inta Witsec. I gotta hit the road and try'n figure out who set me up fer this before they find me and kill me. Right?"

Jack nodded. "Right."

"And that's it, then."

"Yeah."

D cleared his throat. "And, uh… yer okay with leaving it at that, are ya?"

Jack stared at him. "Don't we have to?"

"I dunno." D met his eyes. "Do we?"

Jack's mouth opened and closed a few times. "D… what—"

"Jack, I… I done a lot a thinkin' these past weeks, and especially last night. Don't think I slept at all. Just lyin' there thinkin', mostly. Thinkin' 'bout what you gotta do, and what I gotta do, and all the fuckers want either or both of us on slabs. But mostly thinkin' that…. Well, I know how it's s'posed ta be it fer us now. We're s'posed ta part ways and not look back, right?" Jack nodded. "Ya know what I'm thinkin' now?"

"What?"

"Fuck that."

Jack choked out a surprised bark of laughter that was half a sob. He reached out and grasped the back of D's neck, bringing their foreheads together. "Really?" he whispered. He felt D nod.

"You still gotta do what you gotta do. And I gotta do my thing too. But… that ain't forever."

"I'll be in Witsec," Jack said. "I'll have a different name, I don't know where I'll be living...."

D drew back and took Jack's face in his hands. "I'll find you. You hear me?" Jack nodded, a lump rising in his throat. "I'll find you."

"H... how long?"

"I dunno. Could be years."

Jack met his eyes. "I'll wait."

They sat there staring at each other for a long moment. The honking of Jack's cab outside broke into the silence, and D looked away. "You better get goin'."

Jack nodded and got up. Each step heavy, he took his bags outside, held up a "just a minute" finger to the driver, stepped back inside the room and shut the door behind him. D had pulled on his jeans and was standing there staring into space. "D," Jack said.

He looked up, and Jack felt the words rocketing up his throat. *I love you. You don't have to say it back. You already said it, not in so many words. But I want you to know, I want to say it, I want you to hear it and believe it. I love you.* He opened his mouth, then saw the warning in D's eyes and the words shriveled up behind his lips.

They met each other halfway and wrapped up in a tight embrace. *Jesus, just let me get out of here before I lose it completely.* D drew back and ran his thumb over Jack's lips, silencing him. He sighed. "You be careful."

"You too."

"I'm always careful."

"I'll have armed men protecting me; you won't."

"Nope. Just myself."

Jack stood there paralyzed. "Say it again," he whispered.

D cupped his cheek and lifted his head to meet his eyes. "I'll find you," he said, low and implacable.

Jack nodded. He leaned in and D met his lips, quiet and calm. Jack gave his face one last quick nuzzle and then jerked himself away. He turned and opened the door, practically leaping through and slamming it behind him so he didn't have a chance to look back.

D LEANED up against the closed motel room door, his hands flat against its cheap wood veneer as if he could still feel Jack somewhere on the other side. He took a breath, pulled himself together and picked up his cell phone.

"Witsec, Churchill."

"Yeah, it's D."

"Where's Jack?"

"He jus' left. He's on his way ta meet ya."

"Good. What'd you tell him?"

"Nothing specific, but I know he thinks I'm leaving town right away."

"What's your plan?"

"You find Petros yet?"

"No."

"Well, that'll be high on the list. Then I'll see if I can't figure out if anyone's accepted hits on Jack."

"D, you're a wanted man yourself. Won't you be recognized?"

"Nah. I got a few tricks up my sleeve. Besides, I hardly ever work out East. Don't guess the hit on me will be as high priority out here. Might slip by. What kinda security you got set up fer him?"

"He's staying at the Hyatt in downtown Baltimore. Standard protection conditions apply: no one in any of the rooms above, below, or on either side, he travels only by secure elevator, marshals at the door."

"Mmm. Sounds all right. Look, I gave him a personal firearm."

"I'll look into getting him a permit to carry concealed."

"Good. I appreciate yer trouble."

"You're welcome, Dane."

D went still and cold. "What'd you jus' call me?"

"That's your name, isn't it? Captain Anson Dane, late of the United States Army Special Forces."

D sat down hard. "Fuck."

"I don't mean to startle you, but I thought you ought to know that I know who you are."

"Who else knows?"

"Nobody."

"Don't you fuck with me."

"I'm not. Listen, I'm telling you because you ought to know somebody's been digging into your military record."

"Who?"

"I don't know. Listen, you left a print. At that gas station that blew up outside Stockton. It was baked into the gas pump handle."

"Fuck. I don't leave prints."

"You did this time. Now, your identity's been pretty well scrubbed clean, and Anson Dane is dead, isn't he? Last military record is that of an honorable discharge in 1996. Then there's a record of a man by that name dying in a car crash in Redding, California, except when I dug into it a little deeper the vital stats of the body that was recovered from the resulting fire don't match the ones in your military record, and it just so happens that the date of the crash also coincides with the last time anyone ever heard from your brother, Darrell, although property and utilities continue to be paid in accounts under his name."

D sighed. "That print will fuckin' end me."

"No it won't, because I buried it."

"You what?"

"Don't tell me I'm risking my career because I already know that. Look, you put your neck on the line to save my witness's life. What I'm telling you is that when I went back to your military records I found that someone had accessed them recently."

"When?"

"Last March."

D thought back. March rang no bells and raised no alarms. "I got no fuckin' idea who'd do that."

"Well, nobody knows about the connection between the Dane identity and you except me."

"Guess I better stay on yer good side, then."

Churchill chuckled. "You help me keep Jack alive through all this and we'll be good."

"I'll be in touch."

"All right."

"Oh, and uh…," D trailed off.

"What?"

"You take care a him," D said, unable to keep the hoarseness from his voice. "You take care a my Jack." He was laying himself bare, more than he'd ever done, but it somehow wasn't as scary as he'd always thought it would be.

There was a long pause. "I will." Churchill hung up.

D flopped backward onto the bed, his head spinning. *Jesus, now my nuts're in the fire fer sure. Who the hell's been pokin' in my records? And now somebody knows my name. I think I trust Churchill, but anybody knowin' is one person too many.*

Oh, fuck it all. Yer identity was circlin' the drain anyway. You'da hadta give up a lot a shit now that D's hunted by God knows who-all anyhow. And if yer thinkin' a havin' some kinda life with Jack….

He shut down that line of thought at once. It did no good to spin pipe dreams, not yet anyway. He'd meant what he'd said to Jack. But meaning it and making it happen were two different things.

He turned over and pulled a pillow close. It still smelled like Jack. He buried his face in it and sagged into the lumpy mattress, moorless and undone, drifting now without his anchor.

CHAPTER 20

JACK sat waiting for Churchill on a bench in Baker Park, his duffel bag sitting by his side. It was a beautiful day. It'd be fall soon, and the season felt welcome. It felt like home after months in the desert. Soon he'd be back for real, back in Baltimore, the city where he'd spent most of his adult life.

That life seemed like a mirage now. Something imagined, remembered like a story he'd been told by his parents instead of something he'd lived through.

Your old apartment is there. Your practice. Your car, your belongings. You left it all here. Your whole life.

No. You just left your life back in that motel room.

Jack shut his eyes and sighed, the wind lifting his hair off his forehead.

It can't be helped. And it's just for now.

He let himself hear D's voice again.

I'll find you.

"Jack?"

He opened his eyes to find a man standing in front of him. He was tall and thin with startlingly red hair and a prominent Adam's apple. He looked like a math teacher. He was wearing a suit with no tie, his white button-down shirt open at the throat.

"Yeah?"

He smiled. "I'm Paul Churchill." He stuck out his hand. Jack rose and shook it, reassured. "Goddamn, it's good to finally meet you."

"You too." Jack's smile broadened. Churchill was exactly the opposite of what he'd been expecting, and that was somehow comforting.

"Come on. Let's get you out of here." He took one of Jack's bags and they walked to the street, where Churchill's car was at a parking meter. They loaded the bags and got in.

"Where are we going first?"

"First, I'm going to take you to the hotel. You must be exhausted from that long drive."

Jack nodded. It wasn't the drive that had been exhausting. "Yeah."

"Well, the best I can do for now is let you get a shower and some breakfast, because I'm supposed to have you at the U.S. Attorney's office by noon."

"Where they will ask me the same questions eight hundred times."

"Yeah, probably. Look, it's for your own good. Whatever high-priced lawyer the brothers have hired will do whatever he can to make you look like an idiot or a criminal yourself."

Jack ground his jaw. "Let him try. I didn't go through all this just to be broken down on the stand. I've been grilled by some of the toughest, meanest attending physicians on Earth during rounds. I can handle it."

Churchill chuckled. "I've gotta say, Jack, you are a prosecutor's wet dream as a witness. No criminal record. Not only are you not getting anything from testifying, you're actually risking your life. You were a totally innocent bystander to the crime. Plus you're a doctor, which means automatic intelligence and respect points with a jury, and as you say, you're used to high-pressure situations, so it's hard to trip you up on cross-examination. Salie ought to be getting down on his knees and kissing your ass."

"Salie?"

"Yeah, Brad Salie. He's the prosecutor handling this case."

"Is he any good?"

"Yeah, he's good. He's tough. And he's spent the past five years trying to build a case against the brothers." Churchill was steering onto I-70 toward Baltimore. "You want to stop somewhere and get a coffee? Go to the bathroom?"

Jack shook his head. "I'm okay." A few beats went by; Jack could feel Churchill's eyes on him. "What?"

He sighed. "Jack, I know about D."

Jack blinked. "Who?"

"Don't give me that."

"I don't know what you're talking about."

"The hit man who was supposed to kill you but ended up protecting you."

Jack nodded slowly. "Huh. You come up with that all by yourself?"

"No. I've been talking to him on the phone once a week all summer."

That was enough to knock Jack's train of thought right off the rails. "What?"

"He asked me not to tell you, but I don't see any reason why you shouldn't know. I think he's just too used to keeping secrets."

Jack just stared. "Are you telling me you've been in touch with him all this time?"

"Yep."

He didn't know why he was even surprised. "Goddamn him. He never thinks I can handle anything. And after he gave me that big song and dance about how you couldn't know about him."

"No offense, Jack, but I knew you had to be getting help. It wasn't too likely that you could have escaped someone like him on your own."

"Which is exactly what I told him! He said you'd have no choice but to buy it!"

"He wanted to make sure I'd accept that you were out of pocket, which he knew I'd never do unless I was sure you were protected, so he went behind your back and contacted me so I'd know you weren't alone." Jack could only shake his head ruefully. "Does that piss you off?"

"I guess it probably should, but I don't seem to have much piss-off left in me. I'm sure as hell not going to waste what little I've got on him."

"Look, I've talked to the agent who works with him at the FBI, and I know what he's done for them, but... he's still a professional killer, Jack."

"You don't know him," Jack said, flatly. "No one knows him but me."

D CAME out of a Best Buy in Towson with a new laptop under one arm. He got in the car and found the nearest Panera, home of delicious pastries and free Wi-Fi. He'd had the Best Buy geeks configure the laptop. He had to think for a moment to remember the password to his personal server, but once there he downloaded and installed his usual firewall, then sat back and waited while his security suite installed.

Jack is somewhere in this city, right now.

The thought was like passing by a house where someone was grilling in the backyard. You could smell it, but it wasn't yours, and you couldn't just barge into their home and demand a burger, no matter how your mouth watered.

The computer configured to his satisfaction, D opened the browser and typed in the IP address from memory. The network, a blank white screen with a single line of text entry, was as inscrutable as always.

He couldn't sign in as himself. Every hit man in the country was gunning for him. Fortunately, no one, not even X, knew that D was not one hit man but several. When he'd started working for the FBI he'd seen the advantage in cultivating alternate identities through which he could keep track of what was being said or rumored about himself, and it provided additional ways to undercut the business without compromising his primary identity. Since very few people in his line of work knew what anyone actually looked like, it was easy enough to keep separate personas. He thought for a moment, then signed in as Lincoln, identified by a random string of letters and numbers D had to keep in his head. Over a year ago he'd signed into the network as Lincoln and announced that he was taking a sabbatical in Turkey. People got suspicious if any particular person disappeared for too long.

The site didn't have a welcome screen, or a forum, or a chat room, or even any text. It was another white, featureless series of empty windows, except one. A small frame in the lower-right corner identified the users currently signed in. He scanned the names. *Hmm. I know Frost... there's Carver... Dorian, that sounds familiar....* There were a disturbingly large number of handles he didn't recognize, although his profession did have a high turnover rate. His ten-year career was unusually long, and he'd been out of circulation for several months.

He didn't have to wait long. A window opened up on his screen with a message from Frost. He'd actually met Frost in person, as Lincoln, and cooperated with him on a couple of two-man jobs.

Welcome back.

Thanks.

How was turkey?

Hot. Brought back some shiny new toys.

When'd you get back?

D thought fast. *A week ago.*

You hear? Sig's dead.

Seriously? How?

D killed him.

You're fucking kidding me. Why?

Word around the campfire is D backed off a mark. Ran into Sig in LA, killed him.

Yeah? What mark'd he back off?

Some surgeon, witness against the Dominguez bros.

Contract still active on the surgeon?

No, it's taken.

Who's got it? D could only hope Frost didn't think his interest was suspicious. He probably wouldn't. The thing about professional killers was that they were paranoid and isolationist, but gossipy.

I tried to put in a bid but the bros already have a couple vendors lined up. JJ got the close hit.

D sighed. JJ was smart and sneaky, and would be tough to throw off. *Who else?*

First hit went to Carver. If neither of them get him, bidding might open up again, or else the bros will just do it themselves.

What about D? You bid for that?

All the hits on D got canceled. No bounty.

D frowned. That wasn't a good sign. If all the contracts on his life had been withdrawn, that could only mean that whoever had blackmailed him into killing Jack had decided to find him and deal with him themselves, without involving an independent contractor.

Someone's taking that personally, then. You know who?

No, but whoever it is must have balls made of solid iron. D is too damn hard core and I wouldn't touch a hit on him no matter what the bounty was. The guy's a phantom.

D grinned to himself. A perk of having alternate identities was the chance to hear what your colleagues *really* thought of you. *I heard Petros is in town.*

Yeah. The brothers got him in so in case the surgeon gets away he can take care of it. And if he gets bagged, they'll let Petros play with him for awhile first, you know?

D's stomach turned over. He'd seen the remains of people that Petros had played with, and his mind's eye showed him an image of Jack with his eyeballs gouged out, fingers chopped off one by one, slowly disemboweled and burned with hot irons before he was finally allowed to die.

Guess I'll come to Bmore and see how it plays out.

Yeah? I'm in Lauderdale. Got more drug lord jobs than I can handle.

Good luck with that.

Thx. Lemme know if you get some play.

Later.

D signed off and logged out of the network. So JJ and Carver were both on Jack's trail. If JJ had the better position, that meant she'd be taking the higher-risk (and therefore higher-paying) hit, and Carver would likely make the first attempt when security around Jack would be lower.

He had to find Carver. Now.

JACK got back to his hotel room after nine, exhausted. Brad Salie, the federal prosecutor, had taken him through his testimony dozens of times and seemed confident with Jack's responses. "You want some dinner?" Churchill asked, following him into his room. "Room service is on the Justice Department."

Jack shook his head. "I just want to sleep for a year." He flopped backward onto the bed. "When will I be testifying?"

"I don't know. It won't be Monday, at least; they have to do jury selection."

Jack stared at him. "They still have to do jury selection?"

"Well, yeah. That is generally the first step."

"And you couldn't have waited until they'd gotten past all that crap and were actually *starting the trial* to drag my ass out here?"

"Salie needed you here now! He had to prepare you, and once the circus begins he won't have time! Believe me, the brothers have very well-paid lawyers and they will try and drag out the voir dire as long as humanly possible."

"Stalling so that there's more time for me to get conveniently murdered," Jack said.

"That's not going to happen."

"I bet that's what you guys said to all those other witnesses that never made it to trial with these guys." Churchill just looked at him. Jack sighed and sat up. "I'm sorry. I'm being an asshole."

"Don't apologize. You've got good reason. Most of the witnesses I deal with are much worse than you, in more ways than one."

Jack stood and went to the window. He leaned his head against the glass and stared out into the cityscape that surrounded him, seeing only his own reflection with any clarity.

He heard Churchill clear his throat. "You, uh... miss him, huh?" He was keeping his tone pretty carefully neutral, but Jack knew he wouldn't say such a thing if he didn't have a pretty good idea about the situation.

He sighed. "Yeah."

"I'm sorry, Jack, but I have to ask—"

"Yeah. We were. What you're thinking we were, we were."

"Oh."

Jack stepped back from the window and faced him. "You have an opinion about that?" Jack asked.

"No."

"Yeah, you do."

"Just... are you sure that's wise, Jack? I mean, the kind of man he is—"

"You don't know anything about him."

"All right, I'm sure that's probably true. And I get how... that... happened. I mean, you were on the run for your lives, he saved you, you were alone.... It's a lot of stress, a lot of emotion flying around."

Jack snorted. "Boy, you really *don't* know him if you think he had a lot of emotion flying around."

Churchill was quiet for a moment. "Look, I'm about to spend a great deal of time and a considerable amount of money to set up a new identity for you, and I have to worry about your attachments. People you might be tempted to contact once you're relocated, thereby compromising your security."

I will find you. "I won't be contacting anybody. Scout's honor."

"You were never a Boy Scout."

"I was a Webelo for one month. It counts." Jack turned toward the window to get away from Churchill's calm, evaluating gaze.

"Okay. I just had to ask. I'm sorry. It's just that we have to be pretty careful about people who our witnesses have been... involved with, and I'll want to—"

"I love him," Jack said, staring out at the dark harbor. That was the first time he'd said it aloud. He hadn't meant to. It was like the words had spontaneously appeared on his lips and tumbled off without so much as a push. He just had to tell *somebody.*

"Yeah?"

Jack turned around and met his eyes, then nodded. "Yeah."

Churchill looked down at his hands again. "I'm sorry, Jack."

"It's okay." Jack rubbed his face. "Listen, I'm really damn tired and some crying is possible, which I'd prefer to do in private, so...."

Churchill stood up. "I'll leave you be."

"Thanks."

"I don't know if I'll see you tomorrow. You're not to leave this room, though."

Jack gaped at him. "Seriously?"

"Seriously. Look, catch up on your sleep, watch some TV. If you want books or anything like that, we can get it for you."

"How about a computer?"

"I can get you a laptop, but no Internet."

"Shit."

"Sorry. You have my cell. Call me anytime."

"Okay.

"Good night, Jack." Churchill left. Jack went to the door and poked his head out. His room opened onto a small foyer; there were two armed marshals sitting outside. They nodded to him and he retreated, locking the deadbolt and securing the chain.

He retreated to the suite, which was really quite nice except for his solitude in it. *Where are you tonight, D? How far away are you? It feels like you're very far. Right now it feels like light years. Like I'll never see you again.* He went to the window again. *I probably shouldn't stand in front of this window. Somebody with a sniper rifle could shoot me or something.* The hotel was right on the Inner Harbor and his window faced the water; there wasn't a suitable perch for firing for some distance. Besides, the window glass was bulletproof; Churchill had told him so. He resisted the urge to shut the drapes. He wanted the company of that darkness tonight. With the drapes closed, the room felt too much like a cell.

He put his bag on the bed and began pulling out clothes and toiletries. He reached in for his shaving kit when his hand fell upon something unfamiliar, something he knew he hadn't packed.

He withdrew it and smiled, those tears he'd warned Churchill about springing to his eyes. *Had to have the last laugh, huh, D?* Jack chuckled and for a moment he could almost feel him there in the room, smell his skin, hear his rumbly voice, the weight of his eyes on Jack, gauging his reaction to this little gift that he had slipped into Jack's bag for him to find, to remind him.

D CLIMBED the fire escape to the top floor and slung his duffel over his shoulder. He clambered up on the railing, grabbed the edge of the roofline and hauled himself up to the slate surface. This was the highest perch he could find that faced the right direction. He walked a quick sweep around the rooftop to make sure he was alone, and then returned to the spot he'd scoped out earlier in the day. He pulled out a folding camp chair and set it up in the shadow of a large cinderblock chimney, setting his duffel bag to his side and slouching down in the chair.

He'd spent the day tracking Carver. As best he could determine, he wasn't yet in town, which probably meant he planned to execute the hit after the trial had begun. If Churchill was any good at all, he wouldn't let Jack leave his hotel room until absolutely necessary, and a hit man on his first day on the job could tell you that in-transit was the best time to take somebody out.

He pulled the binoculars out of his bag. They were hellishly heavy and had cost a fortune, but they were military-grade and extremely powerful. Any stronger and they'd be telescopes. He held them up to his eyes and looked across the harbor to the hotel, catty-corner from the rooftop where he sat. Standard protection protocols would dictate that Jack be placed in a room facing the harbor, on the second floor from the top, with no one in the rooms above, below, or to either side. D scanned the lit windows on the harbor side, focusing on the fourteenth floor, until he found it. A room with no lights on in any of the four rooms surrounding it. The curtains were open. He zoomed in until the window was large in his sights. He'd chosen a pretty fair perch; the building he was on was thirteen stories tall, so here on the roof he was almost level with the fourteenth floor of the Hyatt, slightly above due to the terrain. He was looking directly into Jack's room. He focused in tighter.

Jack and Churchill had left the prosecutor's office half an hour ago. D hadn't seen them come out, but he'd seen Churchill's car leave the parking garage and had hightailed it here. He ought to have beaten them; they'd have worse traffic than he had.

He sat waiting. Patient. He was always patient. He'd have to be more patient than he'd ever been in his life, for Jack, for whatever was coming. Patient and ready.

Then, there he was. Coming into the hotel room and throwing down his coat, followed by a man who had to be Churchill. He was skinny and red-haired but D liked the look of him. Just the way he stood and held himself, he didn't look like an idiot. Jack flopped onto the bed. They were talking. D couldn't read their lips but Jack seemed irritated. *Probly had it up ta here with all the legalizin' already.* He came to the window and leaned his forehead against it for a minute. D knew that face. It was the *I'm too tired ta keep arguin'* face.

A few more minutes of conversation. Jack was back at the window now, arms crossed, staring out toward the harbor. D held his breath. It almost seemed like Jack was looking right at him, although of course he couldn't see much of anything from inside a lit room. Churchill was talking behind him, then Jack spoke, and this time D *could* read his lips.

I love him.

D's fingers gripped the binoculars tighter. *Naw, yer seein' things.*

Except he wasn't. He knew he wasn't. *He's talkin' 'bout somebody else.*

Who the hell else could he be talking about?

These mental stall tactics were useless, because D had seen what he'd seen, and he knew Jack meant it. He knew because he'd almost said it in the motel that very morning, before he'd seen something on D's face and stopped himself. D had been glad. He wasn't sure he could stand to hear that, because he didn't think he could say it back and he didn't want to see the hurt on Jack's face when he didn't.

In fact, he'd never said it to anyone, not that way. He'd said it to his daughter, of course. But with Sharon he'd skittered by with "Me too" after she'd said it first. That wouldn't do for Jack. He'd have better. Someday.

He watched as Jack turned away from the window. Churchill seemed to be leaving now. Jack disappeared for a moment, then returned to the window and stared out for a moment. D took the rare opportunity to just look at him without the embarrassment of being caught at it. *He's so... jus'. Yeah. He's jus' so.* Jack had jokingly complimented D on his appearance a number of times, probably hoping to encourage even a joking return of the sentiment, but all D had ever been able to do was blush and mutter something incoherent. He couldn't voice what he felt, which was that he could look for a hundred years and never tire of the sight of Jack. Jack, who was opening his bag now. D sat forward a little, a smirk curling his lips. He hoped he hadn't opened his bag during the trip sometime and already found it. That would be disappointing.

Fortunately, Jack was on the far side of the bed, so he was facing the window and D could see everything clear as day as Jack frowned and pulled D's little present out of the bag. He smiled, looking down at the little box of chocolate-covered cherries D had slipped into Jack's bag that morning while he was in the shower. He'd had them for weeks, but every time he thought about giving them to Jack an attack of paralyzing shyness had gripped him and he'd put them aside again. This morning he'd thought, it's now or never.

Jack was grinning now. He sat down on the other bed and pulled out one of the cherries. D watched as Jack carefully bit off one side, sucked out the syrup, and the reached up with one finger to wipe a dribble from the corner of his mouth. He cocked his head and stuck out his tongue to fish out the cherry, which took a few tries. That worked out fine for D, who was just enjoying watching Jack's pink tongue working around inside the little chocolate shell. Finally he managed it, and then he nibbled away at the empty shell until it was gone. He shook his head, chuckling a little, then closed up the box and set it on the nightstand. His fingers lingered on it for a moment. D saw him sigh, then get up and go into the bathroom.

D relaxed. That couldn't have gone better. He spared a brief thought to how creepy he was being, spying on Jack from across the harbor, but he thought it was forgivable under the circumstances.

His cell phone trilled at him. Text message. Probably from X. He let the binocs fall onto his chest and fished his phone out of his pocket.

all ok?
y
hits on j?
2 that i no of
leads?
no one in town yet. undr contrl.
vgood
where u?
here too
come 2 help?
if need.
mayb finly meet.
think so. hav 2 arrange.
how bout rite now?
now?
y
???
can hear ur fingers typin, dumbass.

D heard a sigh, and then... a voice. "Well, shit." A woman's voice. From the other side of the chimney he was sitting next to. He sat there, stunned, as footsteps circled the chimney... and then a woman with blonde hair stepped out in front of him. "That's embarrassing."

D just stared. "It's you."

She smiled back. "And it's you."

He stood up slowly. "I cain't believe it." It was dark on the roof but he could see her fairly well in the glow from the city lights and the moon. She was tall, just a little shorter than he was, and looked strong. She was wearing cargo pants and a bomber jacket with a fleece lining. Her light hair was pulled into a ponytail. "Yer... a woman!"

"Yep." She stuck out her hand. "Megan Knox, United States Secret Service." She looked a little overwhelmed to be standing here face-to-face with him. He knew how she felt. He shook her hand, still reeling a little. "Goddamn, D," she said, biting her lip a little. "It's good to see you."

"You too," he said, still shaking her hand. Finally he let go and they just stood there staring.

He glanced at the chimney. "How long were you gonna sit there bein' real quiet?"

"I don't know. Until you left, maybe. Turned off the keystroke beeps on my Treo; didn't think you'd hear me."

"I got good ears."

"Evidently."

"C'mon. I woulda found you up here."

"Well, you didn't when you checked the roof, did you?"

"Where were you hiding?"

She jerked her head back toward the far corner. "Inside an intake vent."

"Sneaky."

"My middle name."

D was at a loss. They just stood there like idiots for a few moments, then he chuckled. "I'm still kinda in shock here."

"Yeah, well, this is a surprise for me too."

"Well, come sit down."

"Okay. We do have a lot to talk about." She sat on a raised ledge at his side.

"So... yer a Secret Service agent, huh?"

She looked at him. "I never said I was an agent."

"Oh," he said, sensing her disinterest in follow-up questions.

"Who's got the hits on Jack?"

"Shh. We can talk later. He's gonna come outta the shower any minute now and ain't no way I'm missin' that."

"Ooh," she said, and pulled out her own binoculars.

D looked at her. "Hey!"

"What? You'd deny a hardworking girl a little eye candy?"

"This ain't Halloween."

"What's that mean?"

"Means I ain't sharin' my candy. Gimme them glasses."

CHAPTER 21

D AND X (*Megan, her name's Megan*) sat on the rooftop until the light went out in Jack's room. D felt self-conscious watching him with her sitting right there next to him, although she was quiet and didn't appear to be paying him any attention. He fidgeted in his chair as Jack came out of the bathroom with a towel around his waist, although she couldn't see a thing without binoculars from this distance.

He lowered the heavy glasses. "All right. Guess leave now."

"Okay." She put her binoculars back inside her coat.

He shook his head. "You wouldn'ta been able ta see him with them puny things anyway. Where'd ya get 'em, the dollar store?"

She handed them over. "Have a look."

D raised the compact binocs to his eyes and staggered back a step, orienting himself. They were at least an order of magnitude more powerful than his. "Damn," he muttered. He could see *past* the hotel into the offices of the buildings beyond.

"They're digital," she said, taking them back.

"Pretty slick."

"I like my toys. Come on; let's get a coffee or something."

THEY sat in a far corner of a deserted all-night diner. The bored waitress sat at the far end of the counter reading a trashy romance novel while a radio crackled faintly at her side. She just left them the coffee pot and told them to wave or something when they needed more, or if they wanted pie.

D shook his head, turning the coffee mug (the big thick kind with caramel-colored glaze, just right) around and around in circles. "Still cain't believe yer sittin' here in front a me."

"I guess it's different for me. I've always known what you look like; I see you all the time."

"Yeah."

She was watching him. "I hope I'm not a disappointment."

He looked at her. "Why would ya be?"

"Well, maybe you were expecting some muscle-bound mercenary guy."

He snorted. "I've known a few a them. To a man they been dumber'n a box a sticks 'n' useless for anythin' but workin' somebody over. Gimme somebody sneaky 'n' clever."

She crossed her arms on the tabletop. "I know what your situation is. Maybe more than you do. But you must have questions about me."

"You sayin' you gonna answer all a my questions?"

"Well… maybe not *all.* As many as I'm able."

"Yer Secret Service."

"Yep."

"But you ain't no agent."

"Nope." She sighed. "I'm one of those people that don't exist."

"Well, we got that in common."

"Yeah. Let's just say I go do the jobs that don't get put in the annual report or itemized in the budget. Things that don't officially happen."

"Uh-huh."

"Last ten years I been on anti-assassination. I pretty much roam around following up on tips and intelligence, some of which I'm given, some of which I gather myself. You ought to know that I sometimes pose as somebody in your line of work."

He frowned. "Under what name?"

"Shelby."

He snorted. "That was you?"

"Yep. I know, I stole that Tempe job from you."

"No, ya didn't. I wanted you to take it. Change a heart. Leaked the contact info and ramped back on my bid so somebody'd swoop in and steal it. Thanks for obligin'."

"You played me!" she exclaimed. "Asshole!"

He shrugged. "Look who's talkin'."

She nodded, chuckling. "Anyway. The nature of my job made it easy for me to move around and, uh… look after you."

D was silent for a moment. "You gonna tell me why? Finally?"

"You saved my life."

"Still don't know how."

"That's a conversation for a later time."

He nodded. He'd suspected as much. "Okay. Then there's only one thing ta talk 'bout."

"Who's got these two contracts on Jack?"

"First hit went to a guy called Carver. Know him?"

"Yeah, he's a lightweight."

"Well, I ain't countin' him out, but he don't worry me as much as JJ. I figure I'll tail him when he gets into town and persuade him to take his business elsewhere."

She nodded. "I'll make some discreet inquiries on Carver's known aliases, see if I can find how he's arriving or where he's staying."

"That'd be good. Then there's JJ."

"I'm not familiar with him."

"Her. And I'm a lot more nervous about her than Carver."

"Why? Is she tough?"

D shot her a wry grin. "JJ is a sixty-eight-year-old woman who's about five-two and no more'n ninety pounds soakin' wet."

Meg snorted. "Seriously?"

"Yep. Nobody ever looks at her twice. I seen her a couple a times off the job and she looked like a Park Avenue mama, all high-heeled and white-haired and with them sunglasses. But on the job? She curls her hair and puts on these sweatshirts with teddy bears on 'em and looks like anyone's grandma."

"Someone no one would ever suspect."

"Or even remember. But damn, she gets the job done."

"How?"

"She is the fuckin' master a chemical assassination. Poisons, nerve agents, injections. It could be in his food, or on the car's door handle, or in the ventilation system, or in the fuckin' water."

"Damn. That's not going to be easy to protect him against."

"You ain't kiddin'. Best hope is ta intervene before she puts her plan in place. She ain't no bonehead like Carver, though. She'll be tough ta find. I'm still thinkin' on that. But she drew the close hit, so she only moves if Carver fails, so as long as I can put off Carver's attempt, she won't do nothin' 'til real close ta the trial." He sighed. "But them two are jus' the beginnin' a my problems."

Meg nodded. "Petros."

"Oh, ya heard?"

"It's all over the place. You'd think the guy was Keyser Soze for all the rumors that run around about him. You know, it's often occurred to me that criminal enterprise would run a lot more smoothly if all the criminals could keep their damn mouths shut, which they seem pathologically incapable of doing."

"Mmm. Makes it easier fer us, though."

"You were never one to flap your lips."

"Why I'm still around."

"I don't doubt it." She leaned forward. "I'll deal with Petros, if you want. So you can concentrate on Carver and JJ."

D regarded her, thinking. Did he trust her enough for that? Did he think she could handle it? He only needed a few moments' contemplation to decide that the answers were yes and yes. "Okay. Be easier if I knew what he was gonna do."

"Has it occurred to you that he could be here for you?"

"Cain't be. He works fer the brothers, it's gotta be 'bout Jack. It ain't the brothers on my personal ass but somebody else who's yet ta show their face. I'm bettin' they got him inta town in case Jack makes it ta the stand and inta Witsec. That is one a his special talents."

Meg seemed to consider this, then let it drop. "What's your plan for after? Assuming no one gets to Jack."

"Well, he'll be goin inta Witsec."

"I can't believe you're content to just leave it there."

D smirked, a hard little half-smile. "Hell, no. I'm gonna fix it so he don't hafta stay in Witsec. Can get his own name back, be a surgeon again."

"That'll be a neat trick. How are you going to pull that one off?"

"I got some ideas."

She seemed to get the message that he had no intention of discussing those ideas just now. They sat in silence for a few minutes, drinking their coffee. When Megan spoke again, her voice was quiet. "And what about after, for you and Jack?" she said. "Have you thought about that?"

D stared down at his coffee. "I thought about it." She was waiting for him to go on, but D wasn't about to talk about his plans for a future with Jack, not even to her. Even if he'd wanted to, which he didn't, speaking it aloud seemed like a risk, like he'd curse his hopes if he voiced them and made them real.

The truth was, he hardly dared think about that future in any kind of detail. Jack had talked about a house and dogs and a garden. D hadn't gotten that far. All he could bear to think about was some undefined future time when he'd see Jack again, and about not having to leave him forever. Past that, everything was vague and cloudy, because he couldn't stand to make it distinct. If he did, and it didn't happen, then he'd have outlines and details floating around inside his head to torment him with what he couldn't have. It was bad enough that his mind kept insisting on reminding him that it was very possible— even probable—that Jack would die, and that all D would have of him would be a grave somewhere.

A grave D would never visit, because if the worst happened, all he could imagine doing was vanishing into the night, cutting all ties to the world, and floating through his existence like a specter, touching nothing or nobody ever again.

JACK blinked awake and rolled over. The bed was ridiculously comfortable. He'd gotten used to the lumpy mattress at the Redding house, and after that a week's worth of anonymous fleabag motels, but this... this was heaven. Even so, he hadn't slept all that well, and he blamed his solitude. He hadn't slept alone in some time, and it felt wrong not to have D's weight in the bed next to him, his body heat reminding Jack of his presence even when they weren't touching. The bed felt cold with only himself to warm it.

He smiled when his eyes lit on the little box of chocolate-covered cherries on the nightstand, but not for long. Cherries were a poor substitute.

He turned over and stretched an arm across the empty, cold space where D ought to have been but wasn't, and likely wouldn't be for a long time. The day stretched out endless before him, a day trapped in this hotel room with nothing to do but brood and really relish the depression that he felt lurking in the corner, waiting to pounce.

He put his hands over his face. *Goddamn. It's all gone. My life, my job, my home, my city, my friends.* He'd done his best through this never-ending ordeal not to think about how much he'd lost and how profoundly his life had changed, and for the most part he'd succeeded, but now there was nothing to distract him from it.

At least I had him. For awhile, I had him. But now he's gone too.

He punched the pillow and pulled another one over his head. *Wake me up when it's time to testify. Maybe when I'm done I'll just walk out of the courthouse and yell for the hit men to come and get me, but make it quick and painless.*

FOLLOWING Carver's car from BWI was not difficult, because he'd rented a red Corvette. D sniffed in derision when he saw the flashy thing pull out of the lot. Carver was new enough at this that he was still getting off on the so-called glamour of being an outlaw with bucketloads of cash. Usually the ones that drove fancy cars and bought jewelry and houses in the south of France didn't last long. Carver wouldn't either, if D had anything to say about it.

His cell phone trilled. "D."

"Okay," Megan said, without preamble. "Car was rented under a different name than he flew under, so he probably used that one for his lodging so it'd match."

"What name's he usin' fer the car?"

"Brace yourself. Slade Thorndike."

D shook his head. "Are you fuckin' kiddin' me?"

"As I live and breathe."

"He get that off a soap opera?"

"Sounds like. Anyway I found a townhouse rental under that name on Thames Street."

D's stomach dropped. "Thames Street?"

"Yeah."

"Shit, that's in Fells Point. That's real near where we were last night."

"Well, the courthouse is only a block from the hotel. He could have picked it because of that."

"Maybe, but it's safest t'assume he knows where Jack is. I'll tail him ta the townhouse 'n' deal with it there."

Meg was quiet for a moment. "Are you going to kill him?"

D clenched his teeth. "If he makes me. Gimme that address." D pulled away from the Corvette and passed it, his jaw grinding.

THE townhouse, more of a duplex, was generic in the way of a temporary rental. The security system was a joke; D got in easily through the garage. He made a quick check; he didn't have much time. Carver was no more than ten minutes behind him, perhaps a few minutes more if he was unfamiliar with the neighborhood.

He found a corner near the dining room where he could see both the front door and the door into the garage, so whichever way Carver entered he'd have it covered.

He stood there, still and silent, barely breathing, a SIG Sauer with a silencer screwed into the barrel in one gloved hand inside the pocket of his pea coat. His mind wanted to run back toward Jack. Think about him, what he was doing, how he was feeling. He couldn't let it. That was a distraction he couldn't afford.

He shut his eyes and tried to get back to that place. That place of D, that place where he'd lived for so long, his vault shut up nice and tight, everything smooth and shiny and featureless, not a scratch or a blemish on the surface of his arid desert mind.

Shut it off. Shut it all off. You remember. It's easy.

It was hard to get back there when part of him stubbornly insisted on wondering if that place even existed anymore. Far from being clean and smooth, he was now righteously messy and turned over like soil in a garden just before planting. The vault door hung wide open, askew and half off its hinges, all the secrets it had contained floating around free.

He heard the garage door and took a step back into the shadows. A car door slammed, keys in the lock, the door opening into the kitchen. Carver was making enough noise to wake the dead.

He let his bag fall, oblivious, and walked straight toward D, hand out for the light switch. Before he could reach it, D moved smoothly out of his hiding place, grasped Carver's wrist, spun him around and yanked the arm up between his shoulder blades, pressing his chest against the wall and the muzzle of his gun to his temple. "Quiet, now," he hissed.

"Who the fuck are you?" Carver choked out. He tried to struggle but D had his knee socked right up between his legs and his whole weight leaning on Carver's twisted arm. He wasn't going anywhere.

"You don't need ta know. Now, you listen close ta me and maybe you walk outta here, you got it?" Carver nodded. "You here to do a hit on Jack Francisco, that right? On behalf a the Dominguez brothers?"

"I don't know what you're talking about."

"If you think I'm a cop then yer even dumber'n ya look. Answer my question." He twisted Carver's arm again.

"Yeah. Francisco."

"When was you gonna do it?"

"Who the fuck's askin'?"

D weighed this for a moment. It was true that his name carried a certain reputation behind it. If Carver knew who he was dealing with, he'd probably present his belly like a good little boy, especially since it seemed to be common knowledge that D had already killed a colleague. But if D told Carver who he was, the odds of it staying a secret were small. He just wasn't sure how much it mattered if Carver blabbed all over town that D was in the house. There was no price on his head at the moment, and like Frost, many professionals would shy away from them even if they existed. The only danger to him was that knowledge of his whereabouts would get back to whoever was after him so specifically... and it was likely they already knew. They surely knew that he'd been protecting Jack for months, and it wasn't too likely they'd believe that he would have left Jack here in Baltimore unprotected. They had to be already assuming he was in town. Part of him even *wanted* them to know, so he could get it over with. The sooner they came for him, the sooner it would be resolved, one way or another, and he could concentrate on Jack's issues with the brothers. The thing that worried him most was that they'd come after him before Jack was safely in Witsec, and he'd have to parse his time between protecting Jack and protecting himself. But he had a feeling they wouldn't do that.

Ya know, you could jus' kill him once he tells ya what he had planned. Problem solved.

That was certainly true, except... he didn't want to kill the man.

You don't wanna kill him because Jack wouldn't want ya to.

So?

So, who's runnin' this show, you or Jack?

D didn't know the answer to that, but in the two seconds it took all these considerations to run through his mind, he'd decided what to tell Carver. He was doing all this for Jack, and he wanted to do it as himself. Not as Lincoln, or some other alias, but as....

As the man Jack loves. He loves me. It's crazy and it's hard, and I can't hardly believe it and I sure as hell don't deserve it, but he said it so he musta meant it. He's somewhere in this city right now, with no idea what I'm doin' or why, and he loves me, and that is damn near all I got in the world.

He leaned close and growled in Carver's ear. "My name is D," he said. He felt Carver tense up. "I see it's known ta you."

"What the fuck are you doing here?" He heard the trill of fear inside Carver's voice, and knew he had him.

"I'm askin' the questions. When was you gonna take Francisco out?"

"You want the hit? Buy it off me."

D lowered the gun and pressed it to Carver's leg. "Kneecap," he hissed.

Carver tried to shy away from the gun but didn't have far to go. "All right, goddamnit. I was going to do him long-range from a perch as he went into the courthouse."

D was so amazed that it took him a second to gather his thoughts. "Jesus. I knew you was new at this but I didn't think you was a fuckin' moron."

"Huh?"

"In what universe do they take a witness in a mob trial into the courthouse out in the open? They'll take him in through the tunnels, you fuckin' idiot."

Carver said nothing for a moment. "Oh."

"Yeah. Christ almighty. All right, I ain't got time fer yer sorry ass. Now. I'm gonna knock you out here in a minute. When you wake up, I be gone. You pick up yer little bags, get back in that flashy red cop magnet yer drivin' and head on outta town. I don't care where ya go, but the further you go, the better. You keep your fee on this job."

"But… you don't want the fee?"

"Nope."

"Who's gonna do the job?"

"Nobody."

Carver snorted. "The brothers'll have my head if I skip town with their money and don't do the job."

"If they make a stink I'll arrange fer yer fee ta get returned outta my own pocket, but they gonna have bigger problems than that real soon."

"Why you doin' this?"

"We got a deal?"

Carver was quiet for a moment. "Yeah."

D jerked on his arm again, getting a pained grunt in return. "You listen ta me," he said, low into Carver's ear. "You get gone, and you stay gone. I'll be watchin'. I get so much as a whiff a the salami you ate fer lunch and you won't get the chance ta be sorry 'bout it. You keep yer trap shut about seein' me here. You got it?"

He nodded. "Yeah. I got it."

D shook his head. "You oughta get outta this business. You ain't got the stones." He stepped back and swung the butt of his gun against the back of Carver's head. He slumped to the floor, unconscious. D patted him down and took his guns, then took the rifle he'd brought and his extra firearms, and made himself scarce.

"I THINK they'll be able to finish the voir dire today," Churchill said. He'd come by to have lunch with Jack in his room. It was Wednesday, and Jack was beginning to go stir-crazy. Churchill was doing his best to keep him company, but there was only so much you could do for someone stuck in a hotel room.

"Thank God."

"Yeah, we were afraid they'd drag it out, but the judge isn't having it. He's presided over a few Dominguez trials before, trials that got cut short when witnesses turned up dead. He's moving things right along."

"You think I'll be on the stand by the end of the week?"

"I hope so. You won't be the first witness, but Brad will try to get you up there as fast as he can. We can't get you into Witsec until the trial's over, though, because you could be recalled at any time." He sighed. "I might be able to get Brad to push up your testimony because of the demonstrable threats against your life."

Jack nodded. "You'd think."

Churchill drained his iced tea and sat back. He watched Jack for a moment, and then took a deep breath. "Can I ask you about him?"

Jack was sitting slumped over the table, playing idly with the remnants of his lo mein. "What do you want to know?"

"I don't know. It's... guys in his line of work, they're kind of like urban legends. You always hear about them but never see them, or meet them. I guess I'm curious."

"He's just a man."

"I doubt that."

Jack tossed down his fork and sat back. "Look, if you want to know about D, you'll have to ask him yourself, since you guys are so tight. I'm not telling you a damn thing about him, because it's not my place to talk about him to you and, furthermore, I'm not completely sure I trust you." He seemed to be bracing for an angry response, but Churchill just smiled.

"Good," he said. "That's what I hoped you'd say."

"You're happy that I just told you I don't trust you?"

"Jack, in your position, you can't afford to trust anyone completely."

"I trust D."

Churchill nodded. "I know. I guess he's earned that, hasn't he?"

Jack sat staring into space. "Are you married?"

"Ten years."

"You got any kids?"

"I have two sons."

"And you have a house, I bet. And a car, probably more than one, and this job and all this responsibility, and you probably have friends and co-workers and barbecues in the backyard and aunts and siblings and nieces and nephews and college roommates and all that crap, right?"

Churchill nodded. "Yeah, I do."

"Well, I don't. Not anymore. And once this trial's over I'll never have it. D is all I have, Churchill. Don't expect me to tell you anything about him, or what's between us, because I can't. I can't let it outside myself. Okay?"

"Okay. I'm sorry, Jack. I didn't mean to—"

"I know you didn't. It's just... I'm stuck in this damn room with nothing to do but sit and brood about where he is, or if he's alive or dead, and wonder if I'll ever see him again."

"CHURCHILL."

"It's D."

"Good timing. I just left Jack's... oh wait, you probably know that, don't you?"

D chuckled. "Actually, I ain't watchin' you or him right now, so I guess that makes it good timin'."

"I wish you'd let me tell him you're here."

"It's bad enough you told him we been talkin' all summer. He's probly sore at me."

Churchill was silent for a moment. "D, he misses you so much that I don't think he could be angry about anything you did right now."

D stayed quiet, biting the inside of his cheek, until Churchill's words had passed through his mind and were gone.

"Have you been able to find this JJ person?" Churchill asked.

"No. I'm lookin' under every rock I can think of and as far as I can tell she ain't even in town yet, although she oughta be. She is more'n capable of hidin' from me."

"I'll say it again: give me her description and known aliases and I'll put her on the watch list."

"And I'll say again that I cain't do that. Brothers cain't know that someone's found out about their hits, because if they do they'll jus' call 'em off and get somebody else that we *won't* know about. You gotta trust me. And I got help a that kind, so it ain't all on you."

"Help? From who?"

"Cain't talk 'bout that. Let's jus' say I got some friends in high kinda places. They know yet when he's gonna testify?"

"Brad's hoping he can get him on the stand Friday. That's the first day he's being called to court, anyway."

"So he's leavin' that hotel room on Friday mornin', is what yer tellin' me?"

"That's right. We'll take him by the tunnels."

"Now, if I were JJ, I'd be tryin' ta hit him before then, or on the way. On the way'd be hard and in the hotel room is hard. What route will ya take between the room and the tunnels?"

"The secure elevator here goes directly to the tunnels. We won't ever be exposed."

"Good, that's real good. We're limitin' JJ's options. You watchin' what he eats 'n' drinks?"

"I got a marshal watching as his food is prepared and then he doesn't take his eyes off it until it comes into Jack's room." Churchill hesitated. "What if she's poisoned the ingredients before they get to the kitchen?"

"No, she cain't risk poisonin' people apart from Jack; that'd draw too much attention. She don't dare put nothin' in the hotel's air or water fer the same reason." A thought occurred to D. "What about the cleanin' supplies? She poisoned somebody once by posin' as a hotel maid and puttin' a nerve toxin on the shower nozzle."

"We're not having the hotel staff do any housekeeping. When we need to we'll have marshals take his laundry away. Actually that's standard protection, except for the laundry precautions."

"Good," D said, grudgingly impressed with Churchill's thoroughness.

"How about you?" Churchill asked. "Any sign that anybody's followed you here?"

"Not so far. It's a real good bet they know I'm here anyway. I ain't worryin' 'bout that. They'll come fer me when they want to. I cain't do nothin' 'bout it 'til then, not while I'm lookin' out fer Jack." D sighed. "But I got a feelin' they'll wait ta come fer me until he's through this 'n' safe in Witsec."

"Why?"

"I don't really know what it is they want from me, if it's ta kill me or torture me or jus' make me work fer 'em doin' the kinda work that I normally wouldn't do, but they'd have a helluva bargaining chip as long as he's alive 'n' safe, 'cause I'd do whatever I hadta do ta make sure he stayed that way."

Churchill said nothing for a moment. "You guys are killing me. Both of you. I'm about ready to say to hell with this trial and put you on a plane right this minute with new identities to somewhere remote where nobody'll ever find you."

D sighed. "I wish that was possible, friend." He flipped his phone shut and was about to put it back in his pocket when it rang again. "D."

"It's Meg. Where are you?"

"I'm on 83 comin' back from Towson. What?"

"Meet me at Mercy downtown. I heard it on the scanner, a woman brought in severely beaten. Her description sounded right so I came down to check it out." She hesitated. "D, I think it's JJ."

D blinked. "Who the hell beat her?"

"The police don't know. They found her in an alley over by Lexington Market."

"I'm comin'."

MEGAN was waiting for D at the hospital entrance. "Come on; she's in the ER," she said, heading off without waiting for him to respond.

"What makes ya think it's JJ?"

"She was carrying several IDs in different names and more cash than you'd expect." They came through the double doors into the trauma center. Several police officers were lurking about talking to a doctor; Megan flashed her badge and they were waved through.

D stopped short. The woman in the bed had been beaten to within an inch of her life. Her face was bruised and swollen almost beyond recognition, and one arm was in a cast. "Shit," he muttered.

"Is that her?"

He nodded. "Yeah." He looked at the nurse. "Can she talk?"

"She's a little groggy, but you can talk to her for a minute."

D moved to her bedside, and then glanced back at the nurse and Megan. "Can I, uh...."

The nurse smiled. "We'll leave you alone."

D leaned over JJ's still form. "Hey," he said. "Can you, uh... hear me?" No response. "JJ?" If she could hear him, the use of that name ought to get her attention.

Her eyes opened immediately. She didn't appear groggy at all, but her brow furrowed when she saw him. "D?"

"Yeah, it's D."

She sighed and winced. "Fuck, I shouldn't be surprised. Well, thanks for saving me the trouble of coming to find you."

D was completely lost. "What you talkin' 'bout find me? Who beat on you?"

"Some guys I didn't recognize, but they had a message for you. Said they were letting me live so I could deliver it."

"What message?"

She met his eyes. "They said they weren't going to let me kill Jack Francisco, because...." She swallowed. "Because that's your job, and they still expect you to do it."

Motherfucker. "Well, they gonna be waitin' a long time, because I ain't never gonna kill him."

She nodded. "They said you'd say that, and that you're wrong. You'll kill him. You may not think so now, but you will."

CHAPTER 22

MEGAN was on her cell phone. "Uh-huh. And he's... yeah. Okay." Pause. "Thanks, Pete. Yeah, call me." She hung up and looked over to where D was sitting slumped down in an easy chair in her apartment, one of the generic crash pads the Treasury department kept in cities all over the world for the use of operatives like herself. He was wearing all black, as usual, still had his sunglasses on indoors, and looked like a refugee from a Bono lookalike contest. He was drumming his fingers against the arm of the chair and gnawing on his other thumbnail. "Okay, one of the marshals says they'll probably be ready for Jack to testify after lunch break. The prosecutor's in talking to him now."

He grunted.

"D, you've done all you can." Another grunt. "You ought to try and relax. Have a sandwich or something. Or take a nap. When was the last time you had a good night's sleep?" She wagered that it had been the last time he'd slept next to Jack. "There's nothing we can do until he's off that witness stand."

Grunt the third. "Could go out ta the brothers' house and start shootin' people."

"Uh... huh. Tempting as that is, I don't think that'd be the most discreet course of action."

"Fuck discreet. I'd rather bust some heads."

"That's it. You're switching to decaf." She sighed and sat down on the couch. "There's nothing we can do to protect Jack while he's in that courthouse that we haven't already done, right?"

"Mmm. Guess not."

She watched his profile. She had been watching D for a long time, longer than even he knew. She had long thought that she knew him, as much as a man like him could be known, and had even begun to consider him a friend—a rather strange, one-sided, long-distance friend, but someone who was dependably in her life. But this D, she had never seen. This D who had emotional motives, and who let things affect him, and who showed emotion on his face when he wasn't paying attention. The D she'd known for years was *always* paying attention. "You're still thinking about JJ's message, aren't you?"

He took off his sunglasses and rubbed his nose. "Cain't help it."

"They just did it to throw you off, and look how well it's working!"

"Whoever 'they' are, anyway."

"Well, they clearly couldn't care less about the brothers." She leaned forward. "This is about you. They want *you* to kill Jack."

His jaw tightened. "I won't. I'll die first." Words that could have sounded melodramatic from anyone else sounded like proclamations from the mountaintop coming from D.

"I know. But what's important now is figuring out who these people are. They blackmailed you into taking the hit on Jack, they kidnapped him… now they've followed you here, but haven't done anything to you although they probably could have."

He nodded. "They're stalkin' me. And now I given 'em another card ta play." He pounded his fist on the arm of the chair. "Shoulda kept Jack outta this."

"I think that ship sailed the minute you didn't kill him when you were supposed to." She cleared her throat and hesitated, considering the right phrasing. "Do you think they, uh… know how you feel about Jack? And how he feels about you?"

He met her eyes then, his own narrowed and thoughtful. He held her gaze for a few long moments before looking away. He reached into his pocket and pulled out a small device about the size of an iPod. He turned it on and stared at it.

"What are you doing?"

"I'm watchin' him."

"What is that?"

D sighed. "Tracker."

"You put a *tracker* on him?"

"A course I did! What if he'd gotten kidnapped again or ambushed by the brothers or God knows what else?"

"When did you have time to do that?"

"Tracker's in his gun. Had it there before he took it."

"Well, let's hope he's got it on him."

"He's sposed ta; Churchill got him a permit ta carry. Anyways, it's showin' him at the courthouse, so I guess he's got it."

"They wouldn't let him wear it into the courthouse, permit or not, unless he was law enforcement."

"No, but he'd leave it at the security station and pick it up on his way out, so if it's there, he's there."

She nodded. "What happens after his testimony is over?"

D sighed. "Well, usually he'd hafta stay in town 'til the trial was over in case he got recalled, but Churchill's workin' on gettin' him relocated sooner'n that. Get him outta town. They can always bring him back if he's needed at the trial."

She leaned forward. "And you're really, seriously not going to try and see him before then?"

He looked at her. "No. I cain't."

"Too risky?"

"That, and…." He let his head fall back against the chair and shut his eyes. "I jus' cain't," he murmured. "See him again knowin' I only had a few hours or so before I'd be sayin' goodbye again, for a real long time. Best jus' ta let him go and then take up my business."

Megan hesitated, then reached out and put her hand on his arm. Touching him, even just a casual handshake or shoulder bump, felt so strange after observing him from a distance for so long. It was like waking up one day and discovering you could reach out and touch the people on TV. D turned his head toward her. "I know how hard all this is for you," she said, hoping she sounded sympathetic without being too gooey.

He shrugged. "Don't matter. Gonna be harder before it gets easier, if it ever does get easier."

"But I mean… you've never…." She trailed off. "Never mind."

"What?" He lifted his head and frowned at her.

She took a deep breath. "You've never loved someone like this before, have you?"

He looked away. "Who says I—"

She cut him off. "Don't. Don't insult me."

He met her eyes again and she nearly recoiled at the rawness in his. "I ain't talkin' 'bout this." He stood up and stalked into the other room, leaving Megan staring at nothing and marveling at the vagaries of the male mind.

JACK had been waiting in the witness's room for two hours when Brad Salie entered, looking calm and in control as always. He was a small man with thinning hair and glasses; in fact, he looked like an accountant. But Jack had quickly come to respect him, and his unassuming appearance served him well with juries when they were surprised by his commanding courtroom presence. It helped that he had a deep, booming voice that sounded like it belonged on a man twice his size.

"Shouldn't you be in there doing your Perry Mason thing?" Jack asked.

Brad beckoned him into one of the private consultation rooms and shut the door behind them. "This morning's witnesses are mostly background; Linda's questioning them. I'm sorry we haven't had time to talk this week."

"It's okay. I've been terribly busy watching daytime soaps."

"Carlisle's really going to be loaded for bear when you get up there," Brad said. "You're one of our most important witnesses."

"So I've heard."

"Since all the forensics and the other witnesses corroborate your testimony, all he can really do is attack your credibility, and the reliability of your statement."

"Aren't those the same thing?"

"No. Credibility is whether or not you're lying, and reliability is whether or not what you saw was really what happened. Telling the jury that they should discount a witness's testimony because they're a convicted felon with motive to lie goes to their credibility, but telling them that they should discount the testimony because the witness wasn't wearing his glasses when he saw the defendant fleeing the scene goes to reliability."

"Oh."

"Attacking your credibility is risky, because you're a very credible witness who's risking his life testifying, so going after you too hard just makes him look like a bully, but I suspect he intends to try."

"How?"

Brad sighed. "I think he might drag your sexuality into this somehow."

Jack sat up straighter. "How is *that* relevant?"

"It isn't," Brad said, quickly. "But during voir dire he kept asking potential jurors about their attitudes toward gay men, and he seemed to be favoring the ones who disapprove. The real trick will be how the hell he intends to get that mentioned in court, because there's no way it's legally relevant, but even if he just asks the question and I object and it's sustained, even if his question is stricken and the jury is instructed to disregard, he's still gotten it out there, you know? I really don't know where he's going with this. Dragging it in could backfire for him; if he tries to use your sexuality against you there's a real good chance he'll just come off looking desperate for anything that might possibly taint you as a witness. I just want you to be prepared."

"Okay."

"Attacking your reliability is safer. Carlisle is a big fan of touting the fallibility of cross-racial identifications."

Jack stared. "Seriously?"

"Believe it or not, the idea has some truth to it. There've been several criminological studies that have demonstrated that witnesses have more difficulty distinguishing the facial features of people who are not of their own race. This doesn't mean that cross-racial identifications are worthless, but it definitely gave defense lawyers a big bag of tools to use against eyewitnesses."

"But… these defendants—"

"Are Latino, and you're white, which I know is a bit of a stretch to call them a different race, but I'll lay odds he'll try it. He loves to play little courtroom tricks to demonstrate this too. I remember one case he tried—I just heard about this, mind you—where the defendant was a black man and the witness was a middle-aged white woman. He had her turn her back so she couldn't see what he was doing, and when she turned around again, he'd lined up the defendant with four other black men with the same height, build, haircut, skin tone, and facial hair, wearing the same clothes as the defendant. And she couldn't pick out the defendant, even though she'd been staring at him for hours sitting at the defense table."

Jack blinked. "Damn."

"Yeah, it pretty much destroyed her testimony, even though she'd picked the defendant out of a police lineup. It was a disaster for that prosecutor, who just about blew a blood vessel objecting to this demonstration, but was overruled."

"Well, he's not going to get me on something like that. I'm a facial reconstructive surgeon, Brad. I look at faces for a living."

"I'm counting on that." Brad was quiet for a moment. "Jack… if he brings up your homosexuality, I will do whatever I can to keep him from pursuing that line of questioning. I'm prepared for several avenues he could go down. But I may have to question you on rebuttal to refute things he's implied, if they're allowed to stand. I need to know if you're okay with that."

Jack leaned forward. "You do whatever you have to do to make sure that jury believes me, Brad. You have no idea what I'm giving up to be here and sit on that stand."

"I have an idea."

"No, you really don't. So if it becomes necessary to ask me about my sex life, you go right ahead. I didn't come all this way to have some asshole defense lawyer make it all be for nothing." Jack sighed. "I just want to get it over with."

"Well, you'll get your wish, because I'm calling you after lunch barring catastrophe. I'm going to make it very difficult for him to attack you without looking like an asshole, so hopefully cross will be short and you will be done today."

Jack couldn't fathom being done. This testimony had loomed so large and so all-encompassing over him for so long that it had reshaped everything about his life. The idea that it could just be over and done with in one afternoon seemed ludicrous. "Okay. I'll be ready."

"PLEASE state your name for the record."

"John Edward Francisco."

"And what is your occupation?"

"I'm a maxillofacial surgeon, with a subspecialty in craniofacial surgery."

Brad smiled, that disarming aw-shucks smile that said *I'm just regular folks like you and I don't get this fancy medical jargon either.* "And what is that, exactly?"

"I specialize in facial reconstructive surgery, when there's been trauma, and also in the correction of birth defects of the face, jaw, and skull."

"What degrees have you earned?"

"I have a bachelor of science degree from Dartmouth University, a Doctor of Dental Surgery and a Doctor of Medicine degree, both from Ohio State University."

"So you hold two separate professional degrees, one in dentistry and one in medicine."

"Yes. A DDS degree is required to specialize in maxillofacial surgery."

"You went to dental school *and* medical school?" Brad infused a touch of *can-you-believe-how-amazing-this-guy-is?* awe into his question, clearly for the jury's benefit. They did seem pretty impressed.

"Yes, it was a lot of school," Jack said, smiling a little in what he hoped was a self-deprecating manner. The last thing he wanted was to come off as an arrogant asshole with a God complex.

"And where did you work at the time of the crime, Dr. Francisco?"

"At Johns Hopkins Medical Center."

"In what capacity?"

"I was an attending surgeon."

"The victim, Maria Dominguez, also worked at Johns Hopkins, is that correct?"

"Yes. I'm told she worked in physical facilities as part of the cleaning staff."

"Did you know her?"

"No. I had seen her around, but I didn't know her by name. It's a large hospital."

"Were you aware that her husband, who she was in the process of divorcing, was second cousin to the defendant, Tommy Dominguez, and his brother Raoul?"

"Not at all."

"The day of Maria's death, what time did you leave work?"

"Around six-thirty."

"And where did you go?"

"To the staff parking garage."

"Why did you go there?"

"To get in my car and go home."

"Dr. Francisco, please describe what you saw when you entered the parking garage."

Jack resettled himself in his chair and took a breath. This was it. So far, it had been cake; Brad was easing him into the courtroom setting and establishing his bona fides for the jury. He'd done as instructed and not looked at the defendants or the jury, keeping his eyes on Brad, who stood in front of the prosecutor's table near the jury box so they had a good look at him. Brad had pragmatically advised Jack to play his looks to the female jurors, if he could do so without seeming smarmy or conceited, but Jack didn't really know how to do that except to sit up straight, so that's what he did. "I was about halfway to my car. I had my keys in my hand. There was a van parked against the wall to my right. As I passed behind a retaining wall between me and the van, I heard a struggle. I stopped and looked. There were two men restraining a woman."

"Did you recognize Maria Dominguez?"

"Not immediately."

"Please continue."

"Before I could even open my mouth to call out, one of the men stabbed her here," he said, putting his hand on his upper chest. "Overhand, like this," he said, demonstrating.

"Which of the men did the stabbing?"

"The taller one."

"What did you do when you saw this man stab Maria?"

"I dropped down to a crouch behind the retaining wall, so the men couldn't see me."

"Were you frightened?"

"Yes. I was afraid if they knew I'd seen, they'd come and kill me too."

"What did you do then?"

"I heard car doors open and close, and I heard the car pull out. I looked over the wall and tried to remember the license plate. I called nine-one-one. The woman was lying on the ground by the van. After the car had gone, I went to her to see if I could render aid."

"And could you?"

"Her stab wound was very deep and bleeding profusely. I put pressure on it, but there was very little I could do. The police arrived very quickly, and they brought a gurney out of the hospital to take her inside. I told the police what I'd seen, and what I could remember of the license plate."

"Dr. Francisco, do you see the men who stabbed Maria Dominguez in the courtroom today?"

"Yes, I do." At this point, Jack swung over and looked at the defendants, seeing their faces for the first time since the day he'd seen them commit murder. It was chilling. They were both staring at him with flat, reptilian eyes, no affect visible on their faces, clean-shaven and wearing good-boy suits. "Those are the men, right there," he said, pointing.

Brad nodded. "Let the record show that the witness had identified the defendants, Thomas Dominguez and Carlos Alvarez."

"So noted," said Judge Petersen.

"Dr. Francisco, just a few more questions. Do you stand to gain anything by testifying here today?"

"No."

"In fact, your testimony has placed you in considerable danger."

Carlisle rose. "Objection, Your Honor. The people have introduced no direct evidence that Dr. Francisco's life has been threatened, by my clients or anyone else."

"I'll withdraw the question. Dr. Francisco, what has been your living situation since you witnessed this crime?"

"I've been under the protection of the U.S. Marshals' office."

"Witness protection, you mean."

"Yes."

"In fact you've had to give up your career, your home, your friends and family, all for the sake of this testimony."

Jack sighed. "Yes, that's true."

"Thank you, Dr. Francisco. No further questions." Brad sat down at the prosecutor's table, giving Jack a small, tight nod of approval.

Rod Carlisle stood up and approached the podium. Jack mentally braced himself, because unlike the questions posed to him by Brad Salie, he didn't know exactly what to expect.

Carlisle, unlike Brad, looked like a high-powered defense attorney. He was tall and leonine, with a mane of perfectly coiffed silver hair and a Caribbean tan. His clothes were perfect. He took his sweet time getting up and gathering his papers, as if Jack were not worth his haste and the testimony he'd just given was of no consequence. Jack waited patiently, watching him.

Finally, he stood before the witness stand and fixed Jack with a steady gaze. "Dr. Francisco, are you a homosexual?"

Brad shot to his feet as if he'd just been zapped with a cattle prod. "Objection, Your Honor! The witness's sexual orientation is not relevant!"

Petersen gave Carlisle a withering look. "He has a point, Counselor."

"Your Honor, we suspect that the witness was distracted in that parking garage, and the relevance of his sexual orientation will be clear in a moment."

Petersen sighed. "It had better become clear damn quick. Overruled."

Carlisle turned back to Jack. "Dr. Francisco?"

Jack didn't allow himself a flinch or a fidget. "Yes, I am."

"And are you currently in a relationship?"

Jack sighed. "If you're asking me for a date, Mr. Carlisle, your timing sucks." The courtroom erupted in laughter, and Carlisle flushed. He turned to the judge.

"Your Honor, I'd ask that you direct the witness to refrain from flippant remarks and answer the question."

"Dr. Francisco, please answer Mr. Carlisle's... *question,*" Petersen said, his distaste for this line of questioning evident.

The problem was that Jack didn't really know the answer. He knew what he wanted the answer to be, so he went with that. "Yes, I am."

"Were you at the time of the crime?"

"No, I was not."

"So, you've met someone since you've been in... what was the term? Protective custody?"

Brad jumped up again. "Your Honor, is there a relevant question anywhere in our future?"

"Get to the point, Mr. Carlisle."

Carlisle whirled around in dramatic fashion and faced Jack. "Dr. Francisco, isn't it true that you had arranged to meet up with a male prostitute in that parking garage?"

Jack was stunned by this blatant fabrication, but was spared answering by the seizure Brad Salie appeared to be having. "Objection!" he boomed, both hands going into the air. "Presumes facts not in evidence! Your Honor, defense counsel has no evidence that such a person ever existed or that such an encounter was ever planned!"

"Sustained."

Carlisle wasn't done. "And isn't it true that you were, in fact, receiving oral sex at the time of the crime and were therefore too distracted to have seen anything at all, let alone my clients murdering anyone?"

"Now he's just making stuff up!" Brad yelled. The courtroom was awash in shocked murmurings.

Petersen banged his gavel to quiet the hubbub. "Approach!" he barked. The two attorneys approached the bench, but Jack could hear every word.

"Mr. Carlisle, do you have any evidence that Dr. Francisco was thus engaged?" Petersen asked.

"Your Honor, I am entitled to present reasonable theories as to witness reliability."

"*Reasonable* theories," Brad hissed. "No such encounter was planned or executed, Your Honor, and any attempt to insinuate otherwise is an outright lie, and I will have him censured and disbarred for making false and prejudicial accusations! He is not allowed to just invent people and events that never existed!"

"If I am not allowed to question the witness's reliability then I have grounds for appeal right there," Carlisle said.

"Don't you threaten me in my courtroom," Petersen said. "You will cease this line of questioning immediately and your questions about the witness's sexuality will be stricken." He looked at Brad. "This may be grounds for a mistrial, Mr. Salie."

Jack's heart sank. *Please, don't ask for a mistrial. I can't go through this again.*

"I know it is, Your Honor, but my witnesses are in enough danger as it is. In *fact*, I might suspect Mr. Carlisle of intentionally introducing prejudicial lines of questioning *hoping* to get a mistrial to give his clients more time to bump off the people brave enough to testify against them!"

"Your Honor, this is an outrage—" Carlisle began, but was quickly shushed.

"You've said quite enough, Mr. Carlisle. You don't intend to move for a mistrial, Brad?"

"No, Your Honor, but it still remains that the defense has introduced this idea into the jury's minds and—"

"I know, Counselor. I'll deal with it. Dismissed." Brad and Carlisle returned to their tables and Judge Petersen faced the jury. "Ladies and gentleman, Mr. Carlisle's questions regarding Dr. Francisco's sexual orientation will be stricken from the record and I instruct you to disregard them. Further, there has been no evidence submitted to this court that the encounter Mr. Carlisle described ever took place, nor does this court have any reason to think it did. On a personal note I'd like to apologize to Dr. Francisco for having allowed this line of questioning and subjected him to this accusation."

"Thank you, Your Honor," Jack said. He glanced at Brad, who nodded, looking grim but determined.

"Mr. Carlisle, if you have any *relevant* questions for Dr. Francisco, you may continue."

Carlisle appeared to be totally unruffled by his defeat and went on as if everything was going just how he'd planned. "Dr. Francisco, what is your race, for the record?"

Jack glanced at Brad, who gave him a slight here-we-go eye-roll. "Genetically, there's no such thing as race," he said.

"I'll rephrase. What is your race in the common, non-genetic use of the term?"

"I'm Caucasian."

"And the defendants are Latino, are they not?"

"They are."

"Dr. Francisco, earlier today we heard testimony from an expert in eyewitness identification who informed us that witnesses often have difficulty accurately identifying people of a different race from their own. Are you familiar with this phenomenon?"

"I am, yes."

"Do you still maintain that the men you saw murder Maria Dominguez were the defendants?"

"Yes, absolutely."

"How can you be so positive?"

"Mr. Carlisle, I'm a doctor who specializes in faces, and I have a very good eye for detail. Their *ethnicity* did not affect my ability to clearly identify them. I am positive that the men I saw are your clients." That had been a tip from Brad, to refer to the defendants as "your clients" during cross-examination, to subtly reinforce the attorney's connection to the criminals on trial and his desire to get them off.

"You have a good eye for detail?" Carlisle said.

"I think so, yes."

Carlisle abruptly turned his back to Jack. "What color are my eyes, then?"

Brad jumped up. "Your Honor, the witness has answered defense counsel's questions; this demonstration is argumentative and unnecessary."

Carlisle answered while keeping his back turned. "Witness has touted his eye for detail, I am entitled to test this assertion if we are to accept his identification of the defendants."

Petersen sighed. "Overruled."

"Dr. Francisco? We're waiting."

Jack smiled. *Oral sex in the garage. You asked for this, asshole.* "Mr. Carlisle, your eyes appear to be blue. However, the presence of a thin circle of brown around the pupils makes me think they're probably colored contact lenses. Your eyelashes are unusually short, your lower lip is slightly fuller than your upper, and I suspect you are of Mediterranean descent based on your prominent brow shelf, cleft chin and squared-off jawline. Your earlobes are small and attached and you nicked yourself shaving this morning under the left side of your jaw. You have a small mole on your upper right cheek, a chicken pox scar in almost the same spot on your left, your teeth are veneers, you've had a nose job, and I think you've had cheek implants too." He was sorely tempted to add a smart-ass *Anything else?* but he thought he'd made his point, and rubbing it in would just make him look like a smug jerk.

The jury was smiling and tossing *nyah, nyah* glances at Carlisle, who had clearly not endeared himself to them with his grandstanding. The gallery was tittering. Brad Salie was turning purple with suppressed glee. Carlisle turned to face him, the only sign of distress a slight blush around his ears. "No further questions," he said, and went back to his table.

Brad stood. "No redirect, Your Honor."

Petersen nodded. "The witness is excused."

JACK had to wait until court was adjourned in case he was recalled, but just after four o'clock Brad came hurtling into the witness's room and made a beeline right for him. He grasped Jack's shoulders, beaming. "You. If it weren't really inappropriate I could tongue-kiss you right now."

"Uh, that's okay."

"That was *brilliant.*"

"I can't believe he made that shit up about a male prostitute and a blow job!"

"Oh, and I intend to follow up on that, believe me. I want that jackass at least censured for making shit up. But it might actually have worked in our favor."

"Seriously?"

"Yeah. The fact that the jury found out he was inventing all that just made it very clear to them that he is absolutely terrified of your testimony, or else he wouldn't go to such lengths to discredit you. So what you said must be pretty important."

Jack nodded. "Yeah, I can see that."

"Well, Jack, you're done! How does it feel?"

Kinda shitty, actually. "I don't know. I've been thinking about giving this testimony for so long, now that it's over… I'm a bit lost."

"When are you going into Witsec?"

"I don't know."

"As soon as possible," said Churchill, who had just entered the room. He came up to Jack and shook his hand. "You were really great up there," he said. "Told you. Prosecutor's wet dream."

"Well, he's at least got time to come out for a drink," Brad said.

Churchill looked at Jack. "I don't know. I need to keep him secure."

"There's a bar on the next block that we can get to with the tunnels; we go there all the time. Come on, Churchill! The brothers aren't going to waltz up and pop him in a bar full of witnesses!"

Suddenly, Jack wanted to go out for a drink with the boys. Badly. "Yeah, I'd like that," he said.

"Jack—"

"I've been stuck in that hotel room for almost a week, and I'm going to be there all weekend, right?"

"Yeah," Churchill said, looking glum.

"It'll be fine. One night. Let me celebrate getting all that shit into the court records."

Churchill thought for a moment, and then gave a reluctant nod. "All right. But I'm coming too, with a couple armed marshals."

Jack grinned. "Great!"

Brad clapped Jack on the shoulder. "I've got to file some paperwork and meet with Linda just for a moment. Wait here? I'll come get you within the hour."

"We'll be here." Brad left and Jack settled back into his chair, feeling like he might be rejoining the human race, if only for a few brief hours. Normal people didn't live in hotel rooms and hide in other people's brothers' houses for months on end; they rode the subway and ate lunch in restaurants and went out for drinks with friends.

And their boyfriends.

Jack shut his eyes and pictured himself in a bar. Churchill and Brad were there, and the marshals who'd been guarding him… and he turned his head and there was D, smiling and drinking beer and plugging quarters into the jukebox, even laughing at the off-color jokes and fending off advances from women.

He rubbed his eyes and banished the vision. D was far away, and thinking of him now could only hurt.

"Jack, I'll be back in a minute," Churchill said. "Got to make a phone call."

"Okay," Jack said, barely noticing. He put his head down on his arms, folded on the tabletop, and let his eyes fall shut again, the background noise of conversation and people coming and going fading away. *Just a few quick winks....*

He was asleep within a minute.

CHAPTER 23

D'S PHONE had rung three times before he answered, a measure of his distraction. "Yeah?"

"It's Churchill."

"Yeah?"

"Um… well, Jack's done testifying."

D exhaled. "Good."

"The prosecutor invited Jack to come out for a drink, and me too, and… well, we're going."

He sat up straighter. "I swear it sounded like you jus' said you was' lettin' Jack go ta some unsecured location where he could be shot or poisoned or God knows what."

"He isn't a prisoner, D. He's performed a heroic civic service. The man deserves a little… relaxation."

"He'll be real fuckin' relaxed when he's *dead!*" D exclaimed.

"I think you're being overly paranoid. We will be in a public place in front of many witnesses, most of whom will be lawyers and police officers, we can get there through the tunnels to minimize his exposure, and he will be guarded."

"That don't make it safe. If he were my mark I can think of a half-dozen ways ta kill him in them circumstances and you'd never know it was me or even realize it was happenin' 'til it was too fuckin' late."

"D, Jack wants to go. He's frustrated and he's got cabin fever and he misses you. He deserves some socialization."

That gave D pause. If it were up to him, he'd keep Jack locked in a cage forever, where no one could get to him and he'd always be safe. But much as he might want to, much as he'd sleep better knowing that Jack was safe, he couldn't do that. "Safe" could quickly come to mean "trapped." And trapped things tended to want to escape. "Guess I ain't stoppin' ya," D grumbled. "But I'll be watchin'."

"You do whatever you feel you have to do," Churchill said. He sounded annoyed.

"What I done ta piss you off, now?"

"Oh, I'm sorry, do I sound pissed off? Maybe it's just looking at that man's face day in and day out, that hangdog look that says he thinks he's never going to see you again, when all the time you're right here and you could be spending this time *with* him instead of watching him day and night. Stalking isn't usually recommended as the basis for a lasting relationship, you know."

"It's too risky fer him ta know—"

"Too risky, yeah. Risky for him, or for you?"

"Huh?"

"I know why you won't let me tell him you're here. Because he'd insist on seeing you, and you can't allow that, can you?"

"No, I fuckin' cain't!" D shouted. "I cain't be distracted. I cain't let my guard down fer a single second and Jack is the damn national champion a distractin' me! I gotta concentrate if I am gonna protect him."

"That is *my job* now, D, and I wish you'd let me do it."

"Fer how long? How long you gonna watch over him, and anticipate any threat that might come? I'm prepared ta do it forever; how 'bout you?" Silence. "Yeah. It's *my* job ta protect him. My only job. And I aim ta do it." He hung up, fuming.

Fuckin' guy. Tellin' me what's what.

Except he's right and ya know he is. Jack would insist on seein' you if he knew you was here and you cain't stand ta see him when all you'd be thinkin' 'bout is having ta leave him again, for a lot longer this time.

God. I cain't go on this way. I cain't live like this. I cain't do my fuckin' job.

I cain't protect him like this. I'm too damn... involved. *I think a somethin' happenin' ta him 'n' my guts get all twisted up 'n' I cain't think. I ain't no good ta him like that.*

I gotta do somethin'.

THE bar was full of the after-work happy-hour crowd, ties loosened and hair down, smiling and ordering margaritas and Cosmos and martinis. A lot of them seemed to be lawyers, and all of them seemed to know who Jack was. He wouldn't have to buy a drink for himself for the next twenty rounds, if he didn't pass out first.

Everyone seemed to have heard the story of Carlisle's disastrous cross-examination. "Did you really tell that Armani asshole he was wearing colored contacts?" some lawyer asked Jack.

He nodded. "That color blue does not exist in nature."

"Goddamn, I'd've paid good money to see that."

"Shove off my witness, Byron," Brad said, returning to Jack's side. Churchill was sticking close to him without being too obvious about it, and his two marshal keepers were bellied up to the bar. Jack didn't care. He was riding so high he felt like calling up Raoul Dominguez and telling him to do his worst. "You're quite the folk hero, Jack," he said.

"Whatever."

"You made a lot of friends today among the law-and-order types. You'll sure as hell never get a speeding ticket in Baltimore ever again."

"Not as if I'll actually be living here anymore," Jack said.

Brad sobered. "I'm sorry that has to be part of this."

"Don't be. I knew what I was getting into." Jack drained his gin and tonic. "Hey, let me ask you something."

"Shoot."

"Why did Carlisle risk such a showy maneuver with that eye-color thing? Seems like it was pretty fair odds I'd have noticed his eye color."

"It was a risk, yeah. He's pulled tricks like that in the past, although this particular one was new to me. It's a pretty safe bet for him, though. Witnesses are anxious, they're under pressure, and on the stand they're usually looking at the defendants, into the gallery, at the prosecutor… and if they look at Carlisle, they're not really seeing him. I'm guessing after today he'll think twice before trying that again, though."

Jack laughed. "Maybe." He stood up. "I'm gonna go get a bottled water. Don't feel like getting hammered tonight."

He headed through the crowd toward the bar, craning his neck over the thickening crowds of off-duty lawyers. People brushed by close, and it felt a little claustrophobic. Perhaps he'd gotten used to solitude after all.

Suddenly, he felt something pressed into his hand. He looked around, but no one met his eyes, and it could have been anybody. He made his way to the side of the bar and looked down at the folded-up note in his palm. Jack's eyes narrowed and he looked around again. No one was paying him any particular attention. He set his glass on the bar. Churchill was over with Brad. The marshals were both flirting with pretty women in power suits.

He hunched over a little and made his way to the men's room, pardon-meing through the crush of people, growing more crushing with each minute. He shut himself in a stall and sat down to read the note. His fingers shook as he opened the careful folds. Threat? Request? Fan letter?

We have D.

Jack's insides went cold and slippery, like a fish fresh from the water, flopping on the boat deck and gasping for breath where there was none to be had, the strange sun blinding and burning. "Shit," he muttered.

Come to the alley behind the bar. Come alone. We are watching. Alert no one or he dies.

You have ten minutes.

Jack read the note three times. It was handwritten in generic block letters.

They can't possibly have D. He's far away from here.

And what, they're incapable of finding him and bringing him here? They found you in Vegas, didn't they?

There's no way they captured him. He's too smart. He'd never allow it to happen.

He's human. And he's not exactly on his A-game, is he? You know how distracted you are; don't you think he might be too?

But I'm just me. He's… D. He'd never let himself get that distracted.

Do you know that?

Jack knew that this internal argument was futile, because even if he was ninety-nine percent sure that they were bluffing, that one percent doubt that they might not be wouldn't let him do nothing. He couldn't just throw the note away and dismiss it. What if they really had him? They probably didn't. What if they did? What if he did nothing and they killed him?

They couldn't. He'd get away, or something. They can't kill D.

He isn't Superman, even if he seems that way to you sometimes. They could kill him. If they have him.

They don't have him.

Jack pressed his balled fists to his mouth to stifle a cry of frustration. He struck the wall hard, hard enough to hurt and jolt him back to the situation.

Tell Churchill. Tell somebody.

They said not to tell. They're watching.

They're not watching. It's a trap. They're just trying to get you to come out there alone so they can grab you. It's so obvious. It's an obvious trap.

So obvious it might be real. But I have to walk into it whether it's real or not.

D would have a seizure if he could hear you thinking things like that.

Fuck D. He isn't here. I'm by myself and there's nobody to help me.

It's a trap. D is miles from here.

But what if he isn't? What if he's out there right now with a gun to his head?

Then he's praying you don't come out there. He wouldn't want you to go into that alley even if they do have him.

That isn't up to him. He might be willing to give himself up but I'm sure as hell not willing to let him.

He would yell at you until he was purple that it's a trap, you should know it's a trap, it's obviously a trap.

Get help.

I can't get help.

What would you do to save him? What would you give up?

Everything.

There is no one to help me now.

There is only me.

But I'm not going to just walk out there like a sacrificial lamb.

Jack flushed the note and slipped out of the men's room. A quick glance out at the bar showed the marshals still chatting up the ladies. Churchill was still with Brad, but he wasn't paying attention. He was looking around the room for Jack. *Shit.*

Jack ducked into the coatroom. He grabbed somebody's baseball cap and jammed it on his head. He stripped down to his undershirt and put on someone's leather jacket. His gun was in a holster strapped to his belt; he released the safety strap and checked its load. He pulled the cap further down on his head, ducked his chin down and bent his knees to take a few inches off his height. He slunk through the crowd, unnoticed, and went out the front door.

He walked casually down the sidewalk, heading for the alley. In fact, there were two alleys on this block, one cutting it in half east to west, and another one branching off in a T-junction to the north. It was this shorter alley that ran behind the bar. The bar had a rear entrance onto this alley; no doubt they expected him to use it, which he had no intention of doing.

He walked into the longer east/west alley and paused. He didn't see or hear anyone. He needed a better lay of the land.

He jumped up to grab the bottom rung of the ladder on a nearby fire escape, dragged it down and climbed up to the roof. Crouching low, he slunk across the rooftops until he was over the bar. He took a deep breath and peered over the side.

At first he didn't see anything, but then a slight movement drew his eye. A dark shape of a stranger, standing just to the left of the bar's back door, a glowing cherry of a cigarette marking him. He had his back to the T-junction. Jack peered into the dimness, but didn't see anyone else.

He went back to the fire escape and descended. He walked carefully to the T-junction, eyeing the ground as best he could so he didn't step on anything noisy. At the corner, he shut his eyes and tried to compose himself, pull some of that silent-and-detached armor of D around him. Some of that had to have rubbed off on him, given all the rubbing they'd done over the past weeks.

What the hell do you think you're doing, Francisco? Who do you think you are, Action Dentist? What are you doing skulking around dark alleys trying to rescue a man who would be mad at you for doing it, can take excellent care of himself and probably doesn't need rescuing in the first place?

Jack shut his eyes.

I know who I am. I put people's faces back together. I once gave a man who'd fallen through the ice internal CPR for half an hour straight. I sat in front of ruthless mob bosses, told a jury what they'd done and sent their asshole lawyer to school. And I got a man with a steel-plated heart to tell me things he'd never told anyone.

I don't know what I'm doing. So here we go.

He withdrew his gun, holding it low at his side, and then quickly slipped around the corner into the alley behind the bar.

D CUPPED his hand around the dim display of the tracking monitor to keep its glow from attracting attention. He'd found a perch on a fire escape that overlooked the street and had tucked himself into the shadows of a corner to watch Jack's dot inside the building. This was as close as he'd been to Jack in a week, and watching him through a hotel window with high-powered field glasses just didn't cut it.

He scanned the street, seeing nothing but pedestrians and cars. So far there wasn't anything suspicious, but it was too goddamned exposed; he didn't like it.

He stared down at the roof of the bar, the third rooftop up from the cross street beneath his feet, the demarcations between storefronts indistinguishable from above, just a knobby expanse of gravel-and-tar roofing with ventilation shafts, HVAC units, and random protuberances jutting up like gravestones. *He's in there right now. Havin' a drink. Probly smilin' that smile. Laughin' and bein' congratulated on a job well done. As he oughta be.*

You could jus' go down there and walk in. Surprise him. Imagine the look on his face when he saw ya. He'd grin so wide, and his eyes'd light up, and then maybe he'd even hug ya. You could have him in yer arms again right now. Jus'... go on down. It's easy. Where's the harm, really? He's goin' inta Witsec real soon. You ain't got much time, so take some. Take some time with him.

It was so seductive. And it would be so easy to give in. But he couldn't. He had work to do, and he couldn't afford to take his eyes off his goals. That was how he'd survived more than ten years in a cutthroat business, and how he'd managed to keep his sanity in the meantime. He wouldn't give it up now.

He glanced down at the tracking monitor and jumped. Jack's glowing red dot was no longer in the bar. It was around the corner and moving into the alley—the dark, deserted alley. D whipped out his binoculars and peered into the dimness. There was a man. A dark stranger, standing by the rear door to the bar. His cigarette glowed briefly red. D could just make out his face.

He was on his feet and riding the ladder down to the ground before another thought could pass through his mind.

JACK crept slowly along the wall, his dark coat invisible in the shadows. He was pressed against the same wall where the stranger waited, several storefronts down. He watched him for a few moments; the man didn't move. He crept along the wall until he was about five feet away. He hesitated, sucking in a steadying breath.

Here goes. My first real-life application of all those gun-handling lessons.

He raised the gun to shoulder height, supporting it firmly with both hands. "Don't move," he said. He wanted it to sound commanding and confident, but instead it sounded a bit like the kind of squeaky toy you might give a dog to play with.

The man waiting for him went very still, then slowly turned to face him. He had a dark, swarthy face and glittering rattlesnake eyes, and he didn't seem at all perturbed to have a gun pointed in his face. "Hello, Mr. Francisco," he said. He calmly reached out and slid the heavy security beam over the bar's rear entrance.

"That's *Dr.* Francisco."

"So it is. My apologies."

Jack kept the gun on the man's face. "Where's D?"

The stranger sighed. "You didn't really think we had him, did you?"

Even though Jack had expected this, he felt an untidy mixture of relief, dread, and disappointment. Relief that D was not in danger, dread that he himself most definitely was, and disappointment that he'd screwed up all his courage and come out here for nothing. "No, not really."

"But you came out anyway," the stranger said, nodding. "That was very brave. But foolish." The man took out a lighter and flicked it on.

Jack barely had time to register that this was a signal of some sort before two shapes detached from the shadows and rushed him. His gun was knocked out of his hands. The immediacy of the assault surprised him. *Do something! You learned something from all those Krav Maga lessons, didn't you?*

It was all happening too fast. One of them knocked him down, then another hauled him to his feet. He was punched across the face. *Jesus God that hurts when it's for real.* The pain exploded over his whole skull and made the world fade white for a moment and his hearing cut out. *Shit, D never warned me it'd feel like that.*

Another punch was flying through the air when something clicked over in his brain. *React. Hurt. Take advantage.* Jack stepped toward the man and turned his back quickly, grabbing the punching arm out of the air. He slammed his elbow back into the man's chest and stomped on his foot as hard as he could, then pushed him over onto his side. He was grabbed from behind and, without thinking, he whipped his head back and rammed it into the nose behind him. It hurt him almost as much as it sounded like it hurt the other guy.

The stranger was just watching all of this, silently, hands in his pockets.

His arms were seized and yanked around behind him. The two men he'd managed to hurt—a little—were back on their feet and at his sides. They dragged him to the center of the alley and held him. Jack struggled, but he was pinned.

The stranger appeared in front of him. "That was... not so bad," he said. Without warning, he stepped forward and punched Jack again, harder this time. All the air rushed out of Jack's chest and his knees buckled. The pain was enormous. "I was asked to pass that on by Roderick Carlisle. He's quite put out, you know. He'll never live that down, what happened today. Myself, I thought it was funny. He really is an asshole of astonishing magnitude." He sighed. "We don't have much time. Your minders are probably already looking for you. I think I ought to sedate you for the ride."

"Where are we going?"

"Does it matter?" He pulled out a syringe just as someone tried the bar's back door. Jack heard Churchill's voice, then the door shuddered on its hinges as it was struck from inside. The stranger sighed. "All right, no time. Bring him." He was lifted under the armpits but then he heard two quick spits from behind him, and he was abruptly released. It took a moment for him to realize that both of the men holding him were now on the ground at his feet.

The stranger just blinked, holding his syringe aloft in one elegant hand like it was a fancy cocktail in a delicate glass. His eyes slid past Jack's face to the alley beyond.

Jack turned to see a dark figure approaching, a gun in one raised hand, the dim light glinting off the silencer. It wasn't Churchill. The figure passed in front of the Exit sign of the neighboring building and was briefly silhouetted by the sign's red glow.

Jack's mouth hung open, his injuries forgotten. The pain in his face receded to a dull roar behind the rushing of blood in his ears.

D wasn't looking at him, but past him to the stranger. Jack swung around and realized he was blocking D's shot. "Jack, get down," D said, calm and icy as if he were commenting on the unseasonably cold weather.

Jack lurched out of the way on rubbery legs and D fired, but the stranger had taken advantage of his momentary hesitation and disappeared into the shadows. Jack heard running footsteps but couldn't see where he'd gone.

He turned back around. "D, what the…." The words were swallowed as fast as they could be uttered.

D was gone too. Jack turned in a circle, hearing sirens approaching, and more running footsteps, wondering if he'd hallucinated it. Had D just been here, or had it been a product of his overstressed brain? No, he'd been here. There were two dead bodies at Jack's feet who could swear to it. Churchill and the marshals appeared at the mouth of the alley and ran toward him, one of the marshals talking into a radio. "Jack! Are you all right?" Churchill demanded. The marshals were off in separate directions in the alley.

"Yeah, uh… I saw—"

"What the fuck were you thinking, going off by yourself?" Churchill shouted, grabbing Jack by the coat. "You could have been killed! What made you come out here alone?"

"I got… got this note…. D was here."

Churchill looked at him sharply. "What?"

"D was just here. Right here. These guys had me… this other guy was going to inject me with something…. D shot them. The other guy got away, I guess… guess D went after him…." He snapped out of his daze. "Why the fuck is he here? He's supposed to be far, far away! That was the whole idea! Me here, him… not here!"

"Jack, I can explain…."

Churchill's guilty face snapped Jack to a new level of rage. "You *KNEW?*" he thundered. "You knew he was here and you didn't tell me?"

"He wouldn't let me. He—"

"Don't! I don't want to hear it!"

"Jack, let's get you to a hospital; you're hurt."

Jack shook him off. "I'm not going anywhere! D!" he shouted, walking off toward were D had vanished. "You come back here so I can kick your ass and don't you think I won't! D! I know you can hear me, you…."

Jack's words were abruptly cut off as he staggered against a wall and bent over, his dinner coming up and splashing onto the dirty pavement. Churchill was at his side, one hand on his shoulder. "It's okay, Jack. It's over."

"No," Jack choked, tears streaming from his eyes. "It'll never be over, it'll just go on and on and on—"

"Come on, let's get you out of here. I want you checked out. I should never have let you come here."

"My gun," Jack said, straightening up and wiping his mouth. "Where's my gun?"

"We'll find it later—"

"No!" Jack exclaimed. "I'm not leaving without it. D gave me that gun; I'm not going to lose it."

Churchill pointed. "There it is." He picked it up and handed it to Jack, who took it with both hands and stared at it.

"I never even fired it," he said, blinking.

"That's a *good* thing." Jack could only stare at the gun, hypnotized by its shiny, compact efficiency. "Come on, Jack. The police will handle all this. Let's get you someplace safe."

Jack nodded and let Churchill lead him away.

"THESE two each got it once in the back of the head. Looks like a nine mil. Dead center, each one. That's pretty good shooting in the dark," the crime scene tech said, the last sentence coming out with sarcasm. It was near superhuman shooting and they both knew it. "No ID."

"Shocker," Churchill said, moodily puffing on a cigar. "We'll run their prints. Betcha they've each got close personal friends named Dominguez."

It had been several hours since the shooting in back of the bar. Churchill had pieced together what had happened, except he couldn't exactly tell the local police about D's involvement. He spared barely a thought to the ethics of fabricating a story for them. His priority was the safety of his witness, and somehow that imperative had swelled and expanded until it included protecting D too. There had definitely been a third man in the alley, and it was looking like they were going to pin the shootings of these two on him. They'd been lackeys, and he had killed them to keep them from talking. It was cold-blooded but not unheard of.

The third man's identity was unknown, except Churchill had a pretty good idea who it had been, but maybe if he didn't say the name out loud it wouldn't be true.

Jack had been checked at the hospital, pronounced bruised and battered but okay, and taken back to his hotel room where he was no doubt pacing the floor and muttering to himself.

Churchill could have shot himself in the head for bringing him here. It hadn't seemed like an unreasonable risk. No on-street exposure, a crowded public place, and a security escort three men strong. But their unnamed friend had devised a way to get Jack out of that safety as efficiently as if he'd been pulling out a splinter. So what had Jack done? Pulled a gun and snuck up on the guy. It had backfired spectacularly, but you had to hand it to the guy: he had stones.

Those minutes when he'd realized that Jack was not, in fact, in the bathroom had been… bad. Searching the bar, the growing realization that he wasn't there, that barred back door only telling him that his witness might be already dead. He sighed and wandered off. This wasn't his crime scene. Local PD would handle these guys.

His cell phone vibrated and he pulled it out to find a text message.

Meet across the street by the archway.

He walked down the alley to the cross street. There was a stone arch that led into the courtyard of a nearby building; behind one of the uprights was a shadow a little denser and taller than the others around it. Churchill joined him, barely able to make him out in the dimness. "Why aren'tcha with Jack?"

"I don't stick to him twenty-four/seven, you know. He's in his hotel room with marshals at the door. He's safe."

"Sorry if I don't take yer word on that as too trustworthy jus' now."

"I know, D. You're the only one capable of protecting him and the rest of us can all just go drown ourselves, right?"

Silence. "Ya know who that was in the alley, don'tcha?"

"I'm trying to take one thing at a time here."

"It was Petros."

"Shit, now you've done it. Said the name." He sighed. "You didn't catch him, did you?"

"Gave me the slip. That ain't no mean feat. Fucker's like mercury, cain't pick it up, if ya try it just skitters away like a little... skittery thing." D sounded discouraged. "I'll get X to have another go at him."

Churchill stubbed out his cigar on the ground. "I'll be taking Jack up to Albany on Monday morning."

"Where ya gonna relocate him?"

"D, you know I can't tell you that."

"Ya think I won't find out?"

"Probably, but that doesn't mean I can tell you. This isn't a court of law where you can argue inevitable discovery."

D nodded. "All right." He shrugged his coat closer around his shoulders. "Take me to him."

Churchill blinked. "You... you want to see Jack?"

He was quiet for several beats. "I'd been any later, he'd a been gone. Few seconds is all it takes. I saw it happen, ya know. Minute I realized Petros was in that alley I was runnin' there, but the whole way I saw it. Getting there and him gone, all a them gone. No idea where." He stared at the ground. "I gotta see him," he said, his voice quiet and embarrassed. "I cain't do this no more. Only way I can be sure he's safe is if I'm standing beside him." He lifted his head and met Churchill's eyes, his barely visible in the dark. "I gotta see him," he repeated.

Churchill nodded. "It's about goddamn time."

JACK paced his hotel room, muttering to himself and trying to ignore his throbbing face. He'd been avoiding looking at himself in the mirror. Once had been enough. The pair of bruises on his cheeks and jaw looked like ink stains. His whole body ached; Churchill said it was from unconsciously tensing up all his muscles during the confrontation.

The confrontation. If he closed his eyes he was back in the alley, grunts and cries, the sounds of flesh hitting flesh, his head breaking a man's nose... D's form in the darkness, backlit by the red emergency light like a specter from hell.

D, who had probably been in town this whole time. D who hadn't told him any of this. D who he wanted to kill. D who he dreaded trying to live without.

There was a knock at the door. "It's Churchill."

"Come in."

Churchill used his key and entered. "Got someone here to see you," he said.

Jack stopped pacing and turned his head just in time to see D step out from behind Churchill. He just stood there silently, looking... tired, actually. Worn out, as Jack had only seen him once, when he'd been sick from the infection. He didn't look like he'd been sleeping, or eating. He didn't look good, or wouldn't have to anybody else.

Jack found himself nodding, to keep himself from yelling. "Of course. Of course you're here. And you were in that alley, naturally. You've been here the whole time, haven't you?" D and Churchill exchanged an uneasy glance. "Of course. Did you stow away in the backseat of my cab? Were you hiding under the bench in Baker Park?"

D cleared his throat, his voice raspy like he hadn't used it in awhile. "Jack, I couldn't—"

"No. Why would you? Why would you tell me anything, either of you? Jack has to be protected. Jack can't deal with things like this. Jack doesn't need to know things that don't concern him. Jack is fucking spun sugar and might melt or crack into a million pieces if he hears a bad joke!" he shouted.

"It ain't like that."

Churchill, looking more and more uncomfortable, interrupted. "I'm going to... uh... leave you guys alone. I'll, uh... see you later." He left. Jack barely noticed.

D shrugged out of his topcoat and let it fall, rubbing one hand over his shorn skull. "Jack, I hadta protect you, but I couldn't let you be thinkin' 'bout me bein' out there watchin'. You had other things ta think about."

"Well, I don't now. It's all over." Jack watched him, his anger rapidly bleeding away and leaving only the sensation of being here in the same room with D, relief that they were both alive, near-giddiness at his mere presence that Jack fought down so he wouldn't start grinning like an idiot.

D's eyes ranged over Jack's face. "Jesus, lookit you. They did a number on you."

Jack nodded. "Hurts like a sonofabitch."

He took a step closer. "So... lemme see if I got this right. Yer in the bar. You get a note sayin' somebody's got me and you better come out or they kill me."

"Yeah."

"And you believed that?"

"Not a word of it."

"But ya went out there anyway. Just in case they had me."

Jack was surprised at D's simple tone. He'd been expecting angry reprimands for his foolhardiness. "Yeah, I did."

"And then, my favorite part. You didn't jus' walk out there like a sucker, oh no. You reconned the area from height, determined the best approach, and tried to creep up on the guy wantin' ta take ya."

Jack nodded. "Yeah. I know, it was dumb."

"Dumb ain't the word. Crazy's more like it. Stupid, and foolish, and I thought I'd met some guys in my time who were brave 'n' true, but none a them're anythin' ta you, doc."

He looked up and met D's eyes, standing only a few feet from him now. In them he saw only tenderness, the kind he'd longed to see for so long and which had taken so many weeks to elicit. "Yeah?"

"And when they rushed ya, you broke one a their feet and smashed the other guy's nose inta his face. And all this after what I'm told was a helluva day in court durin' which you made their expensive lawyer stand there with egg all over his face."

Jack felt a slow smile creep over his face. "Yeah."

D reached out and carefully touched the bruise on Jack's left temple. "Well, think it's fair ta say you had one helluva day, Jack."

Jack took the last step that separated them and leaned close, his hands going to D's waist. He stopped when his face was mere inches from D's.

"The day ain't over yet," he whispered.

CHAPTER 24

"DAY ain't over yet."

Jack's words floated between them, a world of promises in his voice. His hands on D's waist were trembling; D could feel the warmth of Jack's breath and smell the gin he'd had at the bar, as well as the antiseptic they'd used at the hospital to clean the lacerations on his face.

Jack tried to smile, but it seemed to get lost halfway to his mouth. The journey from his head to his smile had become rather blocked and cluttered in the past few days, D imagined, but here he was as usual, trying to be positive and upbeat, and he couldn't take it. He pulled Jack close, wrapped his arms around him, and pressed his face into Jack's hair. He felt Jack's body mold to his immediately, as Jack's arms went around his back and clutched tight there. "Jesus, Jack," he breathed. "You gonna be the death a me for sure." Jack sighed, a deep and shuddering release, the tension flowing out on the tide of his breath. D held him tighter. *Goddamn, I been missin' this. How'm I gonna last months, or years, when we gotta be apart?* "Saw them guys had ya and…." He bowed his head down, his mouth against the crook of Jack's neck. "Damn near stopped m'heart," he murmured.

Jack straightened, one hand coming up to cup D's head. "I know what you mean," he said. "That's how I felt when I read that note."

D lifted his head. "Talk later." *Right now I jus' gotta kiss you 'til ya cain't breathe.* Jack's lips were as soft as he remembered, the quiet sounds he made warmed his belly as much, and it felt just as right to hold him as it had before. His hands were on D's neck, pulling him closer. His eyes closed, D felt himself spinning in the darkness, anchored by Jack's mouth, diving deeper there to find all he could of this man who was *his* man, no doubting it now, his as sure as he was Jack's, and he felt the solid lock of their pieces fitting together again, his whole life a solitary odyssey until now, until him, until Jack.

Jack withdrew with a few short kisses. "Hold up," he said, smiling.

D grunted, pulling him close again. "Naw, no holdin' up. Wanna get you in that bed, doc."

"Oh, hell yes," Jack said, his grin widening, "but I'm grimy. I need a shower."

"Hmph," D said. "Guess could use one myself."

"Then you'd better get in there with me."

IN the shower, it was all hands. His own hands, D's hands, hands everywhere until it seemed like there had to be more than four between them. Hands on himself, hands on D, he could barely tell whose hands were whose. Soap and hot water and steam and D's body close against his, the day's tension swirling down the drain with residue of sweat and fear and grime that had lain on his skin.

He turned around to face the faucet to make the water just a tad hotter, and the next thing he knew, D had both arms around his torso from behind and was hugging him tight, his head on Jack's shoulder. Jack went still for a moment and just let D hold him, his hands rising to grip D's forearms. He leaned his head back and rested his cheek against the side of D's head and there they stayed for what felt like a long time. A rite of water and steam, their nude bodies pressed together feet to shoulders, his back to D's chest. Jack turned around and wrapped his arms around D's shoulders; that was better. *Face me, D. Whatever you mean but don't say, face me.*

D's face slid against Jack's, nuzzling close until he found his lips again, the shower water sluicing into their mouths as D's hands headed south to grab Jack's ass, and just like that they were done being silent and relieved. The gentle, cleansing hands became greedy, grabbing hands and the tender kisses became hard and demanding. Jack left off D's mouth and went for his neck, which he knew D particularly liked, while one of D's hands slid around his hips and went between his legs from the front, past his balls, soap on the fingers that were suddenly pressing into him. Jack gasped and hung onto D's shoulders as he worked two fingers inside, riding D's forearm between his legs like a saddle. "You been missin' me, doc?" D rumbled into his ear. In lieu of a response Jack just grabbed D's head and thrust his tongue into his mouth, bucking against D's fingers inside him until it was finally too much and he pulled away. He reached behind him and shut off the water.

"Uh-huh," he said to D's puzzled expression. "You said you wanted to get me in that bed and that's what we're going to do."

"Showers're good too," D said, hopefully, but Jack was already out and toweling off. D followed suit.

"Dry off well, now," Jack said.

"I know, ya hate damp sheets. S'pose ya want me ta blow dry my hair too," he said, rubbing a hand over his nearly bald scalp.

Jack laughed. "I'm going to dry mine."

D straightened up, well dried off, and tossed his towel aside. "Are you fuckin' kiddin' me?"

"I can't get in bed with wet hair. I'll get the pillowcases wet and then we'll have to sleep on them and I hate that. Damp, clammy pillowcases." He shuddered and took the hair dryer out of its jack next to the mirror.

D came up next to him and plucked it out of his hands. "There's two beds, Jack. If you think I'm gonna wait 'round fer you ta dry yer fuckin' hair, yer crazy."

Jack met his eyes and grinned, then stepped right up into D's personal space. "I love that you want me, and can't wait another minute to be with me," he whispered, tipping his head close. "But more than that, I love that you're saying it."

D grunted. "Rather show ya." He dragged Jack out of the bathroom and they stumbled over each other's feet on the way to the bed. Jack turned D around so when they fell together onto the bed, Jack was on top. They scrambled up the mattress until finally, at last, they were twined there together and ready. Jack pressed his pelvis into D's as they kissed, haphazard with enthusiasm, rubbing against each other. He felt D's fingers digging into the flesh of his back and his ass and Jack knew what he wanted. He drew back and looked into D's eyes and saw that he wanted it too. "Show me whatcha got, doc," he breathed. It wasn't quite asking for it, but it was a lot more than he'd been able to manage the first time they'd done this. Jack didn't know if it was the week's absence or just the tension release of the trial being over that was letting D pry himself open another few inches, but he'd take it.

Jack got the lube out of his nightstand and slicked himself well, pushed D's knees up and apart and lay over him, kissing him hard and deep while one of D's hands guided Jack as he pushed in. He tried to go slowly but D wouldn't let him; he grabbed Jack's ass and yanked him in. "Fuck, D," Jack grunted.

"Yeah," D hissed. "That what you want?"

"I got what I want," Jack said and kissed him again, planting his knees so he could thrust forward, D's legs wrapping around his waist now, his head thrown back against the sheets, droplets of water from Jack's damp hair glistening on his chest. He felt wild and powerful; he had to be if this man was willing to spread his legs for *him*, Jack Francisco, mild-mannered surgeon, real nice guy, pretty easy on the eyes, good with people, tastefully decorated apartment and subscriptions to *GQ* and *Men's Health*. Today he felt like more. Tonight he felt like a god, in part because D was looking up at him like he might just be one.

Jack picked up the pace, sweat joining the shower dampness on his face, D's jaw clenched against the moans that Jack could hear anyway, his hands flailing up at Jack's shoulders until they gripped his neck and pulled him down again to kiss him, bite at his lips, hips churning, D muttering now into Jack's ear.

It blasted through Jack like a freight train and he cried out as he came inside D's clenching body, dimly aware of warm damp spreading between them as D followed. His yell of release was half-swallowed by D's mouth and then he sagged, spent, into his arms and the world spun away.

THEY lay there in silence for a long time, shifting positions every ten minutes or so, touching quietly, not speaking. D traced the bruises on Jack's abdomen with one finger, his brow furrowing as he inspected the damage. Jack stroked his fingers over D's architectural skull, his shorn hair cat-soft under his hand.

The sterile hotel air dried the dampness from their bodies and let them chill; they wordlessly pulled back the thick, heavy bedclothes and slid beneath. D drew Jack into his arms and they curled against each other with quiet sighs.

After more than an hour of silence, Jack finally spoke. "Where do I start?"

D grunted. "Guess ya gotta right ta know what I been doin' here." Jack said nothing, just waited. "Couldn't let ya come here ta testify and not come with, ta look out fer you. Ya know that, don'tcha?"

Jack hesitated. "What about you? You were going to figure out who's after you."

"I been doin' that too." D didn't speak for a moment. He didn't know how to explain it without it taking all night, and he had more plans for Jack. "Jack, nothin' much matters now 'cept yer goin' inta Witsec on Monday and I'll be damn glad ta see it."

"That man tonight. That man with the syringe. He was somebody, wasn't he? Somebody significant, I mean. He just had that look, like he was."

D nodded. "His name's Petros. He's the kinda bad guy that other bad guys tell scary stories 'bout."

"He works for the brothers?"

"Not exclusively, but 'round here, yeah he usually does. He's a free agent and a real high-priced piece a work." D thought for a moment. "Nikos Petros grew up in the Greek Mafia, then went inta their military. Did some trainin' with the British SAS. Some people say he spent a few years travelin' the Middle East learnin' the trade."

"What trade?"

"Pain. Pain 'n' torture."

Jack was quiet for a few seconds. "That's what he was going to do to me, isn't it?"

"Probly. Seein's you already testified, if the brothers still want ya dead, it'd be as a warnin'. To make it a good warnin', they'd... well, they'd want ya ta die as slow and with as much pain as possible. Send a message, this is what's waitin' fer anyone dumb enough a cross us."

"Jesus," Jack breathed, shuddering a little. D held him a little closer.

"Don't think on it. Ain't gonna happen now."

"What about you?" Jack said, lifting his head to meet D's eyes. "Did you find out anything more about your blackmailers?"

He considered telling Jack that no, he hadn't. He didn't need to know about JJ, or the message, and D was loath to burden him with it. He looked in Jack's eyes and saw his concern there, and knew that he couldn't keep this from him, not if they were going to be what he hoped they could someday be. "A bit, yeah." He paused to gather his thoughts. "When I got here, I found that there was two people hired by the brothers ta kill you. I dealt with one myself."

"You killed him?"

"Nah, just gave him some real strong encouragement to leave town."

"Oh."

"The other one we was havin' trouble findin'. But then she turn up in the hospital. Got beat up real bad, said she had a message fer me. The message was that no one was gonna kill you, because... because that was my job, and they still expect me ta do it. Told 'em I'd never hurt you, and she said that I would, even if I didn't think so."

Jack was frowning. "So these faceless blackmailers of yours beat up this other hit man... uh, hit woman... to keep her from killing me, so that you could do it?"

"Yeah."

"Well, where the hell were they when those guys jumped me in the alley?"

D had to think about that for a moment. "Huh. That's a damn good question." He arched one eyebrow at Jack. "Possible they never thought you was dumb enough to go out inta that alley inna firs' place."

Jack rolled his eyes. "Maybe they just didn't find out I was going to that bar until it was too late."

"Or maybe," D said, thinking out loud, "Petros sold his services ta somebody else who was willin' ta pay more'n the brothers do."

"You mean... maybe he wasn't going to take me to the brothers?"

"No way ta know now. But if he was workin' fer my blackmailers instead a the brothers... that is troublin' news."

Jack's cell phone went off. He rolled over and answered it. "Hello? Oh hey, Churchill." Pause. "Yeah, he's still here. Hoping to keep him here as long as I can. When are we... oh yeah?" Pause. "Okay. Yeah, I can deal with that. Will do." He hung up and turned back toward D. "Churchill's going to take me up to Albany on Monday morning and from there I don't know where. It's starting."

"Yeah," D said, reaching out with one finger to Jack's face. *It's fer the best. It's what he needs ta be safe. You cain't do what you gotta do fer him if you gotta watch him too. Let him go. Them Witsec guys are good. He'll be safe.*

But how'm I gonna let him go?

Jack seemed to be considering something. "He says I'm to stay in this room all weekend, and they're going to airlift me out on Monday morning from the roof."

"Mmm-hmm."

Jack met his eyes. "Can you stay?" His face was full of boyish hope, excited for a longer reprieve.

"All weekend?"

"Please, D. Stay with me. I mean... come Monday morning, I...." He took a moment, looked away and swallowed hard. "I need to have as much time with you as I can before I'm gone, because it could be a very long time before I see you again." His eyes swiveled back over and met D's again, and the look in them might have knocked him over if he hadn't already been lying down. He drew Jack close again.

"Yeah," he said. "Yeah, I can stay." Jack sighed and kissed him, then tucked himself close again. "How can ya do it, Jack?" D asked after another long silence, not wanting to ask and afraid of the answer.

"Do what?"

"Feel... however ya feel, 'bout me."

"Why not?"

"'Cause a who I am. What I done."

Jack was quiet for a few beats, and then he propped up on one elbow so he could look down into D's face. "I know what you've done."

"Don't it bother you?"

"Yeah, it bothers me. But... I know you, D. You've killed, but you're not a killer. Not really. You did it because you were driven to it, and then because you thought it was all you had, and the more you did it, the more it shut you down so that it was all you could do. If you were a killer, you'd thrive on it. It wouldn't eat you up inside the way it did. The more you did it, the worse you felt, the *less* you felt."

D nodded. "Don't change what I done."

"No. And if somebody just showed me you on paper, what you'd been through and what you'd done, I'd probably say that this man deserved to spend the rest of his life behind bars. You've spent ten years of your life killing bad guys, D. Some people would say you're a hero."

He met Jack's eyes. "You one a them people?"

"I think you know that I'm not. But I can't...." He hesitated, looking away. "I can't set aside what you've done that's good, and the horrible tragedy that drove you to where you were. No one is all good or all evil. You can't change what you've done in the past, not for me or for anyone. But you've already changed who you are now."

"Cain't take no credit fer that," D murmured. "If I changed, it's 'cause a you, doc."

"I don't think so. Maybe I made you *want* to change, but you had to do it yourself. Do you really know how much you've changed since we met?" D didn't know what to say. "Because I see it, and it's astonishing. And how you were with me... you were supposed to *kill* me, you were rough, you were brutal and you made no bones about it. I thought I'd fear you, and I should have hated you, but somehow you made me love you."

D blinked up at Jack's face, his steady blue eyes not letting him go.

"Yeah, you heard me," Jack whispered.

D shut his eyes before Jack saw inside. "Jack, I... I'm not—"

"Shh," Jack said, pressing his forehead to D's. "Just let it be."

Arching his neck, D yearned upward for Jack's mouth and was met halfway, no more words, words that were terrifying and intoxicating and thrilling, words that made him want to curl up into a ball in the corner and sob his heart out, sob out all the poison that still lived there. Just Jack's mouth, the warmth of his skin as he slid over D like he was shielding him from an explosion, his hands roaming over Jack's body, and if only they were larger he could touch more of him at once, if he just moved them fast enough he could feel all of Jack at the same time.

Jack rose up and straddled D's hips, easing himself down, their fingers intertwined... oh God his body was the only heaven D would ever know... when they were joined like this, he wanted to be Anson, go back in time and do it all over, do it differently and then come find Jack as a different man, a whole man with something to give him, a man who could have told Jack that he loved him, right down to the murky dregs of his rotted soul.

JACK got up to go to the bathroom around two a.m. D was sleeping peacefully; Jack wished he could say the same for himself. He'd done no more than doze all night.

He stared at himself in the bathroom mirror, the bruises on his face startling him; he'd almost forgotten they were there.

I told him. Kinda sorta.

Somehow you made me love you.

He hadn't planned that. It just kind of came out. The second he said it he'd wished to take it back, but that wish had only lasted until he'd seen D's face. He looked like no one had ever said that to him before, that no one had ever *loved* him before. Maybe they hadn't. Surely his daughter... but that wasn't remotely the same.

He'd debated it for a long time. Did he *really* love D? Or was he just grateful? Had he just fallen for him out of... some kind of proximity? Being holed up with somebody for weeks at a time could play tricks on a person's feelings. Intense circumstances, fearing for his life, and D did have a certain mystery and sexiness in his persona that was undeniable. It was easy to imagine developing a crush on the man who was voluntarily standing between you and death.

But then he'd remember things. D smelling the sun on his skin. Telling him about the dead bunny. The look in his eyes when they'd kissed for the first time. And this week apart.... What was clear to him now more than ever was that he and D were scarcely two individuals anymore. Being back with him now, back in his arms, hearing his voice... his guts were twisting and he couldn't sleep because he knew it was so brief, just this brief respite before....

Don't think about it now. There'll be plenty of time to think about it after.

Jack washed his hands, took a breath, and went back into the bedroom. He climbed back into bed and curled against D, who flinched and turned over. "Fuck, yer cold."

"Just went to the bathroom."

"Mmmm. Maybe better warm y'up, if yer gonna be in my bed." He slid his arm over Jack's stomach and kissed his neck, then down his throat to his chest. Jack sighed and stretched like a cat under his ministrations, shuddering as he sucked at each nipple in turn, heading south down Jack's stomach.

D settled himself between Jack's legs and rested his cheek against his abdomen, eyes closed, just lying there still and quiet. He lifted his head, resting his chin on Jack's flank, and looked up at him in the faint glow of the city lights outside. Jack lifted a hand to his head; he loved the feeling of D's short hair under his fingers. D was gently stroking the muscles of Jack's stomach. "Mmm," D said, an indistinct sound in his throat.

"What?"

"Nothin', I jus'...." D sighed, resting his cheek against Jack's skin again. "I love yer body," he whispered, quiet like he was hoping Jack wouldn't hear him, his hand now making long strokes up and down Jack's side. "S'like strong 'n' solid, but soft too, and y'always smell so good."

Jack watched the top of D's head, feeling like he might melt. D had expressed tacit appreciation for his physical form but had never said anything like that before. The warmth of D's body and breath so close to him relaxed all his muscles; he felt like it was all he could do to just touch D's head with one hand.

D slid further down, his cheek now resting on the juncture of Jack's hip and thigh. His hand moved into Jack's thatch, stroking the skin there. He could feel D's breath on his half-erect shaft, but he was so relaxed that he didn't feel any urgency about the matter. D slid in a little bit and just let Jack slip into his mouth, still resting his cheek on Jack's groin, sucking gently as one might suck a thumb. Jack felt himself hardening in D's mouth; that slow, gentle suckling was maddening.

"Oh Christ, D," Jack groaned. "God, that's amazing."

D sucked him to orgasm; Jack came with a sigh, his body pulsing, D swallowing and stroking his flank, letting Jack slide from his lips and resting his cheek on Jack's stomach again. He turned his head a little and placed a kiss near Jack's belly button, just one.

"WHO'S 'we'?"

D frowned. He cast his mind back, trying to imagine what Jack could possibly be referring to. Whatever it was had been hours ago, as it was now five a.m. and they were lying sprawled amidst the tangled sheets, practically head to toe, D's head at the foot of the bed and Jack's head resting on his thigh. "Huh?"

"You said when you were looking for that other one who was supposed to kill me, that 'we' couldn't find them. Were you working with somebody?"

The light went on. "Oh yeah. Jesus! Cain't believe I fergot ta tell you. I met X."

"X? Your Deep Throat?"

"Somethin' like that. Yeah, she came 'n' found me soon after I—"

"She?"

"Yep. Her name's Megan. Damn good ta finally see her face."

Jack sat up and crossed his legs Indian-style. "Did she tell you why she's been looking out for you?"

"No, not yet. She hinted she might do."

"So... who is she?"

"Secret Service. But she ain't no agent. She's one a their shadow operatives."

Jack rolled his eyes. "Does *everybody* have shadow operatives? At this point I'd hardly be surprised to find out that the Office of Management and Budget kept a secret squad of black-ops accountants."

D chuckled. "She works anti-assassinations, which brung her in a lotta contact with folks in my business… oh, s'cuse me, my former business," he added, off Jack's look. "She's real smart 'n' strong. I been real glad ta have her help."

"Was she with you last night?"

"No, I didn't get ta tell her 'bout the whole field trip ta the bar. She's tryin' ta track who's been diggin' in my military record, and I think she drove down ta DC—"

"Somebody's been digging in your military record?" Jack exclaimed.

D sighed. "I'm sorry, darlin'. I keep forgettin' who knows what and when, and who told me what and whether or not you were there. Ya been there fer everythin' else, hard ta remember you ain't been privy ta some a these chats." He would have gone on but Jack was gaping at him, open-mouthed. "Whut?"

"Did you just call me 'darlin''?"

D blinked. "Uh… yeah, I guess I did," he said, color slamming into his face. Jack was still speechless. "Sorry 'bout that; it's what I usedta call Jill. Just kinda… slipped out."

"No, no… it's fine," Jack stammered, recovering his composure. He was playing it off casual, but D could see that it had affected him. *Damn, why'd I hafta go'n do that? Shit.* "You were saying? Military records?"

"Right. Was Churchill told me this. Last April some person or persons unknown accessed my record. Means they know my name, my history, lotsa stuff that's been buried awhile. Dunno if anythin' got traced ta me."

"You think this is connected to the people blackmailing you?" Jack asked, all seriousness again.

"Cain't be a coincidence. Anyhow, Megan said she'd look into it. Hopin' she calls today. I know she'd love ta meet you too."

"Yeah, I'd like to meet her," Jack said, that last pronoun slanted slightly.

"I might hafta run ta her place this morning real quick, and get my stuff," D mused.

Jack's head snapped around. "You've been *living* with her?"

"Treasury has apartments that she uses. Why, what's…." D sighed. "You ain't jealous, are ya?"

Jack pulled himself up. "No… well, okay, yes. I mean, you've got this long intimate history with her, and she's saved your life and you somehow saved hers, and now you find out she's a woman, and—"

"And how's that affect me, the queer hit man, huh? Don't that make me *less* wanna sleep with her?"

D GROANED behind Jack and thrust one last time before sagging against his back. Jack hung onto the headboard for dear life, gasping for breath and holding both of them up for a few seconds before losing out to gravity and falling onto the bed, not caring much that he was right on his own wet spot. D slipped out and rolled off. "Holy mother a God," he said.

"Yeah," Jack gasped. "Damn." He turned over onto his back. "Think you buried the needle on that one, stud."

D was silent for a moment, then started to chuckle.

"What?"

"Stud," D repeated, growly and low.

Jack snorted. "You got a better word for a guy who's swept my chimney five times in one night?"

At that, D burst out in honest-to-God laughter, which was an extremely rare occurrence. Jack sat up to watch D laugh. "Swept yer chimney!" D howled. "Aw shit, that is fuckin' rich!" Jack couldn't help but join in D's laughter. He felt giddy, like a kid at an amusement park, finally meeting his favorite cartoon character, just wanting to run up and get a big hug and be carried away to a place where no one ever cried and the world was bright colors and sunshine.

D was calming himself down. "Anyhow, was you doin' the sweepin' a coupla them times."

"Not the point," Jack said, stretching out again with his hands behind his head. "Neither of us is gonna be able to walk tomorrow."

"Who needs ta walk? Dunno 'bout you but I ain't plannin' ta leave this bed."

"What, we just lie here naked all weekend?"

"Somethin' wrong with that?"

"Might scandalize the marshals when they bring in my food."

"Aw, who the fuck cares."

Jack arched one eyebrow at him. "Who are you, and what have you done with D?"

D sobered at that. "I dunno. Not quite sure 'bout that, doc."

Jack watched D's face, outlined by the gray pre-dawn light coming in the window, and wondered for the millionth time just what it would take for D to tell him his real name. *Anson. I know it. I hear it in my head when I look at you. You're still D to me, but I want to call you by your birth name. I want you to feel like it's yours again. What will it take, D? How long will I have to wait? Unless you tell me in the next two days, I'll have to wait a long time.*

He turned on his side and rolled into D's arms, where he was welcomed at once. They lay in silence for a time, something they'd been doing a lot. Jack knew there were many things they could be saying, but weren't, and that was okay. Somehow, it was okay not to say things. "D?" he asked, as he sensed that D was drifting off again.

"Hmm?"

"Am I really going to be safe in Witsec?"

He felt D come to waking again. "How d'ya mean?"

"Well… these guys, they just seem like they can get to anybody, anywhere. If they really wanted to, couldn't they find me in Witsec?"

"Maybe. If they really wanted to. But it'd be a big fuckin' deal, and it'd take a lot, and it'd be real risky. They'd expose themselves t' all kinds a legal shit and it just ain't worth it. After y'already testified, the only thing ta kill ya for is a warnin'. And they ain't goin' to all that trouble jus' fer a warnin'."

Jack sighed. "I know you're blowing smoke up my ass, but I think I'll let you."

"Hey," D said, giving Jack's shoulder a little shake. "Yer gonna be fine."

Something in his tone gave Jack pause. He turned his head and looked up at him. "What do you mean?"

"Jus'… nothin's gonna happen ta you."

"D, you're usually the one preparing for the worst." As soon as he said it, Jack knew. He sat straight up. "You are, aren't you? You're going after them, or something. You've got some kind of plan that you haven't told me about!"

D held out a hand. "Now, Jack—"

"Don't, 'now, Jack' me! Like you don't have enough to worry about with blackmailers on your trail without taking on my problems too!"

"Yer problems is my problems, doc. And it ain't what ya think."

"What is it then?"

D sighed, and sat up as well. "All right, all right. Don't get all worked up."

"Too fucking late!"

"Will ya lemme talk?" Jack made himself shut up and listen. "Okay." D took a deep breath. "I'm gonna fix it for ya, so you don't hafta even be in Witsec no more."

Jack's eyes widened. "You can do that?"

"I think so, yeah."

"You mean… I can go back to being Jack Francisco? *Doctor* Jack Francisco?"

"That's the idea."

"Without the being-killed part?"

"Yeah, that bein' the most important bit."

"How the holy fuck are you going to do that, D?"

"I got it worked out. Kinda."

Jack drew back. "You're not… no. I won't let you kill them all."

"Even if I could kill 'em all, it wouldn't help. No, I got a different idea."

"Tell me!"

"It's best ya don't know."

"Oh, for fuck's sake, you sure love deciding what I should and shouldn't know."

"I don't fuckin' love it, it's jus' the way it is!"

"You're going to arrange it so that the brothers no longer want to kill me *without* killing anybody?"

"Yeah."

"Because I don't want you to kill anybody. Not ever again."

D paused at that. "Really?"

"No. That was the you that was. You're not that guy, not anymore. You're *my* guy now, *my* D, and my D doesn't kill people."

D sighed. "No, he don't."

Jack hesitated. "Exceptions might be made if some horrible torture guy has a syringe to my throat."

"I'll keep that in mind," D said, with a wry smile.

Jack held his gaze. "I wish I could tell you that I don't want you to put yourself in danger for this. Maybe it makes me a horrible selfish person, but I do want my life back. I don't want to live in fear of those men forever. If there's a way to make it go away—"

"I'll take care of it," D said, his jaw tight. "And this ain't fer you, doc."

"It isn't?"

"No." He reached out, tentative, and took Jack's hands. "It's fer us, kinda. 'Cause after that's done, maybe I can finally stop. Jus' stay still, and jus' be that guy a yours, that one who don't kill people."

Jack smiled. "That guy I love?"

D's answering smile, quavery and uncertain, nearly broke Jack's heart. "Yeah. That guy."

"You know that guy is you, don't you? Right here, right now?"

"Is he?" D murmured.

Jack nodded. "Must be, 'cause I love you."

D met his eyes and Jack saw a brief glint of moisture, but then he blinked and it was gone, leaving only D's face, pried open a few more inches, blank without a response to offer, and that was all right. Jack pulled D into his arms and held him as the sun rose outside their window, hoping he'd done the right thing.

CHAPTER 25

"YEAH, gimme a bacon and egg biscuit, hashbrowns, and a large coffee." Megan Knox was no believer in healthy food. Her older brother had been a lifetime healthy-eater, a vegetarian and fitness nut, and had dropped dead of a heart attack at age forty-four. She tore into the greasy food (ahh, McDonald's) as she drove up I-95 towards Baltimore, urgency spurring her to unsafe driving practices like eating at the wheel.

As soon as she'd finished, she took out her cell phone to call D. It took him longer than normal to pick up. "Yeah."

"It's me."

"Where ya been?"

"I'm on my way back now."

"Didja... hey now, cut that out, I'm tryin' ta talk on the phone," he said to someone in the room with him—someone who was giggling—his voice taking on a softer, teasing tone she'd never heard before. "Didja find anything?"

"Oh, yeah. I've got whole bunches of stuff to show you."

"Good. Whyn't you... dammit, you gonna get it you don't quit it!" he said to whoever he was with. She could guess who it was; the grin on his face was clearly audible in his voice.

"Are you with Jack, D?"

"Yeah," he said, and his blush was equally audible. "Some shit happened here too last night. Spent the night in his hotel room."

Megan smiled, hearing more impish laughter in the background and what might have been an actual snort of mirth from D. "Well, it's good you're getting to spend some time with him." No response. "Isn't it?"

"Yeah," D said, quietly. "Real good." Megan could hear the understatement in his voice, and all at once she felt a lump rising in her throat. D had been the only constant presence in her life for nearly ten years. She'd followed him, watched him, helped him and been helped by him, and even though they'd never met until a week ago, there had been times when he'd felt like her only friend. Exchanging their usual terse, cryptic text messages had at times been her only human contact for days on end.

All those years, she'd known his detached manner covered a greater pain. She knew more of his past than he probably realized, and for so long she had watched him descend deeper into a dark pit of solitude to the point that she'd feared he'd never climb out again. That was something she couldn't save him from, much as she might have wished to.

Luckily, someone else had come along who could. Upon discovering D's forced acceptance of the hit on Francisco's life, she had rushed to Vegas as fast as she could, her heart in her throat, praying she wouldn't have to intervene to save Jack's life. She would have shot D if she'd had to, but it would have struck her through the heart to do so. But he hadn't been able to go through with it, as she'd hoped, and so she'd sat back and let things develop, praying for nothing more than for D to get Jack safely to the authorities and get the hell away from the situation.

And then... God, how he had sounded when he'd called her for help after Jack had been taken. "They took Jack," he'd said, and she had heard his emotion where she'd barely ever heard any before. Jack had become important to him. Now, here, what she'd known in her head, she had seen with her own two eyes.

D loved Jack, loved him so much that he'd lay down his life without a second thought. It hung around him like a cloak cut to fit another; it did not rest easily on his shoulders, as if it were stolen and he feared its rightful owner would appear and snatch it away again. He kept telling himself he didn't need to wear it because he didn't feel the cold, he could put it from him and trudge on unprotected, except that was no longer true. His skin had known warmth again, and it remembered, and it couldn't take the bony chill anymore. The cloak would have to be made to fit, and if it couldn't be taken in, D would have to grow to fill it.

So now to hear that curl in his voice that he was there with Jack, spent the night with him and let the warmth seep into his bones, Megan's caution slipped enough for her to feel glad for it. "I'm about twenty minutes out," she said now, these thoughts passing through her mind in a flash.

"Listen, lemme do this: I'm gonna call Churchill and have him meet you at your place. He'll have t'escort ya here anyhow. And could ya bring me my bag? I ain't got no clean clothes."

"I doubt your present company objects to you walking around in the buff."

"Maybe not, but I ain't too keen on you 'n' Churchill seein' my block 'n' tackle."

"Fair enough. I'll see you soon, then."

"Lookin' forward to it." His voice went distant as he took the phone from his ear. "All right, smartass, get that ass on over..." was all she heard before he hung up. She chuckled. Boys.

"THINK that's funny, huh?" D said, grabbing Jack's bare ankle as he tried to get away and dragging him back across the bed. "Cain't a person have a civilized conversation?"

Jack gave in and let himself be dragged. "No. Not when you're talking to your *girlfriend.*"

D yanked Jack half onto his lap, ducked his head in, and kissed him hard, working his mouth until Jack sagged in his arms and opened to him, forgetting what he'd been saying or doing or even thinking. D pulled back, smirking. "My what, now?"

"Huh?"

"Yeah, thought so. Anyhow, she's on her way. Gotta call Churchill ta meet her at her place."

Jack nodded, pulling himself together. "Guess I'll take a shower, seeing as I *have* clean clothes. You'll just have to bivouac in a bathrobe 'til they get here."

D chuckled. "Jesus, Jack. Usin' words like 'bivouac' in casual conversation." Jack grinned, bent down, and kissed the top of D's head before heading into the bathroom.

Jack grimaced at himself in the mirror. He was disgusting. Covered in sweat and hickeys and God knew what else, not to mention the bruises from the fight the night before, other bruises and assorted marks from *later* the night before—he looked like he'd been rode hard and put away wet.

He smiled. *As good a description as any.*

He stepped beneath the hot spray, sighing in contentment. It was ridiculous that he should feel any kind of peace at this moment; after all, he was still wanted dead by a number of people and facing a long separation from D, whose safety he was increasingly worried about, in no small part because the man didn't seem to worry about it himself. And yet it was peace in his heart, and joy, and even hope.

D was here; he'd come of his own free will, and he'd told Jack the truth about things that until very recently, he'd have kept from him. He felt *there* in a way he never had before. Until now, Jack had always had the sense that even though he knew D was emotionally attached to him, and physically attracted, he still had one foot out the door and was hedging his bets with every word, every conversation. But last night... how he'd been, the things he'd said. He was still a close-mouthed, grumpy son of a bitch, but he had seemed like a *committed*, close-mouthed, grumpy son of a bitch. Committed to him, to Jack, and to whatever they might have together in the future. Committed to them actually having a future.

We do. We DO have a future. Someday.

Jack leaned against the tile of the shower, some of the giddy draining out his toes. Someday might be a very long way away.

D WRAPPED up in a hotel bathrobe and paced, waiting for Churchill and Megan to arrive. He didn't want them to come. They represented the world, the world that he and Jack had been holding themselves apart from for months now. He hoped he had the rest of the weekend with Jack and that nothing Megan brought with her would fuck it up, but he wasn't feeling optmistic. He might have to subsist on the meager diet of the memories he'd stored up last night for however long he was forced to fast, without another two days to gorge himself on Jack.

Quit bein' so fuckin' selfish. You got shit ta deal with and better now than later. All yer thinkin' on is more time with him in this room when you oughta be thinkin' on how ta make sure he's safe, not ta mention yer own damn hide, for as much as it's fuckin' worth.

He scrubbed his hands over his skull. *Why's it gotta be this way? Little bits 'n' pieces, one night, tryin' ta cram it all in, all the talkin', all the not-talkin', all the other stuff. Nothin' pure, everythin' tainted by what-next, worries 'bout when the next fuckin' calamity's gonna rain down on our heads spoilin' what little time we got.*

But someday. Someday it won't be like that. I promise you, Jack.

Jack came out of the bathroom stark naked, towelling his hair, smiling when he saw D watching him. He detoured to stand in front of D and slip his arms inside D's bathrobe and around his waist. "There. All clean."

"Maybe I oughta check," D murmured, leaning in, but before he even touched Jack, the flirty smile fell off Jack's face, and he looked away. "What's wrong?"

Jack sighed. "Nothing. Just... you're going to have to leave soon."

D nodded, running his hands up Jack's arms. "Yeah."

"I mean, I knew that, but right now all I can think about is that I might not see you like this for a long time."

"No use dwellin' on things we cain't do nothin' about."

"Are you sure we can't do anything?" Jack said, meeting his eyes.

"What y'mean by that?"

"Let's just *go*," Jack said, his words coming out in a rush like he'd been damming them behind his teeth for too long. "Once I'm in Witsec I'll just tell you where I am and you come join me, and we'll just be anonymous and no one will have to know where we are."

D was shaking his head before Jack had even finished talking. "No, Jack. You think I ain't thought a that? It's real temptin', I know. But them folks're lookin' fer me; they ain't never gonna stop. They come too far and they're too pissed off fer whatever reason. I cain't be with ya 'til that score's settled. And what about the brothers? Might be they trace me ta you, and then where'd we be?" He paused. "Jack, I know you think Witsec's gonna solve all yer problems, but have you thought 'bout the fact that you won't be no surgeon in Witsec?"

"I know," Jack said, very quietly.

"You'll hafta take some job won't draw no attention. You ready ta give up yer whole career that you worked years 'n' years for?"

"I don't care!" Jack hissed. "I mean, I care, but...." He paused, looking away. "It isn't like my life was so great before, you know. I was almost relieved to leave it behind. I was divorced, bored, I wasn't dating, I'd lost a lot of my real friends, and I just felt like I was waiting for something, but I didn't know what." He met D's eyes. "Yeah, I miss my work. And I care about it. But not as much as I care about being with you."

D was nearly struck dumb by *that* sentiment, but he didn't let it show. "That's las' night talkin', and all this drama," he said. "That ain't fer real. Come a time you'd be sorry, and you'd regret it, and I ain't gonna be enough ta make all that go away. I don't want that fer you, y'hear me?" Jack said nothing, eyes downcast. "I ain't gonna *let* you lose what you worked for. It's part a who you are, and I ain't lettin' no part a you get destroyed." He hesitated. "You gotta trust me, Jack."

At that, Jack lifted his eyes and met D's. "I trust you."

D couldn't think of anything more to say. All he could do was draw Jack close and kiss those lips, feel that warm, smooth body in his arms and against his chest, the rasp of Jack's stubble against his own, his damp hair, and the smell of shampoo. Jack drew away after a few moments. "I guess I better get dressed before we end up back in that bed when Churchill and Megan get here," he said.

He started to turn away, but D held fast to his arm. Jack turned back, a questioning look on his face. D just looked at him, his eyes searching Jack's face, unable to ask for what he wanted. *Jus' hold me a little longer, Jack. Tell me again that ya wanna be with me, fer real, cross yer heart 'n' let me know you ain't foolin', cause I dunno how or when it'll happen, but somehow I come ta need ya like air, like blood. Touch me again like ya do with them gentle hands 'n' make me feel like somethin' precious. Say it again that ya love me, 'cause hearin' that was like openin' up some big bottomless well that ran dry years back, and it cain't never be full enough now, I cain't never hear it enough, but once more, one more time, and maybe I'll believe it a little more, and then a little more the next time, 'til someday I believe it fer true enough ta be able to say it back ta you like y'oughta hear it said, 'cause God knows I love you more'n my own life, more'n anythin' in this world, but it cain't get outta me yet cause I still ain't the man I need ta be, the man who's gonna stand before you and declare it.*

D just stood there, mute, but Jack seemed to get the gist of it from his face because he moved close again, wrapped his arms around D's neck, kissed his face, and held him, whispering in his ear words that seemed plucked from D's own head and returned to him, except when Jack said them, he believed.

WHEN the knock came at the door, D and Jack both jumped and glanced at each other, the same thought passing between them: *Here we go.*

Jack got up and peered through the peephole; it was Churchill. He opened the door and stood aside. "Hey, Jack," Churchill said, clapping his shoulder as he passed by. He was followed by a no-nonsense-looking blond woman who had to be the mythic figure he'd so often wondered about with varying degrees of jealousy.

He followed them into the room to where D was sitting on the edge of the bed in his bathrobe. He stood up, appearing exquisitely uncomfortable without his usual armor of black clothing. Jack trailed along behind, feeling useless. Megan was glancing at him. D cleared his throat. "Uh... Megan, this is Jack," D said.

She smiled, a warm smile that took the hard edges from her face and some of the tension from Jack's shoulders. She held out her hand, which Jack shook. "It's really good to meet you, Jack," she said, breaking into a full grin. "Finally. And up close."

"I guess you know a lot more about me than I know about you."

"I'm sorry about that."

"Don't apologize. I'd have to be some kind of an asshole to resent it after you saved my life and D's."

"Ya got my bag there?" D interrupted, clearly eager to get out of the damn bathrobe.

Megan handed him the duffel she was carrying. "Here you go."

"Thanks." He headed for the bathroom. "Back in a few," he said, glancing at Jack.

The door closed behind D, and the remaining three people stood in an uneasy triangle. Jack blinked, looking from Churchill to Megan, who he realized had only just met themselves, and it became suddenly clear that even though all of this was supposedly about protecting him, it was D who was their common thread. He was Jack's lover, Megan's friend, and Churchill's colleague, in a way. "Sit down?" Jack offered, feeling absurd to be playing host in a damn hotel room.

Churchill took the desk chair. Megan sat down on the untouched bed, while Jack hastily drew up the covers on the other bed, acutely aware that it was a bit... well-used. He sat on the edge, his hands clasped between his knees. "How's your head?" Churchill asked.

"It's okay. The bruises are a little tender."

"Churchill filled me in on what happened last night," Megan said, leaning forward.

Jack sighed. "If you were thinking of lecturing me on my stupidity, don't bother. I've had more than an earful from D already."

She shrugged. "I was going to say that you were very brave. But also stupid."

"I'm starting to think that 'brave' and 'stupid' go together more often than not." He met her eyes. "You didn't bring good news, did you?"

She looked away. "Depends on your definition of 'good news'. Given the situation it becomes something of a relative term."

Jack nodded. "Well, that's a non-answer."

"After Monday you won't have to worry about it anymore," Churchill said.

Jack whipped his head around to glare at him. "Are you kidding me? You think whisking me away to God-knows-where will stop me from caring about what happens to D? You think I won't be worrying myself into an early grave over it?"

"No, of course not... that's not what I meant," Churchill spluttered.

Jack rubbed a hand over his face. "Jesus, Churchill. You know, half of me just wants to say fuck Witsec and stay with D."

Churchill's face went slack with horror. "Jack, you can't seriously be considering—"

"What if I said I was? You can't *make* me go into the program if I don't want your protection."

"Jack, D wouldn't want that," Megan said.

"How do you know what he'd want?" Jack exclaimed, rounding on her. He was working himself into what D might call a "hissy fit," but he couldn't seem to stop himself. Everyone was so goddamned busy planning his life for him, the idea of wresting control back into his own hands was seductive as hell. "Watching him from a distance for ten years doesn't make you an expert, you know!"

"Sleeping with him for two months doesn't make you one either," she said, cool as a cucumber.

Churchill recoiled with a wide-eyed "oh no she *didn't*" expression that might have been funny under different circumstances.

Jack watched her face, looking for signs of malice, but saw none. "No, it doesn't," he said. "But I know things about him no one knows, not even you."

"I don't claim to know much about him," she said. "But I know how he feels about you. And the only thing keeping him going right now is the knowledge that in a few days you will be in Witsec and safe and he can concentrate on what he has to do, both for you and for himself. You think the best thing to do is to endanger yourself by refusing protection?"

He sighed. "No. I just... I hate this," he muttered. "It's like a lose-lose situation with some extra lose on the side. There's no win."

"There'll be enough win if you both come out of it alive," Megan said quietly. "Try and think of that."

Jack nodded. "But what does it say that I've reached a point where 'alive' is the best I can hope for? How low can you set the bar before you start wondering what's the point of even *having* the bar at all?"

"Well, 'alive' might not be the most inspiring goal," Churchill said, "but it's a place to start. And preferable to the alternative, right?"

The bathroom door opened, and D came out, showered, dressed and shaved. "All right," he said, coming to sit next to Jack on the bed. "What'd I miss?"

"Nothing," Jack said, gloom circling in his mind like a Halloween fog. The hope and peace of just a short time ago seemed far away. "Just pondering the nature of existence."

D wasn't paying attention. "Megan, what'd you find out?"

She took a deep breath. "Okay." She reached into her messenger bag and pulled out a few files. "I wasn't able to trace who exactly accessed your files. Not directly, at least. I started suspecting that whoever it was wasn't looking for you. No one knows your former identity or that you were ever *in* the military, so it might have been someone researching someone else who just came across your file. So I asked myself who was most likely to have done so? I started to wonder if it had something to do with Major Baldwin."

"Who's that?" Jack asked.

"Man I killed," D said quietly. "First man I killed. The one who helped plan the OKC bombing. Was him… well, that's what started me. On this."

"His death was officially ruled a suicide."

"That's 'cause I made it look like one."

"But if somebody got suspicious and started digging into his life just prior to death, they'd discover that you had an appointment with him the day before."

D nodded. "The officers who wanted me ta kill him arranged that. So I could get the lay a his office and so he'd know my face and not be suspicious when I showed up the next day ta do the job."

"If someone were being thorough, they'd investigate anybody who had contact with Major Baldwin in the days just prior to his death, which would lead them to you, among others. So I did the same. He had contact with at least a dozen officers, civilians, and enlisted personnel according to his appointment calendar, the days before he died, and all of them had their records accessed the same time as yours, D… except all of them saw the Major *after* you did." D sighed, nodding.

Jack was confused. "I don't understand the significance."

"It means somebody worked their way backwards from his death, but when they got ta me, they stopped. Musta found what they was lookin' for," D said.

"I think they did," Megan said. She stared at the file folder in her hand. "D, I don't quite…."

"Just spit it out," he said.

"Baldwin had a daughter," she said. "She's about your age. She has a criminal record, mostly white collar and some criminal solicitation." Megan seemed to brace herself. "Her name is Catherine Baldwin, although she has many aliases."

D was still waiting. "And?"

Megan wordlessly handed him the file folder. D opened it; Jack looked at her picture over his shoulder. She had straight dark hair and a heart-shaped face. Jack had never seen her before. D, on the other hand, clearly had. He jerked as if he'd touched a live wire and sucked in a breath. "Oh sweet Jesus," he rasped.

Jack grasped his arm. "What? Who is she?"

"It's Josey," D choked out. "My fuckin' handler."

THE sight of that face in the folder, a face that had for years been his only reliable point of human contact… D thought crazily about standing on a beach, the tide swirling in around his ankles, the sand shifting beneath him and letting him sink deeper with each wave. His head was spinning, his mind busily rewriting the entire history of the last ten years as it unraveled and re-knitted into a new shape with this new information. He barely felt Jack's hand on his arm, Megan and Churchill's eyes on him. Megan had surely known who this Catherine Baldwin was before handing him the photo; she had to have seen Josey in all the years she'd been spying on him.

They were saying things to him, but D wasn't hearing them. "D," Jack finally said, shaking his arm.

"Huh? Sorry… I'm jus'… fuckin' Christ, I cain't believe this."

"So it had to be her who blackmailed you," Churchill said.

D shook his head. "Seems that way. Went so far as t'have herself beat up ta make it look good too. That's some kinda dedication." He sighed. "But I killed her father, and I guess she wants ta eat my heart or somethin'."

"Do you think she knows you've been working with the FBI?" Jack asked.

"I dunno," D said, looking over at Megan. "You dig up anything on her finances?"

She nodded. "Yeah."

"She got enough?"

"No," Megan said, shaking her head.

"Then she knows."

"That's what I figured too."

Jack put a hand up. "You guys lost me."

D got up and started pacing. He couldn't sit still. "She's got a lotta help with this anti-me operation she's runnin'. That kinda help's expensive just to pay fer their time, not to mention the costs like motels 'n' food 'n' such. Real expensive, 'specially over time. If she's just on a personal vendetta, she'd hafta pay everybody, and she don't got that kinda bankroll. But if she knows I been workin' with the Feds, well… most guys would help her take me down fer greatly reduced rates or even fer free."

"They are keeping this really quiet," Megan said. "I keep my ear to the ground, and I know you do too, and there's been nothing about you except Jack's contract and the fact that you killed Sig back in L.A. She must have a small core group and is keeping everything well under wraps."

"I don't think she hired contractors, jus' muscle. They don't ask as many questions."

"Seems that way."

D handed the file back to her, rubbing at his eyes. His head was starting to pound. "Jesus. I cain't wrap my fuckin' brain round this. She's known since *last spring*?" He thought a moment. "Come ta think of it… that's when she started showin' me witness contracts even though she knew I didn't take 'em. Kept at it, each one worth more'n the last one. Guess she got sick a tryin' ta make the jobs sweet enough and just strongarmed me inta takin' Jack's hit. Why's she so fired-up ta get me ta kill a witness?"

"It's a capital crime in most states," Jack murmured. "Isn't it? Murder of a witness?"

"He's right," Churchill said. "If you killed a witness in almost any state with the death penalty, you'd get a needle in your arm."

"Guess she liked the irony," D said. "Never did think too much a my rules fer what jobs I'd take. Maybe she wants it ta be all poetic justice when I get executed fer killin' a witness." He shook his head. "She couldn'ta been prepared fer it ta go on this long, though. Why's she still draggin' it out? She's here in town, she had JJ give me that message… she could jus' take me out." He sat down again, reaching blindly for Jack's hand. "She don't wanna jus' kill me no more. She wants ta hurt me, bad as she can, fer as long as she can."

"What are you going to do?" Jack murmured, gripping D's fingers with reassuring strength.

D's mind was a blank. Shock had washed it clean of ideas and strategies. "I got no fuckin' idea."

"Well... here's what I propose," Churchill said, speaking for the first time in awhile. "I'm taking Jack to Albany on Monday. If she wants to hurt you, she could try and do it through Jack, so I think you both ought to stay in this room until we're ready to take him up north. After that, D, you can deal with this Josey situation without having to worry about Jack's safety."

D nodded. "Yeah. That's good."

"I think we should move them," Megan said. "She has to know where they are."

"I disagree. She knows and hasn't tried to get to them. They're very well guarded here, she probably knows it'd be futile. Moving them would only expose them, and it'd be very difficult to make sure we weren't followed to some new location on short notice like this."

"I think we oughta stay here," D said. "She ain't gonna try nothin'. Like as not she assumes Jack's gonna hafta stay in town fer the whole trial, like we thought he'd hafta do. We can get him out on Monday before she realizes what's goin' on, and I can go underground ta try 'n' sort out this mess."

Megan nodded. "All right. That makes sense." She met his eyes. "What do you want me to do?"

"I need you to find out if Petros is working for Josey or the brothers. Or both. I got a feelin' he's playin' both sides a the coin on this job. Can ya snoop around and watch him?"

"I'll try. He's pretty slippery."

"Keep an eye out fer Josey too."

"Naturally."

Everyone fell silent. There didn't seem to be much more to say, but no one seemed to want to leave. An air of doom hovered in the air between them, for no good reason D could discern, but he felt it, and he knew Jack did too, by the way he was squeezing D's hand.

Finally Churchill rose. "Well, I guess...." he began, and then he trailed off.

"We'd better be going," Megan finished, getting to her feet.

Churchill came and shook D's hand. "I'll be in touch. Best of luck."

"You too," D said. *This feels like goodbye. Why we sayin' goodbye?*

He moved on to Jack. "Call me on my cell if you need anything. I might stop by tomorrow, but I've got a lot of paperwork to do for your new identity."

"Right."

Megan touched D's shoulder. "I'll call you later." He just nodded, his arms crossed over his chest. She faced Jack. "I hope I see you again, Jack," she said.

He just stood there for a moment and then suddenly hugged her. "Me too," he said. D watched as Jack let her go and she followed Churchill to the door. Jack trailed along after, closing and locking the door after them, pausing first to wave to the two marshals outside. He drifted back into the room, and for a few beats of silence they just stood there.

"You okay?" Jack asked.

D shrugged. "Compared ta what? Jus' one more fucked-up thing ta deal with. Honest, I cain't hardly think 'bout that right now. Ain't like I can do nothin' 'til Monday."

Jack nodded, staring at the floor, working the toes of one bare foot into the carpet. "This is it, isn't it?" he whispered.

"What?"

"This weekend. This is all we're going to have. Ever."

"Jack—"

"Don't bullshit me, D. Don't softpedal it like I'm a little kid who can't handle it." He lifted his head, and their gazes found each other and locked like magnets. "This is it. Monday I'm going away, and after that one of us is going to die. Maybe both. It's too much. There's too many people who want it, and they're too determined." He took a step closer. "This is it for us, isn't it?"

The idea worked like an iron fist around D's heart. He wanted to deny it. *No, Jack. This ain't it 'cause I won't let it be. I won't let that happen ta you or ta me.* But he couldn't, not now when they were right up against it. "Probly," he said, almost too low to hear.

Jack's eyes fell closed, and he exhaled slowly. He almost looked relieved. "D?"

"Yeah?"

"Get those clothes off."

THEY stayed in bed most of the day.

Jack dressed to get the room service inside and then undressed again. They left the cart by the bed and grabbed whatever they touched first.

"What would it have been like?" Jack whispered. Lying on their sides, face to face, just staring at each other for what felt like hours, drifting off and waking again.

D sighed, tucking his hands underneath his head. "Maybe… get a house. Never had no house a my own."

"With a garden."

"Yeah. So's you could come inside smellin' like sunshine after weedin'."

"Would we have had a dog?"

"Hmm. Ain't never had a dog."

"I had one in med school. A Cairn terrier. Sweet little guy who thought he was a Rottweiler."

"Coulda walked him at night. 'Round the neighborhood." He hesitated. "You oughta get one. After."

Jack shook his head. "This isn't about that."

"I know."

His eyes roamed D's face. He knew it so well by now, he felt like he could have drawn every freckle from memory. "Would have been a sweet life," he whispered.

D met his eyes. "Yeah. Woulda been."

CHAPTER 26

THEY sleep hard, long and deep, some part of them always touching. At times wrapped together like siblings in the womb, at other times just a foot grazing a leg. They stir and make love, communion silent, and drift off again still joined. They lay awake in each other's arms, not speaking, sometimes looking toward, sometimes looking away. They let the darkness take them together and lay dead to the world as the sun rises outside their window.

She circles the house like a cat, and just as silent. House, more of an estate. Security like the White House, but she knows a few tricks. He is inside, somewhere. She has followed his trail here, she has seen his car slink inside like a kid coming home after curfew. Petros, perhaps standing at a window and looking out, wondering who might be looking in.

He sits at his desk long into the night in front of a computer. Social Security number gone, a new one with a new name in its place. Fingerprints, erased. Bank accounts, deleted and money transferred into a holding account. Driver's license, deleted and a new one created. Jack Davies, welcome to the world.

She sits in a darkened room, listening to her own thoughts. There's no more time. She can't put it off anymore. She must act now, or it'll be too late. Soon she'll have him before her again, and she won't hesitate.

Today. It happens today.

MEGAN crept back to her car through several acres of wild brush that bordered the Dominguez estate. She needed a new plan. Petros might be in there, he might not be. Lurking on the periphery with high-powered binocs wasn't the most efficient way to determine this.

She'd left her car in a parking lot that served a nearby bike trail; when she returned, there were a few other cars around but no one in sight. She was unlocking the driver's door when she realized she wasn't alone a fraction of a second too late to do anything about it.

His arm was across her neck, a blade at her carotid. "You are sneaky," he whispered in her ear.

"So are you," she choked out.

"I've been trying to follow you for days."

"Same here."

"Make a move and I'll slit your throat."

She swallowed hard, jacking up her visible signs of fear. She knew he'd get off on it. "What are you going to do with me?"

A pause. "Keep you out of the way."

A sliver of real fear slipped down her spine. "Something's happening."

"Soon." He leaned closer. "Get in the car."

JACK opened his eyes. D was lying on his back, his head turned to the window, but Jack could tell he was awake. He slid closer to D's side, leaning in to kiss his neck. D's outstretched arm came around Jack's shoulders and his chest rose and fell in a sigh. "What are my chances of getting some morning sex?" Jack murmured in his ear.

D chuckled, a low rumbling in his chest. "Better'n average," he said, turning into Jack's embrace and rolling him to his back. Jack exhaled in satisfaction as D's weight settled over him, his hips between Jack's legs. He'd never had a clear preference for bottom or top, but he knew that he loved the feeling of D on top of him.

But now, D wasn't making use of his position, he was just staring down at him; Jack's smile slowly bled off his lips as reality came sneaking back in just when he'd thought he was rid of it. "It's Sunday," he said.

D nodded. "Yeah."

Jack shook his head. "I hate Sunday. It's the day before Monday."

"Amen ta that."

For a long moment Jack just stared, letting his eyes slide over every surface of D's face. *If I can just memorize every detail, maybe I'll never lose him.* "I think we ought to get out of this room. Just for a little while."

D frowned. "We ain't s'posed ta leave."

"Churchill lets me go to the restaurant inside the hotel as long as the marshals come with. Let's get some breakfast." He sighed. "I feel like shit, D. But I'll feel better if I can shower and get dressed and have some waffles or something."

D nodded, smirking a little. "Waffles sound good."

"And then we can come back here and have sex all day."

"You jus' fulla plans, ain'tcha?"

"Plans for you, maybe," Jack said, sliding one hand down to cup D's ass. "C'mon, let me up."

Jack showered, making quick work of it. Without D sharing the stall with him there was little reason to delay and every reason to get it over with, even though the hot water felt soothing. D came into the bathroom as he was drying off; they shared a long, slow kiss as they swapped places. Jack dressed in clean clothes and combed his hair. He thought about calling Churchill, but decided against it. If he talked to Churchill, he'd probably tell Jack all about the preparations, and want to give him specifics for tomorrow's itinerary, and specifics felt like Jack's enemy just now. They'd make everything real.

He hadn't really realized how long he'd been sitting on the bed staring out the window until he heard D come out of the bathroom. "Whatcha doin'?" he asked. "Looks like some heavy thinkin'."

Jack started a bit. "Oh... no. No heavier than usual, anyway." He watched D pull on his jeans, T-shirt, and jacket, sad to see his skin disappear beneath the layers. "Want to give the marshals a heads-up?"

"Y'all right," D said. He went to the door and poked his head out.

There was a beat of silence. Jack jumped up. Later, he'd think that it was as if he'd been waiting for it, as if he knew somehow.

"Jack, c'mere," D said, not loudly but firmly.

Jack was already halfway there. He stepped into the alcove outside his room, which shielded his door and the hallway nearby from casual glance. Both the marshals were slumped in their chairs, unconscious. Cups of coffee were sitting at their feet. He crouched in front of one and put two fingers to his carotid artery.

"They dead?" D said, looking up and down the hallway.

"No," Jack said, lifting the man's eyelid. "They've been drugged. Some kind of barbiturate." He looked up and met D's eyes. There was no surprise in their glance, just resignation.

"Back inside," D said. He seemed to have heard enough. He bolted the door and paced, one hand running through his hair. Jack watched him, anxious. D seemed uncertain, like he didn't know what to do, and Jack had never seen him like that.

"What now?" he asked, afraid of the answer.

D met his eyes. "She is comin' ta get us, Jack."

"That seems really insane and risky."

"Damn straight it is, but she don't got no choice. Musta got wind that yer bein' taken away tomorrow and if she wants us both, it's now or never."

"Well, we can't leave this room," Jack said.

"Why not?"

"Because," Jack snapped, surprised D wasn't ahead of him on this, "the elevator's to the right and the stairs are to the left, but we won't know which one they're using so we have a fifty-fifty chance of meeting them coming up if we try to go down!"

D was nodding by the time Jack was halfway through his statement. He watched Jack loading his gun, the weapon's heft reassuring in his hands. "You okay?" he asked.

Jack glanced up at him. "Compared to what?"

"I'm askin' 'cause the best thing fer us ta do is wait here fer them ta come in, then take 'em out so we can leave before anyone realizes what happened."

Jack nodded. "Okay."

"That means you gonna hafta fight. Maybe kill. I don't wanna put you in that position but tryin' ta sneak out before they get here's too risky, 'cause they could be on us before we can get out and this is a more defensible position here."

"I said I'm okay." Jack had a sudden thought. "I have an idea," he said, hauling his doctor's bag out from the closet. It had traveled so far with him, it felt familiar and reassuring. It made him feel like he might still be a doctor. He drew out a small ampoule of sedative and two disposable syringes. "It's quieter than bullets," he said.

D smiled grimly. "Good thinkin', doc. Now you get on over here with me and we'll wait fer our visitors." Jack went across the room; he and D pressed themselves against the wall around the corner from the entryway. D had his gun held up near his jaw; Jack kept his down at his side, hoping he wouldn't have to use it.

"Hope they don't take long," he whispered.

"They won't. They cain't chance leavin' them marshals there too long." They both heard the elevator ding from outside, then footsteps approaching. "All right," D murmured. "Be ready."

Jack nodded, swallowing hard. *Can I do this? This isn't like shooting at a target on a range... but hopefully we won't have to shoot. Jesus, is this what D's life is like all the time?* He went over in his mind what they'd have to do when the bad guys came in. *Wait for them to get in the room. Step out, block the entrance. Raise gun, let D talk.* He nodded to himself. *Wait... we never talked about this plan of attack.* Jack blinked, and realized that he was correct. He and D had not discussed what they'd actually do, but somehow he just knew.

The footsteps had stopped at their door. A quiet pause... *they're getting the room key out of the marshal's pocket...* then an even quieter click as the door opened.

Two dark-complexioned men in nondescript business suits stepped into the room with purpose, guns drawn, eyes scanning the suite. As if they'd rehearsed it, Jack and D stepped out of the corner and blocked the entry. A cloak of calm descended over Jack's mind and he watched from outside himself as he raised his gun and pointed it at one of the men, D covering the other one. "Hands up," D said, his voice low and commanding. Both men froze. "Up, now." They raised their hands. "Guns on the bed." They both tossed their weapons to the nearest bed. "Now turn around, slow." They did, both of them glowering at them. "Where was you takin' us?"

The one on the left sneered. "I'm not telling you anything."

"Huh. Guess I'll jus' shoot you in the kneecap." He lowered his gun.

"All right, all right!" the man said. "Parking garage," he choked out. "Then she'd tell us where to go."

"And how many're waitin' down there?"

"Two more."

"Where?"

"Bottom of the staircase. We were gonna take you down that way."

D nodded, His tongue crept into the corner of his mouth as he pondered this. He tossed a quick nod at Jack. "All right, doc."

Jack handed his gun to D so he could keep them both covered. He quickly withdrew a dose of sedative from the ampoule in his pocket, stepped up and injected first one, then the other in the neck, fast and painless. *This is some kind of Hippocratic violation, I just know it,* he thought, watching as both men collapsed to the ground, unconscious. *It's them or us.*

D was already moving. He slung his messenger bag over his shoulder, tucking his second gun into the back of his pants. "C'mon, Jack. We gotta move."

Jack grabbed his duffel and shoved his doctor's bag into it. D was already heading for the door. He poked his head out, looked right, then left, and motioned Jack to follow. "We'll take the elevator, right?" Jack asked.

"No, stairs."

"But they're waiting at the bottom of the stairs!"

"Yeah, I know. But if we take the elevator we're gonna hafta walk by 'em ta get ta my car anyhow, and they'll see us comin'. We take the stairs they be expectin' their friends ta come out with us, might not realize we're alone long enough for us ta get the jump on 'em."

Jack nodded, seeing the logic but not liking the idea of the confrontation that would mean. "Can't we just... you know. Sneak by?" Everything was moving so fast, he just needed a minute to catch his breath.

D sighed. "No, Jack, we cain't sneak by. These aren't movie bad guys who don't got no peripheral vision and we can just slip past while they're lookin' the other way. You want yer life, you gotta fuckin' *take* it."

"Okay," Jack said. "But... don't kill anyone."

That made D pause and stare at him. "All this goin' down and yer still worried 'bout my soul?"

"Someone's got to."

D's face relaxed for a brief second and Jack thought he might smile, but then he was back to all-business. "C'mon, let's go." They slipped into the hall and were into the deserted stairway within seconds.

D moved fast, but silently. It was all Jack could do to keep up. By the time they reached the door into the parking garage at the bottom, his thighs were screaming at him and his shoulders ached from holding the gun ready to fire. D didn't seem affected.

They stopped at the door into the parking garage. D motioned for Jack to be quiet, and he leaned up against the door, listening. Jack did the same; he could hear voices on the other side, muffled.

What's takin' them so fuckin' long?

D's probably putting up a fight.

Better not damage them. She wants them both intact.

You want to knock them out for the trip?

Yeah. I got some chloroform.

You're so fuckin' old-school.

Hey, if it ain't broke, don't fix it.

The men either turned away or moved a few paces, because their voices became difficult to hear. Jack pressed his ear closer to the door but couldn't make out what they were saying. He looked up at D to ask if he could hear anything, but the question died in his throat.

D was looking down at him, not paying attention to their would-be kidnappers. His expression was flayed open and laid bare with raw emotion, fear and hope and sadness and tragedy written across his features in broad, deep strokes that seemed to deepen the lines on his face and push his dark eyes back into their sockets. Jack's breath caught and he couldn't look away. D looked like he was already mourning Jack, eaten alive by it from the inside out until he was nothing but a hollow skin.

He lifted a hand and stroked Jack's face, his fingers trembling slightly. Jack swallowed hard and gripped his fingers. *We're going to be okay, I know it. I know it because you won't let it be any other way, and I trust you. I trust you enough to place my life in your hands without hesitation, and even if we both die, at least we'll be together.* He hoped D could see his thoughts because he didn't dare speak.

D squared his jaw and nodded briefly, then glanced at the door again. "On three," he mouthed, and held up three fingers.

Jack took a deep breath, and prepared himself for his first field test.

MEGAN'S arms and legs were tied to the hard aluminum chair. Her head hung down, her shoulders were lax. The pain made it easier to fake helplessness, but she wouldn't be faking it for too much longer at this rate.

Petros was walking behind her. Just back and forth. Letting her wonder when he'd strike again. The blood was congealed on her face and her bare chest, each cut precise, deep enough to bleed and hurt but not deep enough to incapacitate.

"So," she rasped. "Are you ever going to ask me anything?"

He chuckled. "No."

"This is just your happy fun time, then?"

"Something like that." He came around in front of her and casually struck her backhanded across the face. At least it *looked* casual. What it felt like was being hit with a two-by-four. Megan let her head rest against her shoulder as if she lacked the strength to lift it up again. "I've been asked to keep you occupied."

"We could just play cards or something," she said, her voice coming out somewhat slurred through her bloodied mouth.

"I am playing cards," he said, and struck her again on the other cheek.

D LOWERED the last finger, raised his gun and nodded to Jack, who nodded back. He burst through the stairwell door and whipped to the left, where the two men waiting to cart them away stood smoking, and now staring. They reacted quickly, much more quickly than he would have thought, but he was still able to get one of them right between the eyes with the butt of his gun. The man went down like a puppet with its strings cut. The other man turned toward him and raised his gun, but then Jack hurled himself forward and pistoned his shoulder into the man's midsection. He grabbed Jack's shoulders and brought up a knee into his stomach. Jack went down to one knee and D took advantage of the man's distraction to swing his gun against the back of the man's skull.

Both men down, he hauled Jack to his feet. "C'mon," he said. "Car." Jack stumbled along, recovering himself as they ran. D already had his keys out and the doors unlocked when they got there; Jack flung himself into the passenger seat as D got into the driver's and started up the engine. "You okay?" he barked as he backed out.

Jack nodded. "Just need to catch my breath."

D spun the wheel, resisting the urge to stand on the gas pedal and fly out of there as fast as he could; such an escape would only attract attention, which he didn't need. He watched the rearview mirror as he neared the garage's exit; so far, no one was behind them.

His relief didn't last long.

As soon as they hit the street outside, a car came flying out of a side street, heading unmistakably toward them. "Shit," he muttered, and tromped on the pedal anyway, careening around the corner. "Hang on," he grumbled.

Jack was twisted around to look out the rear window. "How'd they know?"

"Either one a them guys in the garage came to and sounded the alarm or one a the guys in the room did." D spun the wheel and zipped through a red light and around another corner. "Does it fuckin' matter? And getcher ass down!"

No sooner were the words out of his mouth than three bullets came zinging through the rear window, shattering it, several more hitting the car's body. "Jesus!" Jack yelled, curling into a ball with his hands over his head. "I thought they wanted us alive!"

"They're tryin' ta stop the car." D sped east, swerving in and out of honking cars and cutting people off left and right.

"Oh shit... now there's two," Jack said, peering around the headrest and yanking his seat belt around him.

D took an exit onto the highway, waiting until the last possible moment to swerve onto the ramp. He swore he felt the car tilt onto two wheels for a few hair-raising seconds. "We gotta switch," he said.

"Switch what?"

"You gotta drive. Unless you think you can hit their tires with a bullet."

"Switch? Are you insane?"

"Here. Put your foot here by the gas pedal." D switched hands on the wheel and got his left foot on the gas pedal, moving his right leg into the passenger footwell.

"Oh shit oh shit," Jack kept repeating under his breath, but he did as D asked. He got his foot near the gas, reached over and grabbed the wheel with his left hand.

"Okay, on three. One, two… three!" D flipped over into the passenger seat just as Jack slid over and got into the driver's. The car barely shuddered. "Good," D said, drawing his gun. He aimed out the hole where the rear window used to be and squeezed off a few shots. "Fuck, hold it steady!"

"I'm doing my best!" Jack yelled. "Do I look like a stunt driver to you?"

D tried again. The two cars pursuing them were still on their tail. He didn't recognize any of the men in them; none of the four men they'd taken out at the hotel were in the cars. *Shit, she's got more muscle than I thought she'd have.* Hitting the tire on a moving vehicle was a lot harder than they made it look in the movies, but D finally scored a solid hit on one of the cars. It veered toward the center, out of control.

The other car accelerated and drew up even with them. The driver fired a few shots at the driver's side. "Shit!" Jack kept yelling, his head ducked down. D fired back but didn't hit anything but the side of the car. The car began edging closer, forcing them to the right. "Fuck… he's gonna push me off the road!"

"Pull ahead or fall back!" D yelled.

Before Jack could do either, their pursuer slammed into their left side, hard. Jack swerved right to get away and ended up taking an exit. "Fuck," Jack muttered, muscling the car down the ramp.

"Get back on the highway!" D said, but it was too late. Jack had to swerve right to avoid cross traffic and now they were back on surface roads. He looked back. Their pursuer was right on their ass. "We gotta try'n lose this guy, doc."

"All right," Jack said, his jaw clenched grimly, his hands clutching the wheel. "Hang on."

D grabbed the oh-Jesus bar above his window as Jack whipped the wheel around, taking turn after turn, running lights. D half-hoped that a cop would stop them, but on the other hand he didn't want to be responsible for a dead cop. Their pursuer was having trouble keeping up; Jack's car cornered better.

D had no idea where they were. Somewhere in East Baltimore. Wherever it was, it wasn't a very welcoming landscape. Industrial wastelands and abandoned warehouses loomed like giants' playhouses outgrown and left behind. Jack was watching the buildings speed by as he took turn after turn until, finally, their pursuing car was a few turns behind and out of sight.

"Okay, get off the road and quick hide somewhere, hope he goes on by us," D said.

Jack nodded and took a hard turn into some kind of old brewery-looking building— a bit too hard of a turn. The tire caught on the broken curb going in and they both felt the pop as it blew. "Fuck me sideways," Jack swore, manhandling the steerless car behind a large tank-like structure. He slammed the brakes and they both jerked forward, D bracing himself on the dashboard. "I'm sorry—" he started, but D cut him off.

"Jus getcher gun, we gotta move. Ain't gonna take 'em too long ta figure out where we gone." He'd reloaded both his guns; now all they could do was leave the car and try to hunker down and call for help. He hated calling for help, but it was him and Jack against at least four pissed-off thugs, likely more than four, and he couldn't protect Jack against that kind of resistance.

They ran across the deserted yard and busted in the door to the warehouse. The morning sunlight slanted in the high windows; the place was empty save for a few lonely pieces of rusty equipment. D led Jack across the room to an office; they sat against the inner wall, hidden from view. "Now'd be the time to call Churchill," D said. Jack pulled out his phone and flipped it open, then swore. "What?"

"No signal."

"Shit."

"Maybe if we got higher up?"

D didn't like that idea. He liked this little hidey-hole just fine; it was defensible. But they couldn't just sit here forever, and the odds of them walking out without help weren't good. "Yeah, okay."

They got up and left the office. There was a metal staircase nearby that led up to the rafters and a door to God knew where, but it was the best option. They climbed quickly; the door at the top turned out to lead out to a catwalk that led from the warehouse to some kind of storage tank about a hundred yards away. Jack tried his phone again, but the look on his face told D what he needed to know. "Well, we cain't get no higher," he said. "Back inside."

They retreated to the office. "Now what?" Jack asked.

D hit the wall with a clenched fist. "I don't fuckin' know." He met Jack's eyes, those trusting blue eyes looking to D for answers, for safety, for a plan. "I'm sorry, Jack." He swallowed hard. "I'm so fuckin' sorry I ever got you inta this."

"It isn't your fault. I'm the marked-for-death witness, remember?"

"Yeah, but these guys are after me, not you. Only reason they give a shit about you is because I do."

Jack sighed. "You risked your life for me half a dozen times, D. I guess it's my turn now."

"That ain't your job."

"The hell it isn't." Jack grabbed D's hand, his eyes blazing. "You're my guy, aren't you?"

"Am I?" D asked, sounding like a little boy to his own ears, searching Jack's eyes.

"Yes, you are. No matter what happens, 'til the day I die." Jack took a deep breath. "Just as long as I don't die at your hand."

D frowned. "Jack—"

"That's what she wants, isn't it? For you to kill me?"

"I'd never hurt you."

"I know. But...." He looked away for a moment. "I think we both know that there's things she could do that might make you want to kill me, to stop me from hurting."

Yes, D did know that. He'd lost considerable sleep pondering what he'd do in that situation, which seemed like just the sort of thing Josey might be planning. "Maybe."

"I need you to promise me you won't."

"But... Jack—"

"No, D. No matter what she does to me, you swear that you won't kill me. Even if I beg you to. Whatever happens to me, I don't want my blood on your hands, because you'll never be able to wash it off."

Jack's words were burning D's skin like a branding iron. "It don't matter," he said. "If it came ta that, I'd follow right after you."

"Just promise me." Jack was gripping D's fingers so tight it was starting to hurt. "I won't help her hurt you. I won't be part of it. Don't let her make you do it."

D nodded. "All right," he choked out. "I promise." He stared at Jack's face and wondered if he'd ever hold this man again, make love to him or wake up to the sight of his face on the pillow at his side.

Voices outside the warehouse, running feet. D and Jack just sat there huddled inside the office, fingers interlaced, waiting for their fate to find them.

The door to the warehouse was kicked in. "D!" a voice yelled. "You in here, asshole?"

D peeked around the open door to the office. Two men with large guns were standing at the door. They'd find them in mere seconds either way, and if he acted now, at least he could thin their numbers a little. "Nope!" he yelled, and shot one of them in the chest. He ducked back inside as the other man opened fire with the automatic, the hail of bullets shattering the glass windows above them. Jack had his arms over his head. D popped his head up again and shot the man with the machine gun, but only winged him. Four more had joined them, and for an agonizing few seconds all he and Jack could do was try and make themselves as small as possible as Josey's men poured automatic weapons fire into the small office.

Abruptly, the firing stopped. "D?" came a new voice. A female voice.

Josey.

"Motherfucker," D whispered. Jack grabbed his face and turned it toward him. "This is it," he stammered.

D nodded. "'Fraid so."

Jack swallowed. "Son of a bitch," he whispered.

D drew Jack's face close and kissed him hard. "Follow my lead, and don't try nothin'," he murmured. "This shit's for real." Jack nodded.

D took a deep breath and got to his feet. He faced out into the warehouse through the shattered windows. "Josey," he said. Jack was getting up to stand at his side.

She walked forward a few paces. She looked just the same. Practical, flint-eyed, and no-nonsense. "Well. Here's the infamous Dr. Francisco." Jack squared his shoulders a little, but said nothing. "Why don't you both come on out here and be sociable?"

Hope was quickly draining from D's body. No one knew they were here. No one even knew anything was wrong. He was hopelessly outgunned and almost out of ammo. Josey had six men with her. If it was his time to pay the bill come due for his many crimes, he'd pay it gladly. The best he could hope for now was that he could somehow convince her to spare Jack's life. He took a deep breath, grasped Jack's hand, and walked out of the office with him to stand before the woman who would be his executioner. They stood there and waited as one of Josey's men patted them down, relieving them of their weapons.

Josey's eyes flicked to their clasped hands. "Hmm. I really wouldn't have guessed that you swung that way, D." D stayed silent. "You've dragged this out quite a bit longer than it was supposed to go."

"How *was* it supposed to go?" he asked.

"I'd think that'd be obvious. You kill Francisco, I make an anonymous tip, you're arrested and executed for the murder of a witness."

"That's really it?"

She shrugged. "You're the one who likes elaborate plans, not me. Yes, that was it. Simple, straightforward, with an element of poetic justice. At first I was angry that you didn't kill him, but now it's all worked out so much better than I could have possibly planned."

"Your father deserved what he got," D said, the words out of his mouth before he could stop himself.

Josey barely reacted. "I've no doubt. He was a mean son of a bitch who never gave two shits about me. You think this is about him? Well… it's partly about him. I was already wondering how to handle the fact that you were ratting out my operatives to the fucking Bureau when I discovered that you'd killed my father. You might say it was the straw that broke the camel's back."

D gritted his teeth. "I know you got some sorta plan, but I won't kill Jack."

"That's what you think."

"I'm tellin' you, I won't fuckin' do it."

She took a step closer. "But you've already done it. You're doing it right now."

D's eyes narrowed. "What the fuck're you talking 'bout?"

"You killed him when you loved him, D. When you did that, you gave me a way to hurt you."

Without taking her eyes off D's face, Josey raised her gun and shot Jack in the stomach.

MEGAN knew she had to make her move soon, or she'd be too weak. She didn't know how much blood she'd lost, but there was a not-inconsiderable pool beneath the chair at her feet. Petros had only been playing with her so far, though. Little cuts, not-so-little cuts…. He hadn't taken anything off yet, and he hadn't pulled anything out. That'd be the next stop.

There was only one thing she could do to get out of this, and he hadn't given her the opportunity. All he had to do was lean close…. Fuck, she had to get moving. Somewhere D and Jack were in danger.

As if obeying a subconscious desire to obey her wishes, Petros moved in front of her. "I suppose that's enough of the preliminaries," he purred. He leaned in close.

Megan lifted her head, which she'd been allowing to sag down to her chest, and smacked her forehead as hard as she could into Petro's nose. He recoiled and fell on his back.

She drew a deep breath, rocked back, and threw herself forward, planting her feet hard to flip her entire body, chair and all, the front rung landing across Petros's neck. He made an amusing gurgling noise. She tilted forward, increasing the pressure across his throat. "Where'd they take Jack and D?"

He just glared at her.

"Where?!"

No response.

"Fine, have it your way." She slid her bound arms up and over the chair back, grabbed his straight-razor from the table nearby and sliced herself free. "I'll find them myself." She'd taken no more than a couple of steps before dizziness overtook her. That burst of energy to free herself had taken just about everything she had left.

She heard Petros throw off the chair and get to his feet behind her. *Last chance, Megs.* She tightened her grip on the straight razor and whirled around, swinging it in a flat arc across his neck.

He stopped short, his eyes popped wide. Nothing happened for a moment, then a wide mouth opened in his neck and blood poured down his chest. His hands went to his throat but the cut was far too deep for that. Megan watched, gasping, as he slumped to the ground, blood spreading out beneath him.

She went down to her knees, the world graying out around her. She crawled across the floor to her coat and fumbled for her cell phone, forcing her vision to clear enough for her to dial. "Churchill," said the blessedly unharmed-sounding voice on the other end.

"It's Megan—"

"What's wrong?"

"Something's going down right now. She's making her move on them right now. Help them."

"Are you hurt?"

"Shit, yeah. Just killed Petros."

"Where are you?"

"Dunno...." She slid to the side and lost it for a moment, her last vestiges of consciousness allowing her to bite her tongue hard and bring her brain back.

"Hang up and call nine-one-one. You've got GPS locate, don't you?"

"Yeah."

"Do it now. I'll take care of Jack and D."

Megan thumbed the end button and stared dumbly at the keypad. *Who'm I supposed to call?* She faded, the glowing numbers lighting her down into unconsciousness.

To D, it all happened in slow motion. Josey's arm coming up, sure and quick, firing just as he realized what she meant to do. Turning toward Jack, seeing the bullet strike him just above the waist on his left side, Jack's face going slack, his mouth a wide O of shock, D reaching out toward him in a helpless, involuntary gesture as if he could yank Jack back to wholeness with the pure force of his will.

Shock wiped D's mind clean of any other consideration as he rejoined the world and everything sped up to normal time again and Jack was on the floor, his hand over his stomach, blood beginning to seep out between his fingers.

He skidded to his knees and hauled Jack into his lap, pressing down on the wound. Jack was making a high-pitched, keening noise, his teeth clamped shut tight while his wide eyes rolled up toward D's face.

Josey stepped closer. "That wound isn't fatal. Well, I should say that it is, but it'll take a few days."

D's rage was too large for his body to contain it. "You motherfucking *bitch,* I am gonna tear yer fuckin' eyes outta yer skull!" he shouted at her, nearly unintelligible, spittle flying from his lips. Jack choked out an anguished moan of pain and D pulled him closer, one hand on Jack's head holding it to his own chest. The blood was flowing steadily, but not quickly. It was a precision shot, intentionally placed to cause as much prolonged pain and suffering as possible before causing death from excruciatingly slow exsanguination. Jack's hand fluttered in the air like a bird with a busted wing before grabbing onto D's forearm with panicky tightness. "Yer gonna be okay, baby," he whispered to Jack, pressing his cheek to the top of his head. "You jus' hang on, try not ta move." Jack gurgled, his chest heaving.... Jesus, she'd even managed not to hit his lungs, which would have hurried his death along more quickly.

"He isn't going to be okay, D."

"Shut the fuck up!"

"Don't give the man false hope; that's just mean."

"I WILL GET UP THERE AND RIP YOU APART WITH MY BARE HANDS!" D screamed. He could feel tears pouring down his face and he hated it that she was seeing him so bare, so raw, but that was the least of his worries at the moment.

"Can you stand to watch him die like this? Long, slow, and painful?"

"Don't you even fuckin' think it," D said, his voice choked, trying to hold Jack steady.

"You can end his pain right now, you know."

"I won't do it."

She sighed, a sad and resigned look-what-you're-making-me-do sigh. "I didn't think you'd crack that easily." She raised the gun again and shot Jack in the lower leg. Jack screamed, writhing in D's arms as if trying to get out of his own skin.

D clamped his arms tighter around Jack's torso and gradually became aware that he was screaming "*stop it stop it*" over and over again without having been aware he'd started. Jack fell into a limp semi-daze, shaking and shuddering, whistling moans leaking nonstop from his throat.

"You're the only one who can stop this, D."

He stared up at her, a stranger to the hate he felt for her. He'd never hated so fiercely or so hotly in his life. "I'll do whatever you fuckin' want; jus' stop hurtin' him. Let him be and I'll go quietly. You can torture me long as you want, jus' let Jack go."

"I think you know that isn't how this works."

"Why you hate me this much, huh? Why you gotta put him through this?"

"Rats who run to the Bureau deserve no less, D. Everyone should know it."

Jack was tugging on his shirt. D looked down at him, his face fish-belly pale and covered in sweat and a few stray blood droplets. "You promised," he whispered.

"Jack, I—"

"Don't you do it," Jack said again, the last words lost in another groan of pain, Jack's body trying to curl in on itself like a pill bug.

D looked down into those eyes, clouded as they were with pain, and felt Jack's love for him through his whole being, lighting the long-banked fires inside him and illuminating him from within. Jack who'd risked so much for him, Jack who'd stuck by him, Jack who was now willing to suffer in agony for him, Jack who he did not deserve.

Josey was crouching by their side. She had another gun in her hand. "This gun has one bullet in it. Don't even think about using it on me or any of my guys, because they can shoot you dead before you get the shot off and he will suffer for your mistake. Take it, and show me what happens to people who love you."

D stared at the gun. It was calling him, its voice low and seductive. *He will never hurt again. He will never be in danger again. He will never live to grow tired of you and realize how unworthy you are. He will be out of pain, beyond her reach.* The gun was peace, the gun was normality, the gun was everything he'd been for ten years.

The gun could save them both.

He reached out and took it. Jack's hand grabbed his shirt. "No," he cried, weakly.

"It's okay, Jack." His voice sounded very far away. The gun felt so familiar in his hand. It felt like home. He looked up at Josey, who was nodding as you might to a child who'd pleased you. He smiled at her.

D lifted the gun and pressed the barrel under his own jaw.

Jack's tugging on his shirt grew more urgent. "No, no," he repeated.

"Shh, Jack," D said. "It's gonna be okay."

The smile had fallen off Josey's face. D guessed that this wasn't part of her plan. "Don't be stupid," she said.

"What's stupid? I'd rather die than kill Jack."

"You do yourself in, D, and I swear no one will ever have suffered the way he will."

"Bullshit. You cain't risk the time and energy ta torture him when I'm not around ta witness it, not ta mention the risk of *you* goin' ta the chair for murderin' a witness. Witsec knows who you are, ya know. Jack's found dead and they be comin' fer you."

"You're willing to bet the rest of his short life on that?"

"Yes," Jack croaked, his hand wrapped around D's, his watery eyes fixed on Josey. D pulled him closer to his chest.

"You're bluffing," Josey said, but she didn't look too sure of that. "I'll just take the gun back."

"Wanna find out how fast I can shoot myself before you can get this gun away from me?"

She stood up and paced off a few quick circles. He'd put her off her game, which was about as much as he could hope for at this point. He could feel the wetness of Jack's blood on his legs, the constant low groans of pain straightening his spine. It was kill Jack or kill himself, and that wasn't a choice at all. "D," Jack whispered. He looked down at him, the face of the only person he'd ever loved, his precious life spilling onto the dirty warehouse floor.

He stroked Jack's hair with his bloodstained free hand. "What, darlin'?"

Jack was shaking so violently now that his teeth were chattering. "I don't regret anything," he said, his lips twisting like he was trying to smile.

D smiled back. "You the only thing I don't regret," he said.

Josey sneered at him. "You won't do it. You don't have the guts."

D steeled himself. "Watch me."

A shot rang out, and for a moment D wondered if he'd shot himself before he meant to, but the shot wasn't from his gun. He looked and saw one of Josey's men on the floor. For the briefest second, everything was suspended; even Jack's tight-lipped groans of pain were silent.

Then all hell broke loose. The door to the warehouse was kicked in and four Kevlar-wearing men with Marshal's badges around their necks poured in, shouting for everyone to get down, get down, freeze, throw down their weapons, and other mutually exclusive commands. Another marshal came clattering down the stairs. Gunshots were fired. Josey's men started falling. One of the agents was spun around with what looked like a shot to the arm.

Josey whirled, snarling, her gun raised. D had put his single bullet between her eyes before he even knew he was going to fire. She fell, eyes wide and staring at them, without another word.

D hugged Jack to his chest and felt like sobbing out loud as Churchill strode into the room. He could have sworn a halo of golden light and a flourish of trumpets accompanied him. The other marshals had three of her men on their knees in cuffs; the other ones looked dead or wounded. "It's okay, it's okay," D kept saying, talking both to Jack and himself. He cupped Jack's face. "Yer gonna be okay now, doc. Cavalry's here."

Jack cried out in pain, a little blood coming to his lips. "'Bout fuckin' time," he choked out.

D laughed, light-headed with relief. Churchill knelt at their side. "Jesus," he said.

"He's shot in the left abdomen," D said. "He'll be okay but we gotta get him to a hospital. Got a flesh wound in his calf too."

"Are you hit?"

"Naw, I'm okay. How'd you fuckin' find us?"

"Tracker in Jack's gun. I found it the first day he was at the hotel when I swept for listening devices. I assume you put it there. Made a note of the frequency in case I needed to use it myself. Megan just called me; Petros grabbed her and done a good number on her to keep her out of the way so she knew something was up." Churchill rattled all this off at lightning-quick speed. D's brain wasn't exactly firing on all cylinders and he was still catching up to the fact that he and Jack weren't both about to die.

"Good timin' there," was all he could muster.

Churchill grabbed his arm. "D, they're calling for backup. You've got to get out of here, now."

Jack, who'd been watching them with half-glazed eyes, came back into himself at this. "What?"

"In about three minutes this place is going to be crawling with police, FBI, paramedics and forensics and you can't be here. I can't protect you with that much law around." He handed D his car keys. "Take my car. I saw yours had a flat."

D just stared at the keys. He couldn't say goodbye to Jack like this, here and now, and leave him bleeding on some godforsaken warehouse floor. "Christ, I cain't do this. I cain't jus' leave Jack like this!"

Jack grabbed his arm. "You have to go," he said. "D… they can't find you. You've got… all that to do," Jack said, his halting voice laced with barely suppressed agony. "You gotta stay free, you gotta go."

"It's my turn to look out for him now," Churchill said.

D nodded helplessly. "Okay, okay… just…." He looked at Churchill helplessly.

"I'll give you a minute," he said, and backed off.

D looked down at Jack, staring back up at him with his eyes full of tears. "Didn't think it'd be like this when we said goodbye," Jack said.

"Fuck, no," D choked out.

"I'll be okay," Jack said, an obvious effort going into making the words clear and distinct.

D pressed his forehead to Jack's, wishing he could just pass his thoughts and feelings directly into Jack's brain without having to resort to inadequate words, for which he'd never had a talent anyway. "Jack," he whispered, drawing back to look in his eyes again. "You been the fullest, luckiest blessin' a my life," he said, seeing tears drip onto Jack's upturned face.

Jack was clutching handfuls of D's shirt. "I love you," he croaked.

"I'll see you again," D said, trying to sound certain and emphatic but fearing he only sounded pleading.

"I'll be waiting." Jack pulled him down again and for a few too-long, too-short moments they said nothing, breathing each other in for the last time. D eased Jack down onto the warehouse floor and knelt at his side, a shaky breath escaping him as he pressed his face to Jack's chest for a moment, feeling Jack's hand rest on the back of his head. He met Jack's eyes one final time and they both nodded, as if something had been resolved, then D hauled himself to his feet and turned away, walking as fast as he could toward the door, hearing Jack call his name just one time before the warehouse door closed behind him.

CHAPTER 27

THE first thing Jack was aware of was the breeze. The cold breeze. There was a hurricane-force arctic wind blowing straight up his nose. He raised a hand, which felt like it was encased in concrete, and batted at that damned breeze only to encounter a plastic mask strapped to his face. "Urf," he said, not really sure what word he meant it to be, since what he really wanted to say was "get this goddamned oxygen mask off my face."

"Someone's awake," said a woman's voice. A face appeared over him and removed the mask. "Can you hear me, Jack?"

"Mmm," he said, nodding. He looked around. Hospital, machines, tubes, people in scrubs. "M'I having surgery?" he babbled.

The nurse smiled. "You've already had it. You're in the recovery room. Just lie still, okay? Try to relax and let your body wake up."

Jack blinked, consciousness returning. "What time's it?"

She checked her watch. "Almost six."

"Still Sunday?"

"Yep, still Sunday."

Jack didn't have the energy for any more questions. He lay back against the pillows and let his eyes close, then popped them open again. He didn't like what he saw when they were closed.

D with a gun to his own head. D holding him, crying, shouting. D saying goodbye, D walking away. Jack stared at the ceiling, but the image of D's face had followed him from behind his eyelids and he was still seeing it. Looked like he'd be seeing it whether he liked it or not.

He didn't feel a thing in his side, where Josey had shot him. He imagined he'd feel it plenty later when the drugs wore off. *I was shot. Twice. Huh. Imagine that.* The thought held little power. So he'd been shot. Great.

It had been a strange sensation. At first there hadn't been any pain, just this tremendous pressure and then hot warmth, wetness on his skin, and then he was looking at the ceiling of the warehouse... and *then* the pain had hit, rolling over him like some kind of earth-moving equipment, squashing rational thought and pulverizing his resolve. He couldn't really remember. Pain was like that. It was so intense when it was happening, but later you couldn't really recall the exact sensation.

He wanted D. He wanted him to walk in the room and smile that little slantwise smile, cutting his eyes to the side and back again. He just wanted to hold his hand, that was all.

But he couldn't have that, because D was gone. For the foreseeable future.

For weeks—months, even—this had been looming. The Separate Time. The Time of No D. They'd both known it was ahead, but it had always seemed so vague, like it would someday come but never *really* come. Even this past weekend, when it had been breathing down their necks, it hadn't felt quite real.

But now it was here. It was real. Jack had been rudely thrust into it without any kindness or consideration. He'd always assumed there'd be *time*. Time to say things, do things, discuss things, time to *prepare*. Once, there had been all the time in the world. Then the marshals were drugged and there were car chases and somehow they were saying goodbye on a dirty warehouse floor, Jack's blood on D's face, and it was *there*. Ugly and demanding and ready to rip them apart, grind them up and let them wonder how long it would last.

Jack drifted off, feeling only relief as oblivion claimed him again.

WHEN he woke again, it was morning. He was in a regular hospital room, and Churchill was sitting in a chair next to the bed, reading the paper. "Hey," Jack croaked.

Churchill jumped and tossed the paper aside. "Hey yourself," he said. "How are you feeling?"

Jack wasn't quite sure how to answer that. "Uh… all right, I guess." He tried to sit up a little but that sent a bolt of pain up his left side and he flopped back down again. "Been better."

"Well, the doctors say you came through the surgery fine. The bullet went through you. Tore you up a bit, but they fixed it. You got lucky."

Jack shook his head. "Wasn't luck. She shot me that way on purpose."

Churchill frowned. "What do you mean?"

I mean, she meant for me to slowly bleed to death while she tortured me, until D couldn't take it anymore and killed me to put me out of my misery. That's what I mean. He flapped a hand. "Doesn't matter." He sighed. "Is it Monday?"

"Yep. And just as soon as your doctors say you're stable enough, we're moving you to Albany just like we planned. I'm hoping that's within a few days here."

Jack didn't want to leave Baltimore. This was where they'd last been together, where he'd last seen him. The last place D would know where he was. Once he left that link would be cut, and they'd both be finally, truly alone.

Churchill leaned forward, his face sympathetic. "I know you're probably feeling ambivalent about that."

"I know it's time."

Churchill was staring at his hands. "I'm so sorry, Jack," he murmured.

Jack frowned. "What for?"

"They never should have been able to get to you," he said in a rush. "Witsec has never lost a witness who followed the rules, never. I've never had anyone compromised."

Jack sighed. "It was my understanding that Witsec had never lost a witness who'd actually been relocated. I was still in limbo. Besides, they were after D, not me."

"Still. My security was inadequate."

"No security is adequate if they're determined enough," Jack said. "And they were."

"I just… you're hurt, and what you went through…. I'm just sorry, is all."

Jack smiled. "Thanks." A sudden thought occurred. "Hey, is Megan okay?"

"Yeah. She was supposed to call nine-one-one but she must have passed out before she could. We were able to find her with the GPS in her phone because she'd left it on. She just needed some blood and fluids; she'll be okay." He hesitated. "Petros cut her up pretty bad. She looks like she went five rounds with a grizzly bear."

"She saved our lives. If you hadn't come when you did... D was about to shoot himself."

Churchill leaned forward. "Why was he going to do that?"

Jack struggled to sit up again; Churchill rose and helped him, propping pillows behind his back and taking his seat again once Jack was settled. "Because," Jack said, staring at his hands, "Josey wanted him to kill me, and I made him promise he wouldn't, no matter what. It was the only way he could take away what she wanted."

"Which was?"

"Him suffering. He was like a doll she was taking apart just to see it in pieces. Only thing to do was take the doll away." Jack shook his head, tears fuzzing his vision. "It was all going to be over, right there. Jesus." He pressed the fingers of one hand to his face. "Jesus Christ, I almost died."

"But you didn't," Churchill said, quietly. "And you're not going to. You're going to heal up and start over and you're going to live a long, boring life."

Jack snorted laughter through his tears. "Boring. Sounds like heaven."

Churchill looked toward the door, his face brightening. "Well, speak of the devil," he said as Megan walked in. Jack had to stop himself from gasping. She *did* look like she'd gone five rounds with a grizzly bear. She had cuts on her face and neck, and what skin he could see of her arms. Both sides of her face were bruised and her eyes were swollen. She was walking with a bit more caution than usual.

"Had to come see you before I left," she said, smiling and coming to Jack's bedside. He reached up—carefully—and embraced her, mindful not only of his own injury but of hers.

"Where do you think you're going?" Churchill said severely.

"Home. Signed myself out."

"You got your doctor to agree to that?"

"Who says he agreed? I'm fine. All I'll do here is lie in bed and moan, and I can do that at home."

She pulled back, but Jack hung onto her hand. "Thank you," he said, trying to communicate how much he meant those words with his eyes.

She smiled and touched his face. "Don't mention it. The both of you lived, bad guys didn't, that's thanks enough."

Silence fell among the battered trio. They looked at one another with veiled expressions. No one needed to say anything; the ghost of D that stood among them was doing all the talking.

Finally, Megan drew herself up and took a deep breath. "Well, I better be getting along. I'm sure I'll have things to do pretty soon but for the time being there is a couch with my name on it."

Jack smiled. "I think some serious TV-watching is in my future too."

She smoothed his hair back. "You be safe, Jack. I'll look in on you from time to time."

Jack nodded. "And... if you see...." He couldn't finish, but he didn't need to.

Megan just laid her hand on his shoulder, giving it a quick, reassuring squeeze. "I will."

MEGAN took the elevator, feeling like a wimp for doing so when her apartment was only on the second floor, but she thought her recent ordeal might excuse her.

There was no part of her body that didn't hurt. She'd received several units of blood and overnight IV fluids but she was still wiped out. A long period of sleep sounded like just the thing. She'd have to lie low for awhile. People tended to remember women who looked like they'd been on the receiving end of a bison attack.

Jack's doctors had said that he could be moved in the morning. Off to Albany, or at least that's what Jack thought. What he'd soon be finding out was that *every* Witsec protectee was taken there. "Albany" was the code word the Marshals used in public for whatever city they'd picked to relocate their witness, so if they were overheard by the wrong person the security of the witness's location would not be compromised. She had no idea where Jack was destined to land, and neither would anyone else outside Witsec. Jack wouldn't be told where they were going until they were en route.

She unlocked the apartment door. All was blessedly quiet. She went to the bathroom and examined herself in the mirror. It was pretty bad. Her face was swollen from both sides and heavily bruised, darker circles ringing her eyes, and the cuts on her neck and arms were angry and red. She already had an appointment with a plastic surgeon to clean up the damage so she wouldn't be left with scars.

She tossed some cold water on her heated face, avoiding her stitches, and went back into the living room. "Jesus Christ," she gasped, one hand flying to her chest as she stopped short.

D was sitting in the corner of the room, partially concealed by the armchair, his knees drawn up to his chest and his eyes staring blankly forward. He looked... not all there. *My God, has he been sitting there since yesterday?* All evidence pointed to yes. His clothes were stained with Jack's blood and his face was pale.

"D!" she exclaimed, going to his side. "My God, what... how long have you been sitting here?"

He dragged his eyes up to hers. "All night, I guess."

"Are you all right?"

He nodded. "You seen Jack?"

"Yeah, I just came from the hospital."

A little life came into his eyes. "Is he all right?"

She sat down next to him, her back against the wall, and drew her knees up to mimic his position. "He's all right. He had surgery, came through just fine." She hesitated. "He'll be leaving town in the morning. He wanted me to tell you... well, you know."

D nodded. "Tomorrow, huh?" He sighed. "Guess that's it, then."

Megan nodded. "That's it."

She waited, not speaking. She felt the tension leave D's body gradually; a whispery tremor began in him, transmitted to her through their touching shoulders. His head dropped down and he seemed to curl inward. Megan slid one arm around his shoulders and folded her legs Indian-style, so she was ready when he slid sideways and went boneless, surrendering to his emotions for what might have been the first time in his life, melting into her lap and weeping as she knew he'd never done in front of Jack or anyone else, ragged sobs that bore the weight of so much pain, not just the pain of losing Jack but of losing his daughter, his life, his soul, and his idea of himself as a man. She held him as best she could, feeling like a poor substitute, rubbing his back and making meaningless "shhh" noises. He had one arm wrapped around her knee and the other fist clamped to his mouth, useless barrier though it was to this bottled-up expression, these tears that were like the bleeding of a deep, wide tear, messy and directionless.

She did not calm him, or try to reassure him with words. He'd have to calm himself, and eventually he did. He fell into limp silence, exhaustion in every line of his body, sadness in every crease in his face.

Megan held him loosely across her lap, her head tipped back against the wall, the debt she owed this man hovering just over her shoulder, growing insistent (as it always did) when presented with a situation from which she could not save him, or a trouble she could not help.

Perhaps it was time for that debt to show its face.

He'd been quiet for a few minutes now, but she knew he hadn't fallen asleep. She could feel the waking in his muscles, and the hitches in his breathing.

So she began.

"Before I was a person that doesn't exist," she said, "I was regular Secret Service." He didn't react, but she felt him shift a little and knew he was listening. "I worked my way up to protection detail. I was damn good at it. Eventually I was assigned to the Secretary of Defense. I lived in Georgetown with my husband and my two boys." At that, she felt him flinch, no doubt with surprise, as she'd never referred to her family before.

"One night a man broke into our house with a gun. He tied up my husband and my boys and threatened to kill them if I didn't tell him the Secretary's itinerary for the next week. I couldn't tell him, because I didn't know. Only the SAC had that information. He didn't believe me. He shot my husband in the leg to convince me he meant business. I begged. I got down on my knees and begged him to spare my family's lives. I tried to invent an itinerary, but I was so terrified that I wasn't very convincing. I didn't know what to do." She sighed and let her eyes close, the terror of that long-ago night at her fingertips, asking to be let back in. "He was about to shoot one of my sons when a rifle shot came through the window and killed him on the spot."

She let that sink in for a moment. D didn't move.

"I think you know that man's name."

He sighed. "Cy Rugerand."

"Yes."

"It was just a job," he whispered.

"It doesn't matter, D. You saved not only me but my family when you killed him."

"Didn't know I'd saved nobody."

"Oh, I think you did. You couldn't have seen us from where you were but you had to know he had someone in there that he was threatening."

D hesitated a long time before answering. "Yeah, guess so."

"If all you were hired to do was kill him, it would have been a lot safer for you to wait until he came out and shot him on the street. By doing it through the window, you were establishing a trajectory and giving away your position on the rooftop across the way, which could have left you vulnerable if any forensics were found there, plus you were making it impossible to pass it off as a mugging, or really as anything but an intentional hit. You couldn't have been *planning* to shoot him while he was inside the house; that's insane. No one does that because it's too risky. You were going to shoot him coming or going, but you changed your plans when you saw what was going on."

She let her hand rest on D's arm. "You shot him when you did to save us, even if you didn't know it was us you were saving."

D stayed quiet.

Megan shut her eyes again and rested her head against the wall. "Nothing was the same after that. My husband left me and took our sons away. I didn't fight for custody. They're better off with him and I didn't trust myself anymore than David trusted me. I was too dangerous. I'd put them all in jeopardy, and he couldn't live with it. Neither could I. I don't see them more than a couple of times a year. It hurts, but they're safe, and that's what's important. David remarried. She's a math professor and she loves the boys, and they love her. I'm okay with that. As long as no one ever tries to hurt them again because of me." She looked down at D's profile. "I asked for a transfer out of protection and got into this. Made it my business to find out who'd killed Rugerand. When I found out it was you I did some digging and figured out who you were, and what had happened to you." She sighed. "Almost ten years I've tracked you. Watching you take some jobs and leave others, seeing what kind of man you were or if you were a man at all, or just a monster who killed for money."

She looked out the window at the afternoon sunlight. The sky was blue; it was a beautiful day. Too beautiful to be sitting here holding a blood-soaked, heartbroken man on her lap while she spilled her guts.

"I would be yours if you wanted me," she finally said, after a long pause. "But I know you don't. I'm okay with that. I know about that secret lockbox in your gut, the one where you keep all the sludge and tar and pain. And I know you found the person who had the key to open it. I'm still looking, I guess." She shrugged. "Or maybe I'm not looking at all. Some things are best left locked away."

D stayed where he was for a few beats, then sat up and resumed his position at her side, back to the wall. He stretched out his legs and rubbed at his eyes, then stared at his hands. "I'm in love with him," he murmured, almost to himself.

Megan nodded. "I know. That means I'll be watching out for him now too. Anyone you ever care about, D. Anything you ever need."

"It was just a job," D said, his voice rough.

She smiled. "You don't get it, do you? It doesn't matter. You made a choice, and that choice saved me and my family."

He finally lifted his head and looked at her full in the face, but whatever he planned to say died behind a horrified expression. "Oh my God, what the fuck happened ta you?"

"Petros had a go at me. I'm fine."

"You ain't fine; you look half-dead. You oughta be in the hospital."

"I checked myself out." She squared her shoulders a little. "Punched that psychopath's ticket, though."

D hesitated, and then smiled a little. "Killed him?"

"I'd like to take credit for superior strategy, but it was more or less a reflex."

"How?"

"Straight razor to the throat."

D looked impressed. "Damn. That's old-school."

"Well, he did go pretty medieval on my face," she said, grimacing.

"That's for fuckin' sure. You want some ice or somethin'?"

"I'm okay. They gave me some Darvocet at the hospital."

He was silent for another few moments. "Megan, look… whatever debt y'owe me, you done paid it back and then some. You saved my life and Jack's when you called

Churchill. We'd both be lyin' dead on some warehouse floor right now if ya hadn't. That ain't sayin' nothing 'bout all them times you saved my life before, or how ya helped us out in Tahoe."

"A life debt isn't a mortgage, D. You're not done after thirty years plus interest. It's never over; it'll never be repaid."

"Well, then... I owe you one a them life debts now too. So I guess we jus' keep payin' each other back 'til somebody cries uncle."

"I'm game if you are."

"'Fraid I'm gonna be real busy fer the next foreseeable future."

"Well, you know how to reach me." She stood up and extended a hand to help D to his feet. "Let's not rush off just yet. We could both use a shower, some clean clothes and some food, I'm guessing."

D put a hand on his stomach. "I am kinda hungry. Guess... I dunno. Now I know Jack's safe, well... it's a load off my mind fer the time bein'."

"I brought your things back from Jack's car. You left it at the warehouse."

"Right. Thanks." He started toward the bathroom, then turned. "You give Jack back his things too?"

"Sure did."

"Good," he said, nodding. "Hate ta think a him without that doctor bag."

THEY ordered a pizza and ate it sitting on the floor by the coffee table, not talking much. Megan was feeling a little wrung out from her confessional. She'd been rehearsing how she'd someday tell D what he'd done for her for years now, but when the time had come all her preparations had gone out the window and the facts had come spilling out in a blunt, declarative flood. She felt hollowed out; the space within herself where she'd stored all her secrets and all those words she knew she'd someday say to him was empty and echoing. It was a good kind of empty, though. Unlike the kind of empty that she knew had taken up residence inside D.

D drank half a bottle of beer at a swallow. "Goddamn," he said. "That hit the spot."

She nodded, mouth full of pizza. "Grease and carbs always hit the spot."

He fiddled with the edge of his paper towel, a thoughtful expression on his face. "Thinkin' I might crash here tonight if that's okay."

"Sure."

"I wanna get goin' but I'm fuckin' beat. It's like I been tensed up fer months now and suddenly it's gone and I'm like some kinda wet noodle, all floppy."

"I know what you mean."

"I don't even know where I'm goin' first. Might be best fer me ta stick 'round here. I'm gonna need some sources fer what I got planned, though. And the brothers got family workin' all over; gonna hafta do some travelin'."

"You're still not going to tell me what you've got up your sleeve, are you?"

"Best ya don't know."

She shrugged. "Have it your way."

D shook his head. "Yer jus gonna magically show up like ya do anyhow, don't know why I'm botherin' ta try'n keep shit from you."

Megan grinned, as much as she could with her bruised face. "You want to know how I always find you?"

He narrowed his eyes. "What, you really gonna tell me?"

"Well, we don't have many secrets left, do we? Might as well go for broke."

"Yeah, I'm dyin' ta know, actually."

She took a deep breath, wondering how he'd take this. "You have a transmitter implanted in your body."

His brow furrowed. "No, I don't."

"Yep."

"I fuckin' don't! Ya think I'd know somethin' like that!"

"Not necessarily."

"How the hell'm I s'posed ta buy that you somehow implanted a—"

"Wasn't me that implanted it. It was your... former employers."

"My former... what?"

"You were special ops, D. Let's just say that the army likes to keep track of its assets." D looked gobsmacked. "Let me guess," she said. "Just before you were promoted to special ops, you had some kind of minor medical procedure that required general anesthesia, right?"

D was nodding, his brow still furrowed. "Had some bridge work done."

"Yeah, that's a popular one. While you were out they implanted a transmitter in one of your bones, probably your jaw since your gums were already opened up. A small, nonmetallic transmitter with a forty-year lithium power cell. Nontoxic and high frequency, detectable via satellite from virtually anywhere."

"Motherfucker," D said, rubbing his jaw.

"The device is deactivated when an asset retires, dies, or otherwise leaves, as you did."

"But you got it reactivated, right?"

"I have prevented a lot of assassinations in my time. There are a lot of people at the Pentagon who owe me favors."

"Who's to prevent somebody else from trackin' me with this fuckin' thing?" D said, looking like he wanted to rip his jaw out of his skull to be rid of it.

"Oh, no. The frequency is key-code encrypted. It was actually quite difficult to gain access to it. I made sure no one else ever could, though. I had your encryptions purged from the system once I had them."

D still looked troubled. "I don't like the idea a some bug in my head lettin' you track me. No offense meant ta you, but I ain't one ta be on no leash."

"I know." She thought for a moment. "If you want me to shut it down, I will."

He opened his mouth quickly, probably to say "hell yes," then shut it again, thinking. He heaved a mighty sigh. "Better not. You gonna be lookin' in on Jack, I guess?" She nodded. "You might need ta find me. Was already thinking we oughta set up some kinda weekly check-in, so if I miss it you know somethin's up. Guess... be good if you was able ta find me," he said, grudgingly.

"I think so too."

He held her eyes for a moment, and then got up. "I'm gonna sack out. Be leavin' in the mornin'... if yer okay, that is," he added.

She flapped a hand. "I'm fine." He started to head to the second bedroom. "D?"

"Yeah?"

"Can I ask you something?"

He turned back. "Shoot."

Megan considered her phrasing before speaking. "What is it that you want, ultimately? Once you're done with the brothers, and say you've gotten Jack free of Witsec. What are you hoping for then?"

He leaned against the wall. "Well, he wants... ya know, a life. A garden and a dog and... normal stuff."

She cocked her head. "Is that what *you* want?"

"What I want is ta give him what he wants." He sighed. "I jus' hope I remember how." He turned and went into the bedroom, shutting the door behind him

"CAN'T I ride in a wheelchair?"

"No. You have to go on a gurney. You just had surgery, for Christ's sake."

"Yesterday."

"Gurney."

"Fine." But Jack at least insisted on getting out of bed and onto the gurney himself, which he did very slowly and carefully.

Churchill walked at his side as he was loaded into an elevator and taken to the rooftop helipad, where a medevac helicopter was waiting. "The helicopter will take us to the airport," Churchill said, "and we'll fly from there."

"I can fly?"

"The government has planes with medical equipment; it'll be just like being back in your room."

"Swell." Jack held onto the edges of his gurney, feeling acrophobic all of a sudden, as they loaded him into the helicopter. Churchill got in next to the pilot and a flight nurse climbed in and tucked himself next to the gurney. Jack stared out the window at the Baltimore cityscape. *I wonder if he's still in town, or if he's halfway across the country.* Jack was struck by the absurd hope that D was still in town, and that he might by chance look up and see the helicopter leaving. One last goodbye, even if he didn't know Jack was on board.

The nurse was putting a headset on Jack, cutting off most external sound as the rotor blades started up. "You okay, Jack?" Churchill said, tinny through the headset.

Jack nodded. "I'm okay." *Just shot full of holes and heartbroken. No big thing.* He reached out and touched the window glass with one finger as the helicopter lifted off, zooming away from the hospital faster than Jack expected. Within a few minutes, the city was receding as they headed for BWI.

Goodbye, D. I miss you already.

JACK woke up in yet another hospital room. As before, Churchill was sitting in a chair by the bed, except now it was night, and this wasn't Baltimore. "Jesus, did I sleep the whole flight?" he rasped.

Churchill gave a start and dropped the book he'd been reading. "Oh, shit... uh, yeah. The nurse gave you a sedative so you would."

"Is this Albany?"

He grinned. "We were never going to Albany, Jack. We always say we are in case we're overheard. It's our little code word."

"Oh. Where's this, then?"

"Welcome to Portland, Jack. Your new home."

"Maine?"

"Oregon."

Jack stared.

"I know; it's far."

"Jesus."

"You'll be here in the hospital for at least a week before we can take you to your new house."

"Where am I going to work? Do I have a name? What about money? How am I—"

Churchill held up a hand. "Shh. There'll be time for all those discussions later. Everything's taken care of; you don't have to worry." He got up and came closer. "But if you'd like to know your new name, here it is." He handed Jack a driver's license.

He stared at it, an Oregon license, with his face on it next to a name that was only half his. Jack Davies. Generic. Everyday. Ordinary.

Safe.

There had to be a zillion guys named Jack Davies in the country. How would anyone find him with this name?

Especially people he wanted to find him?

D WAS checking around for anything he'd forgotten when Megan shuffled out of her room in a bathrobe, looking even more bruised and battered than the night before, if that were possible. He felt another surge of anger at Petros for the job he'd done on his friend.

Friend. His only friend apart from Jack. And now the only friend he could see whenever he wanted to. After years of being alone, the idea of being so again had lost its appeal, and he was glad that she was in his corner, at least.

"You heading out?" she said, the words half-swallowed in a huge yawn.

"Yeah. Headin' up ta New York. Brothers got a big presence up there; gonna sniff 'round a bit, find a place ta crash, scout things out."

"I'll be here for at least a week. After that, I don't know. You got my cell."

He nodded, patting his pocket for car keys, and coming to an embarrassingly obvious realization. "Oh, fuck. I don't have a car."

She held out her keys. "Take this one. Treasury issue. I'd advise you to swap the plates as fast as you can." She shrugged off his objection before he'd even voiced it. "They'll send me another one. Don't worry about it."

He took the keys. "Well... all right." They stood there by the door in awkward silence for a moment. D felt something else was required, but he was ill at ease in this situation.

Megan just smiled, then stepped close and hugged him. D hugged back after a moment's hesitation, being careful of her many injuries. "You take care. Keep me posted."

"Will do. And, uh...."

"Soon as I'm back on my feet I'll look in on him. You, uh... have a message you want me to give him?"

D considered that. "No. I cain't tell Jack nothin' he don't already know. Not through no third party, anyhow. Not even if it's you."

"Understood."

D let his eyes linger for a moment on her battered face. "Thank you," he said, hoping she could hear the many layers and vast depths of his gratitude.

She sighed. "Get out of here before you embarrass both of us," she said, shoving him out the door. He picked up his bags, one with clothes and one with guns, and headed out.

He found Megan's nondescript Taurus in the parking lot and climbed in, that old sense of beginning a new venture lending lift to his rotors as they spun faster and faster. He backed out and turned the car's nose first to the street, then to the highway, then to mighty I-95, north to New York.

D shook out his mirrored sunglasses and slid them onto his face, letting the miles accumulate between him and the emotional, wrenching days he'd spent in Baltimore, each click of the odometer stripping him back, closer to who he'd once been, freezing his mind and focusing his thoughts onto one goal, one target, one plan.

A grim little smile creased his lips as morning broke over Maryland, a smile that meant only one thing: that someone was going to be very, very sorry.

CHAPTER 28

Three months later...

JACK was watching a little boy, about three years old, try to pick up a pumpkin that was at least as big as he was. The boy had curly blond hair and was wearing overalls and a bright red hoodie. His little arms didn't even reach halfway around the pumpkin, but he was screwing up his face and giving it the old college try.

A man came up to the boy and crouched at his side. He was wearing jeans and a gray cable-knit turtleneck sweater with expensive-looking leather gloves. He had casual stubble and his hair was mussed in that weekend-suburban-dad way. He owned the world and knew it. "You like that one, sport?" he said to the little boy.

"Daddy, this one!" said the boy, pointing and looking up at his father, who could do anything, lift anything, give him anything, and towered so high that he blocked the sun. "This big one!"

"Okay," the man said, chuckling. A prettily plump woman came up with a wagon in tow, a girl of about six hanging onto her hand. The dad lifted the large pumpkin and put it in the wagon with the two were already there. "All right, that'll be plenty for jack-o'-lanterns," he said. "Let's find some tiny ones and then we'll go to Aunt Sharon's house."

"Up!" the little boy cried, bouncing on his tiny feet. The father reached down and swung the boy effortlessly up to his shoulders and hung on to his legs as they walked away, unaware that Jack was watching them go.

He looked down at the pumpkins scattered all around the field, waiting to be chosen for exalted Halloween duty.

Why am I here? Why the fuck do I need a pumpkin? I don't have anyone to help me carve it or tease me about what a bad job I'm making of it.

He looked around at his fellow pumpkin-shoppers. Families, couples, kids, grandparents. His eyes snagged on a pair of men in jeans and colorful sweaters, joking with each other and play-shoving as they debated their pumpkin choices. As he watched, the men caught hands and squeezed briefly, then let go.

He sighed and picked up a good-sized pumpkin. What the hell. Single people need jack-o'-lanterns too.

"HEY, Jack!"

Jack looked up from the intimidating pile of books and magazines sitting at the information desk, waiting to be reshelved. Lydia was coming out from the backroom, pulling on her coat. "Yeah?"

"You're on recovery tonight?"

"Sadly, yes."

"Well, we're going out to Skully's. Do you want to come?"

"I'll be another half-hour at least. Can I meet you there?"

"Sure," she said, beaming a wide smile at him. Terrance, the manager, was waiting at the front door to unlock it so Lydia and the other booksellers could leave. "See you in a little while."

Jack nodded, tossing her an absent wave as he quickly sorted the books into piles by area of the store. Fiction, sports, kids, history…. He frowned at a large coffee stain on an expensive coffee-table book about stained-glass windows. Another one for the damaged pile, he grumbled to himself. Goddamned customers.

"I'll just be twenty minutes or so, Jack," said Terrance as he headed for the cash office with his arms full of register drawers. "Do what you can."

"Okay."

"And can you check the tables?" he called from across the store.

"Sure." Jack left the desk and went to the rear of the store, where several reading tables sat near the Psychology section. It was a frequent dumping-ground for customer castoffs. Indeed, there were several piles of books and a few empty coffee cups waiting for him. Jack gathered everything up and took it back to the service desk, his mind pleasantly blank.

Churchill had offered him several choices of employment, for all of which he was extravagantly overqualified. Even so, the idea of working somewhere where he didn't have to make life-or-death decisions had its appeal, at least at this stage of his life in which he was still recovering from a serious injury and adjusting to not only a new name but a new existence.

This job had been his choice. Bookstores had always been among his favorite places, and while he knew retail was hard work, surely book retail would be more pleasant than, say, electronics or cars. So far, he enjoyed the job. He was an ordinary bookseller and cashier, and the work was peaceful. His co-workers laughed when he used that word to describe it, to which he could only reply that peace was a relative term.

He'd worried that his age would set him apart from his co-workers but soon found that wasn't the case. The sellers ran the gamut of ages from the predictable college students and young adults to forty-year-olds to one feisty retiree who wore garish pentacle jewelry and Birkenstocks to work and could tell you anything you wanted to know about Tarot cards. No one blinked an eye to find a thirty-six-year-old man working as a bookseller.

He'd spent a week in the hospital, and then another three weeks regaining his strength in an ordinary two-bedroom apartment which the Marshal's office had thoughtfully furnished in a style Jack thought of privately as "temporary-housing chic." He'd had thoughts of spiffing the place up a little, but every time he got close to doing so, something stopped him.

You won't be here that long. Don't get too comfortable.

Which could just as easily be true as not. He could be here another two weeks, or another two years. A lot of things about this situation were difficult. Not being able to do his work. Getting used to a new identity. Being separated from the man he loved. But that uncertainty… the more time went by, that was becoming the thing that kept him awake. Not knowing how long his exile would last, or if it would ever end at all.

His co-workers greeted him warmly when he finally made it to the local bar where they often gathered for drinks after shifts. He was mildly dismayed to see Geoff there. He hadn't expected to see him here since tonight was his night off. Geoff was twenty-eight and took every opportunity to chat him up. He clearly had… motives. Geoff was a nice enough guy. Good-looking too. But Jack just couldn't go there; not now.

It didn't help that his co-workers were forever trying to fix him up. He hadn't told anyone that he was gay, but somehow they all seemed to know. He avoided Geoff's eyes and took a chair next to Gloria, his favorite co-worker. She was twenty-two and heavily Goth, and Jack had no idea why, but he adored her. "Hi, handsome," she said as he sat down. "How's tricks?"

"Oh, you know. Sell some books, shelve some books."

"You're breaking Geoff's little heart," she muttered.

Jack glanced over at him. "He'll live."

"All night he's asking if you're coming, when you're coming, and now here you are and you give him the brush-off."

"He just doesn't give up."

"He might if you told him you were spoken for." Gloria knocked back a shot of something.

Jack stared. "How did you know that?" he whispered. He had never breathed so much as a syllable even suggesting that he might be attached.

She met his eyes. "I didn't until you said that. I suspected."

He sagged. Walked right into that one, Francisco. "Oh. Did you also suspect I'm a moron? Because I am."

"Piffle. Sooooo," she said, leaning closer so their conversation could be at least semi-intimate. "Who is he?"

Oh God. The words "long story" don't even begin to cover it. "No one you know."

"I didn't think it was anyone I knew; I was asking who he is."

"I… can't really talk about it."

Wrong answer. Jack could all but see the curiosity level jack up a few notches in her eyes. "You can't talk about it? Why not?"

"It's complicated."

She eyed him. "Don't tell me he's one of those married, closeted guys. No, wait… he's a Baptist minister, right? And he runs one of those bullshit ex-gay re-education programs and shouts from the pulpit about the evils of the hell-bound queers. And he works for the Pat Robertson campaign."

Jack had to chuckle at the picture she painted and its total lack of resemblance to reality. "Yep, you got it. Hit the nail on the head. But it really gets me off when he cries out to Jesus while he's fucking me."

Gloria laughed. "Fine, don't tell me."

He stared at the table, wishing for a beer. "It's not that I don't want to tell you," he said. "It's just complicated. And it's hard for me to talk about him or even think about him, because I can't be with him right now."

"How long since you've seen him?"

"Three months."

Her eyes widened. "Shit."

Jack nodded. "Seems like longer sometimes. Thinking about my time with him... I don't know. Sometimes it doesn't feel real, like I must have dreamed it." He sighed. "I don't even have a picture of him."

"When are you going to see him again?"

He met her gaze. "I don't know. Maybe never."

She shook her head. "Jesus, Jack."

Jack jerked himself out of the conversation. "I really can't talk about this."

"I'm sorry," she said, her eyes sympathetic. "Whatever the hell's going on with you, it can't be good."

"Hi, Jack!" Jack and Gloria both looked up, surprised. Geoff had ventured around the table and was standing over them, all puppyish enthusiasm and wide-eyed hope. Jack felt like shit. "How's it going?"

"Fine," Jack said, neutrally.

"You need a beer?"

"Buzz off, Geoff," Gloria snapped.

Geoff's face fell immediately. It was almost comic. "I just... uh, sorry." He slunk back around the table, chancing one more glance at Jack.

"That was uncalled for," Jack said, quietly, although he was secretly grateful.

"He'll live."

MEGAN sat in Jack's living room, the lights off, waiting for him to come home. *I should just walk up to the guy, or wait 'til he's home and ring the damn bell. I'll probably give him a heart attack.*

All of which was true, but the stealth mode was hard to give up, especially now, and part of her wanted to see how he'd react.

The keys turned in the lock and the door swung open, Jack silhouetted from the dim light from the streetlamps outside. He had a messenger bag over his shoulder and a scarf wrapped around his throat.

Megan reached over to the lamp at her side and clicked it on.

Jack didn't make a noise or waste a movement. Fast, almost too fast for her to see, he had a gun out from somewhere and he was around in a tight circle, the gun up and pointed at her. She grinned. "Good. You've been staying sharp, I see."

He sagged, breath whooshing out of his chest in a rush. He lowered the gun. "Jesus Christ, Megan!"

"Of course if I'd really been a bad guy I wouldn't have turned on the light; I would have just shot you."

"I guess it's a good thing you're not a bad guy, then," Jack said, slipping the gun back into his bag. He tossed it aside and crossed the room to embrace her. She hugged him back, reassured by how solid he felt in her arms. "Goddamn, I'm glad to see you."

"Me too. I would have been here sooner, but I've been... a little busy."

He pulled back and she saw his eyes flick all over her face. "Your surgeon did a good job," he said. "Your scars are barely noticeable."

"Yeah, well even barely noticeable is a bit of a liability for me. Do you think they'll keep fading?"

"Sure." He turned her face to one side and palpated her most visible scar, a vertical line near her ear. "This one might never go away completely. Are you using any creams or vitamins? I can recommend something."

"Yeah, I'm using every product known to man."

"That's all you can do, then. Make sure you drink lots of water all the time. Hydrated skin heals better and minimizes scar tissue formation." He smiled. "Feels weird to be giving medical advice. These days, the only advice I give is which mystery writer a customer should read next." He put down his messenger bag and unwound his scarf. "I guess Churchill must have told you where I am."

"Yep."

"How'd you get him to do that?"

"A good blow job is very persuasive." She busted out laughing at the stunned expression on Jack's face. "I'm kidding. I wrangled an appointment to the Marshal's office as a special consultant on anti-assassination tactics."

"And what does this consultant job entail?"

"It entails me coming to Witsec once in awhile and saying smart things. Oh, and having access to their database."

"Nice." He was making coffee. "So...."

"I haven't seen him," she said, her voice quiet with understanding.

He nodded, quickly. "Sure, whatever."

"Jack, it's all right to want some news. It's been three months." She sat down on his couch. "All I can tell you is that as of two days ago he was alive and all right. He texts me once a week, just to let me know he isn't dead."

He came into the living room and handed her a cup of coffee. "Well, that's something."

"He's pretty deep underground. I don't know how he's doing with his plan, whatever his plan entails."

"I thought he might have told you more than he told me."

"No, not really. Just the goal. Get the brothers off your back."

"I wish I could do that myself. I hate that he's out there endangering himself for my sake."

"I know you do. But we both have to let him do this. It's a way to—"

"Atone," Jack finished.

She nodded. "Yeah. Atone." She cocked her head, watching Jack's profile. "Jack... are you all right?"

He sighed, fidgeting with his coffee cup. "Compared to what?"

"You're having doubts, aren't you?"

"No!" he said, too quickly.

Megan cleared her throat, proceeding cautiously. "Is that 'no' meaning 'yes'?"

Jack started to deny it again, then hesitated. He shook his head. "I don't know," he said, quietly. "I guess it's just that... well, a lot of things that weren't important then are starting to seem important."

"Such as?" She thought she knew, but she wanted to hear it from him.

He snorted. "Oh, nothing significant. Just little things, like that he's killed people. A lot of people."

"Bad people."

"That makes it right? What if somebody decided I was bad? Plenty of people would think so, because I'm gay. That would make it okay for them to kill me?"

"There's a difference between judging someone bad because they raped a five-year-old and judging that someone's bad because he's gay."

"Is there?" Jack sat back. "Do you know what his final job was?"

She nodded. "An art dealer who was laundering pieces looted by the Nazis."

"Right. That guy probably never hurt anyone in his life; not physically, anyway. He was an art dealer. Did he deserve to die?"

"You know, it wasn't D who thought he deserved it. He didn't hire himself for the job, you know."

"No. But he sure as hell judged the guy bad enough to take the job and cash the check." Jack rubbed his face with one hand. "None of this mattered... then. Now all I can think about is whether it was real."

"You're not sure it was real?"

"I don't know what to think!" he exclaimed. "Sometimes I wake up and for a minute I'm sure I must have dreamed it all. Did it really happen? Does he even exist? If I told anybody in my life now they'd never believe me. I wouldn't believe me, either."

"It was real, Jack."

"I know it was. I've got the scars to prove it. That's not even the scary part." He didn't go on.

"You're not sure what you felt was real," Megan said, quietly.

"It felt real at the time. It was just him and me against the world. Not in some Kerouac, misunderstood way but a very real, bullet-ridden way, and everything was polarized and refracted and it had to be one way or no way. I had to love him so I wouldn't fear him. I had to make him love me or he'd desert me."

"Is that how it was?"

"No. Maybe. I don't know." He leaned forward and put his head in his hands. "I don't want it to be, but I'm afraid it might be. And now everything we went through, even the good stuff, the talking and the sex and the protecting, it all feels tainted by some nebulous truth that I'm not even sure exists."

"You're overanalyzing this."

"Oh, you think?" he snapped. "That is my special gift." He dropped his hands, and she saw how tired he was. Tired of thinking about this. "Sometimes I have this secret shameful little hope that he just never comes back. Then I won't have to find out. I'll be able to just keep those months we had together in my head, and look back and remember him without having a reality to mess it up. I'm terrified of him coming back after doing God knows what to make me safe and finding out that what I felt wasn't real, or even worse, that it was real but it isn't enough to keep us together. I'd almost rather never see him again than get him back and lose him the way everybody else in the world loses relationships. Break up like regular people. We're not supposed to be like that. We're supposed to die in a hail of bullets or part tragically and pine forever. We're not supposed to reunite only to split up over money or intimacy issues or sexual boredom or whatever else splits people up." He slumped in his chair, his eyes falling closed. "What I had with D was the most intense, most exciting, most passionate connection I've ever had with another person in my life. But I'm afraid that if we try for anything more permanent, we'll lose it." He glanced at her. "God, made quite a speech, didn't I? Sorry."

"No, it's okay. Everything you said, it's all valid. Those are all legitimate concerns. But of all those words, only two really matter."

"What?"

"'I'm afraid.'"

He nodded, sighing. "Yeah."

"You just have to ask yourself if you're going to let that fear win. It'd feel awful to lose him in some mundane way, or find out that what you had wasn't what you thought it was. But I have to think it'd feel worse never to try."

He rolled his head on the chair cushion to look at her. "You're right, of course. Like I could ever just give up on it now because it's scary. Isn't it always scary?"

"Oh, yeah." Megan sat up straighter. "I have to be on my way, Jack."

"So soon?" he said, frowning.

"Never a dull moment." She got up. "But I'm glad to find you well and safe. I'll be sure to pass that along."

He stood up and walked her to the door. "Can you pass something else along?"

"If I'm able."

"Tell him... tell him to meet me on Christmas Day. I can't see my family, I have nothing else to do. Tell him I just need to see him, even if it's only for a few hours. Tell him I begged and got down on my hands and knees and made a shameful spectacle of myself."

She smiled. "Meet you where?"

Jack looked away. "He'll know where."

She nodded. "Okay. I'll tell him."

December 25, 2006

JACK'S stomach was in knots as he drove through Redding after six-plus hours on the road from Portland. He could have flown, but given travel times and security procedures it was almost quicker to drive the near seven hours that would bring him from his home in Portland to the house his dreams still placed him in.

He'd round the corner and he would or would not see a car in the driveway. *Even if you don't see a car, he could still be there. He could have hidden the car. He could have taken a cab. He could have dropped in from the sky.*

He rounded the corner. No car in the driveway.

It was almost noon. He might arrive later. If he'd ever gotten Jack's message at all, or if he had any intention of honoring his request. Jack thought the chances of D showing up here were no better than even, if that. But it wasn't like he couldn't show up himself; if there was even the remotest chance, he had to be here.

He parked his car in the driveway and just sat there for a minute. The place looked the same, if a bit overgrown. All that gardening for nothing.

He got out and went around to the little chink under the foundation where they'd hidden a spare key. It was there. Jack went to the front door and took a breath, then unlocked it and stepped into the surreality of memories that had started to feel disjointed from too much handling.

For all the time he'd spent looking back on his time here, actually seeing the place again was... odd. He'd misremembered a few details that now felt more real in the incorrect recollection than here in reality. He set down his overnight bag (optimistically packed) and stood there, the stale air filling his lungs.

He went into the kitchen. Coffeepot, kitchen table, patio doors. The backyard, unkempt and forlorn. He saw his own shadow learning to shoot, learning to fight, that day that D had smelled the sun on him. They'd cleaned the kitchen before leaving; nothing remained of their time except possibly fingerprints, although Jack wouldn't have put it past D to have wiped the place down like a crime scene.

He steeled himself and went to the bedroom.

The bed had been slept in. He would have bet money on it. He'd made the bed himself before they left, with his usual anal-retentive precision. Someone had made it, but it was crooked and a little disheveled-looking. He would not have left it like this.

But it was not the bed that caught his attention; it was the note that had been left on it.

He had no idea how long he stood there staring at it. *He's already been here. He intentionally came on a day he knew I wouldn't be here so he could avoid me. He slept in the bed.*

He's not coming.

He picked up the note with numb fingers and sat down to read it.

12/24

Jack,

Merry Christmas, bud. Sorry I can't be there with you having some eggnog or whatever. I just can't do it. I'm not strong like you. I couldn't be there and see you and spend a day with you and then leave again. Leaving you on that warehouse floor felt like part of me tore off and stayed behind and I can't just visit that part until I get to sew it back on for good.

Nice of you to invite me, tho. Megan said you're doing ok. Working at a bookstore. Kinda made me laugh a little to think of you there. She said you looked real good. All healed up, not so much as a limp. That was a load off my mind.

I'm doing okay. Things are going about like I thought, except it's taking longer, but don't everything always? Damn frustrating, but I can't rush it or it's all gonna fall apart. I know you're probably curious about what I'm doing, exactly, but I can't tell you. Just one thing I want you to know is that I kept my promise. I haven't killed anybody and if all goes like I plan, I won't have to. Thought you'd want to know that.

Damn, but I miss you awful. Seems like every dark-haired guy on the street turns into you. Not that I'm looking, ha ha. I don't look at other guys. If I had any kind of way with words maybe I could tell you all kinds of nice things about how I feel and what I think and all that, but I don't have to tell you I ain't that guy. All I can say is you got no idea how tempting it was to stay in this house and wait for you, but I gotta be strong if we're gonna have a chance later.

Don't be mad at me for ditching you. I know you'll understand.

Can't believe I wrote this much, damn. Looks like something of you rubbed off on me, doc.

There's stuff I'm still waiting to say to you, Jack. Things I want you to know. But I'm damned if they're going in a fucking note.

See you soon (I hope),

D

Jack read it three times. Maybe there was some kind of code embedded in it that would lead to some secret location where D was waiting for him.

Oh God, you really have drunk the Kool-Aid with all this cloak-and-dagger stuff, haven't you?

If there was a code, which he doubted, he didn't get it.

He put the note aside and flopped backward onto the bed, kicked off his shoes and burrowed under the covers. He buried his head in the pillow and smiled; a faint smell of D remained.

Jack got out of bed and stripped naked.

This is weird, Jack.

Fuck weird. He was here, he was right the hell here.

He got back into the bed and shut his eyes, imagining D right where he was lying, just the day before. Possibly only hours before, depending on what time he'd left.

He rarely allowed himself the luxury of remembering the sex he'd had with D. It was too depressing. He'd jerk off to gay porn instead, or imagine getting a blow job from Anderson Cooper. D was not willingly allowed into those fantasies, probably for much the same reason D had refused to meet him here.

Now, he just went with it. He let it wash over him and wallowed, his mind sinking deep into a mudbath of erotic memories. Within seconds he was painfully hard.

That slow blow job he gave me at the hotel in Baltimore. The first time I topped for him, that little look over the shoulder he gave me, his hips in my lap....

He hadn't even gotten to the really good stuff before he was going off.

Shit. That was some kind of a record.

Relax. You can do it again in a few minutes.

He sighed.

Merry Christmas, D.

INTERLUDE

VALENTINE'S DAY. Just pour lemon juice in my eyes.

Everybody was buying cards, and schmoopy books about lurve. This holiday wasn't exactly gangbusters for bookstores, but some guys had cottoned onto the fact that a good book or a DVD lasted a lot longer than flowers, so it was certainly busier than usual.

Jack was putting in an hour at the register, being his usual charming self and chatting with the customers. *Stay busy and don't think about it.*

Gloria came behind the registers during a lull. "Brought you a latte," she said, handing him a cup.

"Thanks. I'm off in an hour anyway."

"You wanna go out? We can do the Single People Anti-Valentine Fatwa thing." Her eyes were full of understanding behind all the black Goth eyeliner.

Jack shrugged. "I don't think so. I just want to go home and stare at my cell phone."

"You think he might call?"

He sighed. "Not in a million years."

She rubbed his arm. "I hate to see you looking so down in the mouth," she said, sticking out her lower lip. Jack had told Gloria a little more about his situation since first admitting it to her months before, just enough so she understood the situation but not enough to give anything away. She straightened up, putting on a smile. "You ever think maybe you ought to just get laid?"

Jack snorted. "Frequently."

"You could walk into a gay bar and take your pick, you know. He wouldn't hold it against you."

"No, I don't think he would. I might, though."

"Jack, it's unreasonable to expect you not to get any at all during an involuntary, open-ended separation."

"I know. Maybe I'll get to that point. Just... it's too soon."

"Okay, I get that." She patted his arm again. "And if you'd like to dip your toes in the other side of the pond, you know I'm available."

He laughed. "Thanks for the offer."

"I like to think of it as a public service."

"Just doing your part for the good of gay America, is that right?"

"Hey, a lot more of your people have taken the occasional poke at their hags than they'll admit, you know."

"If you say so."

"Just, don't be too sad tonight, okay? And call me if you find yourself doing anything remotely resembling drunk-dialing."

"Who would I drunk-dial, Gloria? I don't even have his number."

JACK trudged home, head down, eyes on the ground. Nothing in the mail but bills, that stranger's name shouting up at him from the address labels. *Someday, someday it'll be Francisco again. He said so, and I believe him.*

That belief was becoming a mantra, a point of faith with about as much empirical evidence as intelligent design. The note D had left him in Redding had been re-read nearly to tatters, its contents long since memorized and examined until the words had started to lose meaning. Five months now, soon to be six, and although he'd imagined it would probably take at least this long, maintaining his equanimity was no small task. He hadn't even heard from Megan since Christmas.

He stopped at the top of the stairs. There was a package on his welcome mat.

Trying not to get too excited, Jack approached casually. Had he ordered something from Amazon? That was a distinct possibility. He was a slave to those damn daily Gold box deals. But this package was not from Amazon. It didn't have the smiley on the side.

He bent and picked it up. It was hand-addressed, and he knew that writing, except there was no street address on it. It must have been hand-delivered, which meant either Churchill or Megan had brought it, since they were the only ones who knew where he was. "Shit," he muttered, fumbling for his keys and finally shoving his way into the apartment.

He dropped his bag and coat, already tearing at the package. What on earth would D send him on Valentine's Day?

When he saw the box, he just stared for a moment, and then choked out a laugh that was trying not to be a sob. "Jesus, D," he said. "For all you gave me shit about it you sure love giving me damn chocolate-covered cherries."

There was no note. He hadn't really expected one. It was enough to know D was thinking of him. Jack tore the wrapper off the box and opened it. A whole box this time, not just the tiny four-piece he'd left in his suitcase back in Baltimore. Several dozen. Plenty to stretch them out for weeks.

Fuck that. Eat them all tonight, in one sitting. Eat them until you puke.

CHAPTER 29

April 2007

RUIZ'S house smelled of laundry and machine oil, with a slight undertone of chile peppers. It was dusty; the man's family had stirred things up quite a bit while they packed, their faces tight, their eyes darting to D every few moments. He could tell them he wasn't going to hurt them a dozen times and they still had looked at him with that frightened-puppy look on their faces, waiting for a sudden kick, the strike of a snake they'd been tiptoeing around.

This is the last one. Just this one more really oughta be enough. Then I can go to Raoul, and then... I can go to Jack and all this'll be over. It better be enough, 'cause I don't think I can fuckin' take much more a bein' away from him.

He heard the front door open and Ruiz's cheerful voice calling out in a mixture of half-English, half-Spanish. "Carida!" D heard him step further into the house. "Juanita?" he called, sounding a little uncertain now. There was a long pause. "Dios mio!" he exclaimed.

No doubt he was seeing the mess. The family had thrown things around quite a bit while they packed. It must have looked like the place had been ransacked.

"Juanita! Pedro!" Ruiz yelled, his voice full of alarm now. D heard his footsteps approaching the living room and braced himself. He'd done this six times now and it never got easier. Ruiz burst through the doorway and stopped short when he saw D, sitting in the recliner with his gun held not-casually across his knees.

"Hello, Ruiz," he said, calmly.

Ruiz stared. "La sombra," he murmured.

D didn't speak much Spanish but he knew what "la sombra" meant. He'd heard that's what the boys were calling him now. "If you say so."

"Where is my family? My wife, my son?"

"They're just fine."

Ruiz advanced on him. "If you've done something to them—"

"I ain't hurt your family, Miguel, and I ain't gonna. But I might hurt you if ya don't back off," D said, shifting his gun just a little. "Your family's just got a head start on ya. You'll see 'em soon."

Ruiz was nodding. "This is what happened to all the others, no? Esteban, and Casanas, all of them."

"You don't know what happened yet, but you will."

He sat down in a chair opposite D. "If you kill me, okay. Just let me talk to my family first, so I know they're all right."

"I'm not going to kill you. But you are going to do exactly as I say. And then I'll take you to your family, and I'll never trouble you again."

Ruiz was shaking his head. "I don't understand. What is it you want?"

"Information. That's all. I want to know everything you know about the Dominguez operation. Any murders you participated in. The locations of any bodies you helped bury. Your personal knowledge of their criminal activities. You and I are going to spend a long time documenting everything you know."

"You're crazy, amigo. You might as well kill me. I can't go against the brothers."

"The others did. Esteban, Casanas, and all the rest."

Ruiz stared. "They... they did?"

"They did. I have boxes full of the evidence they all gave me."

"And... none a them are dead?"

"Nope. They're all living comfortable lives with new identities in countries far from here. The brothers won't find them, any of them, just like they won't find you. I'll see to that. Do you believe me?"

"No," Ruiz said, without hesitating.

D nodded. "I didn't think you would." He pulled out his cell phone and sent a quick text message. Thirty seconds later, the phone on the table next to him rang. Ruiz jumped. D pressed the speaker button, motioning for Ruiz to greet the caller.

"H... hello?" Ruiz said.

"Miguel?"

Ruiz's eyes bulged. "Tristan? Es que usted?"

The man on the other end, Tristan Casanas, chuckled. "Soy yo, viejo amigo."

"Pensé que estaba muerto! Y ahora este hombre dice—"

"Debemos hablar Inglés."

Ruiz glanced up at D. "All right. English. But, this is really you, no? Not some kind of trick."

"How many people know your home number, eh?"

This seemed to give Ruiz pause. "Where are you?"

"I made it to Espana, Miguel!"

Ruiz was leaning forward now. "You are there? You are really there?"

"Si! What did I always say, eh?"

"That someday you would return to the mother country and open a cantina," Ruiz recited in a sing-song voice, smiling wryly at the phone.

"I have my cantina!"

Ruiz looked gobsmacked. "That's... I can't believe it, Tristan!"

"The man. La sombra. He is there, no?"

Ruiz glanced up at D. "He is here."

"You can believe what he says. He sent us here."

Now Ruiz looked like he was waiting for the punch line. "He... he did?"

"He gave us money enough to come here. New papers, new passports, new names so they can never find us. I know you want to be free of that *hijo de puta*," Casanas said, his voice dropping as if he were afraid the brothers were listening in. "They want us to think there's no way out. Have us trapped, like a rabbit in a snare. I didn't believe it either, when I came home to find *la sombra* in my house, my wife and daughter gone.... Then I got this call too, except mine was from Esteban."

Ruiz straightened up. "Esteban? Where is he?"

"I shouldn't say, amigo. But he is safe and has a new life, like me. I agreed to make this call so you could escape too. You can, if you trust *la sombra.*"

"How can I?" Ruiz said, shaking his head. "It sounds like… some kind of trap."

"I know. You must trust me that it is not. Miguel, have I said the word?"

Ruiz glanced at D again. "No," he said, quietly.

"Believe me. I am sitting in my cantina now. We are washing the glasses for the evening. Soon the place will be full, and there'll be music, and Estella will come and bring the baby and we will dance like we are free. I don't look over my shoulder every day now, Miguel. I wish this for you. I got you into the business of blood, but I didn't tell you that you'd be just as stuck there as I was. Now I can help get you out."

There was a long, pregnant pause. Ruiz stared at the phone, his hands gripping and squeezing each other. D knew that he was weighing the likelihood that Casanas was telling him the truth. The word he'd referred to was a danger code word. If any member of the brothers' organization was being coerced into saying something untrue, or designed to trap another member, there was an innocuous but uncommon word they were to slip into the conversation. D didn't know what it was, nor did he want to know. But the fact that Casanas had not used it when he could easily have done so had to be weighing heavy on Ruiz's calculations.

In fact, everything Tristan Casanas said was true. D had procured new passports and identification for him, his wife, and small daughter and paid for their passage to Barcelona, with a pretty substantial chunk of money in their pockets to get them started. In return, he had gotten two crates of meticulously documented and described evidence of criminal acts perpetuated or ordered by Raoul and Tommy Dominguez, acts of which Casanas had personal knowledge. The two crates had been added to the dozen or so D had gotten from the previous five Dominguez family members he'd relocated over the past six months.

The first one had been the hardest, because he hadn't had anybody the man would trust to vouch for him. There had been no one to make a call from a safe place, to verify that D had indeed given him a new identity and moved him overseas. So he'd had to carefully observe the men who worked for the brothers, looking for the just the right man to approach, and he'd had to enlist Megan's help to give the whole thing an air of governmental security.

After that, it had been cake. D had been, frankly, amazed at how willing these men were to give up the brothers lock, stock, and barrel in exchange for a chance to escape. Not just to avoid jail time, or for a lesser sentence, but for honest-to-God freedom someplace they could never be traced, where no revenge could be taken on them.

After the first one vanished, there was barely a ripple in the organization. It wasn't that unusual. He'd split, and no doubt he'd be found. Or he'd gotten on the wrong side of someone and ended up dumped by the side of the road. And the fact that he'd packed all his clothes and personal items? Waved off.

The second one had caused some concern. The third one was like a bomb going off. Now men with families were vanishing. Wives, children, pets, the works. This was no accident. This was no coincidence.

When he'd worked up Casanas, the man had laughed himself nearly into hysterics to learn what was really behind all the disappearances. He'd harbored deep hatred for the brothers, far more than any of the others. D hadn't asked why; it didn't matter. But

Tristan Casanas had gleefully told D how little progress Raoul had made in locating any of his missing men, and how paranoid everyone was becoming over who was next.

That was music to D's ears. It meant his plan was working. Now, Ruiz was the last one. After him, there'd be enough.

Ruiz took a deep breath. "Gracias, amigo," he said to the phone. "I will see you around the bend, yes?"

"Si, Miguel. Buena suerte, my friend." He hung up.

Ruiz looked up at D. "What do you want of me, you man with no name?"

D smiled a little. "You and me are going to spend some time together, Ruiz. You're going to answer a lot of questions, draw me some maps, and make some videos. And then you'll be on a plane."

BEING inside Raoul Dominguez's house—although "mansion" was a more appropriate word—was oddly reassuring. All the months he'd spent guarding Jack against this man's machinations, all the months he'd worked to get men out from under his thumb, and getting into his private home had been almost laughably simple. He'd used the old servant's-entrance trick and disguised himself as a member of the catering crew for Raoul's daughter's Quinceañera party. He'd picked up a crate of wineglasses and walked right in. Then he'd shed the waiter's jacket and slipped upstairs to the man's private study. He had a theory about why Dominguez had not beefed up his personal security, but he'd find out if he was correct soon enough.

Now, he was waiting. Dominguez was set to see his wife and children off on holiday to Jamaica right after the party. Dominguez himself would not be joining them. He was too busy chasing ghosts. After tonight, he could stop.

D didn't know when Dominguez was likely to come in here. Tonight, after the party? Not until the morning? It didn't matter. He'd waited this long; he could wait a little longer.

He was sitting in a wing chair in the shadows, where he'd be concealed from view until Dominguez was behind his desk. He let his head tilt back against the chair and thought of Jack, as he so seldom let himself do. It broke his concentration and churned up all kinds of emotions to let his thoughts dwell on him, so he normally avoided it, but the end was so close now.

All the more reason ta keep yer head about ya and not let yerself get distracted, he told himself, but he just couldn't seem to do it. The very high probability that he'd be seeing Jack in a few short days was just too much to put out of his mind entirely.

He'd imagined scenario after scenario for how it would happen. He'd imagined Jack's face when he opened the door to his apartment to see D standing there. He'd imagined lying in wait for him to come out of work. He'd imagined having Megan fetch him to meet at some private spot where they wouldn't have to worry about anyone looking askance. He'd thought that maybe he ought to just let himself into Jack's apartment and wait for him to come home.

He still hadn't decided how he'd do it. Walking back into someone's life was no small task, as it turned out. Logically, he ought to just call him first and let him know he was on the way. But somehow that lacked... drama. Why drama was required, he didn't know. He just knew that calling first felt wrong.

D checked his watch. It was after midnight. The family ought to be in their limos on their way to the airport by now. The sounds of partying below had given way to the sounds of cleanup. He saw a catering van leave, then another.

Footsteps were approaching. D steeled himself, then had to smile. *How much steelier do you even get than normal?* he heard Jack say, in that teasing voice that dared to challenge D's oh-so-serious self-perception.

The door opened. He heard Raoul's heavy footfalls enter, then the door shut and locked. Perfect.

Raoul walked around to the desk. He wasn't looking around. He picked up a folder of something and looked at it, then out the window, then back... then froze.

D knew that he was only dimly visible in the dark office, further shadowed by the deep wings of the leather chair in which he sat. Raoul wouldn't be able to clearly discern his features. D didn't know what he'd expected, but Dominguez was cool as a cucumber. He slowly put the folder down, then sat in his desk chair, never taking his eyes off D. "I have been expecting you," he finally said. His voice was like charcoal, burned and ashen.

"I know."

"How you know?"

"You didn't take any special security precautions with the house. You could have kept me out if you'd tried."

"You would eventually bring to me your demands. You have shown you can get to my men, anywhere and anytime you like. Man like you, so careful as to make men disappear like they were never born. Man like you must have a plan. Something he wants, something he wishes me to know that I will give him. Wishes me to know I am in his power."

"You don't really believe I'm in your power."

"How can I not?"

"Because right now you're using your foot to activate the security measures around this room and trap me here, alerting your muscle." Raoul blinked. "Too bad I disabled it. Thought it was best we talk alone."

A long pause spooled out between them. Dominguez could not have missed the gun lying across D's knees... nor that it was his own gun, stolen from the top desk drawer. "What do you want?" he finally asked.

"Nothing you'll miss. Nothing it'll hurt ya ta give me."

"Then why this... this siege?" Dominguez said, leaning forward a little. The light slid over his eyes and D saw his cold intelligence, his hooded rage. "Months have you labored to demonstrate yourself to me. Why, if it is such a trifle you ask for?"

"I want you to be real clear how serious I am."

"Man like you is nothing but serious." Dominguez steepled his fingers before his lips. "Petros, he spoke of you."

"Did he?"

"Said of all men who walked the earth, there were very few he respected and even fewer that he feared. You were one."

D didn't show his surprise on his face. "I ain't had no idea he even knew who I was."

"He knew."

D watched Raoul's silhouette against the slated exterior lights. "You know what I came here for, don't you?"

The man sighed. "I have heard talk that you are not long for your profession. Some say you lost the taste. Others say you went soft. Still others say you fear capture. But... the truth is not of these things, is it not?"

"You think you know, then?"

"I think I know men like you. Skill and coldness, this is what is needed. When something to live for is found, they lose these things. Leaving the business of death means you have rediscovered what is joyful in life, yes?"

D said nothing.

"I tell you what you come here for. You have come to force from me an oath that I will not harm Jack Francisco. Him who you love. To make sure I agree, you take my men from me, and from them you take what they know. You will now tell me about the evidence you have, the crates, the envelopes, the films and videos of what they have told you. You will tell me how if anything happens to your man or to yourself, all of it goes to the FBI. Away I fly, join my brother behind bars, my organization smashed to pieces by so much revealed." Raoul shook his head. "So much time and effort, la sombra. All you had to do was ask."

"I needed insurance."

"Dr. Francisco can do me no more harm. I might have taken my *venganza* in time. Perhaps not. Perhaps seeing you retired, no more killing men in my business who escape the law, perhaps this is reason enough for Francisco to remain free and safe. A man like you bereaved, with nothing to live for, on a vengeance quest of his own...." Raoul chuckled. "That I need like I need a hole in my head, you see?"

D allowed himself a tiny smile. "Guess I coulda jus' called."

"I ought to kill you where you sit for those six men lost."

"Maybe so, but uh... I oughta warn ya that—"

"You've taken steps against any such action of mine. Yes, of course you have." He sighed. "You could tell me where they are."

"If I did, you'd kill me."

Dominguez cocked his head back and forth. "Perhaps yes, perhaps no. I may find them myself, you know."

Now it was D's turn to chuckle. "You won't. And I've taken steps fer that too. Minute one of 'em goes missin'—"

"Yes, yes. All contingencies covered." Raoul stood up. "You may tell your doctor to come out of his hidey-hole. He is safe from me and anyone who works for me. I will make it my business that he is safe. No one will come for him."

D rose to his feet. "I gotcher word on that?"

"My word. Bolstered by all that evidence you have at the ready. How many banks is it split between?"

D smirked. "Fourteen."

Raoul nodded. "You are nothing if not thorough, Mr. Dane."

All the air went out of the room, or at least out of D's lungs.

Dominguez smiled. "Preparations are not only yours to make. And is it not time for you to take that name back?"

IT'S over.

It cain't be over. Musta forgotten somethin'.

You ain't. You spent months settin' this up. Yer jus freaked out Dominguez was a step ahead.
What if he goes back on his word?
Yer ready for it. You got the goods on him.
But Jack'll be dead. Helluva chance ta take.
Was always gonna be a chance, whether he brought it up or you shoved it down his throat. You lettin' that chance steal away what you want? What Jack wants?
I wanna hide. Safest ta do nothin'. Let him stay there safe. Any chance, small as it is, is too much chance.
Then if he gets hit by a car in a week, won't you feel like a dumbass? Take what fate's given ya, asshole. Everthin' you ever had's been taken away. Now you been given something. You better take it if ya know what's good for ya.
Guess... guess there ain't nothin' more ta do.
Just go get him.

D CONSULTED the scrap of paper Megan had given him, and then headed up the stairs to the second level. Jack's was apartment C. *A... B... here it is.*
He stood before the door, feeling uncharacteristically nervous. *Hi. Uh... how are ya?*
No, no.
Hello, Jack. I'm back.
Shit, that fuckin' rhymes. Sounds like fuckin' Sesame Street.
Hi there. Off with yer clothes.
Nothin' like gettin' right ta the point, huh?
D ran a hand through his hair. He probably wouldn't have to say much; if he knew Jack, he'd say enough for both of them.
He took a deep breath, and knocked.
And waited.
And waited
Shit, he ain't home.
But Megan said he wasn't workin' at Borders tonight.
Don't mean he can't go someplace else, dumbass.
He stepped back from the door, casting his eyes about as if Jack might be hiding nearby, waiting to spring out and surprise him.
For want of a better idea, D headed back the way he'd come, thinking vague thoughts about parking in an unobtrusive spot and watching for Jack to return, *then* going to the door. He got out his keys as his feet hit the sidewalk, but as soon as he came out from beneath the shadow of the corridor, he felt himself being watched. He turned toward the parking lot.
There was Jack, about thirty feet away. Messenger bag across his chest, keys in hand, sunglasses held in his teeth. His mouth dropped open and the sunglasses fell to the ground, then the keys dropped to the grass with a muted jingle.
D's breath caught, the sight of him slamming into his stomach like a cannonball. *Goddamn, I fergot how fuckin' beautiful he is.* Jack had been primarily an idea to him during their separation, a motivating force, by necessity pushed back from being a flesh-and-blood man so D wouldn't miss him too badly.

Now, even with Jack way over there, D could suddenly smell his skin and taste his lips again, as if he'd been kissing him not five seconds before.

Jack looked shellshocked. He shut his eyes tight, then opened them again. D smiled, and of all the thousands of first words he'd imagined himself saying, what came tumbling from his mouth was something he'd never even considered.

"Hey, darlin'."

Jack's face.... D was hard pressed to describe it, but "imploded" came close. He stumbled forward, nearly tripping over the concrete lip of the sidewalk. D strode toward him, his arms opening all on their own, wrapping around Jack when he hit D's chest like one of those snappy metal bracelets that you banged on your wrist. Jack let out a sob; D could feel him shaking, his hands clutching big handfuls of D's shirt. One of his hands slid up to cup the back of D's head. "Your hair's so long," he stammered.

D chuckled. *Of all the things ta comment on first, he picks my hair.*

Jack pulled back and grabbed D's face in his hands, his face wet. "Goddamn, are you real? Or have I just finally gone nuts?"

"Might have, but I am really here, doc."

"Oh, Jesus," Jack breathed, and yanked D's face forward to kiss him, hard and desperate. D gave himself up to it, not caring if anyone saw, if anyone drove in, if anybody was peeking out a window. His arms snaked around Jack's chest, his reassuring heft in his arms, the warmth of his body seeping through D's permafrost and melting still more of it, melting him all the way through as he could now allow. He teased Jack's lips open with his tongue and wallowed, gorging himself, rolling in riches that no longer had to be saved for a rainy day, because no cloud would ever darken the sky again.

They broke off, foreheads together, both breathing hard. "You're back for good?" Jack whispered, sounding like he was afraid to ask.

D nodded. "It's all done, Dr. Francisco. You're a free man."

"But... how? How did you—"

"Shush," D said, with a quick headshake. "Time enough for all that. Just lemme bask for a minute before ya start in with all them questions you wanna ask." Jack fell silent and they stood there, wrapped up tight, for a few moments. "Missed you bad," D said, quiet.

"Me too," Jack said, his hand on D's cheek. "Just tell me one thing, okay?"

"What?"

"Is this for real? Are we... can it...." He stopped and started over. "Are we really going to be together?"

D smiled. "Well, fer now, it looks that way. 'Til we start gettin' on each other's nerves, anyway."

Jack laughed, a quick, surprised chuckle. "God, all I wanted these past months was the chance for you to get on my nerves."

"Guess yer in luck, then."

He drew back and looked in D's eyes again, his own shining. "I can't believe you really came back, D."

D sighed, and slid his hands up Jack's chest to cup his jaw in both hands. "Anson. That's my name. Anson Dane." It was so easy to finally say it.

Jack smiled, slow like the dawn breaking, and D felt a lump rise in his throat. "It's nice to meet you, Anson."

D pulled Jack close again and hugged him tight, burying his face in Jack's neck, smelling like sun again today. He shut his eyes and saw his vault, its door hanging wide, wrenched from its hinges, all its contents spilled out and flown away like birds into the sky, the peace of its emptiness filling him with the knowledge that he would never need it again.

264 | Jane Seville

CHAPTER 30

THIS is like a movie.
> *No, it's like the end of a movie.*
> *Except it's actually the beginning.*

Dr. Jack Francisco, fully in possession of his birth name, medical credentials, a brand-new driver's license and reissued Social Security card, had a helpless, doofy smile on his face as he drove down an endless stretch of two-lane blacktop through the Colorado mountains. The sky was blue, it was a warm June afternoon, and he was driving a bright red 1968 Mustang convertible.

He'd just about shit himself when D had driven up in it looking like a movie star, one arm stretched out across the bench seat, smirking underneath his mirrored sunglasses. "I thought you were going to rent a car," Jack had said, his eyes bugging out of his head.

"Did."

"I didn't know Avis rented vintage Mustangs," he said, grinning as D popped up out of the car, vaulting over the driver's side door without opening it like he was in a James Dean movie.

"Don't," he said, swaggering over. "I found this vintage car rental place. Thought it'd be… ya know. Fun."

Jack arched an eyebrow. "I'm trying to reconcile the idea of you making a decision based on fun and it isn't working."

"Hey, if this was up ta me we'd be flyin' ta Baltimore and be there in six hours, but no. You wanna *drive* cross-country fer 'fun.' So it's gonna be fuckin' fun, goddammit."

"I'm just trying to make up for our *last* cross-country drive."

D had sobered. "Yeah. Wasn't so fun."

"Well, we made that drive knowing at the end we'd be separated. This time we're doing it knowing at the end we'll be together," Jack said, smiling.

Which was how Jack now found himself in this last shot of a movie, driving off with the setting sun at his back. D was slumped down in the passenger seat, his crossed ankles propped up by the rearview mirror, making his long legs look like they stretched for miles. His head was resting near Jack's arm, and ever so often he'd lean against him in a way that might have been accidental. What swelled Jack's heart was that he seemed relaxed. Peaceful. At last.

The past two months had flown by so swiftly it made Jack's head spin. He hadn't been prepared to come back from the gym and find D standing on the lawn of his apartment complex. For all the time he'd spent waiting for him, missing him and anticipating his return, when it had finally happened it had been so unexpected that it took him completely off guard. For a moment, he really thought he was seeing things, but then he was in D's arms again and knew it was real.

They'd staggered up to Jack's apartment and hadn't come out for two days. Frantic and nearly beside themselves, the first time they'd tried to make love it hadn't worked out at all. They were too impatient, too eager, and D had mounted Jack too fast, and it had hurt. Jack had cried out and pushed him away, and D had pulled back, losing his arousal, apologizing all over himself. Jack had tried to reassure him but he'd seemed suddenly lost, and to Jack's shock he'd burst into tears. Tears he'd been storing up for ten years, Jack suspected.

So he'd spent his first night back with D just holding him until they'd both fallen asleep.

He'd woken the next morning to find D propped up on one elbow, watching him, smiling a little. "How do you feel?" Jack had asked.

"Like a new man."

"You *are* a new man, Anson." And they'd reached for each other and then, just bliss. A whole day and night's worth until they'd been forced out of the bedroom in search of food.

And then, chaos.

First, the phone calls. Jack had put in his notice at Borders. "Just tell 'em ya quit and you ain't showin' up no more," D had groused.

"I can't do that. I have to give work my notice. Do you know how much of a bind it'll put them in if I just stop showing up?"

"That ain't your problem."

"Hey, I like that job! I'm not going to leave them in the lurch if I don't have to! I don't have to, *do I?*" D had to admit that no, there was no rush, so Jack had worked his two weeks. This did allow him the pleasure of dragging D to the bar so he could introduce him to Gloria and his other co-workers, unable to keep the proud smile from his face as he took D around, saying, "This is my partner, Anson" and watching D fumble his way through handshakes and small talk and all the questions everyone had.

Then, there had been the phone call he'd been dreading, to Churchill to tell him that he didn't require Witsec's services anymore. Churchill hadn't said much about it. Jack suspected that he knew at least part of the truth, and when Jack told him that he was no longer in danger from the brothers, Churchill seemed to buy it with a minimum of protestation.

After which followed the endless paperwork of reclaiming his own identity, not to mention procuring one for D. Megan knew some people and pulled a few strings and got D issued a new birth certificate and a new Social Security number. So he was Anson Dane again. "But isn't Anson Dane supposed to be dead?" Jack asked.

"No law sayin' there cain't be more'n one Anson Dane," D had said, examining his brand-new driver's license. "So yeah, he dead, but I ain't. I got a different SSN, different place a birth, Megan even made me a year younger. Far's any authorities are concerned, I ain't the same Anson Dane that was in the Army and died in that car crash."

Both of them back on the grid, Jack had called Johns Hopkins to ask if they could use a maxillofacial reconstructive surgeon. They'd invited him back at once. Then it had been about if he really *wanted* to go back to Baltimore. Long conversations ensued.

"But what about you?" Jack asked D, curled up with him in bed. "It's not like you can get a job at Ace Hardware."

"Why not? Sounds good ta me."

"Be serious."

"I got plans. But they ain't dependent on me bein' anywhere particular. I go where you go, Jack."

Jack had sighed. "Where do I want to go?"

"I dunno. You tell me. You wanna stay here?"

"No."

"Back ta Baltimore?"

"No," Jack said, abruptly. He blinked, feeling D's surprise.

"Ya don't?"

Jack turned over in his arms and met his eyes. "No. I mean, we have to go back for a little while. I've got things in storage there. But…." He thought for a moment. "I think I want to go home."

"Home? Where's that?"

"The only time in my life I ever felt really comfortable, really at home, was when I was in med school. I think…." Jack imagined himself back there, in that city, and it felt right. "Yeah, I think I want to go back there."

D chuckled. "You wanna move to *Ohio?*"

"What's wrong with Ohio?"

"Nothin'. Jus' never heard nobody say they wanted ta move there."

"Anyway, it isn't Ohio, it's Columbus. It's just… different."

"If you say so."

"But we still have to go to Baltimore first."

"Sure 'nough. Get plane tickets tomorrow."

"No, let's drive."

"Aw, shit, Jack. That'll take a week."

"I know. That's the idea." He leaned in and began kissing D's neck. "C'mon," he purred. "Been so hectic since you came back. Be nice to have a week just to ourselves, don't you think? Take our time… stay in swank hotels… no rush, nothing to do, nobody chasing us…."

D was growling low in his chest as Jack's hands moved over him. "Sounds good ta me," he said, closing the topic and Jack's mouth with his own.

Which was how they'd ended up here, on their third day on the road, in the middle of Colorado. They were heading for the infamous Stanley Hotel. "It's the hotel from *The Shining*," Jack had said, pointing out the location on the detailed trip plan he was making on the computer.

"There gonna be creepy ghost kids? I ain't down with that shit."

He looked up at D, grinning. "Don't tell me big, tough Anson Dane is afraid of a few ghosts."

"I'm afraid of anythin' that don't go down with a bullet, doc."

Jack couldn't let an opening like that go by. "Oh yeah?" he said, grabbing D's hand and bringing it between his legs. "What about this?"

He smiled to himself at the memory of what had followed. Not that he lacked other reasons to smile at the moment. They were driving east on Highway 34 through Rocky Mountain National Park on their way to Estes Park, their stopover location this night, and it was so beautiful that it was hard to concentrate on the road at times. He heard Anson sigh, then his hand slid from his own lap over to Jack's knee. He reached down and laced his fingers through D's. "Fuckin' amazin'," D said, the first time either of them had spoken for hours.

"I know."

"How far to the hotel?"

"Estes Park is on the far side. Couple hours, depending on the traffic through the park."

"Maybe we'll see a bear."

"I want to see a moose."

"Do they have moose here?"

"I think so."

The road got busier and busier the closer they got to the campgrounds and visitor's areas of the park. D sat up straight so he could see better. They saw moose, all right. They sat in a half-hour traffic jam caused by people slowing down to look at a large moose sauntering along the side of the road. D whipped out a camera and snapped photos. "You're such a tourist," Jack laughed.

"Fuckin' moose, Jack! Look at that sucker! He's huge!" He pointed, grinning like a child, looking back at Jack with his face full of open wonder.

Jack smiled, watching D, a lump rising in his throat.

THEY pulled up to the Stanley just before seven, the sun low amidst the peaks. D whistled. "Nice place," he said, looking up at the hotel's impressive white façade.

A valet hurried up to take the car keys, and a bellhop appeared out of nowhere and took their overnight bags. Jack looked around as they entered the lobby, a cavernous wood-clad space that made Jack feel like he ought to be wearing something from the Hammacher Schlemmer catalog. They went to the reception desk. As usual, Jack smiled his way up to the clerk while D lurked behind, his sunglasses still on his face, looking generally impenetrable. "Good evening, gentlemen," the clerk said. Jack's gaydar went haywire.

"Hello. I have a reservation. It's under Francisco."

"Let's see.... Oh yes, sir, you have reserved one of our suites for tonight only, is that right?" he said, his eyes flicking past Jack to D.

"That's right, yes."

"Welcome to the Stanley," the clerk—his nametag said Charles—said, his lip curling slightly. Jack had been through this a million times with clerks, waiters, and other service employees. It was that slight loosening of the inflection that said *Clearly you two are a gay couple; we won't mention it but it's obvious, so I'm just going to flirt openly with you because that's what's expected.* Jack barely noticed anymore, but it made D uncomfortable. Charles processed Jack's credit card, then slid their room key across the desk. "Please let us know if there's anything we can do to make your stay more pleasant," he said.

D stepped forward and grabbed the key off the counter before Jack could even open his mouth. "Thanks," he said, the word sounding like a death sentence. Charles' flirty eyes went a bit cautious. Jack just shrugged, smiling ruefully, and followed D to the stairs, the bellhop trailing them.

Their suite faced the back of the hotel. Its large windows looked out onto a spectacular view of the surrounding peaks. Jack tipped the bellhop and they were alone again. "Nice view," he said.

"Don't care 'bout the view," D said, turning from the window and pulling Jack into his arms.

Jack grinned and returned D's urgent kisses. "Don't you even want to shower first? I'm all travel-grimy."

D walked them over to the bed. "Smell mighty fine ta me," he said, nuzzling his face into the crook of Jack's neck.

Jack had no further objections. D grabbed the hem of Jack's T-shirt and yanked it off over his head, then pushed him back onto the bed. Jack propped up on his elbows and just watched while D unbuckled Jack's belt and pulled his jeans off, focusing on his task with a determined single-mindedness that Jack found utterly charming. *I am going to get this man undressed as quickly and efficiently as possible, just watch me.*

Once he had Jack naked, D clambered up on the bed and knelt over him, looking down at his body. "Mm," he said. "Lemme lookit you," he breathed, his hands going to Jack's belly, petting the skin, stroking the hair that thickened south. Jack lay beneath D's roaming hands, gazing up at his face and seeing there D's desire for him, its brash directness still a novelty. Since his return D had become a good deal more comfortable with letting that desire show, and with expressing his appreciation for Jack's body. The body itself had changed a little too. Jack was slimmer and more toned than he had been when they'd parted, which D had noticed the first day he'd returned.

"You been workin' out, doc?" he'd asked, his hands stroking the firm muscles of Jack's chest.

"Exercise is great for sexual frustration," Jack had said.

Jack reached up and pulled D down into his arms, arching up to meet his mouth. D stretched out and wound them together, the heady sensation of D's clothed body up against Jack's nude one speeding their breath. D dug a hand beneath Jack to grip his ass while Jack massaged D's groin through his jeans. "Get these off," he muttered in D's ear, and within a few moments D was coming back into his arms, gloriously naked.

"God, you feel good," Jack breathed. D was sucking on his neck and writhing against his body in a way that let Jack know he'd been thinking about doing this to him all day. "Where's the lube?"

"Oh, you want it, huh?" D growled against Jack's skin.

"Yeah," Jack said, anything else he might have added lost into D's mouth. D slid off the bed and went to his suitcase, pulling the lube from a pocket on the side. Jack sat up as D returned, reaching out to yank him close, crushing their mouths together as he pulled them both back on the bed. His blood was pounding through his body, rising to the skin, heating and flushing him all over. Too impatient to take time, he pulled D between his legs and arched his hips against him. He felt D slick himself quickly and then he was pressing deep and entering Jack's body, his eyes closing, sucking in a hissing breath while Jack watched his face. This was his favorite part, seeing the guardedness fall away from D's features, watching as the sensation of being inside Jack overwhelmed the face he wore around all day and shattered it, revealing the naked need and vulnerability beneath. Knowing that it was him who could make D feel like that, himself and nobody else, not for D's whole life, was intoxicating.

D leaned close for a kiss, but Jack stopped him. He didn't feel like kissing. He didn't want to make love, not right now. He didn't want to exchange deep, tender caresses during a long, slow coupling. He wanted to get fucked, by the only man he'd ever been to bed with who could do it right. Right now, Jack just wanted D to drill him through this mattress until he couldn't walk. And he could let D see that. It was okay. D would still respect him afterward. He'd still love him. He might not say it, but that didn't mean he didn't feel it.

Jack was just starting to spiral upward when D suddenly pulled out and seized Jack's waist, flipping him over as easily as one might a pancake on a slick skillet. He didn't pull Jack to his knees but just tilted his hips up, then entered him again, propping himself over Jack's back, the whole bed jouncing with his thrusts, pressing Jack's body into the mattress on each downswing. "That what you want?" he hissed, his mouth near Jack's ear, swiveling his hips down and forward and making Jack see stars.

"Yeah," Jack could only gasp, his hands clutching the edge of the mattress. He arched his back, laying himself bare to be flayed raw, D's skin hot and damp against his, drops of his sweat falling onto Jack's back.

"Goddamn," D groaned, holding tight for a moment, buried deep and straining together, before going at him again, rearing and bucking like he was riding a bronc. Jack cried out, strangled through the filter of his arousal, everything else going away, nothing but the heat, the breath, the sweat and the sex. "Goddamn, ya kill me," D said, nearly unintelligible. "So fuckin' fine."

"D," Jack gasped. "God... yeah...." He didn't even get to finish the sentence before he tipped over and yelled out his release, the warm wetness blooming between his stomach and the hotel's bedspread.

D's arm was around Jack's neck now, holding him up and close. "Aw darlin'...." He felt D go rigid and thrust deep. a lump rising in Jack's throat at the intimacy of this act, a sometimes terrible intimacy, frightening in its strength.

D sagged onto Jack's back, arms wrapped around him, still inside him but softening now. They were both breathing like they'd run a mile. Jack pushed up, D's weight heavy on him, and they turned over to their backs, D slipping out, their limbs tangled together. "Jesus Christ," Jack gasped. D could only grunt incoherently. They just laid there for a few minutes while their heart rates returned to normal. "I don't get it," Jack finally said.

"Whut?"

"How the hell you learned to fuck like that when I'm the only man you've ever slept with."

D chuckled. "Must be a natural." He sighed and propped up on one elbow to look down at Jack. "Or could be I jus' got a real good inspiration," he said, running his hand across Jack's chest.

Jack arched an eyebrow. "You don't have to use smooth lines on me, you know. You got me already."

D smiled, a slow smile like spreading sweet syrup. "Yeah, I do."

For a few dopey moments, Jack could only smile back. The rumbling of his stomach jerked him back to the present. "Food. Need food."

"I ain't leavin' this room."

"Room service?"

"Now yer talkin'."

JACK woke up with a start, swallowing a gasp. He stared into the dim room, the sunrise just touching the window with pale gray light, listening to his heart pound. He turned his head and saw D sleeping, turned on his side facing away. There had been a time when the slightest movement or noise would have woken him instantly, but he'd relaxed a lot in the two months since his return.

Jack let out a breath, rubbing one hand across his face. It'd been a few weeks since he'd had the nightmare, the one he'd started having not long after D's return. Nightmares in which D went on killing rampages, shooting, stabbing, chasing. Shadowy figures fell under his hail of bullets. In his dreams, Jack shouted for him to stop, but D didn't listen.

You didn't have to be Freud to figure out what it meant. D might think he was sparing Jack the details, but the not-knowing was much worse. His imagination conjured scenarios that probably far outstripped the reality.

At first, Jack hadn't argued too much with D's refusal to tell him what he'd done to secure Jack's safety. "It's done, you're safe, that's all that matters," D kept saying. Jack found this somewhat insulting, actually. Did D think he was too sensitive to handle it? Did he think Jack couldn't be trusted with it?

No. It wasn't either of those things. It had to be that D had done something—possibly several somethings—he didn't think Jack would approve of. He swore he hadn't killed anyone, and Jack was pretty sure he believed him, but that still left a lot of unsavory space to fill in the realm of things Jack might not approve of.

He'd been surprised, and irritated, at D's initial refusal, but in the euphoria of having him back and just not wanting to spoil it, he'd let it go. He'd brought the subject up again about a week later, and gotten the same song-and-dance. He'd let it go again. He knew D, and he thought if he didn't press the matter, D would come around to telling him the whole truth on his own, but the more he pressed the issue, the more persistent D's resistance became.

I've got to let him start feeling secure in this relationship. He probably thinks that whatever it is will drive me away, and if he tells me, he'll lose me. When he starts believing that I won't leave him, no matter what, he'll tell me.

That little voice that insisted on asking what Jack would do if D had done something so awful that Jack actually *couldn't* stay with him because of it was under a gag order most of the time, so it had taken to expressing its doubts via Jack's nightmares.

He laid there, unable to sleep, until D stirred at six a.m. on the nose. He rolled over, stretching, and tossed an arm across Jack's chest, grumbling sleepy nothings. Jack sighed, letting his arm fall around D's shoulders.

D turned his head into Jack's chest and began kissing the bed-warm skin His hand was laying sleepy strokes down Jack's side, growing bolder as he woke up. Jack laid his hand on D's head, his fingers tangling in the sandy curls. D loved morning sex. It was his favorite time to "get mushy," as he called it. The drowsiness seemed to strip him of his residual macho-man inhibitions and let him do things like kiss his way down the center of Jack's chest, as he was doing at the moment. Jack sighed and let his eyes fall closed, grateful just to be ministered to right now.

D slid further and further down in the bed, pushing the covers back with him until they were both bare-ass exposed in the dim morning light. He settled between Jack's legs and lifted them up by the knees, hooking them over his shoulders and wrapping his arms around Jack's thighs, trapping Jack in place as he lowered his head and sucked him deep. Jack hissed, his hips wanting to thrust but unable to do so because D had him pinned. "Oh Jesus…," he breathed, clutching the sides of his pillow, yanking up on it until it threatened to swallow his face.

"Careful there," D said, lifting his head. "Don't wanna suffocate yerself."

Jack wrapped his arms around his pillow-encased head, growling in frustration. "Don't stop," he groaned.

D murmured something Jack didn't quite hear and was back at it, with a vengeance. Jack's eyes rolled back in his head and he wondered if he had any blood left in his skull. He came with a surprised grunt, spilling into D's mouth, his torso rising off the bed with the force of it. D rose up over him, smirking and wiping his mouth. "Was that my wake-up call?" Jack said, weakly.

"Predictable joke, doc," D said, starting to lower himself onto Jack.

"Nope," Jack said, stopping him. "Your turn," he said, motioning for D to keep crawling until he was kneeling over Jack's face. He stroked him a few times, then reached around and gripped D's ass, bringing him down to his mouth. He heard D groan above him, his hands braced on the wall, and relaxed as best he could as D began taking short strokes into his mouth. He knew it wouldn't take long and it didn't; D never had much staying power in the morning. Within a minute he was blasting his orgasm into Jack's throat and sagging in a heap at his side.

"Christ," he gasped, pulling Jack tight to his side. "You gotta be the king a fuckin' blow jobs." He paused. "Not that I got much basis for comparison."

"So how do you know I don't give sucky blow jobs?" Jack said. D made a face. "Uh, no pun intended."

"Ain't possible."

"Why not?"

"'Cause if they get any better'n that, nobody'd live through 'em."

Jack laughed. "And you say you're no good at sweet talk."

They just lay there for a few minutes, not speaking, lying in a tangled heap of naked limbs. D's hand left slow strokes up and down Jack's upper arm while Jack's finger traced meaningless patterns on the taut skin of D's flank.

I need to know what he did.

D stirred, stretching like a cat. "Well, c'mon, Jack. Wanna get on the road by eight we best get our asses in gear, huh?"

AFTER showering and dressing, Jack and D headed down to the hotel restaurant for breakfast. Jack was quiet, working out in his mind how to reintroduce the subject. He couldn't believe he'd let it go this long. To be fair to himself, the two months since D's return had been something of a whirlwind, and D had been gone for part of it. He'd had to take two separate weeklong trips away from Portland to wrap up the loose threads of his old life, collect some things from storage, dispose of some stockpiles he'd left around the country, close up some financial accounts and undergo some debriefings with the Bureau. Jack had been studying a lot, reading the back issues of his medical journals that he'd let slide, and prevailing upon the surgeons at the local hospital to let him observe some surgeries. You didn't just step right back into the delicate procedures that were his specialty after more than a year away without some preparation.

All this on top of the many logistical preparations to be made for the trip to Baltimore followed by the move to Columbus had taken up a lot of time, and suddenly two months had gone by and they were leaving, and not another peep had been uttered by either of them about what had happened during their long separation.

272 | Jane Seville

D was looking at him as they stepped off the elevator and handed their overnight bags to the porter. "What's wrong?"

Jack shrugged. "Nothing."

"Ya got that look."

"What look?"

"Somethin's on yer mind."

"Nothing's on my mind."

D sighed. "Have it yer way."

They walked silently to the restaurant, were seated and poured coffee, and sat there waiting to place their orders. "All right, there's something on my mind," Jack said.

"Told ya there was."

"Yes, you were right. Bully for you."

"What is it?"

Jack sighed, holding D's gaze across the table. "You're really never going to tell me? Not ever?"

D had to have been thinking on this subject too, or else he suspected what was troubling Jack, because he didn't need to ask for clarification. "We been over this, Jack."

"So we'll go over it again."

"I told you. I took care a things. You don't gotta worry about it no more."

"How? How did you take care of things?" Jack asked, leaning forward.

"I took care a things," D repeated, his jaw starting to tighten.

"Do you not get that what I'm imagining is probably way worse than anything you did?"

"I told ya I didn't kill anybody."

"I believe you. But there's plenty that could have happened without you killing anyone."

D fixed him with a hard stare. "Don'tcha trust me, Jack?"

Jack sat back. "Oh, no. No, you don't. You do not get to make this my fault that I just don't trust you enough. I trust you. But I can't go on not knowing; I need you to tell me how you did this."

"It don't concern you," D snapped, and seemed to immediately realize his mistake. He shrank a bit in his chair and looked away, picking up his water glass.

Jack felt his whole face go stony. "It doesn't concern me? No, wait... it *doesn't concern me?*"

D said nothing, just stared down into his water glass. Jack nodded, his hands clenched together on the tabletop. "Okay, I got it. Loud and clear. Things that were done for my benefit don't concern me. Things you did that you are clearly conflicted about don't concern me. My own damn partner's fucking close-mouthed Cosa Nostra routine doesn't concern me." He stood up. "I'm not hungry. I'll be in the car when you're ready to go."

He stalked out of the dining room, forcing himself not to look back to see if D was following him. Halfway across the lobby his arm was seized.

"Jack, come on."

"Come on, what?"

"It's...." He glanced around, then leaned closer. "Please. It's jus' better if ya don't know. Ya gotta trust me."

Jack shook his head. "This isn't about me trusting you, Anson. You've told me things about yourself that you said you'd never told anyone else. Why is this different?

Now, when we ought to be sharing *more,* why can't you share this? What is it you're afraid of? Whatever it is you did to help me can't possibly be worse than the things you've done that I've already forgiven you for. But this? Not telling me anything? This, I might have a hard time forgiving." He shook off D's arm and headed for the door. He could hear D coming along behind, but he didn't speak again.

Their car was fetched for them. D loaded their bags into the trunk while Jack checked out, and within a few minutes they were on the road again.

Jack pulled into a gas station in Estes Park. Nobody said a word as he got out and started fueling up. D went into the food mart and came out with some bottled water and a bag of snacks for the road. He got back in the passenger's side and waited.

Jack finished gassing up and got behind the wheel again. He just sat there, staring into space.

"I sent his men away," D finally said.

Jack didn't respond.

"I picked six. Some a the lieutenants. Important guys. Guys I knew might like ta get out a the business. I set 'em up with new identities for them and their families. Paid for 'em ta get outta the country and disappear." He hesitated. "Before they went, they told me things. Where bodies were buried. Locations a secret stashes a drugs and shit. Signed affidavits and videotaped statements. Finally I went ta Dominguez and said look, I got a shitload a evidence against you in fourteen different safety deposit boxes all over the country, and unless you want all of it sent ta the FBI, you leave Jack Francisco alone."

It really was a beautiful day, Jack thought. Even sitting here at the gas pumps. The breeze off the mountains was cool and fresh. He tilted his head back and took a deep breath. "That's it?"

D nodded. "Yeah, that's it."

Jack nodded. "You could put him away for the rest of his life. You could dig up those bodies, let their families bury them. You could smash his whole operation. Right?"

"Yeah."

"And you're trading all that for my life."

"I'd trade a lot more'n that fer your life, Jack."

Jack turned and met D's eyes. *He'd die for me. He's all but said it. But I don't need that from him. I need him to* live *for me.* "Any crime he does from now on will be on our heads."

D shook his head. "Them crimes, they're gonna happen no matter what. If it weren't him, it'd be somebody else. Man like him, it's like them lizards can grow back a leg. Cut him off, somebody come up in his place. I cain't stop what he's doin', or undo what he's done. But I can save you, Jack. If I done nothin' else of any good in this world, I will a saved you, and that's enough fer me."

Jack felt tears rise to his eyes. He couldn't look away from D's face, laid bare before him. "Anson…," he began.

D frowned and looked over his shoulder. Jack cocked his head, hearing sirens approaching, a lot of sirens, and approaching *fast.* They both turned in their seats and looked back out to the street in time to see a blue pickup truck barrel around a curve of the four-lane state highway and toward the intersection. It was going ninety miles an hour at least. The truck smashed into a minivan, spinning it around, and careened through the intersection, turning over and flipping three times. "Jesus Christ!" Jack cried. They both jumped from the car and ran toward the crashes, plural.

Jack headed for the t-boned minivan. People were running to the scene from all sides, and the police cars that had been chasing the truck roared into view, stopping short and laying rubber on the road. A woman inside the minivan was screaming, but she didn't appear hurt. Her husband, who'd been driving, was in bad shape. Jack pushed his way to the car. The driver's side was smashed; he couldn't get in. He ran around to the other side and opened the passenger door.

"Hey! That guy's getting away!" somebody said. Jack glanced over his shoulder and saw the driver of the pickup, miraculously unhurt, running from the scene. Jack and D exchanged a glance and a nod. D took off after the driver while Jack yanked the screaming woman from the car.

"Sorry, ma'am," he said. "I gotta get in there." He leaned over the driver, who was gasping and choking, bleeding heavily from a cut on his neck. It wasn't arterial spray, but it was pretty bad. He slapped a hand over the wound, released the seat belt and dragged the man back out of the van and onto the pavement, swallowing hard when he saw a large gash in the man's thigh, pumping blood steadily. *Shit.*

A cop ran up. "What the hell are you doing?" he said. "Don't move him 'til the paramedics get here!"

Jack barely spared him a glance. "I'm a doctor, and this man is bleeding to death," he snapped. "He's got broken ribs and I think he's punctured a lung." The man's wife was wailing, trying to get closer, held back by a matronly woman.

"But... couldn't he have a spinal injury or something? You aren't supposed to move him without a backboard!"

"His arms and legs are moving; he isn't paralyzed. And it won't matter much if he bleeds out, will it? Now shut the fuck up!" A woman was handing Jack cloth diapers from a bag. "Thanks," he said, pressing the cloths to the wound. He beckoned to the cop. "You, hold these," he barked. The cop knelt by the man's head and held the cloths. "Hold them tight, now." The cop nodded.

Jack moved down to the man's thigh and tore his pants open. It was a deep gash, messy and bloody. He glanced around. Quite a crowd had gathered. "I need a bottle of water and pocketknife!" he said. A young man in biking clothes tossed him a bottle of water, and a sketchy-looking kid came forward and handed Jack a switchblade. The cop shot the kid a look, but the kid just shrugged.

Jack rinsed the wound and opened the switchblade. "What are you doing to him?" the man's wife screamed. "Don't cut him!"

Jack ignored her and dissected the wound just far down enough to see the gusher. He reached in, prompting more than a few groans from the crowd, found the severed blood vessel and clamped it tight with his fingers. He sat back on his knees and shut his eyes, visualizing the slippery tube between his fingertips, concentrating on keeping hold of it. It was like trying to keep a grip on an oil-soaked strand of pasta. Pasta that was pulsing in your hands.

"What are you *dooooooing?*" the wife kept yelling.

"I'm holding his femoral artery closed, lady," Jack said. "And it's really slippery so please shut up and let me concentrate!" He could hear the ambulance approaching. The paramedics would have clamps.

"He gonna live, doc?" Jack looked up, startled to hear anybody but D call him that, but it was the cop who'd spoken.

"He's lost a lot of blood," Jack said. "But he's breathing and hopefully we've got this bleeding under control."

The crowd parted to let the paramedics pull up and rush to the scene. "What's going on?" one of them said, looking at Jack's bloodstained clothing.

"He's got a femoral bleeder; I'm holding it closed right now. You got a clamp?" The paramedic reached into his bag and handed him one. Jack took a deep breath, bent close and switched the clamp for his fingers. "Okay. That neck wound's bad but it's slowing. I think he's got a collapsed lung."

"Okay. We'll take it from here, Doctor," said the paramedic, correctly deducing Jack's profession. Jack rose to his feet and backed away, allowing the paramedics to prep the man for transport to the nearest hospital. The cop who'd been keeping pressure on the man's neck wound got up too, and came to shake Jack's hand.

"Hey, that was... that was good work, there," the cop said, gruffly. "Guy probably woulda died you hadn't been here."

Jack smiled weakly, feeling a little shaky. There was a smattering of applause from the crowd. Jack barely heard; he was looking around for D. He pushed through the onlookers and headed back toward the blue pickup truck.

Coming back down the road were two police officers, leading the cuffed driver between them. D was following along behind, touching a wound on his forehead. Jack trotted up to him. "Are you okay?"

"Yeah. Fucker got in one good lick with a piece a two-by-four."

"You know this guy?" one of the officers said to Jack.

"Yeah, he's my partner," Jack said, not caring if anybody had a problem with that.

"Well, it isn't every day a civilian dives right in and takes down a fleeing suspect. Tell him to stay out of official business. He could get hurt."

Jack couldn't help but laugh at the idea of D being in danger from some punk in a pickup truck. "He isn't exactly a civilian, officer."

One of the cops put the driver in the backseat of a cruiser while the other one turned to face them. "You aren't?" he said to D, who just looked chagrined.

He reached into his back pocket and pulled out his wallet, flipping it open so the officer could see.

"FBI?" the cop said, arching an eyebrow. "What the hell are you doing out here?"

"Thought I was on vacation," D grumbled. Jack put a hand to his mouth to conceal his amusement. That badge was exactly seven days old, and D wasn't actually an agent—more like a consultant—but this officer didn't need the details.

"So, why were you chasing this guy?" Jack asked, putting on a suitably serious face.

The cop sighed. "Routine traffic stop. He took off."

"Why?"

"Turns out there's a bench warrant out on him."

"For what?"

The cop gave them a blank look. "Unpaid parking tickets."

D snorted, shaking his head. Jack stared. "This guy led you on a high-speed chase and nearly killed a man, not to mention himself, over unpaid parking tickets?"

The cop shrugged. "Helluva world, ain't it?" He tipped his hat. "Thanks for your help." He climbed into the cruiser and they were off. Local police were clogging the intersection now, more paramedics arriving to tend to less seriously injured drivers.

Jack and D just stood there for a moment, looking around at the carnage. "That guy gonna be okay?" D asked.

"I think so," Jack said, watching as the man he'd helped was loaded into the back of an ambulance. The man's wife got in with him, still crying, immediately seizing the man's hand. She looked out the back of the bus and her eyes met Jack's across the street. She smiled a little. *Thank you,* Jack saw the words on her lips. He nodded and lifted a hand. "Come on," he said. "Let me wash out that cut."

He led D to another ambulance nearby. The paramedics gave him some antiseptic and a bandage. He cleaned the small gash on D's forehead, taking his time about it, letting his fingers linger on D's skin.

It can all be over, just like that. You're driving down the road and some asshole smashes your car, and you're dead. Or someone you love is dead. It's all a goddamn crapshoot. D was watching him, and Jack saw similar thoughts passing behind his eyes. "You have fun playing cops and robbers?" he asked, quietly.

D sniffed. "Caught up to him a couple blocks away. Tryin' ta get over a fence into an alley. Drug him back down and he put up a bit of a fight, but, well...." He shrugged. "Just a dumbass kid. Thinks he's never gonna die and it don't matter ta him if anybody else does."

Finished with D's cut, Jack just stood there and looked at him. "Didn't think I'd be saving any lives this morning," he said.

"Didn't think I'd be catchin' no bad guys." He met Jack's eyes. "You were some kinda hero today, darlin'."

"So were you."

D flushed. "I ain't no hero."

"Well, you're *my* hero." Jack took his hand and pulled him up off the back end of the ambulance. "C'mon, let's get out of here."

"Ain't they gonna want our names and shit?"

"Probably. Let's get out of here before they find us. We'll call the police department later."

They went back to their car, still sitting by the pumps at the gas station. Jack popped the trunk and got a clean shirt. D waited by the car while he went into the gas station's bathroom, scrubbed the blood from his hands, and changed out of his bloody shirt.

He returned to the car and slid in behind the wheel with a sigh. D got in and buckled up, looking over at Jack, who was still just sitting there. "What's wrong?"

"I don't know. I mean... shit just falls from the sky, doesn't it?"

D nodded. "Yeah. Gotta dance quick so it don't getcha."

Jack smiled and started up the car. He backed out from the pumps and headed for the road.

"Jack?"

"What?" he said, his voice clipped. He was concentrating on navigating around the police cars and ambulances.

"I love you."

Jack forgot his preoccupation. He stopped the car and turned to meet D's eyes. They were full of calm certainty. D's hand crept across the bench seat toward him. Jack grasped it tight. "Yeah?" He hated that needy little tone that crept into his voice, but D had never said that to him before. He knew it was so, but it was hard not to want to hear it.

D nodded. "Yeah."

Jack leaned over and kissed him, lingering a bit past the point of politeness, not caring who might see. "Thanks," he whispered against D's lips.

D pressed another kiss to his lips, and then drew back, smiling. "Let's get the hell outta here, doc. Before a riot breaks out or a plane crashes."

Jack grinned and pulled the car into the open highway, pointed its nose east, and set off down the road, his hand still clasped tightly in D's on the seat between them.

EPILOGUE

Six months later…

"WELL, looky here! Don't you look all spiffy in that suit there." Special Agent Frank Boorstein grinned and elbowed Agent Blansky as their newly minted Academy graduate, Special Agent Ernest Hough, came into the breakroom, clearly trying to be unobtrusive. He could not accomplish this, since the entire office had known he was arriving this morning and had been lying in wait for him.

Hough blushed, his baby-faced cheeks going splotchy scarlet. "Thanks, Frank," he muttered.

"Guess they musta liked you when you were just a pencil pusher here if they asked for you back with a shield in your pocket."

Hough shrugged. "Guess so."

"Welcome to the big leagues, Ernie," said Blansky. "Got your gun?"

Ernie nodded, pulling his jacket open to show the gun in its holster. "I even know how to shoot it and stuff," he said, cocking an eyebrow.

"Hoo-hoo! Someone's already too big for his britches!" Boorstein laughed.

Hough cleared his throat, eager to change the subject. "So what's this task force they want me for? It was all very hush-hush."

Boorstein sobered. "They'll brief you on that soon. Who are you riding around with to start?"

"Uh…." Hough consulted a piece of paper. "Don't know him. Agent Dane?"

Blansky and Boorstein exchanged a look. "Damn. They're really throwing you into the deep end if they're making you start off with Mr. D," Boorstein said.

Hough looked at them, apprehension coming into his face. "Who is he? He must be new."

"Been here 'bout six months. And he isn't an agent, technically. He's a consultant. But this is his task force and he runs it like a goddamned forced labor camp."

"He's a hardass, huh?"

Boorstein answered with uncharacteristic seriousness. "Mr. D could send General Patton running to his mama. You should see him handle the perps we bring in." He lowered his voice a little. "Word around the campfire is that Mr. D's so good with the criminal element because he used to be one of them."

Ernie was looking more and more apprehensive. "And they want me with this guy on my first damn day?"

"He probably asked for it. He's pretty choosy about who gets onto the task force. Might be he wants to size you up."

"Great."

Boorstein looked up. "Oh, speak of the devil... yeah, here he is."

Hough turned in time to see a tall man striding down the corridor, wearing jeans and a black jacket over a black T-shirt. He was just taking off his mirrored sunglasses as he headed for the breakroom where they were all standing. "Shit, here he comes," Blansky said. "Don't piss him off; he's on edge. We had a case go real bad last night and Mr. D takes things personal."

Hough swallowed hard as the tall man entered the breakroom and stopped, hands on his hips. His eyes were sharp and cold and his squared-off jaw looked like it was in a permanent state of clench. "Where's that fuckin' incident report, Frank?" he bit off, his voice low and growly.

"I e-mailed it to you this morning," Boorstein said.

"Coroner called yet?"

"Not yet."

"Fuck, I gotta go down there and get the report my fuckin' self?" Mr. D muttered, shaking his head at the floor. "Ain't like we don't know the cause a death," he said, his voice going quiet. His eyes fell on Hough, who looked like he was fighting the urge to fall back a step. "Who the hell're you?"

"Special Agent Ernest Hough, Mr. D... uh, Mr. Dane."

"Oh, yer that new guy I'm s'posed ta fuckin' babysit, like I ain't got enough ta do."

"I have worked here before. I, uh... I did analysis before I went to the Academy, and uh... Frank and Jim here know me, and, well...." He trailed off. Mr. D was just looking at him flatly.

"I look like I fuckin' care 'bout yer life story? Find out soon enough if yer gonna stick 'round here long enough fer me ta wanna know where ya been in life. Frank, you got review board tomorrow for dischargin' yer weapon and don't lemme hear that yer givin' them no shit 'bout it."

"You don't have to go up for review when you fire your weapon; why should I?" Frank grumped.

"I don't gotta go 'cause I ain't a pansy-ass Super Special Agent like yerself and I'll shoot who I see fit and anybody who wants ta ask me why. Now you call me when the coroner get his thumb outta his ass, y'hear?" He turned and walked out without another word.

Hough blew air through his teeth. "Nice first impression, asshole," he said, mostly to himself.

"Don't worry about it. You wouldn't impress him no matter what you did."

Blansky, who'd been quiet during this exchange, finally spoke up. "You guys want to know something about Mr. D?"

Boorstein and Hough drew closer. "Yeah, sure," Boorstein said.

Blanksy smiled. "He's gay."

Boorstein couldn't help it; he laughed out loud. "You're shitting me."

"Swear on my mother's grave."

"He's gay?"

"Queer as a three-dollar bill."

"How do you know?"

"'Cause I overheard him talking to Myerson about his schedule. Turns out he only lives in that loft downtown when he's working a job with us. When he isn't working he lives up in Columbus. Got a house with some surgeon."

"Jesus, who'd be able to live with Mr. D?"

"I don't know, but he must have balls of steel."

Boorstein smiled. "Maybe not. Mr. D might be a hardass around here, but I bet he turns into a teddy bear when he's home with this surgeon guy. Wait, you sure it's a guy? If he just said surgeon, that could be a woman, you sexist asshole."

"No, it's a man. Mr. D was asking Myerson when Franco's trial is supposed to start, because he was trying to plan a vacation. Myerson asked where he was going. Mr. D said that this Jack had a big surgery coming up next week and after that, he wanted to take him someplace."

"Oh," Hough said. "That's nice of him."

"Yeah, we'll see how nice you think he is the first time he makes you cry." Boorstein shook his head. "I just can't picture Mr. D sucking anybody's dick."

Blansky drew back, horrified. "God, why would you *want* to? Jesus, Frank!"

"Well! Can you?"

"No, and I don't want to start!"

"You suppose he pitches or catches?"

Blanksy threw up his hands. "I'm not listening to this anymore. Come on, Ernie. I've got your passwords."

D WALKED into Myerson's office without knocking. He was on the phone and looked up, irritated, but just motioned D into a chair. He flopped into it with a frustrated exhalation. He ached all over, and not just in his body.

Myerson hung up. "You look like shit."

"I should look like shit after what I let happen."

"I'm just going to record 'it wasn't your fault' onto a tape and loop it over and over again."

"That won't make it any less my fuckin' fault."

"I'm not going to win this argument, am I?"

D ignored him. "I got nothin', Paul. Fuckin' nothin'. I got no clue who done this. I ain't never seen anythin' so…." He stopped and started again. "I never seen nothin' like that before. Whoever done this, they ain't playin' by the rules."

"There are rules?"

"More like ways a behavin' that make sense. Ways a minimizin' yer risk and maximizin' yer profit. But they ain't doin' that. It's like they don't care what happens to 'em, or if they get caught, and that is fuckin' scary cause you cain't predict what they gonna do." He rubbed a hand over his face. "It's like…." He let the words die off, the ones that were to follow just too disturbing to let into the air.

"What?" Myerson prompted him.

"It's like they're getting off on it," D said. "You want somebody dead, you do it fast and safe. What they done took time, it took will. They had ta have the stomach for it, and that'd be one helluva scary-ass stomach. It was risky, and professionals ain't down with risk."

"You're saying you don't think this was a professional job?"

"Christ, I don't know what I'm sayin'."

"You're about to fall over dead, D. Look, why don't you go home? You were going to go back to Columbus tomorrow, weren't you?"

"Yeah, but that was before—"

"Go. It's mostly cleanup and forensics now. Go on home and take your week. See Jack. You know you're easier in your mind when you've seen him."

D examined his fingernails. He had been thinking about Jack a lot since the death of Jennifer Nang the night before. It was all too easy to imagine Jack suffering a similar fate, given how close he had come to doing just that. His mind dwelled on Jack, safe in Columbus and blissfully ignorant of D's torment, and the image of him there in their home, sleeping peacefully, exerted a powerful pull on D's heart. "Yeah," he murmured. "Think I'll do that."

Myerson just stared at him. "You really are upset, aren't you?"

"Makes ya say that?"

"Usually you'd fight me more." Myerson watched him for a moment. "Frank can drive you home."

"That ain't—"

"D, your car was smashed to bits, remember?"

"I can get one from the motor pool."

"Frank will drive you," the SAC said, in that not-down-with-refusals tone of voice. D resigned himself, something he'd had to become accustomed to doing in this new and irritating world he'd gotten himself into where he had to answer to people. Sometimes. Unless they pissed him off.

"WOW. Are you entering the Science Fair?"

Jack just held out his hand for his coffee, keeping his eyes on the MRI scans he was examining. Portia put the cup in his hand and sat down in front of his desk. He took a sip, and then glanced up at her. "Vanilla?"

"Thought you could use some extra sugar today."

"Hmph."

"Jack, you've been over those scans a million times." She was glancing over his desk, littered with reports and diagrams and books and scans, plus a three-dimensional model of a young boy's skull, badly damaged.

He nodded. "I know. I just... want to be ready. It's going to be a very complicated procedure."

"Which is why they wanted you, because you're the best. Ease up."

Jack put down the scans and sat back in his chair. "You're right. I just feel for the kid. Lost both his parents in the wreck, the least I can do is put his face back together properly." He brought himself back to the present. Portia looked tired. "How long did that hip replacement take?"

"Three hours. Kept getting bleeders." She took a drink of her own coffee. "When's the kid's operation?"

"Monday morning. It's gonna be a marathon."

"Isn't The Invisible Man coming home this weekend?"

"Yeah."

"Shouldn't you be at your house being all squirrely like you get?"

"I beg your pardon, I do not get *squirrely*." He made a face at her. "I don't expect him until tomorrow afternoon, anyway."

"So you're not coming to Dr. Avendale's party?"

Jack slapped a hand to his forehead. "Shit. Is that tomorrow night?"

"Yep."

He sighed. "I guess I can make an appearance."

"You could bring D, you know."

"He hates that stuff."

"Jack, you put up with him being gone two weeks out of four, he can suck it up and come to a social event with you."

"I don't *put up* with it, Portia. Our arrangement works for both of us."

"I don't see how. I can't imagine having Andy gone half the time."

"You're not me, and Andy isn't D. We were both bachelors for a long time, you know. No, beyond bachelors, we were practically *hermits*. I guess we both just value our solitude sometimes. Besides, when he's here, he's really *here*. I'm the one whose job creates issues. It really sucks when I get called in while he's home."

"Does he get on your case about it?"

"No, I just resent it." Jack turned his patient's skull over and over in his hands. "Anyway, he needs to do the job he's doing," he said, quietly. "And if that means I have to miss him sometimes, I'll deal with it."

FRANK didn't talk much during the ninety-minute trip from Cincinnati. Mr. D sat in silence, staring out the window, probably resenting having to be driven home like a kid after soccer practice. He didn't bother trying to draw Mr. D into conversation or glean precious nuggets of information about the man. He'd spent countless hours on stakeouts with Mr. D and hadn't had any luck on that score so far; he didn't reckon that an hour and a half in a car would inspire him to get personal.

Besides, he was about to see Mr. D's house. Where he lived with another man. That alone was more than anybody knew or had seen, even if he only got to glimpse the outside.

As they got closer, Mr. D gave him reluctant directions in barely audible grunts, guiding him off the highway just south of downtown into a quaint tree-lined neighborhood with brick-paved streets and modest, old-world houses that probably sold for at least half a million dollars each.

"Here," Mr. D finally said, pointing for Frank to pull up outside a brick home with a detached garage. He put the car in park.

"Well, there you go, Mr. D."

The man sighed. "I s'pose I'd get called a rude bastard if I didn't even ask ya in fer a coffee afore sendin' ya back south," he grumbled.

Frank shrugged. "I wouldn't say no to a coffee."

Mr. D looked at him. "Nor ta getting an eyeful a my private business neither, I guess."

"You want to blindfold me?"

Mr. D grunted. "C'mon, then."

Frank turned off the car and got out, trying not to seem too eager. Mr. D fetched his overnight bag from the backseat and slung it over one shoulder, pulling out his keyring as they approached the house. He unlocked the door and entered, grudgingly standing aside for Frank to follow him.

He didn't know what he'd been expecting, but the interior looked like anyone's house, if a bit higher-end than most. The front room was one of those seldom-used sitting rooms. It was tasteful, but not showy. Mr. D dropped his bag near the stairs and headed into the house without a word. Frank followed along into the kitchen, which somebody had put a lot of money into given the appliances and cabinetry. It was an open kitchen, separated from a casual sitting area by a long island with the range and sink on one side and a bar with stools on the other side. The rear wall was a row of French doors leading out to a patio; the whole room was filled with light.

Mr. D was scooping grounds into the coffeepot. "Nice place," Frank said.

"Thanks."

"Lived here long?"

Sigh. "'Bout six months."

Frank wandered over through the sitting area. Past it was a den that looked a lot more lived-in. A comfy-looking leather couch, bookshelves, a flatscreen on the wall. He picked up a framed photo from the nearest shelf. It showed Mr. D and another man at what looked like the Grand Canyon. They were leaning up against the railing separating them from a very steep drop, blue sky behind them. They weren't touching but they both looked happy and relaxed, smiling behind sunglasses. The other man was handsome and looked friendly; this must be the mysterious Jack. Frank wondered how on earth he'd ever hooked up with Mr. D. He couldn't imagine his impenetrable co-worker looking for love in a bar or putting up a profile on OkCupid.

"Here," Mr. D said, appearing at his side with a cup of coffee. "You take it black, as I recall."

"Thanks," Frank said. Mr. D was looking from the photo to Frank's face and back again. *He won't say anything unless I ask him.* "So, uh… is this your partner?"

A long… very long… beat of silence drew out. Mr. D just looked at him blankly. Finally, he reached out and took the photo from Frank's hands. "I guess you already know that it is," he said, quietly. He put the photo back on the shelf, his finger lingering on it for a moment before drawing away. He put his hands in his pockets, looking at the floor.

"You know… nobody's judging you, Mr. D. No one cares."

His head came up at that. "I look like I'm worried 'bout anybody *judgin'* me?"

"Uh… I guess not."

"Jus'… my own business. Don't care ta bring it inta my job, if that's all right with you. I know y'all wanna know shit 'bout me but I don't care ta have it known, you got that?"

Frank nodded. "We're just curious."

"Oughta spend more time worryin' bout yer fuckin' job and less time bein' *curious* 'bout my personal life." Mr. D stalked back to the kitchen and got out another mug.

Frank followed along. "So… he's a surgeon, right?"

He saw Mr. D shake his head. "I ain't even gonna wonder 'bout how you know that. Yeah, he's a damn good surgeon, one a the best in the state."

"He's, um… a handsome guy."

Mr. D turned around. "You ain't gotta concern yerself with nothing 'bout him, Frank. Got it?"

"Yeah, I got it," Frank said, looking down into his coffee cup. His grand plan to put Mr. D at ease was backfiring spectacularly.

At that moment, both of them heard a car pull up into the drive next to the house. Mr. D shut his eyes. "Shit," he muttered. "All right, I guess you got yer damn wish. You stay the fuck here, got it? You can say how-do and introduce yerself and then you get yer ass gone, hear? You ain't staying ta chat or whatever else, because trust me, he will invite you. You just say 'no thanks, I gotta get back south' and take yer leave. You hearin' me, Frank?"

"I got it, Mr. D."

"Good. You stay right where you are 'til I come back." Mr. D pointed his index finger at Frank's face, then turned and went back into the front room just as Frank heard the chirp of a car being locked outside. He realized that Mr. D wanted him to stay in here so he could greet his partner in relative privacy and warn him that they had a guest.

He heard the door open, then a surprised voice. "Hey! What are you doing home? I didn't think you were coming until tomorrow!"

"Came back early," he heard Mr. D say, muffled, over sounds of fabric rustling and quiet murmurings of the kind that let him know that hugging was going on.

Frank knew it was rude, but he couldn't help himself. He crept to the doorway and peeked around. He saw Mr. D embracing the man in the photo, a tight embrace that reminded Frank that Mr. D spent weeks away from home at a time. *They must miss each other,* he thought.

Mr. D pulled back and Frank was nearly startled into giving himself away by the expression on his face. He looked... relaxed. He looked happy. He looked like a completely different person. He was gazing at his partner with a kind of tenderness Frank would barely have believed him capable, and then he pulled him into a deep kiss. *Okay, that I don't need to see.* Frank stepped back and went to the patio doors. He could still hear their voices, though.

"Where's your car?"

"I kinda... wrecked."

"Oh, shit, are you all right?"

"Fine, not a scratch on me. Car's kinda totaled, though."

"How'd you get home?"

"Uh... one a the guys drove me. He's back in the kitchen."

"He's still here?" Mr. D's partner sounded excited at this prospect. "You mean I finally get to meet one of your phantom co-workers? Which one?"

"It's, uh... Frank."

Mr. D had hardly gotten out this last when his partner, the surgeon, came hurrying into the kitchen with a big smile on his face. His eyes were startlingly blue. "Hi!" he said, holding out his hand. Frank reached out and shook it. "I'm Jack Francisco. It's such a pleasure to meet you! I've heard a lot about you!"

Really? I haven't heard a single solitary thing about you before today. "Nice to meet you, Dr. Francisco. I'm Frank Boorstein."

"Call me Jack. I keep telling D he ought to have some of his friends up for dinner or something...."

"Ain't my friends," Mr. D grumbled.

"Ignore him; he's crotchety. Sit down! Nice of you to drive all the way up here to bring him home." He frowned and twisted around. "Why didn't you just borrow a car from the motor pool?"

Mr. D blinked. "Uh… well—"

"He was up all night on this case," Frank said. "Agent Myerson didn't want to risk him falling asleep at the wheel."

Jack nodded. "I see."

Mr. D took Frank's empty coffee cup. "Wouldn'ta fallen asleep," he muttered.

"Anyway, I'm glad to finally meet one of you. I was starting to worry that none of you existed." Mr. D sat on the arm of the settee next to Jack, who put his hand casually on his knee. Mr. D glanced at it, then got up and moved to the other side of the couch. A quick frown passed across Jack's face, and then he was all smiles again. "Why don't you stay for dinner? I thought I'd be alone tonight, but we can throw a couple of steaks on the grill, and…."

"That's awful nice," Frank said, Mr. D glaring daggers at him over Jack's shoulder, "but I have to head back to Cincinnati." He got up. "But it was really nice to meet you."

Jack got up as well, nodding. "I'd love to have the whole team up to Columbus some day, so I can meet all of you. I mean, sometimes it feels like you guys see more of D than I do."

Frank nodded. "We'd like that. Thanks for the coffee. I'll just see myself out." He shook Jack's hand again, and then headed for the front door. Mr. D followed along behind.

"Thanks," he murmured as Frank stepped out to the front stoop.

Frank nodded. "That's… that's a real nice guy you got there, Mr. D."

He shuffled and flushed a little, to Frank's amazement. "Yeah, I know," he said, staring at his shoes.

"You know, even if all of us got to meet him, and saw your house, and talked to you the way people talk… we'd all still be scared to death of you. So where's the harm?"

Mr. D smirked a little. "Getcher ass back to Cinci. Don't wanna get back ta work and find everythin's gone ta hell, y'hear?"

"Yes, sir."

D SHUT the door after Frank and went back inside, readying a defense for Jack's admonishments that he should have encouraged Frank to stay, that it wasn't polite to make him drive back to Cincinnati so soon, that he'd wanted to talk to Frank some more, and so forth. "I know, I'm a rude son of a bitch," he said.

Jack was shucking his jacket. "You think I care?" he said, coming up to D and twining his arms around his neck.

"Oh, I, uh… thought you'da wanted ta talk ta Frank some more," he said, his own hands finding their way around Jack's waist.

"Sure. But after you've been gone for two weeks I'd rather do this," Jack said, leaning forward and kissing D's lips softly. He drew away, his eyes roaming all over D's face. "Your case go bad?"

D flinched a little and looked away. "Makes ya say that?"

Jack kept looking at him. "It did, didn't it? Really bad." He rubbed his hands up and down D's arms. "You're all buttoned up. You look exhausted." He pulled D back into his arms and D let him, sagging into Jack's strong embrace and exhaling some of the horror into the clean, fresh air of their home. Jack rubbed his back. "Why don't you go upstairs and take a nap? You're half-dead on your feet. I'll get you up later and we'll dig something out of the fridge to eat and then we'll fuck like crazed weasels and you'll feel better."

D sighed, tucking his face into Jack's neck. "You got a real way a plannin' an evenin', doc."

Jack chuckled and kissed the side of D's face. "Get upstairs, now."

"Hmm," D said, pulling back. "Sure I cain't getcha ta come with me?"

"That would kind of defeat the purpose of a nap, wouldn't it?" Jack said, smiling, that twinkle in his eyes that D so missed seeing when he was away.

JACK listened to D's footsteps above his head until he heard them stop at the bed, then the creak of him climbing in. He nodded, then took out his cell phone and dialed Portia.

"You better not be canceling on me," she said, in lieu of a greeting.

"I'm sorry. Anson came home early."

"Oh. Well, in that case," she said, her tone softening, "I guess you have better things to do."

"I don't know. Something went wrong on his last case."

"What?"

"He didn't say anything about it."

"Then how do you know something went wrong?"

"Because of how he's acting. Too normal. He's putting on a front for me." He sighed. "He'll tell me eventually, he always does. He's taking a nap right now."

"Whoa, stop this crazy train!"

Jack grinned. "He was tired. I can't have my fun with him if he keeps falling asleep."

"You're a bad man, Dr. Francisco."

"Yes, and he'd shit a brick if he knew I talked to you like this. I'll let you know if we're coming to Abe's party tomorrow."

"Okay. "

Jack hung up and went into the front room to retrieve his briefcase and abandoned, half-drunk latte, which was now cold. He couldn't face this evening without caffeine. The local coffeehouse wasn't far, and a walk sounded like a good way to pass the time while D napped. Jack put on his coat and headed out.

It was a clear, chilly day. It had been a mild fall, and even now in early December they'd only had a few really cold days. Just having arrived at December felt like a victory. Soon he and D would spend their first Christmas together, and he couldn't help but be excited even if D downplayed it at every opportunity.

His mind wandered as he walked. He thought of Frank, glad to have met one of D's co-workers even if it had been brief (no doubt at D's unspoken insistence), and wondered again what had happened to bring D home early, wearing his "everything's okay" mask.

Don't think about it. No use worrying now. Think about something happier.

His mind grabbed at a random memory, of a time when he and D had made out in an elevator at the Venetian Casino in Las Vegas.

Sunburned from the day at the Canyon, weary from a long drive... why the fuck are we staying in this gaudy monstrosity, again? Oh yeah, it's fun. Fun, sure. It's what you do, it's Vegas. Wanna play craps? Don't know how. C'mon, I know how to play blackjack. Damn right, you do. Looking windblown and casual among the tacky tourists and seedy gamblers. Winning once, twice. Fuck, that's the cost of our room. Where are those free drinks I hear about? Flashing his eyes at D across the table, watching the flush creep up his neck as the thought in his mind traveled across the table to take root in D's. Watching the waitresses eye D, women passing by with their lingering eyes on his tan face, sun-bleached hair. Back off, bitches. That's my man you're mentally undressing.

Past one a.m., the elevator is empty. Pockets flush with cash. Damn, you weren't kidding when you said you could play blackjack. Just got lucky, I guess. Guess so. Think I might do again? The doors closed on them and he moved so fast Jack was caught unawares, shoved up against the wall, grabbing hands and devouring mouths, straddling thighs and shirts untucked, fingers pulling at bared flesh. Fuck, D, there's probably security cameras in here. Good, let 'em see what I got, a deep possessive growl and D's mouth hard on his neck and shoulder, Jack's arms twining like creeper, then the ding and the doors open on them mussed and panting but three feet apart.

Jack smiled to himself at the recollection, along with the memory of what happened once they got to the room.

He turned the corner onto Third Street and went up the block to Cup O' Joe. "Hey, Jack," said Marc, the barista, as he approached the counter. "Latte?"

"Mmm… nah. Gimme a large mocha with a shot of hazelnut, skim, no whip."

"Okay." He rung up the sale. "By yourself tonight?"

"My better half is home asleep. Just got back from a two-week trip."

"Well, tell him I've got some 'regular goddamn coffee' here with his name on it," Marc said, winking.

Jack grinned. "Will do." He picked up the Other Paper and sat down with his drink. Half an hour passed. Customers came in and out of the shop. Jack read some movie reviews and News of the Weird, then looked over the concert schedule. He got out his BlackBerry and noted on his calendar that Jose Gonzalez was going to be playing at the Wexner Center in January. He half-hoped the concert would fall on a night D was in Cincinnati. He'd never go. He hated "that indie crap." In fact, Jack had yet to determine what sort of music, if any, D did like. He seemed equally disinclined toward all of it. In fact, he tended to view most pop culture with a species of dubious contempt that made Jack feel like a prole for watching TV. D had many qualities to recommend him, not to mention physical attributes that would make a man wish to forgive him for the ones that didn't, but sometimes he was just a stubborn, ill-tempered bastard and there was nothing for it.

He got up after an hour or so and left the shop. He took his time walking home, taking a circuitous route around Schiller Park, stopping to pet a few dogs and chat up some neighbors. It was nearly nine by the time he got home. He paused in the entryway, listening for movement, but heard none. D was likely still asleep.

Jack took off his coat and shoes and tiptoed up the stairs. He pushed the bedroom door open a crack; D was sprawled out on his back, arms and legs flung wide; he'd stripped down to his boxers and a T-shirt. Jack came in and shut the door carefully behind him. He sat on the edge of the bed and looked down at Anson, his face quiet in sleep but still bearing traces of the tension he'd sensed there earlier. He felt his own expression soften as his affection for this difficult man rose to tighten his chest. Sometimes he still couldn't believe that they were both really here, living together, that neither of them was dead or permanently maimed, that it had all really happened, that it had really worked for them in the end. It hardly seemed possible that such a horrible time in his life could have led him to the partner he would walk beside for the rest of it.

He smiled to himself. *I think someone needs to wake up.* He slid his hand up the outside of D's thigh, then dipped it between his legs, cupping him through his boxers. D grunted and shifted. "C'mere," he said in a sleepy growl, pulling Jack down with him and rolling him to his back, scooping up Jack's mouth with his own. "Mmm," he growled. "Taste sweet," he whispered.

"I went out for a mocha."

"Nah. Think it's just you," D said, smiling crookedly, lifting one hand to flick a lock of hair from Jack's forehead. Jack melted a little. "And I think yer overdressed, doc."

They sat up and stripped quickly, yanking back the bedclothes and diving underneath, coming back together in a tangle of naked limbs, D's skin deliciously warm and soft against Jack's as they lay on their sides and necked for awhile. They fell into a lull, just lying quietly, looking at each other. "I missed you," Jack whispered.

"Me too."

"I hate sleeping in this bed alone."

D sighed. "I hate bein' in that sterile apartment. Nothin' a you there." He leaned in and kissed Jack again, his hand sliding down Jack's back to his ass, drawing him close, his kisses intensifying. They rolled so D was on top, his hips between Jack's legs, both of them gasping as they rubbed against each other, D's hips rocking against Jack's. D kissed him again. "You wanna come like this?"

Jack shook his head. "Want you inside me."

D nodded and grabbed for the lube, slicked up and pressed in, his face going slack with pleasure as he slid into Jack's body. Jack held his breath, his hands clutching D's flanks, until they were joined again and D sank into his arms with a shaky exhale. He didn't move for a few moments, just lay there like he was savoring the sensation again after weeks of anticipation. Jack shut his eyes and wrapped his arms around his lover's body, glad as always to have him back home, in his bed and in his body where he belonged, safe and unhurt, another job survived.

Slowly, they began to rock together as one, friction inside and out warming them and bringing sweat to their pores, D's mouth hard and insistent on Jack's as his thrusts grew harder and faster. He propped himself up and stared down into Jack's eyes, his defenses leaving him as his body flew to another peak; Jack saw the horror of whatever had happened on this last job show through D's eyes as the rising tide of his passion dragged other emotions up from the seabed to crash upon the shore. He looked confused and even frightened; he was pounding Jack now with panicky intensity. Jack gasped as D stroked his insides, his orgasm peaking fast and hard; he shot upon his own stomach, grasping D's face in his fingers as D screwed his eyes shut and came with a shout, gasping and crying out, then… crying. His face creased and pulled against itself, tears squeezing out from under his eyelids. He fell against Jack, shaking and trying to swallow it back.

"It's okay," Jack whispered, holding him tight. "Let it out."

He wept quietly for a few moments, and then got himself under control. He stayed where he was, head tucked into Jack's shoulder, still nestled inside him.

"What happened, baby?" Jack murmured, letting a seldom-offered endearment slip from his lips. "Can't you tell me? You're so torn up; I hate to see you like this."

D sat up abruptly, pulling out of Jack with a suddenness that made him wince a little. He turned away, wiping at his eyes, and put his legs over the side of the bed. Jack sat up and folded his legs under him, staying quiet and letting D manhandle the words out of his mouth in his own time. "Case went bad," D finally said, his voice low and scratchy. "Real bad."

"You want to talk about it?"

D shook his head. "No. But I think I gotta."

"Okay."

He was quiet for a long time, just sitting there at the side of the bed, his hands gripping the edge, his head hanging down. "Jack, I...," he began, halting. "I think I need... can ya, uh...."

Jack knew what he couldn't ask for. He slid forward and snuggled up to D's back, then wrapped his arms around him from behind. D relaxed a little, his hands coming up to grip Jack's where they rested on his chest. He leaned the side of his head against Jack's for a moment, then straightened up and began to speak.

"Her name was Jennifer Nang. She had a seven-year-old son, Evan. She didn't know what kind of man her husband was before she married him. She left him when Evan was five. We got word through the channels that the husband put out a hit on her and the boy."

"His own son?"

"Weren't nothin' ta him but a prop, a trophy. Knew the best way ta threaten the mother was ta threaten the child. So we take them both inta protective custody. Got folks watchin', but far as we can tell nobody's taken the hit. Ain't too many pros who'll do a child like that. Even we got standards."

Jack bit back a comment at D's use of the pronoun "we."

"Anyways. We was gonna hand 'em off ta some federal marshals this mornin'. They had a safe house set up 'til the Bureau could arrest the husband; they was workin' up a case. Myerson asked me how much muscle ta put on the little cabin where he had 'em. I said two men. If nobody'd taken the hit, weren't much danger yet." D sighed, a sigh of such bone-deep weariness and despair that it made Jack's lungs hurt in sympathy.

"When the men on the door didn't make their check-in, we went out ta see what was up." He fell silent and stayed that way for some time. Jack just sat holding him, feeling deep tremors in D's guts and wondering what had been horrible enough to knock D for such a loop. He was a little scared to hear about it, but he would. "They was dead. Both dead. Mother and child, both our men. The men just shot, but the woman and the boy...." He shook his head. "I ain't never seen nothin' like it. Nobody had."

Another long pause.

"They didn't kill Jennifer. She was tied to a chair, but... they didn't touch her. She was shot once through the head, but they didn't do it." Jack didn't understand, but he said nothing, just let D get around to it in his own time. "The boy, he... he was...." D's body shuddered. "What was done ta that child I couldn't hardly get my mind 'round. What they done ta him. He was beat, burned, tortured, raped, the worst things you could imagine, they done it. And they made her watch it all."

Jack felt like throwing up. "Jesus."

"Made her watch 'til they finally let him die. Then they put the gun near her hand, loosened the rope and left. She worked her hand free and shot herself."

Jack pressed his forehead to D's shoulders, holding him tighter. "Oh my God, Anson."

"Nobody knew how ta deal with it. I had a forensics tech throwing up in the bushes. Went out for some air and one a my agents was sittin' in his car bawlin' like a baby."

"What about you?" Jack whispered.

"Me?" D snorted. "I jus' did my fuckin' job. Put my head down and did it. Jack… I tell ya, whoever done this ain't nobody I ever heard of or seen. Never known no pro ta do somethin' like that. Took hours, what was done. Don't make no sense. Ya want somebody dead, ya shoot 'em or poison 'em, ya just get it done. Ya don't do somethin' like this unless the point is the doin'. Whoever done this done it 'cause he wanted ta do it. That is somebody the sun don't like ta shine on."

"This wasn't your fault," Jack said.

"Coulda put more men on that door. Didn't think they was in no danger yet, but hell was I wrong."

"You aren't all-knowing, D. You did what you thought was best."

"Sound like Myerson. Could be yer right. It's still on my head ta find who done it, though. And I am gonna do that." He squeezed Jack's hands tighter. "I agreed ta come home early 'cause… I jus' had ta see you," he whispered. "Saw her body and couldn't stop thinkin' 'bout how near that was ta bein' you, at my own hand even. Couldn't stop thinkin' how near I came ta pullin' that trigger on you, how much I woulda missed, how much I don't deserve any a this, how many folks I done left in much the same way."

Jack silenced him with his lips on D's cheek. "Shh," he said. "Thought we were past this."

"Ain't no past it, Jack. You think I don't know what ya gave up ta be here with me? The kinda compromises yer makin' in yer own head?"

Jack said nothing, thinking of Raoul Dominguez, safe as houses, to buy Jack's life. "Let's not talk about that now."

"You never wanna talk 'bout that. You afraid a what ya might say?"

Jack sighed. "I just don't know what more there is to say."

D shook his head. "Times it gets ta be too much. Just reminded me again how I almost…." He turned and faced Jack, his hands going to Jack's shoulders. "If I'd a gone through with it I'd be dead now," he said. "Not just 'cause Josie was gonna turn me in. I was right on the fuckin' edge, Jack. Ta think 'bout how close I was ta killin' you," he said, his voice choking and wobbling over those words. "And if I had I'd a never known what I'd really done, who it was that I'd taken from this world or how much the world needed him. Tears me up thinkin' on never knowin' you or lovin' you. Cain't hold it in my mind too long before it burns."

"You didn't do it, because that wasn't who you really were."

D let his hands fall away from Jack's body and into his own lap. He stared down at them. "I don't deserve you, or none a this," he murmured.

"Jesus, D. Can we not do this again? That is just another way for you to disengage. If you don't deserve us then you don't really have to work at being a part of this relationship, do you?"

"Christ, ya know I fuckin' hate it when you talk like a shrink!"

"Then don't make me do it! It doesn't matter if you deserve this or not; you're here and I'm here and this is what we've got. Maybe I don't deserve it, either."

"Why, you got a trail a fuckin' bodies behind you that I don't know 'bout?"

Jack grabbed D's face in his hands. "Look at me. I can't spend the rest of our lives repeating myself. I want to be with you, and to do that I have to learn to live with your past. I'm not going to tell you I'm fine with everything; you'd know I was lying. Nothing's perfect. Neither of us can do anything about what's happened in the past. I'm just…." He paused, surprised to find himself choking up. "I'm just grateful we have each other now," he said past the lump in his throat. "And all we can do is make it good."

D reached up and clasped Jack's hands in his own, bringing them down between them. "I came home early 'cause the whole time I was in that room with those bodies, all I could think about was that I hadta get ta you as soon as I could and tell ya I love you," he said. "Love you so much that… well, don't hardly know what ta do with it most a the time."

Jack smiled, the lump in his throat growing larger. D didn't say that very often. He leaned forward and pressed his forehead to D's. "I love you too," he whispered.

THEY threw on boxer shorts and went downstairs to find something to eat. They ended up sitting on the couch in the den eating leftover Chinese food straight out of the carton with pretzels and Twizzlers on the side.

"I've got a… thing tomorrow night," Jack said through a mouthful of kung pao chicken. "Abe Avendale is moving to Tucson, and he's having a going-away party at his house. I'm more or less obligated to put in an appearance. I'll make it as quick as I can."

"Mmm. Don't hafta."

"You just got home. I don't want to be gone all night—"

"I'll go with ya."

Jack blinked. "You… you will?"

D shrugged. "Yeah, what the hell. Frank says I oughta try talkin' ta some regular folks now 'n' again."

"I knew I liked Frank." Jack grinned. "Well, good then. Oh, and I have some news!"

"Yeah?"

"I talked to my broker and he says that I ought to be able to pay you for half the house in a few months."

D paused mid-chew, then slowly set down his carton of lo mein. "I told ya you don't gotta do that."

"I know. I want to."

"Bought this house fer you. You don't gotta pay me for half."

"I don't *want* you to buy me a house, Anson. It isn't a gift like a new tie or a bike. It's something we ought to share."

"Why cain't ya jus' let me do that?" D said, getting agitated. "Lemme spend this damn money on somethin' good, take away the stain a how I earned it!"

"Fine, you spent it on something good. Now I'll pay you for half with the money that I earned fixing faces. Nothing wrong with *that* money, is there?"

"Why you gotta be so stubborn 'bout this?"

"Because I'm not your little wifey, D!" Jack exclaimed. "I won't be set up in housekeeping like a mail-order bride! I don't need you to support me. Do you know how much money I make? What else am I going to do with it? Buy fancy cars and gourmet coffee?"

"Y'always said ya wanted ta travel."

"I'd love to travel, but you won't go anywhere."

"I gone places with ya!"

"Yeah, we had our little tour, but since you started working it's been all I can do to get you to go down to Hocking Hills for the weekend."

D's face fell. "You don't like Hocking Hills?"

"I like it fine, but…." Jack eyed him. "What?"

"I was gonna take you down there next weekend. Once that boy's surgery's done."

Jack sagged a little. "Oh. Well, that's… nice. But if he has complications I won't be able to leave."

"He'll be fine. We'll go on down and get a cabin and spend the whole weekend in the hot tub."

He nodded. "All right, D. All right."

TWO A.M. and D was wide awake. He lay in bed with Jack in his arms, sleeping peacefully against his chest, his breath stirring the sparse hair there. After their improvised dinner they'd spooned up on the couch under an afghan and watched the news, then Jack had taken his hand and led him back upstairs to their bedroom where they'd made love again, slow and more thorough, leaving any and all troubling discussions aside.

He looked down at Jack's face, his dark lashes lying against his cheek. He lifted a finger and riffled it through the soft hair at the nape of Jack's neck, feeling that still-strange bubble of contentment swelling in his chest, always surprising that such an emotion could be his.

D had never imagined he could be as happy as he was with Jack. Their relationship wasn't perfect. His long absences wore on both of them. His happiness was perpetually tinged with fear that it'd be taken from him, not to mention doubt that he deserved it. His instinct to take care of Jack drove Jack crazy. Jack's recklessness about his own safety and freedom with their private details drove D crazy. And always, always there was the elephant in the room that they both saw but did not discuss: the fact of D's criminal past and what he'd done to ensure Jack's safety.

He had to make himself believe that these things could be overcome. He didn't know if he could change. He often doubted it, and just waited for the day it became too much for Jack, and he'd lose him. But for now, he could just enjoy that surge of joy that came through him when he got home and saw Jack smile at him, that big happy grin that seemed to say that D was all Jack had been missing to make his life complete. He could relax in the company of someone who truly knew him and accepted him, even if he hardly understood how that was possible. He could hear Jack call him "Anson" and feel that the name was his to bear again.

And it was… peaceful. Life with Jack was peaceful, and peace was a strange thing to his soul. Even if Jack was continually trying to drag his ass into a greater participation in the world than he would have preferred. He could stand it if that was Jack wanted.

He'd never dreamt of having the kind of sex life he had now, either. His relations with Sharon had been perfunctory, obligatory, pleasant but sometimes hardly worth the trouble. Sex with Jack, on the other hand, was… well, he wasn't sure he could describe it. It was humbling to know that Jack could have him panting like a dog, groveling at his feet if he so desired. He was powerless before his desire for Jack, and that was scary sometimes, but the payoff was well worth the sacrifice in the self-control department.

He hugged Jack a little closer. Jack stirred and resettled his head in the crook of D's shoulder, then relaxed back into sleep.

He'd almost said it tonight. He'd wondered if now was the right time, and it had almost popped out. *Marry me, Jack. Lemme put a ring on yer finger so the world'll see that yer spoken for. Tell me it'll be 'til death. Promise me.*

There'd be time for that. All this was still so new.

But he had plans. Plans and intentions. First on the list was to protect this man who slept in his arms so trusting, so open. Nobody would ever hurt Jack, ever... and nobody would ever take Jack away from him.

Not ever.

Jack and D's adventures aren't over. Visit www.janesevillebooks.com
for exclusive Web-only short stories, news, and Jane's blog.

JANE SEVILLE owns a bookstore in Columbus, Ohio, and can't believe she's actually written one of these book things she's been selling to others for years. Her coworkers are a little surprised that her first effort is about a gay relationship, but she isn't. She grew up in Syracuse, New York, where her mother directed the local gay men's chorus, and she attended a women's college. Sometimes it's the straight lifestyle that seems alternative to her.

Jane lives in a house too big for her that she got in her divorce. She shares it with a Newfoundland and a pack of unruly friends who come around every few days to be fed. She's a pathological reader and collects cookbooks, of which she has over five hundred. She frequently visits the Columbus neighborhood where Jack and D live, and she's even picked out a house for them. She's waiting to be invited over for dinner.

Visit Jane's website at _www.janesevillebooks.com_.

Lightning Source UK Ltd.
Milton Keynes UK
02 February 2011

166786UK00009B/140/P